PRAISE OF

Château of Secrets

"Intriguing and suspenseful, rich in secrets, hidden tunnels, and heroic deeds—Melanie Dobson's *Château of Secrets* weaves a compelling tale of a family's sacrifice for those in need, and their determination to resist Nazi domination in the France they remember and love. A compelling and beautiful story not to be missed."

—Cathy Gohlke, Christy Award–winning author
of *Saving Amelie* and *Band of Sisters*

"Seldom do I read an entire book in one day, but I did with *Château of Secrets*. I was entranced by the beautifully researched setting and the complex web of characters. Melanie Dobson has written a masterful novel!"

—Sarah Sundin, award-winning author
of *On Distant Shores*

CHATEAU
of
SECRETS

A Novel

MELANIE
DOBSON

HOWARD BOOKS
A DIVISION OF SIMON & SCHUSTER, INC.

NEW YORK   NASHVILLE   LONDON   TORONTO   SYDNEY   NEW DELHI

Howard Books
A Division of Simon & Schuster, Inc.
1230 Avenue of the Americas
New York, NY 10020

This book is a work of fiction. Any references to historical events, real people, or real places are used fictitiously. Other names, characters, places, and events are products of the author's imagination, and any resemblance to actual events or places or persons, living or deceased, is entirely coincidental.

First Howard Books trade paperback edition May 2014

HOWARD and colophon are trademarks of Simon & Schuster, Inc.

For information about special discounts for bulk purchases, please contact Simon & Schuster Special Sales at 1-866-506-1949 or business@simonandschuster.com.

The Simon & Schuster Speakers Bureau can bring authors to your live event. For more information or to book an event contact the Simon & Schuster Speakers Bureau at 1-866-248-3049 or visit our website at www.simonspeakers.com.

Scripture quotations marked (NLT) are taken from the Holy Bible, New Living Translation, copyright © 1996, 2004, 2007. Used by permission of Tyndale House Publishers Inc., Carol Stream, Illinois 60188. All rights reserved.

All other scripture quotations are from The Revised Standard Version of the Bible: Catholic Edition, copyright © 1965, 1966 the Division of Christian Education of the National Council of the Churches of Christ in the United States of America. Used by permission. All rights reserved.

Interior design by Jaime Putorti

Manufactured in the United States of America

10   9   8   7   6   5   4   3   2   1

Library of Congress Cataloging-in-Publication Data
Dobson, Melanie B.
   Chateau of secrets : a novel / Melanie Dobson.
      p. cm.
   1. France—History—German occupation, 1940-1945—Fiction. 2. World War, 1939-1945—Underground movements—France—Fiction. 3. Nobility—France—Fiction. 4. Jews—France—History—Fiction. 5. Family secrets—Fiction. I. Title.
   PS3604.O25C54 2014
   813'.6—dc23

                                       2013043579

ISBN 978-1-4767-4611-1
ISBN 978-1-4767-4612-8 (ebook)

Genevieve Marie Josephe de Saint Pern Menke

1922–2010

PART ONE

All the darkness in the world cannot extinguish
the light of a single candle.

—ST. FRANCIS OF ASSISI (1181–1226)

✑ Chapter 1 ✑

June 1940
Agneaux, France

Candlelight flickered on the medieval walls as Gisèle Duchant stepped into the warmth of the nave. The shadows in the sacristy were the only witnesses to her secret—no one but she and Michel knew the same small room that stored the vestments and supplies for their family's *chapelle* was also a hiding place.

She slid the iron gate across the entry into the sacristy, and after locking it, she set down her picnic hamper—emptied of its Camembert cheese and Calvados—and turned toward the pews.

Five women from Agneaux, the tiny commune at the top of the lane, knelt before the altar, the sweet fragrance of incense blending with the smell of cigarette smoke on their clothing. For centuries, women had visited this *chapelle* to plead with the Almighty to protect their husbands, sons, and brothers as they fought for France. Now they battled in prayer even as the men they loved defended their country against Hitler and his ploy to assimilate the French people into his Third Reich.

Gisèle slid her fingers over the amber rosary beads around her neck, gently fingering the ornamented handle of the brass crucifix in the center. A cross that was also a key.

"Secrets can destroy."

The words of her university professor echoed in her mind. If a secret was powerful enough, her philosophy professor had declared from his lectern, it could demolish an entire army. Or shatter the heart of a family.

The narrow pew creaked as she knelt beside it. Looking up at the crucifix that hung above the altar, she crossed herself and then whispered, "Our Father, who art in heaven, hallowed be thy Name."

Her mind wandered as the familiar prayer tumbled from her lips.

The healing powers of a secret intrigued her, the layers that sheltered families and nations alike. A secret could destroy, like her professor said, but it could also shield a family. Like the tangled hedgerows of brushwood and bramble that fortified the nearby city of Saint-Lô, a secret could keep those you love from destruction.

When did a secret cross over the gray wasteland between protecting one you loved and destroying him?

Last month Prime Minister Chamberlain had evacuated all the British troops he'd sent to France, along with a hundred thousand French soldiers. Michel had been among those evacuated at Dunkirk, and Papa thought his son was safe in England.

But Michel snuck home after the evacuation, and she prayed God would forgive her for her trespasses, that her secret effort to save her younger brother's life wouldn't become a mortal sin.

The women whispered prayers around her, and like many of them, she couldn't confess her sin to anyone, not even to the priest who came once a week to preside over Mass. With the world in turmoil, they all had to guard secrets to protect the men they loved.

Aeroplane engines buzzed in the distance, and she shivered. The German bombers flew over them almost every night now, showing off their power for the citizens of Saint-Lô. Her country refused to be intimidated by their display.

Candles rattled in their bronze holders.

"Deliver us from evil," she whispered as the planes passed overhead. Then she repeated her words.

Unlike Austria and Denmark, France would fight the Nazis.

When the drone of engines settled into the night, the village women silently slipped out the door. Gisèle rose to attend to her duties.

Just as she was the keeper of Michel's secret, she was the keeper of the Chapelle d'Agneaux. While other aristocratic women attended their formal gardens or antique collections, her mother had painstakingly cared for the *chapelle* for two decades. Instead of remembering her mother at the cemetery beside the *chapelle*, Gisèle liked to remember her inside these walls. When she was at the château, Gisèle unlocked the door of the *chapelle* every morning so villagers could pray, and every night she blew out the vigil candles and swept the stone floors.

Outside in the courtyard, the misty breath of the river Vire stole up and over the stone walls of the *chapelle* and the turrets of the medieval château that stood before her, the home of the Duchant family for more than three hundred years. While her family had lost sons and daughters to the guillotine during the revolution and to the wars that were waged across France, this fortress of stone towers and secret tunnels had sheltered many of her ancestors through wars and storms. It had been a solace for her mother. And for her.

Gisèle quickly crossed the gravel courtyard and hurried into the foyer of the Château d'Epines. Sliding off her red suede pumps, she padded across the marble floor in her silk stockings, the handles of the picnic hamper clutched in her hands. If she could store the hamper before she saw her father, she wouldn't have to lie to him.

She snuck past the staircase that spiraled up to the second floor and the entrance to the drawing room, but before she reached the door to the kitchen, her father called her name. Then she heard the heels of his sturdy Richelieus clapping across the marble floor.

She dropped the hamper and kicked it to the edge of the antique console table.

The sight of her father in his brown cardigan and trousers, the familiar scent of applewood and tobacco, usually comforted her, but tonight the fear in his blue eyes wasn't familiar at all. Papa—known in France as the esteemed Vicomte Jean-François de Bouchard Duchant—was never afraid.

She clasped the pumps to her chest. "What is it?"

His gaze wandered toward the tall window by the front door, like he was seeking solace from the *chapelle* outside as well.

"Hitler—" His voice cracked, and he hesitated as if he hadn't yet digested the news he bore.

"Papa?" she whispered, pressing him.

"Hitler has taken Paris."

Her shoes clattered on the marble and she stumbled backward as if the tiles had shifted under her feet. Her hands flailed, searching until they caught the banister.

Paris was a great city, the greatest in the world. How could it bow to a lunatic?

"But the war—" she stammered. "It has just begun."

Papa's shoulders dropped. "The government in Paris . . . they decided not to fight."

She squeezed the iron banister. How could the Parisians refuse to fight?

If the French resisted together, if they refused to cower . . .

They had to resist.

"What will happen?" she whispered.

"Philippe is coming to drive you south, to the manor in Lyon."

"I don't care what happens to me." Her voice trembled. "What will happen to France?"

He hesitated again, like he wasn't sure he should tell her the truth. He might still have thought her twelve, but she was twenty-two years old now. A graduate of the prestigious Université de Caen. She was certainly old enough to know the truth.

She willed strength into her voice. If he thought her strong, perhaps he would be honest. "You must tell me."

He seemed to consider her words before he spoke. "Hitler won't stop until he takes all of Europe."

She released the banister to pick up her pumps, her hands trembling. "I can't go to Lyon."

Compassion mixed with the fear in his eyes. "We must leave. Hitler seems determined to take London next, and his army will march through here on their way to the port at Cherbourg."

She rubbed her bare arms. Lyon was ten hours southeast. "If they've taken Paris, it won't be long before the Germans take Lyon too."

"Perhaps." Papa tugged on the hem of his cardigan. "But Philippe can take you to Switzerland before then."

Hitler's appetite for power seemed insatiable. He'd taken much of Europe now, but she doubted conquering the rest of France and even London would satisfy the German führer. With the French government refusing to fight, they needed courageous Frenchmen—former soldiers like Michel—to stop him.

But ten years ago, before her mother died, she'd begged Gisèle to care for Michel. Even though she was just a girl, Gisèle had sworn, on the crucifix of her mother's rosary, that she would give her very life to watch over her brother. Michel may have been nineteen now, but he was just as headstrong as when he was a boy. How could she protect him from an onslaught of the German army and their bombs?

Papa rang a bell. "Émilie will help you pack your things for the trip."

Seconds later their housemaid rushed into the hall, her white apron tied over her black uniform and her graying hair pinned back in a neat knot. But instead of stopping, Émilie rushed past Gisèle to the front door, a valise clutched in each of her hands.

Papa called out to her. "Where are you going?"

Émilie set down one of her bags. "My sister just called from Cahagnes. German tanks are moving through the town."

Papa swore. Cahagnes was just thirty kilometers away.

As the door opened and then rattled shut, Gisèle slipped on her shoes. Before she left, she had to warn Michel that the Germans were near.

"You must pack your things," Papa said as he glanced at his watch. "Philippe said he would be here within the half hour."

Her chest felt as if it might explode. The Germans might kill them if they stayed, but she couldn't leave without telling her brother. He had to flee as well.

"I need more time," she pleaded.

"*Ma chérie,*" he said tenderly as he reached for her hand, imploring her. "It is not safe for you to stay here any longer."

Her heart felt as if it might rip into two. How could she make him understand without revealing Michel's secret?

He nudged her toward the steps. "I will meet you in Lyon."

Still she didn't move. "You must come with us, Papa."

"I will follow soon, after I hide the silver and your mother's jewelry. If they arrive while I'm here—" He cleared his throat. "The Germans won't harm a member of the aristocracy."

She nudged her chin up. "Nor will they harm his daughter."

A siren wailed and the floor shook from more aeroplanes sweeping low in the valley. Hair bristled on the back of her neck.

Papa turned her shoulders toward the stairs. "Hurry, Gisèle."

"I can't—"

"You don't have a choice."

She knew he was afraid that he would lose her, just like he had her mother, but if she left right now—

She feared they would both lose Michel.

— CHAPTER 2 —

June 2014
Richmond, Virginia

The clock at the back of my classroom ticked past the hour of four, and I shoved my MacBook into its pink-and-brown-striped case.

Don't be late!!!

Tommy Dawson, my favorite third grader, eyed the text on my phone. "Who is that?"

Mrs. Dawson nudged her son. "Miss Sauver doesn't have to tell you."

"It's Austin," I said before I turned off my phone.

He was sending a car to pick me up at five for tonight's gala in downtown Richmond, and he hated it when I was late. It would take a good fifteen minutes to drive home and another forty-five to dress and do something decent with my hair, but I couldn't rush Tommy or his mother.

Tommy plucked his backpack off the hook one last time and lingered beside my desk for a final good-bye before summer break. Mrs. Dawson reached for Tommy's backpack and slung it over her shoulder before she turned back toward me. "When are you getting married?"

I smiled. "On August 10."

"I'm sure it will be a gorgeous wedding."

I maintained my smile, a talent I'd honed to perfection over the past six months. It had to be a dream wedding, the most beautiful one in Richmond that summer, or my first months of marriage would be a nightmare.

Mrs. Dawson handed Tommy a coffee mug, and he set it on my desk. After five years of teaching third grade, I had dozens and dozens of mugs, each one displayed on a shelf in my condo as a happy reminder of the student who'd given it to me. My students knew me and my passion for France well, gifting me every year with trinkets that displayed the Eiffel Tower or the Palace of Versailles or the Cathédrale Notre Dame in Paris. I admired the photo of Mont Saint-Michel on Tommy's mug and thanked him and his mother for the gift.

Then Tommy reached into his pocket and pulled out a miniature plastic lion, the kind that comes in a box along with giraffes and elephants at the craft store. He lifted it up to show me.

"Who's this?" I asked.

"It's Aslan," he stated with certainty, as if I should know exactly who it was.

Mrs. Dawson flashed an apologetic smile. "He's been obsessed with Narnia ever since you read *The Lion, the Witch and the Wardrobe*."

"Narnia is one of my favorite places too." My gaze slipped down to Tommy and the lion clasped in his hand. "My grandmother used to read me the stories when I was about your age."

His eyes grew wide. "Have you been to Narnia?"

I almost laughed until I realized Tommy was serious. "Not yet . . . but perhaps one day."

He rewarded me with his grin.

"We'll both miss you." Mrs. Dawson glanced down at her son as he raced Aslan across the desk. "But I told him that he'd see you next year."

My poised smile began to crack. "Unfortunately, I won't be coming back to teach."

Tommy's lips trembled, and I leaned over, nudging his chin. "But I can still visit, can't I?"

He nodded and then hugged me. Mrs. Dawson finally coaxed him out the door, but the truth was, I didn't want them to go.

For the past nine months, Washington Elementary had entrusted twenty-seven students to my care. This year had been a challenging one, with two students, in particular, who felt quite confident in their leadership abilities. While I loved to teach—and loved the children—I hated conflict.

The year had been spent in a silent battle between two kids who were stronger than me in spirit. I'd had to feign confidence I didn't have, but in the end, I was stronger for it. Perhaps I wouldn't miss the demands of those two students, but I would miss the enthusiasm of the other twenty-five.

When I powered up my phone again, there was another text from my fiancé.

Chloe?

I typed back a quick response.

On my way.

I turned off the overhead lights and rushed to my car.

Thankfully the weeks ahead would be so full of wedding planning and campaigning, I wouldn't have much time to think about missing my kids. Then by summer's end, I would join Austin Vale and his political aspirations in matrimony. Come November, if public opinion held, I would be the wife of Virginia's youngest governor in history, and I'd promised Austin that I'd dedicate myself full-time to this new role. I would no longer be teaching elementary kids, but Austin and I both hoped parenthood would follow soon after our wedding.

My '68 Mercedes roadster had no air-conditioning and the heat was as temperamental as Virginia politics, but the body was a beautiful burgundy color and the convertible top still worked. When I turned twenty-one, my dad had bought it just for me. The doors had gotten dinged up over the past seven years and the fender was slightly askew, but when my dad offered to buy me a newer model, I declined. I liked the mystique—the charm—of the old much more than the sheen of the new.

Austin didn't have the same appreciation or affection for mystique. He'd asked me twice to replace my vehicle with a newer model, something more trendy, like a BMW or an Audi. I'd compromised much in our relationship, but I wasn't trading in my car just because it had a few bumps and bruises. It had taken a few weeks of finagling, but Austin and I finally reached an agreement that worked for both of us. I drove the roadster to and from school. When he couldn't pick me up for political events or meals with his parents, he sent a driver in a shiny sedan.

The sunshine lit my path home this afternoon, and the river beside the road seemed to beckon me. *Come play.* But there would be no time to kayak this weekend. Almost every minute was scheduled. Tonight's gala. A luncheon tomorrow in the Fan. Dinner at the Vales' plantation home. Sunday would be church downtown with Austin and then a golfing fund-raiser at the country club. Every event, Austin said, was another brick mortared on the monument of his campaign, each stone solidifying what his manager told the press. Austin Vale may have been young, but he was passionate, articulate, and qualified to lead the Commonwealth of Virginia. And his future wife would be leading alongside him.

Event-hopping was exhausting at times, but I understood the importance of it. We were a team, working together to win this governorship. What bothered me most about the election process was when Austin and I talked about our wedding. Instead of a ceremony, sometimes it felt like he was helping me coordinate another meet-and-greet. With the bloated guest list, half of whom I didn't even know, we would be meeting and greeting half of Richmond the same day we said our vows.

The local media had been mesmerized by our story from almost our first date, a year ago. Austin Vale, the successful attorney and son of the Honorable Richard Vale, a justice of the Supreme Court of Virginia. Chloe Sauver, granddaughter of a French war hero and daughter of a French nobleman who now owned the largest investment management company in the Commonwealth of Virginia. My mom was an accomplished business owner in her own right, but the political powers that be ignored her successes with the popular Bliss Bakery.

Austin and I had met by accident, when he literally bumped into me and my chai latte at a local coffee shop. When he asked me to dinner, I hadn't known he was being courted as a candidate and he hadn't known about my family. I'd fallen almost immediately for the charming attorney who brought me flowers on our first date and asked me a dozen questions, the man who stopped by every week for lunch at my school in those first few months of dating and called for no other reason than to inquire about my day.

The morning after Austin announced our engagement, the national media became fascinated with the minutiae of our relationship. The morning shows were enchanted by our wedding plans, speculating on the cake, the flowers, even our choice of music for the reception. But when the tabloids came out each week, my heart sometimes felt like it would bleed, the doubts inside me fighting against the truth. The tabloids couldn't have cared less about our wedding plans, speculating instead on our faithfulness, as if either Austin or I had the time or desire to be cheating on the other.

Thankfully, there would be no media on our honeymoon. I didn't know where we were going, but Austin had promised it would be a million miles away from cameras and campaigning. Secretly, I hoped he was taking me back to France.

I pulled into the garage under my condo. Tonight I couldn't get hung up on the details for the wedding or our honeymoon. Instead I had to focus on getting ready for this gala. A new dress was waiting for me in my closet, a cobalt-blue affair that Austin handpicked in Manhattan, along with some strappy black stilettos to go with it. I tossed my casual skirt and blouse into the laundry bin and began the transformation.

Austin's driver was on time, but I wasn't. It took an extra fifteen minutes to finish my makeup and torture my long hair with the flatiron. The mirror displayed an elegant woman with eyes the color of her dress and blond hair tucked behind one ear, but I felt a bit like a broken gift hidden under pretty paper and a bow. Sometimes I felt . . . well, sometimes I wondered if I was the right woman for Austin Vale. And if he was the right man for me. He said he loved me, that he was confident in our relationship and our future. Why couldn't I be confident as well?

With our wedding a little over two months away, it was much too late to reconsider. Our months of dating had been a firestorm of sorts—a romantic inferno. He had literally swept me off my feet the night he proposed, wading across a reflecting pool at the Madison Inn to our dinner waiting on the other side. Dozens of candles reflected in the pool and rosebuds dangled along the patio's trellis, sweetening the air. Before we ate, Austin got down on one knee, and my doubts faded in the lights.

No one could ever guess at my fear of living in the spotlight for the rest of my life or my haunting doubts about Austin's love.

But tonight wasn't the time for soul-searching. I'd have to do that later on the river, a paddle in my hands.

As I slid out of the town car and into the lobby of the Jefferson Hotel, my cell phone began to play the first bars of "Do You Hear the People Sing?"—one of my favorite songs from *Les Misérables*. I glanced down at my mother's picture on the screen and stuffed my phone into my beaded handbag. I'd have to call her back later tonight. Or first thing tomorrow.

I rushed through the lobby, and by the time I entered the elegant ballroom, the orchestra had already started playing. Hopefully Austin wouldn't notice I was late.

Chapter 3

Philippe tossed her two suitcases into the luggage compartment of his new cabriolet, and then he opened the passenger door, waving her inside. "Hurry, Gisèle."

Instead of moving toward the car, she turned toward her father. He stood dazed in the courtyard, like one of the winged statues displayed at the Louvre. He should have been flying away from the château with them, but he couldn't seem to move at all.

Her cousin waved toward the car again. "We have to get through town before the tanks arrive."

The stained glass on the *chapelle* glowed in the moonlight, not twenty meters from where she stood. Michel had sworn her to secrecy, but perhaps she should still tell Papa . . .

Her father still hadn't moved. She understood the fear that seemed to paralyze him—more than twenty years ago, he'd lost both of his brothers and a cousin to the Germans during the Great War. Then, less than a decade ago, he'd lost his wife. Now the Germans were threatening his home and the rest of his family.

If Michel refused to leave, Papa wouldn't leave either.

Stepping away from the car, she pleaded. "I must visit the *chapelle*, Papa. One last time."

But it was Philippe, not Papa, who responded to her plea. "You can pray at a chapel in Lyon."

She shook her head. "I can't wait."

Philippe brushed both hands over his short hair, frustrated with her delay. "Then pray in the car."

"He's right, Gisèle," Papa said, urging her forward.

She eyed the *chapelle* one last time. She could sprint toward it, but Philippe would follow her and so would Papa. She doubted they would force her into the car, but they would never allow her to be alone in the sacristy.

Papa finally stepped forward, kissed her cheeks. "I will see you before the week ends."

A bomb exploded to the east, the night sky sparking near the town.

"Come with us now," she begged her father one last time.

But he pushed her into the seat and closed the door.

"Soon," he mouthed on the other side of her window.

Over her shoulder, she watched him at the end of the drive, waving to her. She rolled down her window and waved back, her heart in shreds.

She felt like a coward, running away when her brother—and her father—needed her.

Philippe rode in silence beside her, under the long row of beech trees that lined the entrance to the château. His gloved fingers circled around the steering wheel, his eyes focused on the narrow road lit by the moon as he sped through Agneaux, turning left toward the city of Saint-Lô.

She and Philippe were distant cousins and they both looked like their ancestors with hair the chalky tan color of the Norman beaches and eyes the same light blue of the English Channel. Her father and his mother—Corinne Duchant Borde—were technically second cousins, but she called his mother Tante Corinne.

Philippe's father had been killed during the Great War, but Tante Corinne and Gisèle's mother had been dear friends. Today Gisèle, Michel, and Philippe were the last descendants of the Duchant bloodline.

Philippe had asked her father twice to marry her, to reunite the Duchant family again through matrimony, but she didn't love him the way a wife should love her husband. Whenever Philippe brought up the subject, Papa had stalled, saying she must finish at the university first.

Now Gisèle had her diploma and her own desires for the future, desires that didn't include wedding her cousin. The Germans had muddied her plans to lounge on the beaches in Brittany for the summer and perhaps, to her father's dismay, obtain a position teaching literature in the fall. Papa couldn't understand why she would want to work, but the thought of living on her own, supporting herself even, thrilled her. And women did it these days. Her friend Odette had begun working in Paris last year and telephoned almost every week, begging Gisèle to join her.

Had Odette left Paris before the Germans arrived?

As lights flashed again in the distance, Gisèle retied the laces on her most sensible brogue shoes and clutched her sweater over her chest. They were two kilometers from Saint-Lô now, and on the other side of the city, the main road curled south toward Lyon. The Germans may have been bombing, but she prayed the tanks hadn't arrived in the town yet.

Philippe glanced over at her. "Your brother is the lucky one, hiding out in England with your mother's family."

"Lucky for him," she whispered.

"Your father should have sent you to England a long time ago."

"There was no reason for me to leave." She slowly unfolded her arms. Philippe didn't need to know that her father hadn't spoken to the Eckleys since her mother's death. "None of us guessed that Paris would surrender."

They rode through the forest and then over the stone bridge, the Vire flowing underneath. They trailed the river as they drove into Saint-Lô. Ahead was the tall steeple above the cathedral, a proud symbol of their faith in God and in France. Their government may have failed them, but she prayed God would not.

The main road was crammed with people. Dozens of cars and horse carts, bicyclists, and crowds of people fleeing on foot with their luggage in hand or strapped to their back. Her heart raced. How were they supposed to get out of town before the Germans arrived?

Philippe honked his horn, and the pedestrians divided like the Red Sea. But a truck blocked the road.

Philippe opened his window. "Get out of the way," he shouted out, the gasoline fumes flooding into the *coupé*. The truck didn't move.

Another explosion ignited the sky, and Gisèle gasped. People fled from their automobiles into shops on both sides of the road.

Smoke poured into Philippe's window. Coughing, she waved her hands in front of her. "They're going to kill us all."

He honked again. "Now would be the time to pray."

She clung to the cross on her rosary beads and closed her eyes, begging the Almighty for a way out.

Something exploded on the left, and her window shattered. She froze on the seat, too shocked to even scream.

Philippe leaned over, pushing her door open. "Get out."

"But—"

"Please, Gisèle."

She stumbled onto the sidewalk, the smoke suffocating her. Villagers screamed around her, some colliding into each other as they fled. She didn't know in which direction to run.

"Philippe!" she screamed.

In the clamor of the crowd, she heard Philippe call her name, his voice muffled. She tried to run around the car, but the crowd pressed up against her and she tripped over the handles of an abandoned bicycle.

"Philippe," she said again, this time a whisper. It didn't matter how loud she screamed. He would never hear her.

In the blackness, the smoke, she ran west. Back toward the safety of her home, toward her father and brother.

Hundreds of people dashed back over the bridge alongside her, but on the other side of the river, she ducked into a narrow passage between the towering hedgerows. Her legs burned as she ran down another passage and then out into the forest of tangled hawthorns and apple trees.

Branches slapped against her body, the thorns snagging her arms and clothes. She shielded her face, rushing past the dozens of wooden beehives among the trees. She didn't stop until ahead of her, concealed in the forest, she saw a cottage. The home of her friends, André and Nadine Batier.

An aeroplane dipped over the trees, and she shivered. The château was still a kilometer away.

If the Batiers hadn't run away, perhaps she could wait with them until first light. Then she would meet Philippe back at the château.

— CHAPTER 4 —

A crystal chandelier rained shards of light over the crowded ballroom. Columns of red, white, and blue balloons swayed at the front, on each side of the podium. There were two rows of chairs along the walls and in the middle of the room was an open space crowded with several hundred people. Under the archway at the back of the room, a buffet table teemed with hors d'oeuvres, but no one in the room seemed to be eating.

I eyed the table of food from afar. No one on Austin's staff wanted to insult me by explaining protocol, but on nights like this it would have been nice if Olivia Larson, Austin's campaign manager, handed me a brief list of the dos and don'ts. The most pressing question being, was the candidate's fiancée allowed to eat the stuffed mushrooms and crab wontons? Or was she simply to stand and smile?

It seemed such a waste to leave all that food on the table, especially when I'd had no time for either lunch or dinner. My tight dress wouldn't allow me to do anything except nibble, but it wouldn't pay for me to pass out during the function either.

Austin's parents were at the front of the room, and as I inched toward the buffet, Mrs. Vale eyed me from afar. With her slow nod of greeting, I knew she was scrutinizing my appearance as well, from my heels up to my hair. Like I was a package for display.

Perhaps I should have worn a bow.

Austin stood near his mother, hemmed in by admirers. With his wavy black hair parted on the side, his tuxedo a perfect fit, he breathed confidence. I admired him for a moment, like the hordes of women who gawked whenever we went out. Then I stepped closer.

His familiar laughter sounded genuine, his gaze focused on the man he spoke with, like his colleague was the only person who mattered in the world. The older constituents liked to compare his charisma and his appearance to JFK's. The younger ones said he looked more like Patrick Dempsey. Personally I thought he was even more handsome than either man.

When Austin's gaze met mine, he greeted me with his smile, his gaze admiring my dress. After clapping the shoulder of his friend, he turned and kissed me on the cheek. "You look amazing."

I smiled back. "Thank you."

"I was worried."

"I'm sorry." I reached for his hand, lacing my fingers through his. "Last day of school, you know."

"I thought your day ended at three."

"Tommy Dawson stayed after. He—"

Austin's attention wandered over my shoulder. Fifteen seconds into the conversation, and I'd already lost him. He let go of my hand, stepping around me to greet one of the trustees from the University of Richmond. Sighing, I inched back toward the banquet table. Sometimes it seemed as if I was the only person who couldn't hold his attention.

But it was only a season. After the wedding, we'd have a whole week together, not a constituent in sight. And then a lifetime of nights to ourselves.

I reached for a plate on the table.

"Chloe!" Olivia, the thirtysomething woman whom Austin had hired to be his campaign manager, was barreling down on me. Olivia was an organizational wizard, but unlike Austin, she had little concern for her appearance. Her glasses had crept an inch or two down her nose, and the hair she'd tied back was falling out in frizzy chunks. It was as if she singlehandedly severed every ounce of stress that might infect Austin before it festered.

Olivia retrieved the plate from my hands and returned it to the stack. Then she reached for my wrist and tugged me toward the side of the room. "I've been looking for you."

"I was with Austin," I said as if I'd been hanging out for an hour.

"The program starts in twelve minutes," she rattled on. "Dr. Everett is going to speak about the future of the party for ten minutes, and then he'll introduce Austin. Austin will introduce you."

"I know." I shook my arm to free it from her grasp. "You emailed me the schedule."

"When Austin says your name, I want you to smile and give an elegant wave to the cameras on your left." Olivia attempted to demonstrate a wave that wasn't the least bit elegant.

"Like this." I showed off my well-rehearsed smile and wave.

"Exactly." Olivia glanced down at her tablet. "Austin will speak for a half hour and then the orchestra will start playing. You'll move up front for a dance with the candidate."

"Who is also my fiancé."

"Right." She tapped her tablet.

Of course I was right. Why did I feel like I had to convince Olivia—and Austin's family, for that matter—that I was more than a campaign volunteer? Austin was the one who'd pursued me. He was the one who'd proposed.

Olivia's phone buzzed and when she twirled on her heel, I leaned back against the column. Perhaps my "pretty package" analogy was all wrong. On nights like tonight, I was simply a prop. The room quieted when Dr. Everett took the stage. He leaned toward the microphone to introduce Austin, but before he spoke, the music from *Les Misérables* echoed across the room. Swearing under my breath, I dove into my beaded bag, muted my cell.

The doctor made a joke about the interruption, and my cheeks warmed as the people standing nearby chuckled. Hopefully Austin wouldn't find out whose phone disrupted his event. He wouldn't find it nearly as funny as my neighbors.

The ringing stopped, but the phone continued to vibrate in my hand. I glanced down at a text from my mom.

CALL ME! ASAP

The capital letters screamed back at me, and my heart began to race. What if something had happened to my grandmother?

With apologies to those around me, I ducked my head and carefully backed out of the crowd, grateful my new heels held steady as I exited through the arched doorway behind me. I would be back inside the ballroom in five minutes for my obligatory wave.

In the hallway, I called my mom back. She answered on the first ring.

"Is Mémé okay?" I demanded.

"As far as I know, she's fine."

"And Dad?"

"Chloe wants to know if you're okay," she called out. There was a muffled response in the background before she spoke to me again. "Your dad says everything is fine."

I took a deep breath, my heart slowing back to a normal pace.

"Where are you?" my mom asked.

"At the fund-raiser downtown. I have to get back inside—Austin's about to introduce me." I leaned back against a wall. "I thought it was an emergency."

"It is an emergency," she replied. "Is your passport up-to-date?"

"My passport?" I replied, agitated. Clearly we had different definitions of *emergency*. "My passport is not a matter of urgency."

"But is it current?"

"Yes." Just last summer, right before I met Austin, my best friend, Marissa, and I had kayaked through Costa Rica. But Mom and I would have to discuss my passport situation later. It wouldn't be long before Austin took the stage. "I have to go—"

The following sigh would have impressed all twenty-seven of my third graders. "Between school and the campaign, it's never a good time to talk with you."

"I'll have more time starting Monday."

"Oh, good." Mom paused. "Because your dad and I need you to do something next week."

I drummed my fingers against my dress. "What exactly do you need me to do?"

"We need you . . ." She hesitated. "Well, we need you to go to France."

"France?" The word came out as a shout. I stepped farther back into the hallway. My father was from France, and I'd spent two summers after college touring Paris and southern France. I loved everything about the country, but I couldn't go back now, nine weeks before my wedding.

My mom talked faster now. "Have you heard of Riley Holtz?"

"The name sounds familiar—"

"He's won all sorts of awards for his documentaries about historical events and he wants to film part of his new documentary at the château."

I switched the phone to my left ear, confused. The Château d'Epines was my grandmother's childhood home in Normandy, a grand fortress of beauty and legend that had captivated me since I was a girl. I'd only been there once, when I was eight years old. My grandmother wanted to honor her brother, Michel, with a tombstone in the family's cemetery, by the old chapel. My parents wanted to go with her, but for some reason, Grandpa hadn't been able to travel with us.

My family had spent an hour with a priest at a chapel, honoring Michel's life, and then we'd left without going inside the château. Philippe—my third cousin, multiple times removed—lived there with his wife and son. I remembered Dad saying he wished someone would remove Philippe from our family altogether.

But Philippe was gone now and so were the three wives he'd accumulated over the years. His son, Stéphane, had lived at the château until his father's death. After he moved to Paris, Stéphane sent regular letters to my grandmother, asking if he could return to the Château d'Epines.

My dad hadn't wanted to visit his childhood home since that trip years ago.

I tightened the grip on my phone, trying to focus. I only had two minutes, maybe less, before Austin took the stage. "What does the documentary have to do with the château?"

"Mr. Holtz wants to hear the stories from World War II."

I leaned back against the walls, which were striped with a muddy yellow and white. I knew plenty of stories about the château but very little from the years during the war. "I wish Mémé could tell him."

"Me too."

It was too late to ask her now. Even though her body was plenty strong, her mind had failed. "Why can't Stéphane handle it?" I asked. "Or the caretakers Dad hired?"

My mom cleared her throat. "Your dad doesn't want Stéphane back on the property, and this gentleman wants to talk to someone in the family."

"Then Dad should go—"

"He has to be in DC on Tuesday."

"This Tuesday?" My retort came out as more of a squeak.

"We thought you would be perfect—"

"I have nine weeks to plan a wedding!"

"The planning will be here when you return."

My mind whirled. Going back to the château was a dream of mine, but the timing was terrible. Austin would be frustrated if I even entertained the idea of leaving the country, and I couldn't blame him. The next weeks were pivotal to the campaign.

"I would go in a heartbeat if I could, Mom, but there's so much to do—"

"Your dad really wants you to do this," she whispered.

"But why now—" Austin's voice thundered over the speakers, and I rushed out of the hallway. "I really have to go, Mom. Austin's about to introduce me."

Slipping my phone back into my bag, I hurried back toward the ballroom, but as I neared the door, one of my stilettos rebelled and my ankle teetered. My hands flailed until I caught myself on a railing, and with my ankle throbbing, I reached down and freed my foot from the straps.

The audience laughed at Austin's opening joke, and for the first time, I hoped he would forget he was engaged.

Unfortunately, he didn't.

"It's an honor to introduce my lovely fiancée to all of you," he said. And then I heard him say my name. "Chloe Sauver."

Applause swept out the doors, into the hall. If I stumbled into the ballroom now, flustered and limping on one shoe, I would only create a spectacle, and there was nothing Austin hated more than attention being diverted from the campaign. Better for the audience to think—

Well, I wasn't sure what they would think, but they hadn't come to the gala to see me anyway. Austin would continue on just fine without me, and I would apologize to him after everyone was gone.

I leaned my head back against the wall. My parents' request had rattled me.

How could they ask me to visit France next week? They knew I loved France—that I'd dreamed about exploring the Château d'Epines—but life had collided with my dreams.

If I couldn't talk my parents out of this plan, Austin would do it with his perfect mix of charm and reason, explaining perfectly well why someone else would have to entertain this filmmaker in Normandy.

～ *Chapter 5* ～

*G*isèle woke with a jolt, sunlight stealing through the dormer window in André and Nadine's guest room. The room was quiet, but instead of celebrating the silence, it terrified her. Where were the German bombers? And where were Papa, Philippe, and Michel?

Her arms and legs were bruised, and last night Nadine had helped her bandage her bloodied knees. Then her friend had loaned her a pink nightgown to wear to bed. On a chair near the window, Nadine had draped a fresh blouse and skirt for her to borrow.

Gisèle closed her eyes again.

If only she could be more like her mother—the former Lady Serena Eckley. The Vicomtesse Duchant after she married Papa. Her mother would have faced the Germans with courage and strength like she had in the previous war, but right now, Gisèle felt nothing but fear.

Forcing herself to rise, she smoothed her hair and stepped across the creaky floor to dress in her friend's clothes. They were a size smaller than what Gisèle wore but a much better alternative than the smoky, torn clothing she'd arrived in last night.

Her forehead against the windowpane, she scanned the tips of the trees for Nazi planes, but only puffs of cumulus clouds hung overhead. As if the heart of France hadn't changed overnight.

Had the Germans already taken Saint-Lô? The Batiers' property stretched into the trees, all the way down to the river, and collided with her family's property line. Most of the townspeople avoided this patch near the river due to the dozens of beehives along the path, some of them built centuries ago. Neither André nor Nadine tried to persuade them otherwise. The previous owner of their home had been an avid beekeeper, but André and Nadine had never officially kept bees. Even without the Batiers' assistance, the insects continued to flourish between the hawthorns.

André and Nadine had bought the house three years ago, days after André accepted a position as a teacher at the secondary school in Saint-Lô. The house had been a disaster with its crooked shutters and crumbling fireplace and unpainted wooden walls. Apparently the previous owner had been more enamored of beekeeping than housekeeping.

Michel helped André repair the fireplace, and in the following months, before Nadine's parents moved down to Grenoble, Gisèle assisted Nadine and her mother in painting the exterior a creamy yellow color, straightening the shutters, and planting a garden. There were few places more beautiful now than the Batiers' backyard in springtime, but she couldn't linger here.

In the clarity of morning, she knew what she had to do. She would sneak back to the château and tell Michel all that had happened. Then she would meet Philippe and leave with him and Papa—if Papa still remained.

Michel had enough food and apple brandy to last at least three days. Her brother didn't want to leave, but she would convince him to go to Switzerland as well. Perhaps they could meet on the other side of the border. Or perhaps the British would come to their country's rescue and they could return home.

Her door inched open, and she turned to see her dear friend standing in the doorway.

"I didn't want to wake you," Nadine said. "But it's almost ten."

She glanced back out the window. "Do you have any news?"

"I'm afraid not much of consequence." She looked out the window. "The aeroplanes haven't returned this morning."

Gisèle pressed her fingers against the glass. "I suppose that is the best of news right now."

"Come eat." Nadine was small in stature, but André had nicknamed his wife "Flambée." Not because of her temper—Gisèle had never seen her friend angry—but because she was passionate about her garden, her home, her family. Her charcoal hair was coiled at her neck, and her olive skin was flawless. Years ago, she'd been confirmed in the Catholic Church, the faith of her community, but it would have been impossible to hide the Jewish heritage in her features.

The three of them had stayed up past four, until the skies grew quiet, listening to the BBC on the wireless even though there was little news reported during the night.

André and Nadine decided not to run—they had no automobile and knew they wouldn't get far on their bicycles. Besides, André said, Nadine's family was in southern France and his family had moved to Morocco. There was no place for them to go. So they hunkered down in their cottage to see what would happen next.

Gisèle followed Nadine down into the living room. Nadine paused, lifting the corner of the curtain as if she were checking for the Germans before she turned toward Gisèle. "I'm afraid of what they will do if they stay here."

For a moment, Gisèle flashed back to her years in primary school, before Nadine and her family emigrated from Austria.

Even though she preferred riding her bicycle up the long path like the other children, her father insisted that their chauffeur drive her to school. Most of the kids in her class shunned her, refusing to play with the "queen from the castle." She wasn't a queen and never thought of herself as nobility in those years. She viewed herself as a Norman girl who happened to live in a big house. A lonely Norman girl who had only her family and her father's horses for company.

Then Nadine arrived in Saint-Lô when they were both eight, and they became instant friends. They'd eaten lunch together every day, jumped rope on the playground, and stayed up late giggling on the rare occasions when Gisèle's parents allowed a slumber party in the château. When Gisèle lost her mother, Nadine cried with her until no more tears would come, and even now, ten years later, Nadine sometimes mourned Gisèle's loss. But her mother wouldn't want them to grieve right now. She would want them to stand up to their enemy.

But how could they fight the Germans on their own?

Nadine rolled her hands over her belly and for the first time, Gisèle noticed the slightest bulge in her friend's abdomen. She met the eyes of her friend and saw the anxiety in them. "Nadine?"

She nodded toward the closed door of the office, the buzz of the wireless seeping out to the living room. "André doesn't know yet."

"Why not?"

"At first . . ." She swallowed. "At first, I wanted to be certain, and then when I confirmed it, I was scared. It's a terrible time to bring a baby into the world."

Gisèle thought of the joy a child would bring to all of them. "The baby won't know it's a terrible time." Just like she hadn't known there was a war when she was born. Until her mother died, she only remembered peace and happiness in her home.

"I pray the fighting will be done before she's born," Nadine said, the strength of her desire pressing through her words.

"How do you know it's a she?"

A gentle smile lit Nadine's face. "Just a hunch."

From the next room, she heard the crackle of a voice. Nadine nodded toward the office door. "André's been glued to the wireless all morning."

"Perhaps there is new information."

Nadine pointed toward the door. "You go listen with him. I'll bring lunch."

Gisèle knocked on the door, and André told her to come in. Nadine's husband sat on a padded footstool, his head almost resting on the small speaker of the wireless. His light brown hair was messy, and his wire-rimmed glasses crept down his nose.

The announcer said the French people were fleeing south by the thousands, the French army running alongside them. The French people had been assured that their army was strong enough to resist a German attack, yet everything was crumbling.

As the news broadcast ended, Nadine set a tray with small sandwiches on the desk along with a pot of coffee. "It is too late for us to fight."

André shook his head. "It is never too late. The people in France won't let the Germans stay here."

Nadine collapsed onto a chair. "But what do we do now?"

"We may not be able to fight them with weapons." André reached for his wife's hand, and with his other hand, he pounded his chest. "But we can fight them with our hearts."

Nadine shook her head. "The Germans care nothing about hearts."

"It doesn't matter if they care," André insisted. "It matters that we care about our country. About our fellow man."

Gisèle poured a cup of coffee and took a sip. "Sometimes, I fear, our hearts can steer us wrong."

"We will fight for the good in France," André said. "No matter what happens, we will know we did the right thing."

His words resonated with her. No matter what happened, she needed to fight for what was good as well.

They listened to the BBC, eating their chicken salad sandwiches, but it was the same news. France was still running, reeling, from the German blitzkrieg. And then there was news from London about Winston Churchill, the new prime minister in Britain.

She didn't want to know what was happening in England. She wanted to know what was happening right here, on the streets of Saint-Lo. And at the château.

When the announcer finished, Gisèle stood.

"Please stay with us," Nadine begged her.

"Philippe will be waiting for me," she said as they walked toward the front door. "And I must check on my father."

"Surely the Germans will be gone soon," Nadine said before Gisèle kissed both of her friend's cheeks.

Gisèle tried to smile as she whispered, "Long before your baby is born."

"I pray so."

"What will you name her?"

Fear flickered in Nadine's eyes before she returned Gisèle's smile. "It depends on André, of course, but if it's a girl, I want to name her Louise, after his mother."

Perhaps by the time Louise was born, the world would be righted again. "It's a beautiful name."

"With that name . . ." Pride flashed in her eyes. "No one will ever question whether or not my daughter is a Frenchwoman."

— CHAPTER 6 —

Leaning my head back against the wall, I sank onto the floor of the ballroom and surveyed the damage. A half hour ago, Austin's supporters began trickling out, leaving behind a room littered with plates, napkins, and fancy toothpicks pierced into remnants of food.

At least someone had eaten tonight.

I tossed my sandal toward a chair but nailed a plastic cup on the floor instead. Red wine streamed onto the flecked carpet, and I watched, mesmerized, as the river grew hairline passages of fingers and toes. I should have run for paper towels, mopped up the mess before it stained, but it was half past two in the morning. Somewhere back around one, my energy had begun spilling out like the wine. Now there wasn't a single ounce left in me.

Closing my eyes, I breathed in the blessed silence. My hunger pangs had been numbed, the need for sleep replacing my need for food. Olivia drummed up a chai latte for me around midnight, but the effects had been minimal. No amount of caffeine could replace the benefits of a decent pillow.

The door creaked open on the other side of the room, and in the dim light, I watched Austin moving toward me. I'd botched up his introduction, but I made it for the first dance of the night.

Barefoot. He hadn't said a word about either faux pas. Instead he smiled and I smiled, and for about three minutes, in the magic of the music and the lights, I had his attention.

"Dr. Everett was the last one to leave." Austin turned a chair around to sit beside me. "You think it was a success?"

Somehow his tux had managed to stay wrinkle-free for the entire event and his wavy black hair remained set perfectly in place.

"It was a blockbuster of a night," I said, coaxing my fingers through the stiff spray in my hair. "These people adore you."

He took a long sip from his bottled water. "I tried to introduce you, but you seemed to have disappeared."

A headache clustered over my eyes, and I pressed my middle fingers against my eyebrows. "I'm sorry."

The pout in his smile reminded me more of a kid like Tommy Dawson than of a confident candidate or movie star. "Better to ditch me here than at the altar."

"I didn't ditch you." I pressed harder on my brows, as if I could massage the pain away. "My mom texted and said she needed to speak with me. I thought it was urgent."

"Everything is urgent for your mom." He set his water bottle beside the chair and reached for my left hand, tugging it away from my face. Then he entwined my fingers through his. "What was it this time?"

"Something about a filmmaker shooting a documentary in France. Mom wants me to meet him at the château."

He leaned forward a few inches. "When does she want you to go?"

"Tuesday," I said, "but don't worry. I told her I couldn't do it."

He eyed me for a moment before speaking again. "Is this a documentary about World War II?"

At my nod, he leaned closer, his eyes intent on mine. "When will it air?"

"I have no idea, but it doesn't matter. There's no way I can travel to France next week."

His elbows propped on his legs, he held up my hand. "These are important details, Chloe."

"I have a thousand important details I'm trying to pull together. It's impossible to keep track of them all."

"That's why you hired a wedding coordinator. To help you with the details."

If only it were that easy. I, not the coordinator, would be responsible if everything went awry on August 10. Or, heaven forbid, if I picked out the wrong colors or plates or dresses for my eight bridesmaids—only two of whom were actual friends.

His eyes narrowed slightly, and I knew exactly what he was doing—developing some sort of a plan. "Would he be interviewing you?"

I wished I could read his mind. Why did he care if I did an interview on World War II? "My parents want me to tell him some of Mémé's stories, but it doesn't matter. I only have nine weeks to pull this wedding together."

Nine weeks to achieve perfection.

"So you run away for one of those weeks and get some rest," he said with a shrug. "You'll come back refreshed and ready to tackle what's left."

He drummed on my hand as I processed his words. He made it sound so simple, this running away. I cocked my head, studying him. "You really think I should go to France?"

"I think you should consider it."

Something else was going on behind that smile. I was exhausted, but if I was going to dig, I needed to do it now. Even though we'd be together all day tomorrow, we'd be surrounded.

"What's the real reason you want me to go?"

This time he shrugged. "I want my fiancée to relax."

"And . . . ," I said, pressing him.

He took a deep breath. "And that reporter at the newspaper keeps hounding Olivia for your grandfather's war records. No one can seem to find them."

I yanked my hand away from his grip. "It's none of the reporter's business—"

"That's not how he sees it, especially since we keep telling the press that you're the granddaughter of a war hero." He put his hands on the floor. "If we tell him you're being interviewed for a documentary on the war, it might deter him for a bit, at least until after the campaign."

I rested my head back against the wall. I'd never asked Olivia to tell the media about my grandfather, but she wrote about him in my bio and then touted his military service.

I'd certainly never refuted his record, and it was much too late to tell Austin that Henri Sauver wasn't actually my biological grandfather. Henri was the only father my dad ever knew, and I was proud of him.

Grandpa had passed away fifteen years ago, but Mémé told me he was an officer in the Armée de Terre before the occupation— and a member of the French resistance after it. They'd met, she said, in Saint-Lô. Right after the war. And moved to Virginia.

I didn't remember Grandpa talking about his years before or during the war and as I grew older, I wished I knew more about his story—their story. Unlike Austin and the media, I didn't even particularly care about Grandpa's war record. I wanted to know the stories of how my grandparents met. And why they traded a château in France for a trilevel in Fairfax, Virginia.

Austin's reasoning for the needed PR was more viable than his urging me to vacate. He had no problem energizing the younger voters, but neither he nor Olivia was convinced that the younger crowd would turn out en masse at the polls. His competitor was a devoted family man with twenty-five years of experience, and Austin needed more than Virginia's millennials to elect him governor. The campaign needed to show that he was grounded. That he respected those generations who fought in the wars before him. His family's military roots were shallow—one grandfather was a conscientious objector and the other had married his first of four wives in order to dodge the draft for Vietnam. Even though the details were sparse, my grandfather's record provided Austin with at least the appearance of roots.

"You'll charm both the videographer and the viewers," he said.

"I'm no expert on World War II."

"I'll have Olivia put together a cheat sheet for you."

I cocked my head. "Methinks you are trying to get rid of me, Governor."

"I hate it when you call me that," he said, but he didn't mean it.

I glanced up at the light glowing from the chandelier. When Mom called, I thought traveling to France would be impossible until after the election, but perhaps it was plausible, even beneficial, for me to go.

Olivia was a pro at creating buzz even when there wasn't much to buzz about. A couple press releases about an upcoming documentary, along with an interview or two about the war, might convince Virginia's older generation that Austin was astute enough to be their governor.

"If Gisèle knows you're going, perhaps she would remember more stories," he said.

"Mémé rarely remembers anything these days, but I know a few stories about my grandfather."

"All we need are a few crumbs to throw to the media," Austin said as if he'd already decided I was going. "Then we won't have to worry about the records."

I wanted to know these stories, every one of them, but it had nothing to do with distracting the media.

"*The château was magical,*" Mémé told me when I was younger, after she'd read me one of the Narnia stories. "*Like Cair Paravel.*"

She'd told me stories about her and her brother swimming in the lake when they were children. About the gardens and her father's horses and the glowworms that lit their path in the summer. She told me about her parents and how she adored them, but whenever I asked her about the war, she would tell me about my grandfather's work. When I asked what she had done during the war, she'd change the subject.

Austin reached for my hand again and gently squeezed it. "Go and enjoy the French food and the wine and give this guy a few good sound bites for his show. You'll come back refreshed and ready for the rest of the campaign season."

"And for our wedding." I don't know why I felt like I needed to remind him, but I did.

"Of course." This time he let go of my hand. "The wedding."

✎ Chapter 7 ✎

The relentless rhythm of jackboots pounded across the valley and latched on to the beat of Gisèle's heart. Even though an hour had passed, the rhythm still echoed in her mind, defiant and strong as the soldiers marched along the river path. The path that led to her home.

The soldiers were gone, but she remained hidden behind the swollen trunks of the beech trees, praying that Papa had fled and that Michel remained hidden.

She scanned the herds of butterscotch-colored cows grazing on the grassy hill across the river and the forest above them. To her right, the cathedral in Saint-Lô towered above the hills, and to her left, up on the cliff, was her family's château. Even though wars had raged in the valley for centuries, the Château d'Epines, protected by the forest and cliffs and stone walls, remained strong.

Before the French Revolution, her family's property had stretched across the Batiers' land, all the way to Saint-Lô. Life turned upside down during the revolution and several of her ancestors across the country had been beheaded. When radicals came for the head of the Vicomtesse Jeanne Duchant, she crawled into the hollowed-out trunk of an enormous elm tree and hid. Leaning back against the crusty bark of a tree, Gisèle petitioned the Blessed Virgin Mary for the protection and patience that had been gifted to her ancestor.

The French government had thought their country was as formidable as her family's château, but somehow the Germans had found a chink in their armor. Michel and other Frenchmen might have to hide now, but eventually they would fight. Like they had in the Great War.

Papa said there was no reason for the Germans to linger in Saint-Lô since they were intent on reaching Great Britain. The port of Cherbourg was a hundred kilometers to the north, and after the Germans took the port, they'd fight for England across the Channel.

But why were the soldiers still here?

A black speck appeared above Saint-Lô, and she ducked back into the forest. A yellow engine gleamed in the light as one plane and then a dozen of them flew low over the valley, each one touting a hooked cross on its tail as if they were fishing for the enemy.

Closing her eyes, Gisèle sank into a bed of leaves and buried her head. If they dropped a bomb on her beloved home, she couldn't bear to watch it.

And if they dropped a bomb—what would happen to Papa? And Michel and his men?

She prayed they were all safe, that Philippe had gotten out of Saint-Lô and Papa had fled during the night. And that Michel hadn't left the tunnel.

A minute passed, perhaps two, and the sound of engines had faded. She rose and looked back over the valley again.

On the other side of her house were fields to the north of the river—farmed by the Polin family, who rented the property from her father—and to the south was a forest filled with treasures: a small lake and caves and a medieval guardhouse that she and Nadine had deemed their meeting place when they were twelve.

The planes would spot her if she stepped onto the river's path, but in the darkness she could hide. She knew every step of the valley and the forest on the other side. If she waited until night, the Germans would never catch her.

She crept back under the cover of the hawthorn trees. They were in full bloom, the white petals like flakes of snow icing the thorns. Bees buzzed among the fragrant blossoms, and they seemed as unafraid of her as she was of them. As long as the sweetness of the flowers quenched their thirst, she didn't have to worry about the bees' sting.

Birds hid among the hawthorn branches, protected by the thorns, the melodies of their songs the only clue to their presence.

She wondered what it was they sang about. Perhaps it was their hunger or their fright or even their love. Whatever it was, they seemed oblivious to the dangers above them and on the ground. If only she could be oblivious alongside them. Still, the serenity of their song calmed the rhythm in her heart, the hours passing slowly as she waited.

The steady cadence of their song reminded her of her two years in the convent boarding school near Coutances, the familiar prayers flowing from their lips with the music. She hadn't appreciated the music as a child. Sometimes she and her friend Odette were downright awful.

The nuns in their boarding school had known French and Latin and a little English, but not a word of German. Odette had learned German from her grandfather and taught the basics to Gisèle so they could share their secrets without fear of a nun discovering their plans. They had been perfectly naughty during their middle-grade years—salting the porridge of the mother superior, hiding the prayer books of their classmates. When the others sang their morning hymns, she and Odette replaced the words with the lyrics from "Parlez-Moi d'Amour," giggling about treasures and kisses, bitterness and love.

The nuns may have suspected that she and Odette were the instigators of trouble, but they weren't caught until one windy afternoon in March when they were both fourteen. After they borrowed two horses from the stable—and got themselves lost in the forest—the mother superior whipped them both with a switch and sent them home for a week of reflection.

Papa spared her another round with the rod, but he insisted that Gisèle spend a miserable week in isolation and reflection. There had been no riding for her in the hills near their house, no wading in the lake below the château. Even Michel—the boy who'd never let rules stop him—was disappointed in her.

In hindsight, Papa was probably more afraid of her getting injured than disappointed in her for taking the horses. After a week of eating alone in her bedroom, she decided to tolerate the rules at school until summer break. The next year her father sent her to another boarding school, one where she rode horses every day.

During the summers, she'd ridden her horse up into the trees on the other side of the river. When she was fifteen, she'd been fond of a boy who lived in the woods—a boy named Jean-Marc Rausch. He and his parents used to come to the Mass at the *chapelle* long ago, but after she left for the university, she never saw him again.

Had he and his parents moved before the war? And what had become of him and her other classmates and of Odette in Paris?

The birds' song faded as darkness fell. Gisèle crept out of her hiding place and followed the river until she reached the steep bike path up to the château. In the moonlight, she could see the gray walls of the château, but there were no lights on inside. The other servants, she assumed, had fled like Émilie. Were Papa and Philippe waiting for her in the darkness?

She scanned the empty courtyard and driveway in front of the château. Perhaps Philippe had hidden his *coupé* in the carriage house or—she shuddered—perhaps he and Papa had gone on to Lyon without her.

Two towers soared over the stone castle, and she eyed the one on the far side of the house. Thorns from the rosebushes pecked at her arms as she snuck through the formal garden and around the old masonry oven that hadn't been used in a century or two. At the base of the tower, she clambered around the hedges and jimmied the top of a window until it opened.

The lock had been broken for years—it had been an easy way for her to sneak in and out at night to meet Nadine, before her friend married André. Her heart pounding, Gisèle lifted one leg onto the windowsill and then pulled herself through, into the small study.

"Papa?" she whispered in the darkness.

Accounting ledgers, newspapers, and the *Farmers' Almanac* were piled up on the side of Papa's desk, and his wireless stood against the wall beside it. When she was younger, she'd been afraid of the dark, and in the evenings, she'd often draped herself over the damask chair beside the desk and pretended to read while he pored over his books. Really she'd been watching him, fascinated as he calculated his figures and talked business on his black telephone and thumbed through *La Croix*. In the cadence of his work, she found comfort. After her mother passed away, she'd known her father would take care of her.

But if Papa had already left the château, she would have to care for herself. Like she'd wanted to do in Paris.

She lifted the telephone receiver from the cradle, to call Tante Corinne and see if she'd heard from Philippe, but the line was dead. Sighing, she dropped the receiver back onto the brass bands.

She leaned back against the open window, the warm moonlight casting shadows over the office. In the silence of her home, she listened to the sound of her breathing. Was Papa someplace inside the house? Or were there Germans hiding upstairs?

No matter how much she hoped the Germans had kept marching down the valley, she didn't know for certain, and she hated this, the feeling that her home was no longer a safe place.

Something moved behind the desk, and her breath caught in her throat. Clenching her fists, she willed herself to be strong, but her courage dissolved within her. She turned to flee back out of the window until she heard the softest of meows from under the desk. The trappings of her breath slipped out as she ducked under the desktop.

The source of her fear was crouched in the dark corner. A kitten.

"How did you get in here?" she whispered as she gently pulled him out into the light.

The kitten reached up with its paw and batted her nose.

She cradled him close to the window, brushing her face over his soft gray fur. On his neck was a white fleck in the shape of a star, and she could feel his tiny ribs through his skin.

"If Papa found you, he would put you right back outside where you belong," she said, scolding him.

She scratched his chin, and he purred back at her. A kitten could do nothing to protect her, yet somehow it made her feel more secure, bold even, to have it near. She dug through the top drawer of Papa's desk until she found the flashlight he kept for when the electricity failed. Then, the kitten in her arms, she crept through the large dining salon, past the long table and massive fireplace with the three lambs carved on the mantel. On her left side, a row of windows framed the courtyard, *chapelle*, and long drive. On the other side of the room four windows overlooked the river valley and the grassy hill and forest across the valley.

"Papa?" she called out again as she tiptoed into the foyer. No one responded, but the front door was partially open.

Had someone been here, or had Papa left the door open when he left?

She closed it.

On the other side of the foyer was the kitchen, and when she stepped inside, she flipped on the flashlight and set the kitten beside the brick fireplace. Copper pots hung neatly on each side of the mantel and two cast iron kettles rested along the hearth. The fireplace was built when the château was renovated in the seventeenth century, but their cook only used the white gas oven her parents had installed before she was born.

Gisèle stared at the spokes on the range and then looked at the three drawers beside it. She should make Michel some bread or something else, but how was she supposed to feed her brother when she didn't even know how to light an oven?

She sighed. Just because she wanted to help didn't mean she was able to do it.

Opening up the refrigerator door, she removed a pint of milk and trickled it into a bowl for—

She looked back down at the kitten as he lapped up the milk. "What should I call you?"

There were too many silly pet names—Fluffy, Tiger, Smudge. But this kitten was smart, hiding from the Germans. Shadow— that's what she would call him.

Then she scanned the contents in the refrigerator. There was a tub of butter, along with salami and cheese. On the counter was a half loaf of *pain noir*, the hardy black bread their cook liked to bake. It wasn't much food, but she hoped it would sustain her brother until the Germans left.

She set the flashlight on the counter and reached for a glass goblet to fill with water when the door to the kitchen swung open. Shadow leapt up on the counter, and she dropped the goblet as she whirled around, glass shattering across the floor.

Someone stood at the door, but she couldn't see their face. Sweeping the flashlight off the counter, she shined it toward the door.

"Émilie," she said with a sigh, her heart calming. "What are you doing here?"

The older woman tossed her valise onto the wooden table that stood before the fireplace. "I tried to walk to Cahagnes, but didn't get far."

Gisèle sank back against the counter. "I'm sorry."

"It's no matter," Émilie said, eyeing the salami and cheese on the counter. "I don't know what is to become of us, but in the meantime, I can help you and your father."

"I need you, but . . ."

Her gaze fell to the kitten lapping milk on the floor. "You better take that cat outside before Vicomte Duchant sees it."

"Papa's not here."

Émilie's eyes welled up with worry. "Where is he?"

Gisèle swallowed hard, trying to calm the fear that sparked fresh inside her. She didn't tell Émilie about the soldiers she'd seen marching toward the château. "He was planning to head south, after Philippe and I left, but we didn't get past Saint-Lô. I spent the night at the Batiers."

Émilie glanced back toward the door. "Is his automobile still here?"

"I haven't checked the carriage house yet."

"What about Philippe?"

"I don't know." She couldn't consider the possibility that he'd been injured, but the bombs had been falling and people stampeded in their frantic attempt to escape them.

"It will not be safe for you here," Émilie said.

"I'm afraid no place is safe in France."

"Perhaps I could stay and help you find your father?"

"I will go check the carriage house." Gisèle rapped her knuckles on the stovetop, the loneliness beginning to fade away. "Can you bake some bread tonight?"

"It doesn't seem right to bake . . ."

"I want to take it to those who are hungry." She paused. "Like my mother used to do."

Émilie tilted her head slightly, studying Gisèle's face. "Your mother used to take food every week to the children in the orphanage."

Gisèle nodded. When she was younger, she'd sometimes joined her mother to deliver the baskets of fresh vegetables and bread. "I'm not going to the orphanage."

Émilie opened the refrigerator. "But we can pretend you are."

Gisèle picked up Shadow. The world outside might be spiraling, but here inside the château, perhaps she and Émilie would find peace. Until Papa or Philippe returned, it would be their refuge in the storm.

— CHAPTER 8 —

Saturday night's dinner was supposed to be a casual affair, but Austin's mother wore pearls with her ivory cocktail dress and coral cardigan. The table was set with antique silver and crystal goblets and folded napkins on the china plates. I wore the same yellow sundress I'd worn at today's luncheon, but still I felt underdressed.

Mr. and Mrs. Vale anchored each end of their dining room table. On one side, Mrs. Vale sipped a mint julep with shaved ice. On the other, Mr. Vale drank his bourbon straight up. I sat across from Austin's older sister, Lisa, and Austin faced his brother—a sixteen-year-old skateboarder officially named Lawrence, though for some reason unknown to me, everyone called him Vos.

Lisa's husband, Wyatt, was absent from the meal. I'd only seen Wyatt twice in the year since I began dating Austin, but in his absence Mrs. Vale touted his successes as a busy executive, as if the family could somehow take credit for his accolades.

Marissa had tried to talk me out of coming tonight, tempting me with an evening out at Tarrant's instead to celebrate the end of the school year. Marissa thought I spent way too much time pandering to Austin and his campaign. Before he proposed, she'd tried to talk me into breaking up with him, saying I should be with

someone who loved me much more than Austin ever could. Now
that we were engaged, she tolerated him, but sometimes I wondered if an undercurrent of jealousy drove her to dislike him. Still
I missed hanging out with my best friend. I'd asked her to celebrate at the gala with me last night, but she declined. Even though
we were on the phone, I knew the exact moment she'd rolled her
eyes.

"A gala is work," she informed me. "You need an official
'Hooray—summer is finally here' party that doesn't involve politics."

I promised to celebrate with her next week, but now I'd have
to reschedule. I didn't need a coordinator for my wedding. I
needed one for my life.

Mrs. Vale cupped her manicured hands and held them out to
her daughter. "Please pass the green beans."

Lisa reached for the bowl on the sideboard behind her and
passed it along. The beans were followed by Virginia ham, rosemary potatoes, and French bread from Patty Wilson's chain of
boutique bakeries.

Lisa began buttering her bread. "I wish I could go to New
York with you on Tuesday."

I glanced up at her and then over at Austin, confused. Just an
hour ago, after a conversation with both Austin and Olivia, I'd
texted my mom with the go-ahead to buy plane tickets. She'd
booked me on the first flight out on Tuesday, through New York,
but I hadn't even told Austin it was a done deal.

Lisa smiled at me as if she was conspiring. "We could storm
Fifth Avenue together in search of your trousseau."

"I won't have time . . ."

Lisa glanced at Austin. "Does Starla still own a shop in Manhattan?"

He choked on his bite of ham.

I poked my fork into a potato. "Who's Starla?"

Austin took a long sip of water, recovering before he replied. "An old family friend."

I turned back to Lisa. "I'm only flying through New York."

Now Lisa seemed confused. "Aren't you going with Austin to the fund-raiser?"

I put down my fork—I didn't know anything about a fund-raiser.

Austin lifted his glass of sweet tea. "Chloe's leaving for France on Tuesday."

In his ambiguity, it sounded as if I were going on vacation.

Mrs. Vale took the potatoes from Lisa. "Why in the world are you going to France?"

"I think it's fantastic," Lisa said. "You can storm the shops in Paris instead."

Austin winked at me. "An excellent idea."

"Perhaps I will," I said, trying to match my voice with the lightness in his, but I wasn't letting him off the hook. I'd wait and ask about the fund-raiser when we were alone—there was no sense in pointing out my ignorance in front of his entire family.

Mrs. Vale dished a small serving of potatoes onto her plate. "Austin tells us the wedding plans are going well."

"Yes, ma'am," I replied.

Vos snorted at my formality, but even after a year of dating Austin, I wasn't quite sure what to call her. *Mrs. Vale* didn't sound right. Neither did *Katherine*. Austin and Lisa called her *Mother*, but I figured I needed an invite to use that title. And even if she suggested it, I wasn't sure I could say the word. Katherine Vale was nothing like my mother. For the moment, I was sticking with *ma'am*.

"Lisa can help you finalize the décor for your reception. She has excellent taste."

"Mother!" Lisa sputtered. "Chloe has wonderful taste too."

If Mrs. Vale had been sitting beside me, I was certain she would have patted my hand, but instead she indulged me with a strained smile. "I'm sure you do, dear, but it's good to rely on the experts for something as big as this."

Austin reached for my hand instead, as if his touch would erase her insult.

"Patty Wilson told me she will make your cake," Mrs. Vale said.

I glanced at Austin. "But my mother was planning—"

"For heaven's sake, Katherine," Mr. Vale interrupted, "it's her wedding. Let her choose who makes the cake."

Austin looked at his dad. "Patty and Robert are some of our largest contributors."

"And they will continue to contribute, even if Patty doesn't bake your damn cake," Mr. Vale said. "Robert has much bigger reasons to have you in office than to secure business for his wife."

Mrs. Vale stabbed one of her potatoes. "But Patty makes the best cakes in Richmond."

Heat rose to my face. It was one thing to insult me, quite another to insult my mother. "I don't think—"

Austin squeezed my hand a bit harder than necessary. "Perhaps this isn't the right time to have this discussion."

"It's only a cake," Vos said as he rolled his eyes. "I'll make it."

I slowly chewed a piece of the ham. While I loved Austin, dinners like these might drive me mad. Perhaps after the wedding I could use whatever excuse Wyatt had contrived to go AWOL. In my absence, perhaps Mrs. Vale would begin to sing my praises.

The doorbell rang, and the housekeeper bustled down the hall to the door. Seconds later, the former runner-up for Miss Virginia—Megan Browning—stepped onto a different kind of stage, the theater of the Vale family dining room. Her blond hair was smoothed back into a neat ponytail and she wore a fitted shirt over black leggings. Even though she was almost twice his age, Vos gawked at her.

Megan shifted her briefcase into her left hand, breaking the awkward silence. "I didn't mean to interrupt your dinner."

Mr. Vale threw his napkin onto the table and pushed back his chair. "Megan's helping me write an opinion for Monday morning."

"But you've hardly eaten . . . ," Mrs. Vale said.

He lifted his plate from the table. "I'll finish in my office."

Vos leaned slightly to watch Megan's backside as she disappeared down the hall.

"Lawrence," Mrs. Vale snapped from the other end of the table. "Pass the potatoes."

Vos glanced away long enough to retrieve the silver platter in front of him and pass it along to his mother. Mrs. Vale added another spoonful of potatoes to the pile already on her plate.

I shifted uncomfortably on the hard seat. The family liked to pretend Justice Vale wasn't sleeping with his law clerk, and I tried to ignore this fact with the rest of them. The thought made me queasy. Megan had graduated from George Mason University two years ago with her degree in law, but I doubted Justice Vale had hired her for the degree. Silently I wondered how much he paid her to assist him.

I glanced over at Mrs. Vale and her lips were pressed into a tight line. How could she live like this? How could they all continue to pretend? My parents had been married for thirty-two years, but if my mom thought Dad was cheating, she would never let him—and certainly not the woman he was sleeping with— back into our home.

Mrs. Vale stood and clapped her hands. "Who's ready for dessert?"

I looked down at my plate. Like the rest of the family, I'd barely begun to eat, but she left us no choice. "I'll help you clear the dishes," I said as I stood.

Twenty minutes later, Austin and I leaned against the banister of their deck, looking down at the lights of Richmond.

He reached for my hand. "You know I love you."

"I do, but I wish you'd told me about the fund-raiser in New York."

He covered my hand with his. "I thought I did."

"I would have remembered——"

"I'm sorry, Chloe. It's been so crazy." He squeezed my hand. "I wish you could go with me. It's a formal dinner and dance at the Plaza."

"Are you leaving Tuesday morning?"

He nodded.

I smiled at the thought of the two of us indulging in first class together, dreaming about where the future might take us. "Perhaps we can fly together. It would be like stealing away for a whole hour."

"I wish we could," he said, squeezing my hand again. "But my flight's going into LaGuardia."

I sighed. I had to go through John F. Kennedy for my connection to Paris.

"We'll drive to the airport together," he promised. "Just the two of us."

I heard Megan's laughter below the patio, and my stomach

churned. I inched my hand away from his. "How can you tolerate your father's—*behavior?*"

Austin leaned forward, his arms resting on the banister, his voice low. "Dad will do what he wants to do."

"But he's cheating on your mom," I said, my voice clipped. I didn't care if Megan or Justice Vale or anyone else in the family heard me.

"It's not really cheating if Mom knows."

"That's disgusting, Austin. He's on Virginia's supreme court, for heaven's sake. He's supposed to be a pillar of all that is right."

He stood up, pulling me close. "It's how they do their marriage."

"It's not how we will do our marriage," I said, melting into him.

"We'll be more like your parents." He stroked my arm. "I need you, Chloe. You know that, don't you?"

"You just need a wife . . . ," I said, teasing him.

He kissed the top of my head. "You're stuck with me for life, for better or worse."

"Mostly better, I hope."

He pulled me in front of him, and I leaned back against his chest. "It will be the best," he promised.

And I believed him.

Chapter 9

Rain pecked at the dozen panes on Gisèle's bedroom window, and she pressed her nose to the glass, trying to spot any Germans patrolling the river valley below, but the valley was still. Her gaze went up to the gray sky and then to the tower of Saint-Lô's cathedral.

She'd slept little last night. The family's Delahaye was sitting in the old carriage house that had been remodeled as a garage, but there was no sign of her father. She tried to cling to the hope that Philippe had returned after the bombing and taken Papa away with him. Perhaps they were both searching for her. Once the telephone lines were restored, she told herself, both Papa and Philippe would call.

Still, she felt scattered, not knowing whether she should stay and wait for Papa and Philippe or go look for them. Life, it seemed, had tipped over on its side, cracking into tiny pieces. Somehow she had to fit it back together again.

After she went to the carriage house, she visited the *chapelle*—both to pray and to leave the black bread and a letter for Michel on the ledge, telling him all that had transpired. If he hadn't left yet, she would take him Émilie's food this morning.

Last night she'd taken a hot bath with lavender bath salts, cleaned her wounds, and washed her hair with the honey-scented shampoo her mother had loved before setting her hair with curlers. She had blue eyes, like her mother, but the skin under her eyes was tinted purple from her restless night.

This morning she splashed water on her face and quickly powdered her nose and cheeks before studying herself in the washroom mirror. It seemed trivial to be concerned with her appearance, but her mother would have told her to face this day— and any Germans in it—with dignity. She'd been born into an aristocratic family, Mother would have said, and the enemy would never respect the lineage of her family if she didn't respect herself.

She powdered her face again.

Émilie was already bustling in the kitchen, and Gisèle drank a cup of coffee before eating the last slice of bread, slathered with jelly made from the hawthorn berries. As the rain drizzled down the window, the two women kneaded the rye and wheat flour together to make four more loaves of bread.

It felt strange to be in the kitchen, working alongside the woman who'd been her mother's favorite servant. The camaraderie eased the loneliness in her heart, and Émilie seemed to be enjoying her company as well.

Émilie talked about her father, who'd worked at the Palais-Royal until his death in 1934, and about her sister and nephews, who lived in Cahagnes. They both talked of the family members they'd lost a little more than twenty years ago, when France defeated Germany during the Great War.

Gisèle had been born only three months before the Great War ended, so she only knew the stories her parents told her, but Émilie remembered well the horrors of that war, the millions of young men France lost to the battles, the blood of their countrymen spilling over French soil.

"We must defeat the Germans quickly this time," Émilie said as she pounded the dough in front of her.

Gisèle mimicked the way Émilie pounded her bread. "What will happen if we don't defeat them?"

She sighed. "I fear this Hitler will make us pay dearly for the past."

"Half of France wasn't even alive during the Great War."

"It won't matter to him."

Gisèle had read the first part of Hitler's book *Mein Kampf* when she was at the university. One of her professors extolled the honesty of Hitler's struggle, the fervor of his words, but the hatred in the man's writing—his soul—appalled her. Hitler asserted that the Aryan race—the blond-haired and blue-eyed men and women—was elite. The Jews were parasites, dirty, wily, repulsive, liars. The mortal enemy of the master race.

She couldn't finish reading the book.

Hitler might make the French pay for the Great War, but there was something more sinister about the man than revenge.

Gisèle turned over the dough in her hands. "I am going to bike into Saint-Lô this morning, to see if I can find a pay phone that works."

Émilie stopped kneading. "You can't go alone."

"I won't be gone long."

Émilie turned over the dough in her hands, studying Gisèle for a moment before she spoke again. "What other food will you need to take to the orphanage?"

Gisèle pressed her lips together. The only thing her brother had ever requested was the local Calvados, but he couldn't live forever on apple brandy. "Some cheese, I suppose, and hard-boiled eggs or meat."

The exhaustion in Émilie's eyes fled with her smile. "You remind me of your mother."

Her words warmed Gisèle to her core. "Thank you."

"You must take more than bread and cheese." Émilie opened the pantry door and rustled inside it before she shut the door with a loud huff. "But we are lacking in almost everything."

"How do we get—" Gisèle started to ask, but Émilie kept talking.

Émilie moved up into the hall and Gisèle followed her to the front door. "I will go ask the Polins for some eggs and carrots from their garden and perhaps some flour."

The Polins lived farther up the lane, in the house where their family had lived for almost fifty years while they farmed a portion of the land for the Duchants.

"Will you return?" Gisèle asked. She hated this feeling of desperation, but she needed Émilie even more than she had the last time she'd walked out the door, on the way to her sister's house.

Émilie stepped outside and opened her umbrella. "I won't be longer than an hour."

The rain tapered into a drizzle until the summer sun chased it away. Gisèle zipped up her boots under her slacks and retrieved her bicycle from the carriage house. Months ago she would have put a saddle on Papillon Bleu, her Anglo-Norman mare, but Papa had sent away all their horses when Germany began to threaten the Maginot Line. In hindsight, Papa should have insisted their entire household relocate to Lyon when he sent away their horses, but he hadn't really thought the Germans would make it this far west into France.

She wouldn't linger in Saint-Lô this morning, only long enough to learn if the Germans were gone. And if they were, she would search for a working pay phone. If Papa were in Lyon, he would be worried sick about her.

The sun warmed her bare arms as she pedaled under the narrow lane of elm trees up into Agneaux. One main street divided the village, and it was strewn with clothes and toys and broken bicycle wheels. She pedaled quickly through the commune, along rue de la Cavée, until she crossed the bridge into Saint-Lô.

A rank of tangled hedgerows, twice her size in height, usually fenced in animals and gardens on both sides of the street, but she didn't hear the bleating of sheep or the bellowing of cows or even dogs barking today. Instead of automobilists and bicyclists clamoring up and down the road, automobiles sat abandoned in the middle of the road and bicycles lay on the sidewalk.

The earlier mayhem had diffused into an eerie calm.

Instead of pedaling into the town center on the road, Gisèle found a break in the hedges and biked along its bumpy backside. There was a telephone booth near the police station. She would call Tante Corinne from there.

Peeking through another break in the hedgerows, she surveyed the cobblestone street between the shops and primary school. Glass and debris covered the sidewalks and empty vehicles.

Had everyone in town fled or were they all hiding in their homes?

A troop of German soldiers marched from around the corner, into the street, the silver butts of their rifles gleaming in the sunlight. Their heavy boots pounded together on the stone.

Then a dark gray tank rounded the corner, a soldier perched above an enormous machine gun.

She watched as the gunner scanned the high buildings on both sides of him first before turning toward the hedgerows. Gunfire popped on the street, and she ducked back under the thick hedges with her bicycle, losing herself again among the rows.

The Germans, it appeared, were in no hurry to leave Saint Lô.

CHAPTER 10

"Hello, Mémé." I bent to kiss the bony cheek of my grandmother.

Officially, she was the Honorable Gisèle de Bouchard Duchant Sauver. Hers was a lofty title for a little woman, but in spite of her age and illness, my grandmother still had the elegance and often the attitude of a French noblewoman. The air of superiority sometimes flared in her later years, but we all adored her, even when she liked to tell us exactly what we should—or should not—do.

"She escaped again yesterday," Pamela James, her saint of an aide, said from the other side of the bed. "I found her petting a cat—"

"Not just any cat," Mémé said, spanking Pamela's hand. "His name is Shadow."

Pamela's smile was strained. "I found her petting *Shadow*, down by the pond."

"I went to see Papillon Bleu." Mémé scooted herself farther up on her mound of pillows. "But I wasn't going to ride her until today."

My grandmother hadn't ridden Papillon Bleu or any other horse in two decades, but I wasn't going to remind her. "Now, Mémé, you can't go riding without Pamela."

A stream of French poured from her lips, telling me it was none of my business when she rode a horse or with whom.

"Pamela needs your help," I insisted.

Mémé scrutinized Pamela as if to ascertain whether or not the woman before her really required her assistance.

I sat down on the stool beside her bed. I had been glad to skip the golf tournament this afternoon to visit my grandmother. On the table beside her was a black-and-white photograph of our entire family, a small jewelry box, and a glass of water. "Guess where I'm going this week?"

"Who are you?" she asked.

I kissed her forehead. "Someone who loves you."

She looked over my shoulder like she didn't see me, toward the front door of her apartment at Meadow Glen. "I'm thirsty."

I held the water glass up to her, and her hands shook as she took a sip. Then she patted my arm. "Much better. Thank you, dear."

Pamela stepped toward the door. "I'll get her some lemonade."

I leaned toward my grandmother, whispering as if I had a secret. Like she used to do with me when I was in grade school. "I'm going to Normandy."

"Normandy?" Her eyes grew wide, and I could see the lucidity battle her confusion. "The Château d'Epines . . ."

Relief filled me with her words. For that fleeting moment, her mind was with me.

"There's a man meeting me in France." She was watching me closely, so I continued. "He wants to know what happened at the château during the war."

"The château is such a lovely place," she mused. "You must

take your friend down to the lake. Most people don't even know it's there—"

"Did you meet Grandpa at the château?" I asked, trying to help her focus.

Her stiff fingers tugged at the blanket over her chest. "We used to swim in it."

"You and Grandpa used to swim?"

"No." She shook her head. "Me and Michel."

I smiled as I imagined her, years younger than me, splashing in a lake with the younger brother she adored. They probably jumped off logs and paddled in a canoe and hunted for frogs and perhaps even snakes on the shores. It seemed to me that Mémé wasn't afraid of anything.

"And Nadine used to swim with us too—before they took her away."

I leaned closer. "Who is Nadine?"

Her gaze wandered to the wall in front of her, to the cards and artwork drawn by the grandchildren of the many students and colleagues she'd befriended over the years, and her fingers began the familiar rhythm of moving the amber rosary beads that hung around her neck. "No one knows what happened at the lake."

Mémé began to rock against her pillow, and I reached for her hand. I wanted to offer her comfort, not distress, but something I said had upset her. This was why we couldn't talk about the past. The memories confused her.

Tears began to fill her eyes. "Poor Papa. He . . ."

I wanted to probe, but the pain in her eyes pressed me to stop. "We don't have to talk about it."

"There was nothing but good in him," she said, rocking faster now. "Nothing but good . . ."

Pamela shuffled through the door, and I turned around. Worry creased her eyes.

I gently stroked my grandmother's hand. "It will be okay, Mémé."

She jerked her hand away and threw off the blanket. Then her gaze found my face. "We must find her."

I looked up at Pamela again, wondering who we must find, but she seemed just as confused as me.

I tucked the blanket back across Mémé's chest. "Do we need to find your friend?"

"No." Her small hand reached out and took my arm, the strength in it surprising me. "We must find Adeline."

I swallowed hard. "Who is Adeline?"

"The girl." Her voice grew more insistent. "You must find the girl."

"Where should I look for her?" I asked.

Her blue eyes seemed to pierce me. "In the hawthorn trees."

Her head fell back against the pillow, and she swept her hand from mine, bracing it on her chest as the fire in her eyes began to dull. Her eyes closed, and I watched the blanket slowly rise and fall. Then her eyes fluttered open again, and her gaze darted back and forth between Pamela and me before it settled on my face.

She tilted her head. "I'm sorry, dear. Who are you?"

I picked my handbag off the floor. "Michael's daughter."

She looked over at Pamela again, confusion wrinkling her forehead. Pamela leaned down and pulled the blanket back over her chest. "You must rest, Mrs. Sauver."

She threw the blanket off her chest again. "But it's time for us to ride."

I kissed her cheek, blinking back my tears. "Perhaps you can go riding tomorrow."

Chapter 11

The ring of the doorbell startled Gisèle, and she almost sliced her finger with the paring knife. Across the table, Émilie was chopping leeks, and Gisèle saw the fear mirrored in her eyes. But perhaps the news wasn't bad this time. It could be the Polins or even Nadine with good news for them.

"Be careful," Émilie warned her, as if Gisèle could somehow ward off the Germans with her caution.

Shadow trailed her to the window beside the door. There wasn't an automobile in the courtyard, but she saw a bicycle. And the blond curls of a young woman standing on the flagstone outside.

Opening the door, she hurried the woman inside. Lisette was barely seventeen, but she had stolen Michel's heart two years ago. When Michel left with the Armée de Terre, Lisette began coming by often to visit her.

Gisèle kissed Lisette on both of her cheeks and then escorted her into the salon.

"Have you heard any news of Michel?" Lisette begged as she sat on the couch across from Gisèle.

She wished she could offer her the comfort of the truth. Instead she shook her head.

Lisette dabbed her cheeks with a white handkerchief. "I wish he would send a letter."

"We haven't received a letter from England in months," Gisèle said.

"Surely the Germans will let us get mail."

Gisèle hated the resignation in Lisette's voice, as if the Germans would bring an end to their problems. "The Germans will be gone soon," she insisted.

"I don't think so." Lisette folded the handkerchief on her lap. "They've begun moving men into the courthouse in Saint-Lô. They want to make it their headquarters for all of La Manche."

Gisèle shuddered at the thought of all those soldiers she'd seen remaining in the city. "How do you know?"

"Someone told them my uncle had been a translator during the Great War so they knocked on our door. He was too ill to leave the apartment, but I could translate for them."

The telephone rang out from her father's office. For a moment, Gisèle ignored it, as if Papa would answer the call. Then she leapt to her feet.

The telephone lines had been restored.

She excused herself and hurried toward the office.

Trepidation filled her along with a bit of excitement as she reached for the black receiver. "Hello?"

"Gisèle?" It was Philippe on the other end of the line.

"It's me!" she exclaimed, so glad to hear his voice. "Is Papa with you?"

"Are you safe?"

"Yes, but I—"

"I've been trying to call." His words rushed out. "I searched all over for you."

"I went to the Batiers' house."

The line clicked. "Who?"

"My friends' home. Is Papa with you?"

There was a scratching sound on the line and then she heard a muffled voice. The Germans may have restored their telephone lines, but it seemed they might be listening to their calls as well.

"What did you say?" he asked.

"Papa," she repeated again. "Is he with you?"

"No," he said. "I haven't seen him."

Her excitement leached out of her. "Are you in Lyon?"

"Yes."

She fell back into her father's chair, and Shadow jumped on her lap. If Papa wasn't with Philippe, where had he gone?

Lisette stepped into the office. "Is it Michel?" she mouthed.

When Gisèle shook her head, Lisette retreated back into the salon, leaving her alone with her cat and Philippe's voice.

"Did the Germans bomb the château?"

"No, the house and property are safe."

"Good," he said. "Quite good."

"Is your mother safe?" she asked.

"She's right beside me." Another crackling sound on the line interrupted his words. "We're trying to figure out how to get you here as well. We could marry—"

"I can't leave the château," she interrupted. Her stomach coiled again at the thought of marrying him. "Not until I find Papa."

Then her heart began to beat faster. What if her father was trying to call her right now? "I must get off the line."

He pressed through her retort. "The Germans aren't marching toward the south of France," he said, and she wondered how well those who listened to their conversation understood French. "You will be safe here."

"Papa and I will come soon."

"Gisèle—"

"I must go," she said. "In case he's trying to call."

After she hung up the receiver, she waited by the phone. How could Philippe talk of marriage when her father was missing? He didn't seem to care . . .

Lisette wandered back into the room and sat down across from her. "Was that Philippe?"

She nodded her head, stroking Shadow's fur.

"Michel doesn't like him," Lisette said.

She managed a weak smile. "He and Michel used to fight as children."

"Michel said his cousin will do anything to get ownership of this château."

It was ludicrous to consider Philippe obtaining their property. Papa wasn't even fifty yet, and even when he was gone, Michel would inherit the place, and Lisette would be the new vicomtesse. Decades and decades from now.

And she would come regularly from Paris to visit them and their children, long after the Germans were gone.

— CHAPTER 12 —

Light dappled the ripples in the murky lake water, twinkling like a thousand fireflies at twilight. I dipped my paddle into the sea of lights and pushed the kayak smoothly through it, the steady motion soothing my nerves. For the first time in weeks, I was free—liberated from responsibilities and obligations and all that was required of me.

A small catamaran sailed across the lake from me, its red-and-blue-striped sail fluttering in the wind. The city had been sweltering today, but the breeze drifting over Lake Kendall felt blissfully cool.

Perhaps I should have felt guilty for my desire to escape, but I beat away the guilt with every stroke of my paddle. For this rare hour, I wasn't the fiancée of Austin Vale or the daughter of the Sauvers or even a third-grade teacher at Washington Elementary. For this hour, I could simply be.

When we met, Austin had captured me with his vision of the future—our future—but somewhere along the line, I'd forgotten exactly who I was, silhouetted by those with greater dreams than my own.

Chaos—in the best sense of the word—had been the backbone of my family life growing up. My dad was raised by parents who loved him but struggled to survive in the United States. He had always been fascinated with numbers. When he was twenty-five, he started his first business—a coin-operated Laundromat that quickly turned a profit. He used the flood of revenue to purchase a second Laundromat a few months later, and then for the next decade, he bought another business each year. When he turned forty, he sold everything and launched a company to invest in other people's businesses.

My parents met when Dad was forty-three. And a multimillionaire.

Growing up, it seemed as if my father was as old as some of my friends' grandfathers. He spoiled me as a child, but thankfully my mother, as she liked to say, kept me from going rotten.

When my parents married, they both were already business owners. Even though their ventures were polar opposites, the world of self-employment required them to work nights and weekends, when they were eating, and practically when they were sleeping. The results of their enslavement were ridiculously successful careers. And a life with few memories outside their work.

Instead of a hectic life like my parents, I'd craved a more simple one, time to enjoy the water and my family and my students. For as long as I could remember, I'd wanted to teach children, discovering ways to make learning stick for a lifetime. Teaching invigorated me, the opportunity to help provide a foundation of education for the kids in my community. Then each summer, I traveled someplace new, steeping myself in history and culture and local food.

But it seemed my destiny wasn't going to involve much simplicity. As long as I could continue to carve out chunks of time like this to savor, I would enjoy the more public ride with Austin.

A branch draped low over the cove, and I ducked under it before sinking my paddle into the water again. The edge trailed in the water, the ripples blending with the light. Mesmerized, I watched as the light danced along the top of the brackish pool.

I hadn't planned to be on the water today, but when I arrived at my parents' summer home, neither of them was here yet. Instead of waiting inside, I hauled my kayak out of the boathouse and paddled across the small lake to an overgrown cove that seemed a million miles away.

And as I paddled, I mulled over my family's stories.

Mémé was usually confused these days, but this afternoon she'd seemed lucid when she begged me to find Adeline. Who was this girl who seemed to haunt her? And what happened to my great-grandfather during the war?

My grandmother had seemed afraid until the sadness overtook her. Something terrible must have happened to her father. If only she had told me years before, when she told me my grandfather had fought the Germans.

Unlike my father's side of the family, the history on my mother's side flowed like a rapid river current. My mother's parents—Lionel and Grace Bishop—had seemingly endless tales from their year of courting. Every payday in the winter of 1954, Lionel had shown up at the bakery to buy a dozen of Grace's coconut macaroons. It took him a solid six months to muster enough courage to ask her for a date, but after another six months, he proposed and they married in an old church in Bethesda. To celebrate every anniversary, Grace still made him macaroons.

My grandparents on my father's side loved each other deeply, but all I knew about their courtship was that they'd met in a café. They'd told me no stories about their wedding day.

I remembered a little about my grandpa—the cinnamon candies he'd kept in his pockets and his fascination for anything that flew. He had a remote-control plane and during the summer, I spent hours at the park with him, flying it above the trees. His knowledge of history inspired me to love education, but somehow the history he discussed never encompassed his own story and I was too young at the time to think about asking for more. It was my grandmother who told me about his service in the military and resistance.

One specific memory from the years before Grandpa passed on rose to the top. It was my grandparents, holding hands as I joined them for a walk along the Atlantic coast. Mémé swatted Grandpa away playfully when he tried to steal a kiss. Then they'd escaped around a dune, ahead of me. When Mémé thought no one was looking, she kissed him back.

I smiled at my treasure of a memory—a simple, stolen kiss that sealed their enduring love, a love that lasted almost sixty years.

Near the shore, I saw the flat head of a snake and then the black sheen of its body trailing behind it. With swift strokes, I paddled away. While I loved the water, I wasn't thrilled about sharing it with a moccasin. Few things above the water scared me, but I was scared of what swam underneath it. Especially snakes looking for trouble.

Perhaps that was why I had a deep appreciation for the kayak. I could play on the water without diving in.

As I neared the dock, my mom waved from the patio of the house.

"Ahoy!" she shouted as she descended the path down to the water, a cooler in her hand. Her ash-blond hair was twisted back into a knot, and she wore a sleeveless blouse that showed off the bronze color on her plump arms. My mom was sixty-four, but she believed that age was relative. A state of mind. Oddly enough, her mind insisted that she hadn't yet hit the big 4-0.

After I beached my kayak, she greeted me with a giant hug. I pulled a chair under a yellow umbrella and kicked off my flip-flops. "I'm glad to see you're pretending to retire."

"We are retired," she said. "On the second Sunday of every month."

I rolled my eyes. "I guess that's progress."

My parents were supposed to be easing their way into retirement, though the pace of their professional lives didn't seem to be letting up. I couldn't envision either of them fully retired.

A catamaran sailed toward our side of the lake, and I could see the chalky outline of a sailor leaning into the wind. Her eyes on the sailboat, Mom reached into the cooler and pulled out a Perrier for me. "Are you excited about France?"

"I'm excited to return to the château," I said. "But I don't know what I'm going to say in an interview about World War II."

Mom pulled a Tupperware container from her cooler and propped it on her lap. "Just tell Mr. Holtz the stories you remember about your grandfather."

She opened the container and took a strawberry from the pile of fresh fruit. It seemed ironic to me that she—the owner of Bliss Bakery—abstained from all refined sugar and artificial colors. Most of her cakes and cookies were chock-full of the processed stuff, but these days she let others bake while she met with brides who wanted one of her prized cakes.

Except for my wedding cake. She was planning to bake it herself. I wasn't sure how I was going to tell her that Austin's mother had asked Patty Wilson to bake one as well.

My mom held out the container, and I popped several blueberries into my mouth. "Perhaps Grandpa has family I can visit while I'm in France."

She shook her head. "He was estranged from them long ago."

The catamaran drew close, and I realized the man sailing the boat in long board shorts was my father. "What is Dad doing?"

"He decided to take up a new hobby."

I understood my dad's love of the water, but he was much too old to be out sailing by himself. "Can't he take up golfing or—I don't know—bunco?"

She laughed. "He'd be bored out of his mind."

Dad lassoed a post on the dock and pulled in his catamaran before retrieving a towel and T-shirt from the dock. He wiped his tanned face with his towel. "I'd give you a hug, but . . ."

I waved both hands. "There's no need."

Mom scooted the cooler toward him with her toes. "Drink something, Michael."

"When did you get a sailboat?" I asked.

"Two weeks ago." He plucked a vitamin-infused water out of the cooler and then he winked at me. "I'm planning to go pro."

Mom rolled her eyes. "He thinks the catamaran scouts are coming for him."

Dad pulled over a chair to sit beside me. His silver hair glistened in the sunlight, but besides his hair, few people would probably have guessed he was pushing seventy-six. He was in better physical condition than half the guys my age, and he worked harder than any other man I knew. "Thank you for doing this interview."

I leaned into the shade of the umbrella. "I wish you could go with me."

He took a long drink and then put the bottle back down on the glass table. "Not this time, I'm afraid." He always seemed to have an excuse as to why he couldn't return to France, but he never explained it to me. "Perhaps someday we'll all go back again for a visit together."

"I saw Mémé this morning." I slowly twirled my toes. "I told her I was going to Normandy."

Dad twisted the water bottle. "What did she say?"

"She talked about the château and her father and then she asked me about a little girl named Adeline."

My parents shared a glance, and I looked between them. "What are you keeping from me?"

"We're not keeping anything," Mom said. "It's just that Gisèle has mentioned this Adeline a few times recently."

"So you were keeping it from me."

Dad shook his head. "She says a lot of things that don't mean anything. We thought she was confused."

"She seemed quite intent on it today."

"I've never heard of anyone named Adeline," Dad said.

I sipped the bubbly water. "She was afraid for her father as well."

Dad glanced back out at the lake. "My grandfather died at the beginning of the war."

"Do you know how he died?"

After Dad shook his head, Mom slipped off her sunglasses and placed them on the table. "Tell her what Mr. Holtz said."

Dad leaned toward me, his eyes intent. "He seems to think something significant happened at the château."

"Like what?" I asked.

"He didn't expound."

I sighed. "I wish he could have given us a little lead time to gather material."

"Apparently he was just able to track us down," Mom said.

"Maybe Stéphane could tell me some stories—"

"That man is not to be trusted," Dad said.

"Why not?"

"His father lost their family's home in Lyon and then he spent a lifetime trying to steal the château from my mother, even as she allowed him to live there without paying a dime of rent." Tears welled in his eyes, and I loved how much he still loved Mémé. Her mind might be slipping, but Dad remembered everything good about her. "Philippe despised her, but she didn't turn him away."

"What was it like growing up in a château?" It was the same question I'd asked when I was younger, but this time I hoped for a better answer.

"I don't remember much," he said, his voice quiet. "I was barely six when we moved to the States."

I had so many memories from my early years of life—coloring with my friends in kindergarten, playing in the ocean in Virginia Beach, my dog who died when I was five. "Surely you remember something," I said, pressing him.

"My mother tells the grandest stories of my childhood there, but all I recall are the tall stone walls." His gaze wandered toward the water. "And a room filled with children, dozens of them . . ."

I glanced up at the contrails of a plane in the sky. "I suppose it's hard to tell the difference between a childhood dream and a memory."

He looked back at me. "Dreams and blurry memories should never be trusted. And neither should the Bordes."

Chapter 13

The spicy scent of incense lingered in the *chapelle*, and the stained-glass windows gleamed from the setting sunlight, warming the blond wood of the benches. Near the altar was a statue of Mother Mary holding her baby, and pictures lined the walls—scenes of Saint Francis holding a lamb, Saint Michel defeating the dragon, Jesus carrying his cross to Calvary.

With the handles of the picnic hamper strung over her arm, Gisèle unlocked the gate across the sacristy and then relocked it behind her. A cabinet to the right stored linens and beside it was a locked closet for vestments. Usually she came to the sacristy after dark, when those who prayed couldn't see what she was doing, but she couldn't wait until nightfall to find Michel. She needed his help to find Papa.

The skeleton key that hung on her rosary also unlocked the large closet in the sacristy, and she pushed aside the tunics, stoles, and robes until she felt the wooden panel in the back. When she pressed on it, the wood swung inward.

Turning on her flashlight, she shone it onto the ledge and saw the food she'd left last night in the picnic hamper was still there, along with her letter. She stepped inside and closed the panel behind her before picking up the hamper.

Steps led downward from the ledge, into the darkness, and her skin bristled as she shined her light below.

Her father used to tell them legends about a tunnel under the property, a place where their ancestors hid during the French Revolution, but she had never known where the entrance was until Michel returned last month from England and begged for her help. Her brother made her swear not to tell anyone, especially their father, that he'd found the tunnel.

Breathing in the cool air, she began her descent. The dirt walls circled around her. She much preferred the open lands around her home to dark, tight spaces like this, but she forced her mind to wander away from its panic, to wonder at those who had come down here long before her. Perhaps the Vikings had built the tunnel after they raided this land, or maybe the Romans built it in the earlier centuries after Christ's birth. Perhaps it had been used as a catacomb.

She shouldn't let her mind wander.

The passage tapered, the cold air chilling her skin, but even with the drop in temperature, her hands were clammy. The sooner she found her brother, the sooner she could get back to the warmth on the surface.

"Michel?" she called out.

There was no answer.

The tunnel diverged into two passages, and she shone her light down both sides. On both sides, the darkness swallowed up her ray of light.

She chose the left passage at first, but it dead-ended into a dozen stone steps, a small pocket door at the top. Curiosity spurred her forward and she tugged on the metal pull. The door cracked open, but it was the tiniest sliver. On the other side was some sort of barrier.

Her breathing grew faster now. What if she was trapped under the earth? What if she lost her way and couldn't get back to the *chapelle*?

What if someone locked the closet door from the outside and she couldn't open it?

What if her brother was gone—and someone else was here instead?

She had to find him quickly and get back up the stairs.

The tunnel sloped downward as she crept forward, and she wondered if she was descending in the direction of the forest or the river. She knew every step of their property aboveground, but it felt so strange to be far below all that she knew.

When the path flattened again, she paused by a small room cut out of the dirt. Blankets and cigarette butts littered the ground. She passed by the room, but voices echoed farther up the tunnel, and she froze, listening to the sound. Then she turned off her flashlight.

Light continued to illuminate the walls in front of her, and she prayed her brother was with the light.

"Michel?" she called again.

The voices stopped, and for a moment, all she heard was her breathing.

"Is that you, Gigi?"

At the sound of her brother's voice, her heart returned to a steady pace. Only Michel was allowed to call her that name. "It's me."

"It's not safe for you to be here." The sternness in his voice frightened her.

She squinted into the light but couldn't see him or anyone else, so she stepped toward the lantern. "I've brought your food."

"Leave it where you are," he said.

"But I need to speak with you."

The shadow of a man emerged in front of her, and she flashed her light on him. Her brother, dark and swarthy, walked toward her as if he were Clark Gable or another one of America's stars who dominated the silver screen. Many of the young women in Normandy pined over Michel Duchant, but he'd always been more enamored of his motorcycle than the idea of marriage—at least until he met Lisette.

He'd been conscripted into the Armée de Terre before he graduated from *lycée* and reported to duty on his eighteenth birthday, ready to slay the dragons like the saint Mother named him after. Sometimes Gisèle wondered if anything ever frightened her brother.

"You can't see the other men who are with me," he said.

She set the picnic hamper on the ground. "I wouldn't tell anyone who they are."

"We're in a war," he said, his voice sad. "None of us can be certain what we will or will not do."

As he drew closer in the tunnels, she could smell sweat and brandy and cigarette smoke, but she didn't care. She hugged him.

When he released her, he clamped his hands on her shoulders. "What is it, Gigi?"

"Émilie and I baked you bread." She nudged the picnic hamper toward him. "You must check the ledge, Michel. I left you a letter last night."

"I thought you'd fled," he said. "We heard the bombs two nights ago. One of our men went out—" His voice cracked with emotion. "He hasn't returned."

She took a deep breath. "The Germans have taken Paris."

His fist shot out, hitting the wall. "This is what we feared," he said as he pulled his fist back into his chest. "The worst of our fears."

"I am afraid for you, Michel."

"Where are the French soldiers?" he asked, rubbing his hand.

"The wireless said they were running south."

"Our government—they are all cowards."

"No one wants the Germans here," she said.

He shook his head. "Some do. They think it will bring peace."

"How can bombs bring peace?" she asked.

"It all depends on who is dropping the bombs." His voice grew stronger. "If our army can't stop them, then we will have to."

His declaration made her shiver, and she trembled. His fervor, she feared, might get him killed. "You must leave here too. Papa said we could get to Switzerland."

"I will not run away." He paused. "Why are you still here?"

She forced a smile. "I promised Mother that I'd take care of you."

"That was ten years ago," he said. "You must leave, Gigi. We will find food another way."

"How many are down here?" she asked.

"Four right now, but with this news . . ." He unclenched his hand. "There will be more."

"Then you will need more food." When they found Papa, he would agree with her.

"I can't put you into harm's way. If something happened to you, Papa would never forgive me, and I—I would never forgive myself." He paused again. "Why hasn't Papa made you leave?"

Tears began to well in her eyes. "He's gone, Michel, and I don't know where he went."

"He left without you?"

"He stayed behind to hide the silver and Mother's jewelry. Philippe came to get me—"

"Where is Philippe now?" he demanded.

"We got separated in the bombing," she explained. "But he called today, from Lyon."

"He is just waiting . . . ," Michel muttered.

"Waiting for what?"

He shook his head. "Nothing."

"You must tell me, Michel."

But he didn't speak anymore about Philippe. "Papa would have tried to hide the valuables down near the lake."

She took a step back. "I will go look for him."

"Not by yourself, Gigi." He glanced back over his shoulder, at the dark corridor. "I will go with you tonight."

"Do you think . . ." She couldn't bear to finish the question, couldn't bear the thought that he might be lying wounded by the bombs.

His voice dipped low. "I don't know what to think anymore."

CHAPTER 14

Austin turned off the ignition in the airport parking garage and intertwined his fingers through mine. "I am the luckiest man in the world."

I glanced out the window, at the red and blue lights flashing along the cement wall. "The security cameras are watching."

He pulled me closer. "I don't care if the whole world knows how much I love you."

His kiss reminded me of all I loved about him—his confidence and passion and fervent dreams for our future. As I sank into him, in the privacy of the parking deck, he held me as close as he could with a console stuck between us.

What was I thinking, going to France weeks before my wedding? Even with Austin's encouragement, even with the allure of visiting the château, I didn't want to leave.

"Perhaps I shouldn't go—" I began to say.

Austin hushed me with another kiss, one that made my toes tingle. "I'll be waiting here when you return," he said. "And then next time you travel to France, we'll be together."

"You will love it in Normandy," I said.

Grinning, he brushed my long hair back over my shoulder. "I would love anyplace if I'm with you."

I kissed him one last time, and with a glance at the dashboard clock, began to inch away. I didn't want to step outside, but my flight left in an hour.

As he removed our luggage from his trunk, I reapplied my lip gloss and we strolled into the Richmond airport like an old married couple, side by side about three feet apart. Together but distracted.

Before we made it to security, a young couple stopped Austin. Nervous, they began to gush about their desire to have him as their next governor. His smile charismatic, he thanked them and then disarmed them by asking the questions he asked of everyone—where did they live and what did they want for the future? As they chatted, I discreetly checked the time on my phone. My flight left in thirty-five minutes now, his in an hour.

He introduced me as his future wife, the third-grade teacher who would champion education reform. I smiled politely and then stretched my fingers over his arm. A gentle tug brought him back to the reality that we were in an airport, trying to catch two separate flights to New York. Others might wait for the candidate, but I was pretty sure the commercial airlines would not.

By the time we arrived at the gate, I was out of breath and the attendant was calling for final boarding.

"Did Olivia send you the research notes?" Austin asked.

I tapped my briefcase. "They're all on my iPad—I'll read them on the plane."

"I'm going to miss you," he said.

I'd only be gone a week, I told myself. After that we had a lifetime together. "I'm going to miss you too."

He pecked my cheek. "Call me when you get to Paris."

I smiled. "I'll call you when I land in New York."

Worry flashed in his eyes. "Someone from the party is picking me up at the airport. I'm afraid they have meetings planned all day for me."

My smile fell. "Of course."

"But I'll send you a text."

I slid my boarding pass out of my purse. "Good enough."

"I'm sorry, Chloe. I wish you were going with me."

I didn't mean to be insensitive to his commitments. I just wasn't quite ready to say good-bye.

"No stress," he commanded, "for an entire week."

The attendant called my name from the podium, and Austin stepped back, pointing his thumb over his shoulder. "I suppose I should catch my flight too."

I shooed him away. "Go."

Before I stepped onto the Jetway, my fiancé was gone.

.   .   .

Steely clouds anchored themselves above the New York skyline, dark and foreboding. Our plane circled the airport three times before the pilot was cleared to land. After the plane parked, hail began to pelt the windows, and inside the terminal the attendant informed me and every other passenger on my flight that we were grounded until the thunderstorm cleared. Pending weather, the next flight to Paris would leave tomorrow morning at ten.

I glanced around the lobby. People were already draped over most of the seats, and both luggage and children had strayed onto the walkway. The weather might keep me out of the skies for the next twenty-four hours, but it didn't mean I had to stay off the roads.

Perhaps I could join Austin at the Plaza.

I wasn't naïve enough to think it would be a romantic evening, but I much preferred spending the night at the Plaza than at the airport. And maybe Austin and I could duck out after the event for a walk in Central Park or even a midnight carriage ride.

I called Austin's number, but his phone went straight to voice mail. He'd probably been whisked off to a meeting the moment he landed.

My luggage would be transferred to my next flight, but I could secure an elegant dress and shoes on Fifth Avenue. And if I called ahead, perhaps I could make an appointment with a stylist to do my hair and makeup.

Smiling, I climbed into the cab. I wouldn't try to call Austin again.

Instead I'd wait and surprise him at dinner.

Chapter 15

Gisèle slipped out of the château after midnight and hurried west, toward the forested hill that dipped down to a lake and ancient caves where Michel loved to hide as a child. Her flashlight trembled in her hand, but she didn't dare turn it on.

The narrow path wound under the stone walls of an old guardhouse to the brick wall that separated the landscaped lawn from the towering oak and beech trees. A rusty iron gate linked the wall, and the hinges creaked when she edged it open.

An aeroplane flew over the château, and she ducked under the canopy of branches until she heard a low whistle filtering through the trees. She whistled back.

"Gigi," Michel whispered.

"I'm by the gate."

Her brother crept up beside her. "We must hurry," he said.

She followed him down the winding path that descended to the lake. Every minute or two, the beam from his flashlight swept across the floor, and then they were covered in blackness again.

"Lisette came by today," she whispered as they walked.

He slowed his pace. "What did she say?"

"She's worried about you."

"You can't tell her where I am," he said, worried.

"Can I tell her you are safe?"

He shook his head. "She must forget about me."

"None of us will forget about you, Michel."

He flashed his light again and they scanned the fallen branches and overgrowth on the forest floor.

"Why don't you like Philippe?" she asked as they neared the lake.

"I want you to marry someone who loves you."

She stopped walking. "You don't think Philippe loves me?"

"Not like he should." He hesitated. "He wants the château."

"But the château will be yours one day."

"Philippe is a gambling man."

Michel resumed his walk, and she fell behind him, trying to sort out the implications of his words. What was Philippe betting on?

The trail flattened, and ahead of them, moonlight trailed across the small lake, like the filmy train of a bride. As they rounded the edge, Michel scanned the rocks and downed logs along the shore. On the other side of the lake was the shadowy entrance to a cave.

Michel ducked inside, and when he flicked on his light, she stepped in behind him.

"Stop!" he yelled, but it was too late.

Against the wall was her father, and she rushed forward. Dark bruises circled around his eyes. Dried blood caked his ears and cheeks. "Papa," she whispered, shaking him.

Michel placed his hand on her shoulder. "Gisèle."

She pushed her brother away. "No . . ."

Her head dropped to her father's chest, listening for the whisper of his heartbeat, but his body was still. "Papa!" she yelled, shaking him as if he might wake again, but there was no life left in him.

Rushing outside, she retched in the bushes.

Papa had said the Germans would respect the aristocracy, that he would follow her to Lyon. That he would be safe.

Michel was beside her again, but this time she didn't shake him away. He put his arms around her and she sobbed on his shoulder.

Had the Nazis killed him for the silver? As if silver was worth more than the life of her father, a hero of a man. How could Hitler's soldiers kill good men, innocent men, as they plundered Europe?

Her entire body trembled as she collapsed to the ground. "I shouldn't have left the château without him."

"This isn't your fault."

She clutched the crucifix that hung around her neck. "They murdered him."

"And they will pay for it," he said, anger teeming in his voice.

She curled over her knees, rocking back and forth. "We must bury him."

"The others will help me retrieve his body. We'll bury him beside Mother."

Michel stepped back into the cave, but she couldn't go back inside. Her hands clasped around the cross, she whispered her prayer as she counted the beads.

Our Father who art in heaven,
Hallowed be thy name;
Thy kingdom come
Thy will be done
On earth as it is in heaven.

Michel appeared back at the entrance, his hand outstretched. She looked down at his palm in the flashlight beam and saw an onyx-and-gold cuff link with a tiny diamond in the center.

He folded his fingers around it. "I'll kill a hundred *boches* to avenge his death."

Her heart seemed to collapse within her. As much as she wanted revenge, she couldn't lose two of the men she loved. "It won't bring him back," she said. "We should both go to Lyon."

His eyes seemed to blaze. "I won't cower, Gigi."

She didn't want him to cower, but she had to protect her younger brother. If he went into Saint-Lô now, the Germans would surely kill him.

"You must wait," she begged.

"You can go with Philippe," he said, his voice broken. "But I have to stay here. I have to fight them."

Her anger collided with her fear as she walked back up the trail beside him, her body numb.

"I will help you," she said before he slipped back into the shadows.

She wouldn't leave her brother here alone.

— CHAPTER 16 —

After the rain stopped, I reemerged onto Fifty-ninth Street, a chai latte in hand. Ahead of me was Central Park, along with the elegant façade of the Plaza, overlooking the trees. Storm clouds still threatened the shoppers who paraded along the sidewalk, but at least I could walk to the hotel without getting drenched.

On my cab ride from the airport, I'd secured a hotel room for the night, along with an appointment at their salon. After checking in, I had four hours to find the right dress and shoes before the artisans began working their magic on my makeup and hair. It was almost impossible to surprise Austin—I couldn't wait to see his face when I walked into the ballroom.

As I crossed Fifth Avenue, a black limousine rolled up to the curb next to the hotel and a bellman rushed forward to open the door. Austin emerged from the car, and my heart leapt. Perhaps it would be just as fun to surprise Austin now, away from the spotlight. In the timing of providence, perhaps, instead of my own.

I pulled my phone out of my bag and quickly typed.

Turn around.

Smiling, I lifted my finger to send my message, but before I sent it, I glanced back up. Instead of walking into the Plaza, Austin extended his arm back into the limousine. Another figure emerged on the sidewalk beside him. A woman.

And she was stunning.

I watched with a mixture of awe and horror as she reached for Austin's hand.

Dropping my phone back into my purse, I watched them laugh together as they strolled up the front steps. What if someone recognized him?

I supposed it didn't matter. Surely she was only a colleague from the party headquarters in New York.

The woman's ebony curls bounced with her laughter, and her white summer dress glided behind her like that of a Greek goddess. I glanced down at my navy capris, wrinkled from the plane ride, and tan-colored blouse. There was no comparison between me and a goddess.

But it was Austin who had kissed me this morning, three hours ago. It was Austin who told *me* how beautiful I was and how much he loved me. As I watched him with this other woman, my head felt like it was about to explode.

There had to be an explanation—but why didn't he let go of that woman's hand?

The bellman opened the door to the lobby, and Austin and his escort disappeared under the golden lights.

Hiking my handbag over my shoulder, I rushed toward the hotel, and the same bellman who'd opened the door for Austin opened it for me. The lobby radiated elegance, with its marble columns and oriental rugs. To the right of the registration desk was a giant fern. I didn't exactly hide behind it—I merely paused beside it and no one seemed to notice, perhaps because they were all staring at the eye candy dangling on Austin's arm.

And how could they not stare? She was more striking than the gold encrusted around the lobby's windows and doors.

I clutched my handbag to my chest. My dad would tell me not to be impulsive, to wait and make a decision after I had all the facts. The woman was probably a campaign manager for a candidate in New York or someone's assistant sent to escort Austin to his meeting. In a few minutes, the three of us would be laughing about the misunderstanding. It would be awkward but understandable. If she wasn't a business associate . . .

I couldn't allow myself to linger on that possibility.

The man at the registration desk slipped Austin an envelope and told him his room—the Edwardian Fifth Avenue Suite—overlooked the Pulitzer Fountain from the eighteenth floor. Austin turned to pick up his suitcase, and I almost wished he would glance up and see me hovering beside the fern.

He didn't notice me.

Now that he had his hotel key in hand, I prayed he would say good-bye to the woman. Bid her a good day. But there was no handshake as they parted ways. Or the kiss of the French on both cheeks. The woman trailed Austin to the elevator and slipped inside.

As the doors began to close, I saw Austin lean down. Even though I knew the scene would haunt me, I couldn't look away. Before the doors shut, I watched the man I was supposed to marry kiss her lips.

The bright colors of the lobby fused together and I felt as if I might faint. *Air.* I needed fresh air. Rushing back out the lobby doors, I collapsed against a column and pounded my fists against the stone, gasping the warm, fume-laden air. The relentless horns of taxis rattled my head. Messy tears flooded my cheeks.

How could I have been so stupid?

I punched the column again. I'd known something was off the moment Lisa mentioned the trip to New York. Or perhaps it was before, when Austin lectured me on the importance of my commitment and then put me on a plane to France.

No wonder he hadn't wanted me to call him during my layover. And why he'd neglected to invite me on this trip. His *meeting* would indeed encompass all of his time.

My head whirled as I pressed against my brows. It was too much to comprehend.

"Are you all right, miss?"

I looked up at the tall form of a uniformed bellhop. My body shook as I tried to right myself. "It's just a headache," I said, pointing to my forehead.

What else could I tell him—that I feared my fiancé was sleeping with another woman? That my relationship, my future, was crumbling before me? He might tell me to ditch the guy, but it wasn't that easy.

"Can I get you some Advil?" he asked.

When I shook my head, he backed away.

I'd given my heart, along with my dreams, to the traitor upstairs. If I ended our engagement now, the media would feast on the story of Austin's indiscretion. My closest friends would pity me, while those who didn't know me—including the hundreds who'd already received a wedding invitation—might wonder what I'd done to make my fiancé unfaithful. Others might joke about a last fling before he tied the knot.

I thought Marissa had been jealous of what Austin and I had, but I'd been a fool. She and my parents would tell me to march upstairs and break it off.

Instead of confronting him, I could take a taxi back to the airport for the night and then fly on to Paris in the morning. Pretend

I never saw him kissing that woman. Guzzle mint juleps all the way across the Atlantic until my heart was numb.

A picture slashed violently through my mind. It was me, thirty years from now, the miserable Mrs. Vale. Like Austin's mother, I would have to tolerate his sorties for the sake of—for the sake of what? Being the wife of a politician or the money that came from being married to a successful man. Or to hold my broken family together by pretending that everything was fine and then demanding that everyone join me in looking the other way while my husband flaunted his latest affair. Instead of standing up to my husband, I would ask our precocious son to pass the potatoes.

No one respected Mrs. Vale—including Mrs. Vale. If I tolerated Austin's unfaithfulness, I would never be able to respect myself either.

If I broke our engagement, I'd be the punch line of late-night jokes and tabloid headlines, but better to be a punch line than the miserable wife of a man who preferred to be with other women.

I wanted to scream. Hurl something through the window. Run.

So many people had compared Austin's charisma and charm to John F. Kennedy's. Is this what Jackie felt like the first time she found out about her husband's affairs? Angry and ashamed.

Perhaps she felt trapped in their marriage, but I wasn't trapped. There was still time for me to walk away.

My heart heavy, I wiped away my tears and stepped back into the lobby. My father and Marissa had both warned me that Austin might be hiding something, but I'd ignored the waving of their red flags.

The elevator delivered me to the eighteenth floor, to a long hall lit with golden wall sconces and masked with mirrors. All it needed was smoke to complete the illusion.

My stomach rolled when I heard a woman laugh in the Edwardian Fifth Avenue Suite, like Megan laughing in the Vales' home. In front of the suite was an alcove with a stiff leather bench, and I sat, wishing I could break down the door.

Instead I pulled out my phone, looked at the text I'd almost sent on the sidewalk. The one asking Austin to turn around.

If I'd sent it, he might have turned and slammed the car door before I saw the woman with him. Years or even decades might have passed before I learned the truth.

My stomach curled at the thought.

Austin's mother might have tolerated her husband's infidelities. Countless politicians' wives before me might have looked the other way. But I could not.

Slowly I began to delete each letter in my original text. Then, taking a deep breath, I began to type again.

I made it to NYC, I wrote. *You here?*

This time I heard his laugh blending with hers. Were they mocking me? I wiped away the last of my tears.

A few minutes later, he texted back.

Crazy storm, huh? I'm here. In meetings already.

So this is what he referred to as a meeting? Bitter, I joined in their laughter.

My phone flashed again with another text.

I miss you.

His audacity infuriated me.

Right . . . I typed. Casual bait to catch my fish. *Whatcha meeting about?*

He texted right back. *Budgets. Boring stuff . . .*

Doesn't sound a bit boring to me.

His reply came at lightning speed. *U ok???*

I stared at the phone for a moment, and the aching in my heart almost drowned out the anger. There was still time to run away. Pretend that everything was fine.

Yet I couldn't do it. Perhaps the meeting really was providential. I leaned back against the wall and closed my eyes.

Laughter no longer bled through the door in front of me, and I wondered what might be going through Austin's head. Usually he knew the game plan of each player around him before he calculated his next move. Perhaps it was good to make him a little nervous.

Slowly I began to type again, anger fueling me. *I'm just great. When were you planning to tell me?*

Sorry, he wrote. *I didn't think budgets interested you . . .*

They do now.

What do you want to know?

This time I didn't hesitate as I typed. *I want to know the name of your girlfriend.*

I leaned back, relief filling me as the words vanished on my screen. The truth was the only thing that would free both of us.

Where are you?!?

I took a deep breath before I texted him back. *Sitting outside your door.*

Seconds later, Austin Vale stood before me in the doorway, dressed in a white robe, the Plaza insignia embroidered on his chest.

"What are you doing—" he demanded, stumbling over his words. I'd never seen Austin flustered before.

"I was going to surprise you." I tucked my phone back into my purse. "Apparently I succeeded."

His mouth gaped open. I'd never seen Austin at a loss for words either.

Standing, I eyed his attire. "Do you always conduct budget meetings in a bathrobe?"

He glanced down at the robe as if he'd forgotten it was on, and then he raked his fingers through his dark hair. What had appeared so handsome to me hours before suddenly looked fake. Plastic. Why had I kissed those lips with such fervor? Lips that told me they loved me and then lied.

He motioned back into the room. "I was just getting dressed for a meeting. I didn't mean to confuse you—"

Inside my heart was crumbling, but I had no choice—I had to cling to the thread of strength dangling within me. "What's her name?"

"I don't know who you're talking about—"

Then she—the woman he didn't know—stepped into the doorway behind him, wearing a matching robe. Her triumphant smile was nauseating. "My name is Starla," she said, mocking me. "Starla Dedrick."

Austin ignored the woman, his eyes focused on me. "This is not what it looks like."

"Of course it is." The bitterness in my laugh made him wince. "How much are you paying her?"

Starla's smirk began to fade. "I think I'll let you two work this out alone."

Austin glanced both ways before stepping into the hallway. Then he shut the door behind him. "You are supposed to be on your way to Normandy," he said as if this problem was somehow my fault.

"You are supposed to be faithful!"

"I don't love her—not like I love you." He looked so genuine, so pathetic. I didn't feel sorry enough to run back into his arms, but I wavered. For the briefest of moments.

Then I remembered. Lisa had asked if I was meeting Starla—the old family friend—to shop in New York. My hands sank to my sides. "How does your sister know her?"

Austin dug his hands into the pockets of the robe. "Starla and I dated in college."

I almost wished that he'd hired her for the day.

"I love you, Chloe." He reached for my hands, but I yanked them away. "Truly."

I wanted to pull every hair out of his head. One at a time. "I can't believe this, Austin."

"I'll never do this again." He took another step forward. "Nothing will change between us."

I picked up my handbag off the bench. "It's already changed."

I rushed back toward the elevator doors. Thankfully, they opened right after I pushed the arrow.

The last sound I heard from the eighteenth floor was Austin Vale, the distinguished gubernatorial candidate from Virginia, banging on his hotel room door, begging his girlfriend to let him back inside.

PART TWO

*Do not judge your fellow until
you have stood in his place.*

—RABBI HILLEL

ETHICS OF THE FATHERS

Chapter 17

Juif. The vile word was woven into the star on the boy's black vest. Eyes wide, the boy stared into the window teeming with croissants and bread, but the branding prevented him from entering the bakery in Saint-Lô.

When the child lifted his head, Gisèle met his gaze. He couldn't have been four years of age, but his face was gaunt, his eyes flush with fear, like one of the prisoners she'd seen laboring along the road into town.

She lifted her hand to greet him.

"Don't encourage him." Turning, Gisèle watched the baker lift a woven basket onto the counter.

"But he looks so sad," she said as she handed him her coupon for bread.

Monsieur Cornett glanced down at the coupon and then looked back at her. "He's manipulating you."

"How do you know?"

"Because he's a dirty Jew."

The baker's words made her cringe, as if the child were a dog or a maggot instead of a hungry boy.

For decades France had been a haven for the Jewish people escaping persecution in Germany and Austria. Thousands of Jews—like Nadine's family—found refuge among the French, but since the Germans had *liberated* the northern districts of her country, they'd inundated France with propaganda about the threat of Jews.

How could anyone believe the Nazis' propaganda, the wretched manipulation and lies? Their frightening obsession with harassing even the youngest and oldest Jews had infected some of her neighbors, their blatant hatred sickening her.

The baker brushed the flour off his apron and disappeared into the back room to retrieve her ration.

The Germans seemed to be everywhere now—living uninvited in the homes of people in Saint-Lô, playing like chums with the children after school, patrolling the streets of the city to enforce order during the day and the curfew at night. They'd set up a headquarters in the town center for the entire French district of La Manche, across from the prison that they'd filled with people brave enough to resist their occupation. And even before her uncle passed away, they'd forced Lisette to work for them.

Still she feared that too many French people had begun to identify with their occupiers instead of fighting against them. Some French men and women were simply resigned to the occupancy, while others joined their occupants in despising the Jewish population, fanning the flames of bitterness until it raged in their hearts. Hatred, it seemed, was a powerful unifier of even the greatest enemies.

Hatred for the Nazis had also unified those resisting them. The more regulations the Germans inflicted on them, the faster Michel's resistance cell grew. Her brother's group now included dozens of men, former business owners, farmers, soldiers, schoolboys who'd become men during the occupation. They left for weeks at a time, wreaking havoc on their occupiers across France.

The Nazis had confiscated most of the wirelesses in the town, but Gisèle had kept hers, listening to it in Papa's office and relaying the information to her brother. Charles de Gaulle was hiding in London, but he spoke regularly to the people of France on the wireless.

"France is not alone," he'd pronounced. "She has a vast empire behind her."

When Gisèle heard his words, hope rekindled in her heart. Perhaps the entire world hadn't given up on them. With the help of others, perhaps they did still have a chance to win back their country.

"Whatever happens, the flame of the French resistance will not be extinguished," de Gaulle had said. Then he urged the resistance to cut telephone wires, sabotage the railways, print underground newspapers that promoted freedom for the French people.

Her brother and his men continued to stoke the embers of their freedom, and when they returned to the tunnels, she provided food and water for them.

The Nazis tried to regulate what the French people planted and what they ate, even from their own gardens. But no matter how hard they tried, it was impossible to monitor every apple and carrot stick.

She and Émilie didn't need bread from the bakery—the families who farmed their property continued to supply flour and cheese and vegetables to Gisèle and Émilie in abundance—but they had to use their ration coupons so the Germans wouldn't suspect. As the months passed, Émilie had taught her how to bake bread and cook the leeks, potatoes, and cabbage. Émilie knew the food they prepared wasn't for the orphanage, but she didn't ask questions. It seemed best for all of them not to question.

She glanced back out the window again and saw the child peeking around the glass. Where were his parents?

Last month the Germans mandated that the Jews living among them—even those born in France—wear the stars on their coats. If Jews refused to wear it, the Germans threatened a penalty of imprisonment, but Nadine thought wearing the badge was a greater threat than refusing. Gisèle was terrified as to what would happen to her friend Nadine if she didn't wear the star. Her daughter, Louise, had been born more than a year ago now, and Gisèle had tried to convince her friend to wear the star for Louise's sake, but Nadine refused.

Until the government began requiring the badges, Gisèle hadn't realized how many Jewish people lived near Saint-Lô. Now their city seemed to glow yellow from the fallen stars. Instead of finding safety, their haven had crumbled.

People wouldn't hate the Jewish people if they were blessed with a friend like Nadine. Nadine Batier was a French citizen, a devout Catholic. Her husband had been one of the favorite teachers at the secondary school until the headmaster in Saint-Lô terminated his position last term, citing the fact that he was no longer qualified to teach. They all knew the truth—the administration didn't want the husband of a Jewish woman teaching their children.

She couldn't comprehend why they would dismiss André because of the blood in his wife's veins. How was his family supposed to survive without work? But the Germans had taken his job away and now they wanted to brand his family.

When Monsieur Cornett returned, he glanced back out the window. "Why is he still here?"

The boy looked away. "Perhaps he's waiting for his parents."

"They were probably arrested last night."

A tremor of fear flared up her spine. "Why would they be arrested?"

"How would I know?" he replied. "They rounded up dozens of people around Saint-Lô."

He handed her the bread and she tucked it under her arm. "Where did they take them?"

The baker shrugged.

She shivered. There had been rumors of the Germans rounding up Jews in Paris, and she'd been afraid they would begin to gather the Jews here as well. Had André and Nadine heard what happened? Probably not—they rarely left their home these days.

She had to warn them.

As she moved toward the door, she ripped a large piece of bread from her loaf and held it out to the boy on the street. The boy stared down at her offering. When his gaze bounced back up to her, she saw fear mirrored in his eyes. Purple remnants of a bruise circled his eye, and for a moment, she flashed back to that horrific night when she and Michel had found Papa's body by the lake, his face battered by the Germans.

Had they beaten this boy as well?

Her heart felt as if it would rip into two pieces.

Instead of taking the piece of bread, the boy turned and ran. Stunned, she stood and watched him disappear into an alley.

Did he think she was trying to trick him?

Someone brushed up against her, an old woman wearing a brown-and-green scarf over her head. She kissed Gisèle on one cheek, and as she leaned to kiss her second cheek, she whispered, "He is afraid."

Gisèle clung to the woman a moment longer. "But why?"

"Because they are watching him."

The old woman continued her walk, swinging a basket in her arms. Gisèle looked up at the windows across the street and then down the lane of shops. Two soldiers stood on the street corner, guns at their sides to maintain order.

Since the occupation, the German soldiers had stood alongside the Russians forced into servitude as guards or soldiers for the Wehrmacht. After two years of *captivité*, the unwelcome presence of both the Germans and the Russians seemed permanently etched into the streets.

Sirens blared around the corner and an ambulance rushed toward her, the lights flashing. She hopped back onto the sidewalk and watched it race up the hill, toward the hospital.

The baker's words echoed in her mind. How many Jews had the Germans taken away last night? And where had they gone?

She prayed the Batiers, like the boy in Saint-Lô, hadn't been among them. She had to check on André and Nadine, but yet . . .

Her gaze wandered back to the alley where the boy had run.

The soldiers were everywhere, and the familiar fears threatened her. But she could not succumb to the paralysis of fear, not if the Germans were planning to take this child too.

Setting the bread in her basket, she waited until the soldiers shuffled down the street, and then she pushed her bicycle into the alley. The boy cowered beside an empty trash can, his head tucked into his knees. As if he could shrink into the wall and she would never know he was there.

She sat down beside him and held out the bread again.

This time he took it.

"Where are your parents?" she asked.

He wiped his face on his sleeves. "They had to leave."

"Are they coming back?"

"I don't know," he said quietly. "They said they couldn't take me with them."

As loudly as her heart cried out for her to hurry to Nadine's, she couldn't leave this child here, alone and hungry.

"Outside of town," she whispered. "There's a home for children."

He shook his head. "Not for children like me."

She swallowed. It was a Catholic orphanage, but surely they would take in an abandoned child, no matter his religious background.

When he finished his piece of bread, she offered her hand. "I cannot leave you by yourself."

He eyed her hand for a moment. "What if they don't want me?"

A tear fell down her cheek. "Then I will find another safe place," she promised.

He took her hand.

— CHAPTER 18 —

"Pretty Woman" blared on the cab's radio as my driver navigated the streets of Paris. "*No anglais*," he'd said when I climbed into the car at the airport, yet as he maneuvered through the morning traffic of Paris, he had no problem belting out the English lyrics to this song.

It seemed so surreal—cruising past the celebrated museums and architectural treasures of this great city as we listened to American pop songs.

From Gare Saint-Lazare, I would board a train to Carentan in Normandy, and Marguerite, the woman hired to care for the château, was supposed to pick me up at the train station. Riley Holtz would arrive tomorrow afternoon to begin filming.

Between my confrontation with Austin and my lack of sleep, my head felt like it had been crushed. My mind raged with anger, but my heart wouldn't cooperate. It just felt shattered.

My phone lit up again, and I glanced down at Austin's number. I'd lost track of the times he'd called and texted since I left the hotel last night. Or was that two nights ago? I'd lost track of time altogether.

I declined his call.

As the cab crawled through a narrow street, I rolled down my window, and the aroma of warm pastries and strong espresso wafted into the cab. Morning had dawned in France.

I was supposed to be calling Austin, telling him I'd arrived, telling him how much I missed him. Instead he was texting me, in the middle of the night from New York, begging me to forgive him.

The memory of him kissing the lips of Starla Dedrick in the elevator looped through my mind. Was she sleeping beside him now as he texted me? Or had he snuck away while she slept?

The moment I saw Austin with Starla at the Plaza, my perfectly structured future had crumbled. I didn't know when I would speak to him again—if I would speak to him again—but there was so much more I wanted to say, conversations I'd rehashed over and over during my excruciatingly long flight across the Atlantic. None of it would change the fact that our engagement was over. There would be no wedding now. No marriage. Austin might become Virginia's governor, but I would not be the governor's wife. In hindsight, I knew I should have seen this coming, but I had thought his indifference to me in the past months was due to the busyness of his campaign. Apparently he had plenty of time for recreation. It just didn't involve me.

How could I have been so stupid?

I closed my eyes, imagining for a moment how he would position this new wrench in his campaign. Olivia would have a cow, no doubt. He'd probably make her handle the announcement of our breakup to the media and his staff. Still, the media would have questions that only he could answer.

Somehow Olivia and Austin would spin this in a positive light, probably making me look like a fool in the process. I shouldn't have cared, but I did.

How long had he been sleeping with Starla? For all I knew, they'd never even broken up after college. Perhaps Olivia had been covering for him all along.

All it would take was a call from me to one of the morning shows to set a scandal in motion. Or I could sell the gritty details to a tabloid. I had contemplated that very thing on the plane, the sweetness of letting the world know that Austin was scum.

But what woman really wanted to let the world know her fiancé had rejected her? It would be bad enough to tell my parents what happened. I didn't want to be part of the world's analysis of why my fiancé had cheated on me. The sweet taste of my revenge would sour quickly and somehow Olivia would position me as the villain instead of the victim.

Is she walking back to me? Yeah, she's walking back to me.

The driver grinned as he sang the final lyrics to "Pretty Woman," and when I glanced up at the rearview mirror, he winked at me. Cringing, I leaned my head back on the seat and gazed out the window at the crowds of Parisians emerging for work. Thanks to my grandmother and my college professors, I spoke fluent French, but I didn't want this man to know I could speak his language.

I wouldn't be walking back to Austin, nor did I have a job to return to in the fall. At some point I'd have to call Marissa and my other bridesmaids to let them off the hook in August, but I would start with my parents.

Still, how did you tell your family that the man you planned to marry was sleeping with another woman? That he had probably loved her all along?

The driver pointed up and I saw the golden Flame of Liberty before we descended into the infamous Pont de l'Alma tunnel where Princess Diana's car crashed when I was in elementary school. In that moment, my heart empathized with the princess—a young woman chosen to marry the future king of England, a devoted wife and mother who played her part well for fifteen years, smiling for the cameras even as her marriage was disintegrating.

Had the prince swept Diana off her feet even as his heart belonged to another woman—a woman the Crown wouldn't permit him to marry?

The next time my phone rang, my mom's picture flashed up on the screen. Either she was worried about me or she knew something—it was two in the morning there and my mom rarely stayed up past eleven.

With a cleansing breath to calm myself, I answered her call.

"Austin was just here, looking like heck," she said. "What happened?"

It took a lot of gall for him to petition my parents. "You don't want to know."

"I do want to know," she replied. "He said you'd fought . . ."

"Did he happen to say about what?"

"It doesn't matter, Chloe. Everyone fights before their wedding. That's why they call it jitters." A woman rode up next to the cab on a bicycle, a girl strapped in a seat behind her. The child's hands were stretched out to reach around her mother's back. "Austin said he's still planning to marry you."

I groaned. "That's awfully kind of him."

"He thought your dad and I might be able to convince you to reconcile."

The driver watched me in the mirror, and I highly doubted his insistence that he didn't speak any English. "We're not reconciling."

"He said there was a misunderstanding. Surely it can be resolved—"

I stopped her. "I don't think so, Mom. I found him in New York with an old girlfriend."

Silence reigned on the other end of the line before she spoke again. "Having dinner together?"

"They weren't dining when I found them."

"Oh my—"

"And he didn't seem the least bit remorseful about their pillow talk at the Plaza."

"I'm—I'm so sorry, honey."

"Me too."

The shock in my mother's voice turned to anger. "If he can't be faithful now, he never will be."

I knew I'd made the right choice, but why did my heart still ache?

When we ended the call, the taxi driver glanced in the mirror. "Do you want to get a drink?" he asked in French.

I continued pretending not to understand him, like he pretended not to understand English.

"Thriller" started playing on the radio, and his attention was diverted to the song. As he drummed his thumbs on the steering wheel, my phone flashed again.

We need to talk, Austin wrote.

I powered off my phone and stuffed it deep into my handbag. Part of me wanted to speak to him again, to say everything I'd forgotten to say at the Plaza, but the thought of talking to him made my stomach churn.

In France, I would have to forget about Austin.

In France, perhaps I would find a little bit of myself.

And for Mémé's sake, I hoped I would find out what happened to the girl she'd lost.

≈ Chapter 19 ≈

The boy clung to Gisèle's hand in the alley as she smoothed back his messy hair. Then she removed the identity document, stamped with an incriminating *J*, from around his neck and ripped it into tiny pieces.

He didn't want to take off the vest, but she finally coaxed him to remove it. She used it to wipe the smudges of dirt off his face before stuffing the vest and slivers of paper deep into the trash can.

"What is your name?" she asked.

When he didn't answer, she knelt beside him. "Are you scared?"

This time he gave her the slightest of nods.

She was terrified, but she didn't tell him. Instead, she gently squeezed his hand. "If anyone asks, you must say you're my brother."

Gisèle prayed quietly as she pushed her bicycle slowly through the town center. The boy walked beside her, clutching her hand, her bread displayed prominently in the basket so the Germans knew the reason they were here.

There were no automobiles on the street; the government was rationing gas along with food. She didn't care much about the gas—she had no need to go anyplace farther than a bicycle ride—but she missed sugar and coffee. Though she could hardly mourn such things when the boy beside her didn't even have bread.

They neared the town center. The stone courthouse that the Germans had taken for their headquarters was on one side of the street, the gray prison on the other. A long red banner was draped over the front windows of their headquarters, displaying a black swastika.

Two soldiers guarded the entrance to the headquarters while three soldiers smoked nearby.

She refused to look at the soldiers, but she knew they were scrutinizing her and her companion. A smile on her face, she leaned down to the boy and whispered for him to laugh. While the soldiers watched, they both forced their quiet laughter.

The Jews in Saint-Lô no longer laughed.

"Halt!" a soldier ordered, and she tightened her grip on the boy's hand as fear gripped her heart. She'd worked hard the past two years not to draw attention to herself, to appear as if she was complying with the law of their occupiers even as she worked covertly to help those resisting. She'd yet to have to stand face-to-face and confront their enemy.

Her teeth chattered as she smiled at the soldier. He looked to be about her age. "Yes, monsieur?"

He held out his hand. "Your papers," he demanded, his French poor.

She opened her satchel and pulled out her identity card. He scanned it quickly and then looked at the boy's neck for his document. Only the smallest children weren't required to wear their papers. "Where is his *Kinderausweis?*"

She sighed. "We left it at home," she explained in French. "I keep telling my brother that he has to wear his card, but you know boys—"

He stopped her and lifted a small radio, asking for a translator. She pretended not to understand his German.

Moments later, a woman stepped out of the headquarters, her yellow scarf flapping behind her. Gisèle's heart plummeted when the woman waved. She'd known Lisette had been conscripted to work as a secretary for the Germans, but she hadn't spoken to her in months. As Lisette rushed up beside her, she prayed the younger woman wouldn't betray her and the child.

Lisette spoke to Gisèle instead of the soldier. "What happened?"

Gisèle pressed her lips together before she replied, trying to steady her voice. "My little brother and I came to town to buy bread."

"Your little bro—" Lisette's gaze dropped and a soft gasp escaped her lips. "He looks like Michel."

"Could you please tell this man—"

The soldier stepped between them, talking rapidly in German to Lisette. Her friend turned back to her. "He's asking about his identity card."

"We forgot it," Gisèle said.

Lisette's eyes grew wide. "You can't forget your papers!"

"But I did."

Lisette chewed at the edge of a fingernail before addressing the soldier again. "She said she will bring the document back to you."

He eyed Gisèle again, ignoring the boy, and she cringed at the lust in his gaze. She'd heard horrific stories of what some of the Nazis had done to the Frenchwomen. A few wooed the local women. Others forced themselves on them.

"Where does she live?" he asked.

Before Lisette could translate the man's words, a dozen soldiers poured out of the prison, and Gisèle stared as they crossed the street. In the midst of them were four men in tattered clothes, their hands tied behind their backs, heads bowed. Her heart raced even faster as she stared at the prisoners, trying to see their faces.

What if they'd caught Michel?

One of the men glanced over at her, and she recognized him—a former banker in Saint-Lô. He seemed defeated with his head down, but fire blazed in his eyes.

The soldier before her stopped one of the guards. "Who are they?"

"Resistance," the man spat.

With that single word, her interrogator grunted at her, telling Lisette that Gisèle must carry her brother's card with her. Then he followed his fellow soldiers and the prisoners away from the town center.

She turned to Lisette. "Where are they taking the men?"

"It doesn't matter," Lisette whispered, nudging her down the sidewalk. "You have to get that boy away from here!"

With a quick nod, Gisèle tugged on the child's hand. They hurried to the north edge of town, trailing about three hundred meters behind the pack of soldiers. She had to get this boy to safety, had to visit Nadine, but her priorities shifted again. Before she did anything else, she needed to make certain her brother wasn't among the prisoners.

The soldiers turned down a narrow lane between the trees, and she hid her bicycle behind one of the hedgerows. She and the boy trailed far behind them, walking among the trees instead of using the trail. The men stopped in a clearing, and she backtracked with the boy almost a hundred meters.

"Wait here," she said, hiding him behind a bush.

The boy didn't argue with her. Instead he sat down and pulled his knees to his chest. She snuck back toward the clearing and watched in horror as the soldiers tied the men against four poles.

She could see the men's faces now. Her brother wasn't among them, but her relief was fleeting. All of these men had families who loved them.

Were the soldiers going to torture these men where no one could hear their screams?

Her stomach reeled again; she felt as sick as she had the night they found their father.

She glanced at the tall oak trees around the clearing. If only there was something she could do. Distract the soldiers in some way and help these men escape. What if she screamed and ran away? Would they follow her?

Perhaps the Frenchmen could run away as well.

But what if the soldiers found the boy in the brush? They would kill him too.

Clutching her arms around her chest, she rocked back and forth, helpless. Was there nothing she could do to stop the Germans?

This time the fear paralyzed her.

The crack of a gunshot exploded in the forest, and the head of one of the men pitched forward. At the second shot, she ran, fear clinging to her like the talons of a hawk.

She would never be able to fight the dragon.

The boy was where she'd left him, his eyes wide.

She held out her hand. "We must hurry."

Together they rushed down the lane, away from the madness. A few kilometers down the road, she found the path where she and her mother had once walked hand in hand, when the world seemed to make sense. She and the boy turned, and ahead of them was the tower of a stone manor peeking out above the trees.

For the first time, she felt his hand tremble in hers. She might not be able to fight the dragon, but she prayed she could rescue this boy.

— CHAPTER 20 —

The Château d'Epines rose majestically above the trees that sheltered it, and I leaned back in my car seat to soak in the beauty—the magic—of the medieval château. Intricate strands of ivy wove around two turrets that climbed above the three stories of stone, and dozens of glass panes shimmered peach in the setting sunlight.

I remembered sitting here with my parents and my grandmother twenty years ago, soaking in the mystery of it all. The château hadn't lost the wonder for me, but after all these years, I still didn't understand. On that trip long ago, why had Mémé and my father refused to go inside?

Marguerite, the caretaker of our family's property, parked the station wagon in the courtyard. She turned off the ignition and stared up at the château beside me. "It is lovely, yes?"

I opened my door and the breeze awoke my senses. "Breathtaking."

"It was even larger, you know, before the war."

"I didn't know."

Marguerite pointed toward the left. "There was another wing on the west side of the house, but Allied pilots bombed it during the German occupation."

"It's so sad . . ."

She nodded. "Thousands of civilians died in Saint-Lô, but the Allied forces had no choice. The Germans refused to leave."

"Refused to leave Saint-Lô?"

Marguerite dumped the keys into her pocket and opened her car door. "They refused to leave our city and they refused to leave the château. The Allies had to almost flatten Saint-Lô and the surrounding villages before the Germans fled."

I needed to read the material Olivia had compiled for me. "I can't imagine how horrible it must have been to have the Germans occupying the town."

"At first, people were shocked by the blitzkrieg," Marguerite said, "but then Hitler commanded his men to be friendly to the French people and win them over with food depots and such until they decided that collaborating with the Nazis would be to their advantage. For two years, they were more like annoying neighbors than tyrants to the people here."

"What happened after those first two years?" I asked.

Marguerite's eyes focused back on the château in front of us. "The Nazi Party began to unravel."

My head tilted back again as my hostess stepped out of the car, my brain dazed from the shock of Austin's betrayal and my few, fitful hours of sleep. Did the filmmaker want to know the stories about the German occupation? If so, I was afraid I didn't have anything to tell him. Once again, I wished my dad had been able to make the trip.

I stepped out onto the gravel drive and glanced behind me. The château wasn't alone on the property. Along the driveway was a second house, a smaller, rambling structure where Marguerite and her husband lived, surrounded by a half-dozen outbuildings. Across from the château was a chapel. The cluster of old buildings reminded me of the ceramic French village Mémé used to display each Christmas on her mantel.

My gaze shifted back to the forest that curved around the back of the house like a warm stole. I wondered if the lake Mémé had told me about was still there in the trees. In the morning, perhaps I could find her favorite place and quiet the racing in my mind.

Marguerite slammed her car door and crossed over to my side. Her trousers and vest were a mossy brown color, her bushy eyebrows hedged above her green eyes. She was a large woman, but the extra pounds didn't seem to do anything to diminish her energy. In exchange for a place to live and a monthly stipend, she and her husband had been entrusted to care for the property and keeping squatters from sneaking into the house.

I slung my handbag over my shoulder. "Do you know where the lake is?"

Her eyebrows slid up. "Do you mean the river?"

I shook my head. "My grandmother said there was a lake in the forest."

She pointed left. "There's a small lake over there, but the path is overgrown."

I heaved my suitcase out of the back of the station wagon and set it upright on the gravel. The pewter-colored cover seemed to be made of titanium, and in my rush to get to France, I'd brought a hodgepodge of stuff—shorts and T-shirts, skirts, dress pants for the interview, even an evening dress, just in case I had a night out in Paris.

When I arrived at the train station in Carentan, a fellow passenger took pity on me and my mammoth bag, carrying it down to the platform. Rolling it to Marguerite's waiting car had been a simple affair, but it had taken both of us to lift it into her car. Now

I eyed the three floors of the château, wondering on which floor I would find my room.

"Are you certain you don't want to stay with us in the farm-house?" Marguerite asked.

I thanked her and then reassured her that I wanted to sleep in the house where my grandmother had lived.

"I don't think anyone has slept here in several years, but I've cleaned the main rooms for you."

A new thought flashed into my head, one I should have considered before I insisted on staying in the house. "What about the utilities?"

"We've kept on the water and electricity, but there's nothing fancy like Wi-Fi."

"That's okay." I had Internet access on my phone and iPad, but the less connection I had to the outside world, probably the better.

Marguerite glanced down at the behemoth of a suitcase. "My husband can carry that up the stairs for you."

"There's no need for him to help—" I started to say. Her eyebrows rose in question as she slid her cell phone out of her purse, and I realized the ridiculousness of my words. "I would be grateful for it."

When she lifted her phone to her ear, I leaned back against the car. I was supposed to be here two full days before the arrival of Riley Holtz to overcome my jet lag and acquaint myself with the château, but with the delay in my flight, it was already Thursday. He would be here tomorrow.

My body was exhausted. My broken heart felt numb. How was I supposed to smile for his camera?

Being here, though, was much better than being at home. My phone hummed and I pulled it out of my purse. This time Olivia was texting me.

Call me, Chloe! We will work this out before the wedding.

My harsh laugh earned me a look of concern from Marguerite, as if she were trying to determine my mental capabilities. I mustered a smile. Olivia was a campaign manager, not a counselor, and there was nothing for her or us to *work out.*

I texted back. *The wedding is off!*

A flood of texts followed, begging me to call her, telling me the wedding could be postponed, not canceled. But standing outside Austin's room at the Plaza, my fingers pressed against my phone, I had made my decision not to overlook Austin's liaisons now or in the future. No matter what Olivia said, I would never marry Austin. The publicity might be messy, but I had no doubt that she had cleaned up bigger messes in the past.

If only Olivia would insist Austin clean this mess up on his own. Perhaps he would change his behavior.

Marguerite closed her flip phone, and I powered mine down. "You need to get some rest," she said.

I reached for the handle of my suitcase. "I'd like to sleep in my grandmother's room."

"I don't know which room was hers, but we've set you up in the master suite for tonight." She pointed at my bag. "Pierre said he will carry it up to the second floor."

Seconds later, a man came rushing toward us, a grasshopper sort of fellow—tall and thin with a white button-down shirt streaked with dirt and underarms soaked with perspiration. The grin spread across his thin lips was so friendly, I couldn't help but smile back at him.

Marguerite introduced us, and Pierre pumped my hand with enthusiasm. "It is a pleasure to meet you. A real pleasure."

"You as well."

He kept shaking my hand. "I hope you find the house to your liking."

"I'm sure I will like it very much."

Pierre's smile started to fade when he looked down at my suit-case and then it dissolved altogether when he tried to pick it up. He set it back on the gravel. "Did you pack a refrigerator?"

I smiled again. "I thought it might come in handy . . ."

He tried to lift it again. "Perhaps you packed two."

Marguerite scolded him. "Stop harassing her."

He wiped the sweat from his brow and heaved the suitcase off the ground before he lugged it across the stone pavers. Marguerite reached for the iron handle on the front door and opened it for him.

I hadn't known what to expect, but my mouth gaped open when I stepped into the entryway of the house. The home might have been vacant, but the elaborate décor remained in residence. In front of me, the hall rose three stories, with a giant tapestry draped over an arched doorway on my right. Beside it, a staircase spiraled up to balconies on the second and then third landing. The marble floors were adorned with oriental rugs of rich indigo, blood red, and deep evergreen.

For a moment, it felt as if I were back in the Plaza.

Marguerite flipped a switch and light cascaded down from a wrought-iron chandelier with electric candles. "The salon is through the arch," she said before pointing left. "And the kitchen is stocked—"

"The woman doesn't need food," Pierre teased. "She carries a refrigerator with her."

Marguerite ignored him. "I'll bring you up a dinner tray."

"That would be wonderful."

While Pierre fiddled with something in the kitchen, Marguerite gave me a quick tour of the rest of the house. There were a total of ten bedrooms on the upper levels, some with furnishings, others filled with boxes, two completely empty. Almost all of them were covered with a layer of dust.

On the main floor, the windows in the salon overlooked a lush valley and river. On the other side was a grassy hill topped with trees.

The salon, Marguerite said, could be transformed into a ball-room or a dining hall, and then she showed me the library, an office tucked into a turret, the drawing room, and a kitchen with a medieval fireplace. I asked Marguerite if I could try my hand at cooking over the fireplace. She said she didn't know—I would have to ask my dad.

Behind the kitchen was a small door, and I followed her downstairs into a wine cellar. There were circular brick bins on the walls that reminded me of a red-flecked honeycomb and large casks of wine stacked on the far end of the wall.

"It used to be a prison," Marguerite said. "Until the Duchants turned it into a wine cellar."

I rubbed my arms. "It feels strange down here."

She flicked off the lights. "The ghosts refuse to leave this place."

I hurried back up the stairs. That's just what I needed in the middle of the night, to be thinking about the ghosts.

Pierre pulled and I pushed my suitcase up the winding stairs of the turret. Then I followed him into a large room in one of the turrets, complete with a sofa, desk, and canopied bed with wrought-iron posts. Exposed rafters lined the ceiling and a dozen narrow windows lined the walls. Pierre set my suitcase near the armoire, and with a quick nod, he scurried back through the door as if he was worried I might ask him to lift something else. When he was gone, I stepped toward one of the windows to see the view, but all I saw were tree limbs and gray shadows from the fleeing sun.

Sinking back into the cushions of the sofa, I stared up at the rafters. The past twenty-four hours had been torture—trying to keep myself from melting down as I traveled across the ocean. Now I had no plane to catch, no taxi to find, no train to ride. And no one around to see me cry.

Tears drenched my cheeks.

I hated this feeling, this not knowing who I was without Austin Vale. I had no idea where I was going. For an entire year, my identity had been entwined with his, and now—now I felt like a lost soul.

Perhaps I shouldn't have gotten on the plane to France—I could have gone to my parents' house on the lake and hidden away for a few weeks. But Austin would have found me there in days, if not hours, and I couldn't face him or my family or friends yet. My family would be kind, telling me things like Austin didn't deserve me or someone better would come along, but I didn't want to hear that. The problem was, I had no idea what I wanted.

The aching in my heart returned, and I lay on the bed, my arms splayed out on both sides.

Austin swooped into my life last summer with an intensity that swept me away, a handsome, charming politician who seemed to be as fascinated by me as I'd been by him.

Perhaps he had found me attractive early on. He certainly acted as if he had, though he rarely pushed the limits of the boundaries we'd set for our physical relationship. I thought he was respecting my desire to wait until we married, but really he hadn't needed to be physical with me. Instead he needed the other assets I brought to the table as his fiancée and wife.

The daughter of a wealthy businessman who contributed heavily to his campaign and would pass along a considerable inheritance to his only daughter and son-in-law.

The granddaughter of a World War II hero.

The elementary schoolteacher willing to give up her career to tout his education reform and raise his children.

The woman who would dote on Austin and smile at dinners and dances and golf tournaments for decades to come.

The wife who would entertain herself while her husband took weekend trips to New York.

I felt sick.

Had Austin seen dollar signs when he looked into my eyes? Had he and Olivia compiled lists of single women in Richmond and narrowed it down to the final three? The morning we'd met in the coffee shop, when he'd spilled my latte . . .

The memory pricked my mind, clearing the fog.

That was why our engagement had been so swift. He and Olivia must have orchestrated our meeting.

A single man his age would probably never be voted in as governor, especially when he was running against an older, much wiser family man. The past year had been a façade concocted by him and Olivia and maybe even Starla to make the media think he was a mature man committed to government and family, and I—

I was nothing but a campaign pawn in order to get him elected.

When I'd agreed to his proposal of marriage, Olivia had rolled me out with great fanfare to the media, and I'd been blinded by all the lights, painfully ignorant of the casting call for a governor's wife. It was as if I were a contestant on *The Bachelor* but no one bothered to tell me about the invisible strings pulling my arms and legs and even my mouth.

What was Austin planning to do with me postelection? Show me off like a horse in an arena? Olivia could braid my hair and decorate my tail with ribbons and parade me around for everyone to see. Then they'd probably put me back in the stall until the next show.

Whether or not he won the governor's house—and whether or not he married another Virginia girl—I suspected Austin would continue to indulge in his trips to New York.

A light blinked outside the window, and it took me a moment to realize that stars had appeared. The château, in all its glory, was a lonely place, and I felt the pangs of loneliness along with the ghosts of the past.

But I couldn't wallow in my pain. I had to press through it.

My eyes grew heavy.

This trip was no longer a favor for Austin—I didn't care one bit about the documentary and its benefit to his campaign. But I was in France and curious about my roots, curious about the echo of stories in the château, curious about the girl Mémé thought she'd left behind.

I had intended to stay awake until Marguerite brought up a tray of food, but if she knocked, I never heard her. Exhaustion won out over my hunger, and I drifted off into blessed sleep.

Tomorrow I would search for answers.

Chapter 21

Gisèle and the boy scuttled through a pair of lofty iron gates, into a grassy courtyard. Three children played on a metal merry-go-round, but when she and the boy approached, the children raced inside the manor.

It didn't deter Gisèle. With the boy's hand cocooned inside hers, she led him to the back of the house and knocked on the wooden door. The curtain lifted in a window by the door, and the eyes of a little girl looked back at her. Gisèle waved at the girl, and moments later, the curtain fell back into place, the lock on the door sliding back.

A nun in a black habit and white veil answered Gisèle's knock. She looked like she was in her midthirties, her face pale without any makeup, her smile kind. Behind her, dozens of children crowded around roughly hewn tables, eating from tin bowls.

The nun's gaze rested on the little boy. "My name is Sister Beatrice."

He gave her a slight nod.

"Are you hungry?" she asked.

When he didn't respond, Gisèle inched him forward. "He's hungry."

The nun put her hand on his shoulder. "One of my sisters will get you some stew."

The boy hesitated until another child came forward and led him to a table.

"Where did you find him?" Sister Beatrice whispered.

"He was in Saint-Lô. His parents . . ." She stepped into the house beside Sister Beatrice. "They can no longer care for him."

The nun watched him sit with the others. "He is one of God's children," she said, resolute.

"He is," Gisèle whispered. Though he no longer wore his star. Gisèle looked back at Sister Beatrice. "My mother was Vicomtesse Duchant from the Château d'Epines. She used to bring food for the children here."

Sister Beatrice smiled. "I remember your mother well. You are blessed with her eyes . . . and her heart."

The nun's words warmed her, but the woman had no idea of the fear that clutched at—poisoned—her heart as well.

"Can this child stay with the others, until his parents return for him?"

Sister Beatrice stepped closer to her. "Why don't you take him home?"

The gunshots from the forest seemed to echo in her mind. The soldiers were prowling the town and the countryside, searching for members of the resistance. If the Germans found the cell hiding under her house, they might kill all of them, including the child.

"I fear it won't be safe for him, so close to town." She looked across the great room again, at the children finishing their stew. The boy picked up his spoon and began to eat. "All he needs is a place to sleep and something nourishing to eat."

Sister Beatrice gently touched her arm. "A child needs more than that."

"That's part of the problem, she said with a sigh. "I don't know what a child needs."

"If his parents were part of the roundup, the police may come looking for him here. And if they find him—" Sister Beatrice's voice cracked. "The French think it is admirable to keep families together when they send them away, but if his parents are gone, they would send him away by himself."

The thought made Gisèle tremble, for André and Nadine and the little girl they adored. "Where are they sending these families?"

"I'm not certain. Perhaps to one of the work camps."

"He is too small. He'd be of no use to them—"

Sister Beatrice's voice dipped so low that Gisèle had to strain to hear her. "The Nazis have no patience for people who aren't useful, especially the Jewish people."

Gisèle thought back to some of the bitter reflections she'd read in *Mein Kampf*, to the deep loathing in the author's heart. "I don't understand why Hitler hates the Jews—"

"It isn't just Hitler," Sister Beatrice said. "He is only unifying all those in Europe who think the Jewish people flaunt their wealth."

The only Jewish people she knew well weren't wealthy, nor could she imagine Nadine or her parents flaunting the little they did have, but Gisèle understood the misperception. Since childhood, she had borne the brunt of meanness from people who'd thought the Duchants needed a good dose of humility. "But there aren't many wealthy Jews in France . . ."

Sister Beatrice folded one of her hands over the crucifix that hung from her neck. "Others hate the Jewish people because they claim to be God's chosen people and then others, I'm told, have hatred in their hearts because Jews were responsible for the crucifixion of Jesus."

Gisèle leaned back against the wall. "It's strange to think that an event that happened almost two thousand years ago could breed such hatred today."

This time a whisper of a smile crept up on Sister Beatrice's lips. "Almost as strange as an event that happened almost two thousand years ago healing lives today."

Gisèle rubbed her hands together. "Can I leave this boy with you?"

Sister Beatrice glanced back at the children.

"I will bring you food and—"

Sister Beatrice interrupted her. "You mustn't bring us any food. In fact, you mustn't come here anymore, at all. Someone may follow you."

"You will take him?"

"We will take him," Sister Beatrice replied. "But we aren't able to care for any more children."

A little girl with blond pigtails stepped up beside her, a bowl of stew in her hands. She held it out to Gisèle.

"Thank you," Gisèle said, smiling at the child. She ate rapidly, the broth warming her, the vegetables giving her strength. She would need it to pedal back to André and Nadine's.

Before Gisèle left, Sister Beatrice took both her hands, and the nun prayed with fervency, pleading with Jesus to protect Saint-Lô's children from the evil in their midst.

But Gisèle feared the Spirit of God had already fled Saint-Lô.

CHAPTER 22

A breakfast tray fit for the queen of England arrived at my door, a few minutes before eight. This time I heard the knock, and I would have answered it except I was in the midst of trying to wash my long hair under the bathtub's finicky spigot. The water did indeed work, and for that I was grateful, but it fluctuated from cold to hot as quickly as the polls in Virginia swung between Austin and his opponent.

With my wet hair wrapped in a towel, I retrieved the tray of food, placed it on the coffee table, and breathed in the aromas of dark espresso and apple butter. Piled onto the tray was a basket of warm croissants, prosciutto sliced so thin it looked like pink tissue paper, slices of honeydew melon, and little white tubs with butter and jam and soft cheese.

As I cut open a croissant, its breath warmed my face, and I slathered it with the butter and then the strawberry jam. While in France, I would not count a single calorie. It was Austin himself who had told me to enjoy the food. Immerse myself in the past. He and Olivia could sweat the future.

When I finished my breakfast, I took the tray down to the kitchen. "I'm so sorry," I said. "I fell asleep last night."

Marguerite waved her hand. "Please don't worry. I had an urgent call and brought it up late."

"I didn't even hear you knock."

"Riley Holtz is scheduled to arrive in Carentan this after-noon," she said as she piled the dishes in the sink. "Do you want to ride to the train station with me?"

I declined. Instead I would search for Mémé's lake.

I found a path on each side of the house—a wide path that appeared to go down to the river and a sliver of a path that slipped back into the forest to the west of the house. I took the path west.

I'd only walked a few yards when I discovered an iron gate, its base anchored in mud. I lifted and pushed until there was finally enough space for me to squeeze through. The trail zigzagged down the hill, and I saw a glint of water at the bottom.

Several trees dipped low over the banks of the lake, while others had tumbled into the water. Sunlight streaked through the leaves above and glistened on the coats of moss below. Magnifi-cent greens and yellows ornamented the browns.

I sat on a flat stone and curled my knees up against my chest. A turtle peeked its head out of the water and then glided along the surface.

I could almost imagine Mémé as a child, skipping along the stones, balancing herself on the slippery trunks that rested in the lake, splashing water at her brother, or sneaking down here to enjoy the solace. Cell phone reception had been sketchy in my room, but down here, there was none at all. I relished the sunlight that snuck through the trees, the simplicity of the warm breeze tickling my neck.

I wished I could paddle around this lake in a kayak or even a canoe, but for the moment, I would simply savor the quiet.

Closing my eyes, I remembered Mémé's laughter when she used to take me to the stables in Virginia where she boarded her two horses. We would ride through the forest outside Fairfax, and she would tell me the stories of Normandy and the hours she would ride her horse along the river Vire.

Grandpa had been the vice president at a local bank and Mémé taught French literature at George Mason University. Every June, when school ended, I would spend two weeks at their house, riding horses, cooking comfort food like coq au vin and bouillabaisse alongside Mémé, paddling on the river nearby. Every Sunday, she took Grandpa and me to Mass, and before I went to bed, she quoted Scripture along with wisdom from her writing heroes.

> *You've never lived until you've almost died.*
>
> —GUY DE MAUPASSANT

> *I have learnt that all men live not by care*
> *for themselves but by love.*
>
> —LEO TOLSTOY

> *For there are many great deeds done*
> *in the small struggles of life.*
>
> —VICTOR HUGO

And her other favorite quote from Victor Hugo: *France is great because she is France.*

I wished I could call her now and tell her that I was at the château. That I'd broken my engagement and didn't know what my future held. I could almost hear her say, "*Ma chérie*, your life is not over. It has only begun."

And then she would say something brilliant, influenced by all the writers she loved. Something like, "But don't live to bring happiness to yourself, Chloe. Live to bring joy to all those around you."

In the distance I heard the chiming of church bells. And I opened my eyes.

Had Mémé lost herself here when she was a girl?

Or perhaps she hadn't lost herself at all. Perhaps she'd found herself by the water.

Perhaps here she'd learned to give her life for others.

I slowly rose to my feet, my sweet memories fading. Riley Holtz would be here in two hours, but we weren't scheduled to meet until tomorrow morning at nine. This afternoon I would explore the property and read Olivia's notes about the war.

A second path meandered up the cliff and I followed it to the south of the house. It ended at a brick wall with another iron gate, but this gate was padlocked shut. I trailed the wall until I reached a portion that had collapsed. Heaving myself up, I climbed over it and began to wade through the tall grass.

On the other side of the field was another brick wall, and behind that the stone chapel with a small cemetery to its side. A girl skipped past the church, her ponytail bouncing behind her. Then I saw an elderly man with denim overalls perched against the brick wall, about thirty yards away.

When I was about halfway across the field, the older man called out to me in French. "You'd best take care where you step."

I froze, lifting my eyes again to meet his gaze. "Why should I be careful?"

When he grinned, I saw a chipped tooth under his dried lips. "You're walking across an old minefield."

What was wrong with this man, smiling at me like that? And why wasn't the minefield surrounded by an electrical fence? Or marked by a giant, flashing Danger sign?

Perhaps there was a sign along the road. Probably no one else ever came up the back way from the lake.

Should I follow my footsteps back to the wall or continue forward?

Before I decided, the girl called out to me. "Don't mind Monsieur Lavigne. He likes to scare people."

I eyed the man again and then the girl, farther down the wall. She couldn't have been more than ten or eleven, but between the two of them, I decided to trust the child.

I quizzed her. "It's not a minefield?"

"It was, a long time ago, but the mines were taken out after the war. There is no need for worry—you won't lose a leg or anything now."

I wasn't sure if that was supposed to comfort me. I didn't want to lose a toe or a foot or any other body part either.

"Come this way," the girl instructed in French, waving me forward.

I took a small step as if to test the ground. "Are you certain the mines are gone?"

She nodded. "Unless you have tremendously bad luck."

I grimaced. "I'm afraid bad luck is chasing me."

She laughed. "You're funny."

I proceeded cautiously until I came to a muddy rut in the field, not ten feet from where she stood. I glanced back up at her before I walked through it.

"A bomb made that hole a long time ago," she said in English. "Nothing will grow on it."

I thought back to the crumbling wall by the gate and recalled Marguerite's words about the bombing of the west hall. "Are there a lot of these holes left?"

The girl shrugged. "My great-grandmother says that one is too many."

"Your great-grandmother is a smart woman."

When I reached the other side of the field, I took a deep breath and settled with my back against the wall. The elderly man had wandered away, but the girl remained, sitting on a log to tie her black shoes. The light brown hair in her ponytail curled down her back, and she wore a short plaid skirt with tights and a red blouse.

"Are you from Saint-Lô?" I asked.

"My great-grandmother lives down near the river." She pointed east. "I stay with her in the summers."

"I used to spend part of the summer with my grandmother." I brushed off my jeans. "Your English is perfect."

She smiled. "What is your name?"

"Chloe—Chloe Sauver. My grandmother lived here as a child."

She popped up from the log. "In Agneaux?"

"In the château. Her name was Gisèle Duchant before she married."

"Grand-mère said she used to be friends with the woman who lived here."

My heart quickened. Perhaps her great-grandmother could tell me more about Mémé's story. Perhaps she even knew Adeline.

"My name is Isabelle," the girl volunteered.

"That's a beautiful name." I stuck my hands into my pockets. "How old are you?"

"Almost eleven."

"It's good that you're learning English."

She twisted the hem of her skirt. "Grand-mère says I don't have a choice."

It was a bit strange to think this girl's great-grandmother and my grandmother were the same age, but since my father was older than most dads, I was used to the gap.

"What is your great-grandmother's name?" I asked.

"Madame Calvez."

"I would like to meet your great-grandmother."

Isabelle checked the watch on her wrist. "She'll sleep for another hour."

"Where were you going now?"

She nodded up the lane, toward the village at the top. "Up to Agneaux to buy bread." She paused. "When I get back, I could take you to meet her."

I wondered what Madame Calvez remembered about my grandmother.

Chapter 23

Gisèle turned onto the empty rue de la Vire and then pedaled toward the river as fast as she could, the words of the baker
and then Sister Beatrice ominous in her mind. Leaning her bicycle against the Batiers' garage door, she glanced over at the lacy
white curtains that concealed the living room. Nadine usually
waved at her through the window, but this time she didn't see
her friend.

"Gisèle!" a voice called, and she turned to see Lisette pedaling
quickly down the lane. She waited until Lisette stepped off the bicycle.

Her breath came in short heaves. "You pedal too fast."

"I didn't know you were following me," Gisèle said.

"For at least half a kilometer." Lisette patted her curls and
then straightened the navy blue scarf around her neck before kissing Gisèle on both of her cheeks.

"Aren't you supposed to be at work?"

"The commander sent me on an errand." The woman's blue
eyes implored her for information. "Have you heard from
Michel?"

Gisèle shook her head.

"How about Philippe?" Lisette asked.

The Nazis had overtaken northern France, but in the south, they'd left France unoccupied in an area known as Vichy. De Gaulle called it a "puppet government," Hitler's cronies pulling the strings, but Lyon, where Philippe and his mother lived, was in Vichy.

"He tries to call about once a week," she said. Though lately it seemed to be more like once a month, and with the Germans listening, they never talked about anything of consequence. She'd stopped waiting for him to return to Saint-Lô a long time ago.

"I keep hoping . . . ," Lisette began. "I just want to know if Michel's still alive."

"You must keep praying that he's alive." Gisèle swallowed. "Thank you for helping me at the town square."

Lisette shook her head. "I don't want to know who that child is—"

"I won't tell you," she said even though she didn't know anything about him.

Lisette glanced up the lane behind her before she looked back at Gisèle. "Is the boy safe?"

Gisèle nodded as she stepped toward the house.

Lisette eyed the front door. "We shouldn't be here."

"André and Nadine are my friends."

Lisette lowered her voice. "Nadine may not wear her star, but the officials know about her parents."

"Her family is Catholic. And French."

"Before she became French—"

Gisèle stopped her. "It shouldn't matter about before."

Lisette waited by her bicycle as Gisèle walked through the picket gate and up the stone pavers that wove a path through the trellises of roses in the Batiers' front yard. She knocked on the front door, her fingers drumming against the frame as she waited impatiently for

Nadine to swing it open and kiss her on both cheeks. When no one responded, she knocked again.

Stepping to the side, Gisèle tried to peer through the window, but the curtain covered the inside. Perhaps André had been able to secure bus passes to Grenoble, where Nadine's parents lived. Or perhaps they had simply taken a walk down to the Vire.

She glanced over her shoulder at Lisette. "They must be out back."

Lisette looked skeptical, but she trailed her through Nadine's garden, to the edge of the property. Red berries ornamented the hawthorn trees, and the air smelled of wood smoke and rain.

"Nadine?" Gisèle called into the trees.

A bee buzzed past them, and Lisette shrieked. Then she pulled her scarf up over her head as she eyed a row of old wooden hives tucked back in the forest. "This place is creepy."

"As long as you don't harm the bees, they won't hurt you," Gisèle said.

"You don't know that."

Gisèle called André's name this time, but still there was no response.

Lisette stepped into the garden. "Perhaps they left before the roundup."

Gisèle had to cling to that hope—she couldn't let herself consider the alternative.

A goldfinch fluttered between the trees, and then she heard a noise. A cry. She swiveled toward Lisette. "Was that a bird?"

Lisette's eyes were wide. "It sounded like a baby."

There was a second cry, dull but persistent.

If it was Louise, why weren't André and Nadine answering her cries?

Turning, Gisèle raced back toward the cottage. On the second floor, one of the bedroom windows was cracked open. She reached for the knob on the back door, expecting to shove it, but the door was already open. She stumbled inside.

The living room looked as if a German tank had plowed through its center. André's prized books had been flung across the floor, torn pages crumpled, as if someone planned to build a bonfire. Legs had been hacked off the wooden furniture, the upholstered pieces slashed, dishes shattered on the floor.

Lisette cursed.

Gisèle steadied herself on the windowsill, trying to force her thoughts to stay present, but they refused to cooperate. Her mind flashed back again in rapid sequence to that terrible day two years ago when she found her father's bloodied body in the forest. The loss that had seared a hole in her core.

The room swayed.

Would she find André and Nadine as she had Papa? She didn't think she could bear the loss of someone else she loved, seeing them bloody and bruised. She knew it didn't really matter how much she could bear, but still, the thought of losing her friends was heart-wrenching. Overwhelming. Whatever she found, she would try to bear it, for Louise's sake and for the sake of her friends, but still—it seemed too much.

Lisette rushed toward the kitchen, and Gisèle yelled for Nadine as she hurried upstairs to the bedrooms. Louise's small bed, carved by her father, was empty, the pink spread unwrinkled on top. Her toys were in a wicker basket in the corner, under the lacy pink curtains that fluttered in the breeze.

In the next room, the bedcovers on André and Nadine's bed were balled up on the floor, clothes piled on top of it. Gisèle looked under the bed, as if a child was stowed underneath, but it was empty.

"Louise!" she shouted.

The child had just begun to walk. Had she toddled downstairs alone? But if the Germans had come, surely they would have taken her with her parents . . .

She found Lisette on the bottom step, a cigarette trembling in her hand. "You wanna smoke?" Lisette asked, holding it out.

Gisèle took a long drag, but the tobacco did nothing to calm her. They had to find Louise.

"I despise them all," Lisette said, her voice shaking along with the cigarette.

"Me too."

Lisette took another drag. "We heard a baby's cry, didn't we?"

"I pray so," Gisèle said as she moved toward the back door.

"And the Germans wonder why the resistance wants them dead." Lisette lowered the cigarette to her side. "If Michel were here, he would know what we should do."

The two women searched the garage, the garden, and back among the hawthorns again. They called for Louise all the way to the river, just in case she'd wandered away, but they didn't hear another cry.

Discouraged, the two women trudged back to the house. Gisèle collapsed against the side of the garage, wiping the sweat off her brow with her sleeve. She would never forgive herself if she left Louise here alone.

Lisette climbed on her bicycle. "I must return to work."

Gisèle kissed her friend's cheeks, but before Lisette began to pedal down the lane, the cry echoed again. Lisette threw down her bicycle.

Gisèle pointed left toward the river. "It sounded like it came from that direction."

Another scream erupted in the forest. "*Maman!*"

Lisette followed Gisèle into the forest, scouring the over-grown tangle of trees until they discovered what looked like an old root cellar among the beehives and brush, camouflaged with river stones and branches. On the moss-covered door was a rope handle.

Gisèle leaned down and yanked it open.

CHAPTER 24

Isabelle led me down to the river, to a paved path alongside a grove of white-tipped trees. Graying wooden hives stood among the trees, their resident bees congregating in the neighborhood outside. Last year one of my students had brought *The Life and Times of the Honeybee* to read to the class, and I had been just as fascinated as my students with the world of beekeeping.

I stopped for a moment, sniffing the blossoms. The scent reminded me of the sweet almond smell in marzipan. I reached for a branch, pulling it closer. Until it stung me.

"Ouch!" I said, shaking my fingers.

"The trees have thorns."

I rubbed my hands together. "I figured that out."

"That's why they call them hawthorns."

With a shiver, I recalled my grandmother's words about losing a baby. In the hawthorn trees. How exactly did one lose a child in these trees?

Not that Adeline would still be here, seventy years later, but I was curious to know where my grandmother's mind wandered and what she remembered. And what happened to this girl.

Isabelle chattered with a seamless mixture of French and English. About her school in Paris and her twelve cousins and how she planned to visit America with her mother when she turned sixteen.

A bee buzzed past my ear, and I almost leapt into the river.

Isabelle laughed at me. "They won't sting you this time of year."

I waved my hands across my face. "You can't possibly know that."

"They've never stung me."

"That's because you don't look threatening to them."

"What does *threatening* mean?"

I stretched out my arms overhead. "Big and scary."

She laughed again. "I don't think you look threatening."

In less than a half mile, we veered away from the river and took a small path between the trees. Old hives clung to tree trunks on both sides. Isabelle didn't seem the least bit concerned about trekking through the city of bees, but I prodded her forward, practically stepping on her heels.

We passed an overgrown vegetable and then flower garden before we reached a white cottage adorned with peeling shutters, the color of their paint blending with the trees. A swing set had been built among the gardens and on the back patio of the house was a glass table with two vinyl chairs.

Isabelle slid open the glass door and slipped inside.

When she reopened the door, she didn't step back onto the patio. Her sweet smile was gone, and worry tugged at her eyes.

"Is something wrong?" I asked.

She tilted her head slightly. "Grand-mère says she can't visit with you."

I tried to hide my disappointment. "Did you tell her that Gisèle Duchant is my grandmother?"

Isabelle nodded her head. "She doesn't want to talk about Madame Duchant."

I smiled at the girl. "Thank you for asking. Perhaps I can come back—"

"She said that you shouldn't return," Isabelle said in a louder voice. I assumed so Madame Calvez could hear.

In the window near the patio, I watched a face peek from behind the curtain. I lifted my hand to wave, but the face disappeared.

"I'll be here for a few more days," I told Isabelle as I backed away from the patio. "I'd love to visit her anytime."

I hurried back through the maze of beehives and trees.

What had happened between Madame Calvez and my grandmother?

.   .   .

I called Marissa and in lieu of being a bridesmaid, I asked if she wanted to go kayaking with me on August 10, far away from Richmond. My friend commiserated for an hour without reminding me even once that she'd told me so.

Then I tucked myself away in my room and searched online for the records of an Adeline who had lived in Agneaux or in Saint-Lô. Nothing emerged so I expanded my search through Normandy and discovered an Adeline who'd been born near here. In AD 980.

The other Adelines I found proved equally futile.

I hadn't expected an easy answer, but like my parents, I began to doubt the validity of a quest for a girl that Mémé remembered only after her mind began slipping away.

Outside the window, a cloud of dust trailed Marguerite's station wagon down the drive. I closed my iPad case and watched as a man stepped out of the car and took off his dark sunglasses to gaze up at the château. He looked to be in his early thirties, and he wore a brown bomber jacket even though it must have been at least seventy degrees outside.

When I realized he might see me, I started to step away from the window but it was too late. The man I assumed to be Riley Holtz waved up at me, and I had no choice but to wave back. Then Marguerite motioned toward the farmhouse and Riley followed her away from the château.

There was no reason to rush out now and greet him. I'd promised two hours tomorrow morning for his documentary, and I'd keep my word.

Chapter 25

Gisèle descended back into the tunnel, but this time she wasn't alone. Louise was in her arms, whimpering in the darkness as Gisèle stroked her soft wisps of hair.

She didn't know how long the child had been alone in the cellar, surrounded by the old equipment of a beekeeper, an emptied bottle in the playpen beside her. If André and Nadine had put her there before the raid, it would have been almost twenty-four hours.

Had the Germans wrecked the Batiers' house, searching for André and Nadine's baby? Her friends must have foreseen what might come, but why hadn't they hidden as well? And why had they left Louise in an abandoned basement instead of someplace she'd be more likely to be found?

When she brought Louise home, Émilie filled the child's bottle with warm milk. Louise guzzled the warm milk and slept beside Gisèle until dawn. Then she crawled into Gisèle's arms.

"*Maman?*" Louise had asked, her eyes wide with wonder.

"Your mother is on a trip," Gisèle said, not knowing how much the girl understood and yet wanting to reassure her.

Louise nodded, her eyes still filled with expectancy. "Papa?"

"He is with your mother."

Gisèle's words seemed to comfort her. Or perhaps it was because Shadow snuggled beside her. Gisèle lay back on the pillow and watched the sunlight dance on the walls until Louise stirred again. In those early hours, she decided that she must hide Louise until André and Nadine returned.

When the tunnel split, Gisèle took the right passage. A voice echoed up the passage, and Louise flinched, knocking the flashlight out of Gisèle's hand. When it clattered to the ground, the tunnel faded into black and the child's cries echoed through the darkness.

Gisèle tried to comfort Louise, but this time she could not be consoled. Her parents were gone, and now Gisèle had her down in this cold, dark tunnel, just like the root cellar where she'd been hidden.

Gisèle fumbled for the flashlight until she found it and when she turned it on, Michel was standing in front of her.

At the sight of the man, Louise's cries turned into shrieks.

"Stop screaming," Michel demanded.

Gisèle bounced Louise on her hip. "Hush," she said softly. "He won't hurt you."

The girl pressed her face into Gisèle's shoulder as if she could burrow inside and disappear, her cries sinking to a whimper.

He eyed the back of the child. "Who is she?"

Sorrow passed over her again at the state of their world. Michel should have been smoking cigars with André the day Louise was born. He should have joined them at the cathedral in Saint-Lô on the day of Louise's baptism. He should have been visiting the Batiers on the weekends and getting down on his knees and playing with blocks alongside her, like any godparent would do. But he didn't know Louise, and she was terrified of him.

"This is André and Nadine's daughter," she said.

The edge in his voice softened. "Louise?"

She nodded.

"Where are André and Nadine?" he asked, his voice laden with worry.

She would have given just about anything to tell him she was caring for Louise for the night, that her parents were out picnicking or on an overnight visit to the shore, that they would return in the morning.

"I don't know. I visited this afternoon, and their house was in shambles. I almost left but—" She swallowed. "Lisette was with me. We heard her cry and found her in a cellar behind her home."

"Lisette helped you?" he asked.

She nodded, and he grew quiet for a moment.

"André must have hidden her before—" His voice cracked. "Before they took both him and Nadine away. They knew I would find her soon."

"But how would you find her?" she asked.

"Gigi," he said slowly. "Our ancestors were beekeepers."

Her mind flashed. She'd known there was another entrance to the tunnel, away from the house, but she'd never known where it was.

Louise clung to her neck. "Why didn't André and Nadine wait in the cellar with her?"

He reached out, and for a moment, she thought he would take Louise's hand, but then he pulled back as if he were afraid of her, as if caring for her could destroy everything he was doing. He put his hand back in the pocket of his ragged cardigan. "The officials would have searched until they found the whole family. Perhaps André and Nadine thought if they just hid Louise, she would have a chance."

She put her hand on Louise's back. André and Nadine had sacrificed themselves for their child. "God forgive me, Michel, but I hate the Nazis. Every one of them."

"The Nazis didn't take them away." His voice grew sad. "It was the gendarmes."

It felt like he had punched her in the gut. How could those hired to protect the French people send innocent citizens away?

"Where did they take them?" she asked.

He shook his head. "I don't know."

She heard the low murmur of voices behind them. "Can you keep her down here?"

He stepped back. "It's not possible."

"But they thought you could protect her," she insisted.

"They thought I would bring her to you."

She trembled. "I can't keep her in the house."

"My men and I are leaving soon, Gigi, but even if we weren't, someone above would surely hear her cries. It would destroy our operation."

"But if the police are looking for her, they will search for her in the château."

"Perhaps Lisette could care for her."

Gisèle shook her head. "She works at the headquarters office all day, but even at night—her neighbors would question where she got a child."

"There must be someone . . ."

Sister Beatrice had asked her not to come back, but perhaps she would change her mind. "I will take her to the orphanage."

"Thank you, Gigi."

"André and Nadine will return, won't they?"

"You must pray for them," he said, but there was no hope in his words.

The burden of war weighed heavily on her. "When will this be over?"

"De Gaulle says soon, as long as we keep fighting the Nazis from the inside."

"And when we do beat them, what will happen?"

She wanted to hear her brother say everything would return to how it had been before the war, but she knew he couldn't promise that—not with their father gone and the country wrecked.

"We will be free again," he said. "But until that happens, we can't stop fighting."

She told him about the men she'd seen killed in the forest, and his temper flared. He asked her a dozen questions, and then, as she pulled Louise closer to her chest, he disappeared back into the shadows.

If André and Nadine had risked their lives for Louise, she would do nothing less to keep her safe, out of honor to them and because, frankly, she adored their daughter.

CHAPTER 26

Marguerite discreetly suggested that I venture up to Agneaux for dinner, recommending two restaurants she thought I might enjoy. Then she offered me the use of their vehicle.

I didn't expect her to cook for me during my stay, but I was in France, and the thought of eating out alone was akin to torture. I envisioned myself surrounded by adoring couples, laughing and lingering over bottles of local wine. And then there would be me, alone for hours with my three or four courses and, even worse, my thoughts.

Scrounging through the refrigerator, I found some leftover ham, cheese, and fruit. And a bottle of red Bordeaux. As I poured a glass, a bell rang overhead, and with my wineglass in hand, I wandered up the three steps and across the hall. When I glanced through an oval window by the door, I groaned. I didn't want to be alone, but neither did I want this filmmaker to invade my space. I moved away from the window hoping he hadn't seen me.

Tomorrow morning, I would put on a skirt and flatiron my hair and perfect my smile. Then I would do his interview and move on.

I stepped back to hide in the kitchen until I heard the grate of the front door. Swiveling, I watched Riley Holtz step into the foyer, and my mouth dropped open.

With a sheepish grin, he pointed at the door handle. "You left it unlocked."

I didn't reply, too stunned to speak.

"It's probably not safe," he said, "considering all the thugs who live around here."

I regained my voice. "So you feel entirely comfortable with breaking into someone's house?"

"It's not really breaking in when the door is unlocked." He smiled again. "I saw you through the window and wanted to introduce myself."

"There was a reason I didn't answer the door."

He stuck out his hand. "You must be Chloe."

I stared down at his hand. "You're a smart man."

He dropped his hand back to his side, eyeing my wineglass. "Drinking alone is a terrible habit."

"Smart and cocky . . ."

I hadn't meant it to be funny, but he laughed anyway.

I put the glass down on a sideboard. "I was only drinking one glass. We're in France, you know."

"Indeed."

I leaned against the wall and studied the man for a moment. He was handsome in a rugged sort of way, with his green eyes and goatee. Nothing like Austin's polished persona. His smile seemed genuine. "Aren't you supposed to be sleeping off your jet lag?" I asked.

He eyed what looked like a diver's watch. "It's only seven and I can't start sleeping until at least nine or I'll be groggy for days."

"I was planning to do the interview with you tomorrow."

"I don't want to work tonight, but I'm starving." He glanced at my wineglass again. "Did you eat dinner yet?"

I nodded back toward the kitchen. "I was just getting ready to put something together."

"Why don't we go out instead?" His smile grew an inch wider. "We're in France, you know."

The way he said it was so casual. Unassuming. I felt guilty for a moment for making the "cocky" comment. I knew I should apologize, but at the moment I wasn't very fond of single men.

But then again, I was assuming that Riley was single. As he waited for me to answer, he looked up at the tapestry that hung from the wall and I dared a glance down at his left hand. His ring finger was empty.

An empty ring finger didn't mean anything, of course. A lot of married men didn't even wear rings. Riley probably had a wife or girlfriend back in California—or wherever it was that he was from.

"I promise not to keep you up late," he said. "We can talk about the documentary if you want. Or we can not talk at all."

As long as he kept the conversation focused on business, I supposed it was fine.

While he waited, I tossed the food back into the refrigerator and drained the last of my glass. Marguerite had suggested a café less than a mile away, so we strolled up the long drive, under the lofty beech trees. The evening light warmed our path and cast webbed shadows around our feet.

In my fog yesterday, I hadn't noticed the cow grazing on each side of the drive or even the village at the end of the road. Time may have stolen the life out of the château, but the land around it seemed to be thriving with the passage of the years.

The restaurant was in a stone house draped with ivy. Two iron lamps lit the stone walkway, beckoning us toward the dark-stained door. Inside, the owner led us upstairs to a room that overlooked a narrow alley. Four tables were crowded into the room, positioned like jigsaw pieces ready to snap together, but we had the room to ourselves.

Each table was clothed in white with two wineglasses by each plate, ready to top off what I'd already consumed at the château. Our server brought us two menus and a bottle of San Pellegrino. I sipped the bubbly water while Riley eyed the menu.

"Are you a fan of *escargot?*" he asked.

"Not particularly."

"Good." His smile eased onto his lips again. "I get concerned when people eat snails."

I glanced down the menu. "What about chicken?"

"I'm not as concerned."

"Then I'm going to order the *poulet à la fermière*."

"What is that?"

I glanced back down at the menu. "It's chicken with cream sauce. A farmwife's bounty, it says, with vegetables and fresh herbs."

"Impressive. Did you learn French from your grandmother?"

"My grandmother and then my dad. He and my grandmother always spoke to each other in their native language and then I minored in French in college."

Our waiter poured us each a glass of red wine and then brought pea soup for our first course. Riley watched me stir my soup, the thin veil of steam rising between us.

"What?" I asked, self-conscious as he studied me.

He picked up his spoon, shrugging. "Nothing."

"What is it?" I demanded.

He took a sip of his wine, and I saw a tattoo etched under his wrist. "I just thought you would be different."

I pushed my hair behind my ear. "Different how?"

"I don't know," he said. His constant smile was beginning to irritate me. "More buttoned up, somehow."

"Like a politician's wife?" I asked.

He shrugged. "I hate stereotypes."

"Agreed." I lifted my wine in a salute. There was no reason to educate him on how I'd ended my engagement with Austin. This way it would be harmless—no questions. "I hate stereotypes and I hate trying to live up to them."

"Fair enough," he said. "Why don't you shatter the stereotype and tell me about your life instead?"

I was supposed to talk about my grandparents, not talk about me. We had the room to ourselves, but I had no desire to tell a filmmaker—and a stranger—my story.

I swirled my wine in its glass. "I'd like to hear about your documentary."

He ignored my snub. "I'm profiling the stories of some of the German soldiers."

His words took me aback. "The German soldiers?"

He nodded.

"But you're in France."

"I've already done my filming in Berlin."

A breeze wafted through the open window and rustled the sleeve of my blouse. Something about the way he said it—or perhaps it was because he folded his arms across his chest—made it seem as if he were hiding something. I refused to be played again. "After all the Germans did, I don't know why you want to do a documentary on them."

The fire in his green eyes relaxed in the flicker of the candlelight. "Hitler was an evil man, but not all the men in the Wehrmacht were evil."

"The Wehrmacht?"

"The German army."

Outside the darkened window a streetlamp glimmered. It reminded me of the lamp in Narnia—the one that beckoned the Pevensie children and lit their path as they returned home. The children confronted evil, but not on their own. They needed the tools gifted to them. They needed one another, and in their darkest hours, they needed Aslan, but Aslan had seemed distant at times in the book.

The novels were inspired, in part, by the three young evacuees C. S. Lewis's family hosted during World War II. Perhaps it was Lewis's own journey of trying to process all the evil that happened in Europe. By the end of his stories, good had triumphed over the evil, but the lives of good people were also lost in the battle. It was a tumultuous journey for those who clung to all that was good.

When I looked back at Riley, he was watching me intently. "What are you thinking about?"

"Narnia," I replied. "My grandmother read the series to me when I was a girl, and I've read one of the books to my class each year."

"They were some of my favorite books as a kid too. We had a big wardrobe in my parents' room, and I kept knocking on its back wall when I thought no one was around."

"What does your documentary have to do with the Château d'Epines?" I asked.

"I'd like to talk to you about the German occupation."

Now I folded my arms. "I didn't even know the Germans occupied the château until yesterday."

"I'll have more general questions for you." He nudged his empty soup bowl to the side of the table. "Then perhaps you can give me a tour."

"Why are you doing this—" I started to ask, but our waiter walked into the room. He cleared our bowls and replaced my soup with a plate of creamy chicken with baby pota-toes, carrots, and leeks. In front of Riley, he set fillets of red snapper, the fish ornamented with sprigs of rosemary and wedges of lemon.

The aroma was intoxicating, but I didn't begin eating. "What inspired you to do a documentary about German soldiers?"

"My grandfather flew a B-24 during World War II." He glanced out the window at the streetlamp glowing across from us. "And I suppose I've always been intrigued as to what sacrifices people will make to protect themselves and those they love. It tells a lot about a person when you find out what or who they're will-ing to die for."

When he smiled again, I wondered if he was always this cheerful.

"I still don't understand why you want to feature the Ger-mans."

Riley's head tilted left, confusion filling his eyes. "Why don't we talk more about it tomorrow?"

My knife slid through the chicken as smoothly as if it were softened butter, and the meat tasted as if it were soaked in butter as well. Ah, well, when in France . . .

He held out his fork with a piece of baked fish on it. "You have to try this."

Wary, I eyed the oil puddled on his offering.

He persisted. "It's my clean fork."

In that moment, I realized that I was still playing for the cam-eras. Chloe Sauver, the candidate's fiancée, would be obsessed with her image and how she portrayed her future husband and family for the documentary. She would never trounce through France wearing jeans and flip-flops. And she certainly wouldn't eat a bite of fish off a stranger's fork.

But I was no longer the candidate's fiancée. There were no cameras here and no one but me seemed to care a thing about image. No longer did I have to play by the campaign rules.

I accepted his offering and enjoyed the tangy mixture of flavors on my tongue. Then I offered him a bite of the creamy chicken.

"Are you interviewing anyone else in Normandy?" I asked.

"A woman named Calvez," he said. "She lived at the château during the occupation."

I put down my fork. "I tried to visit a Madame Calvez earlier today."

Riley's face flooded with concern. "Did something happen?"

I glanced out the window before looking back at him. "She refused to see me."

He didn't seem surprised.

Over our third course—an assortment of breads and cheeses—I tried to probe further into Madame Calvez's story, but Riley refused to say anything else. It was for each person to tell their own story, he said, and his job to honor it. According to him, almost everyone wanted to share their story—eventually. When they were ready to talk, it was his job to share it with the world.

Why had Mémé hidden part of her story from me, until it was too late for her to share it? If only Madame Calvez would talk to me as well as to Riley. It wasn't too late for her to share her story.

Chapter 27

With Louise on her hip, Gisèle picked up the empty picnic basket and began to walk back across the yard from the *chapelle*. They would leave before lunch to cross the river and climb the hill, taking the path through the forest to find the orphanage. Somehow she would have to convince Sister Beatrice to keep Louise. If not, she feared the gendarmes would search for her here.

"I will miss you," she whispered to the little girl. She'd swept Louise's curly brown hair up into a ponytail. Thankfully the child had her father's blue eyes, the eyes of a national.

Louise clutched a fistful of Gisèle's hair in her hand. "*Maman?*"

"She'll be here soon," Gisèle lied. She didn't know what else to do. "In the meantime, you can stay with me."

"More milk," she begged.

"Of course, sweetheart. You may have all the milk you'd like."

She hummed to Louise as they moved across the morning shadows of the château, to the safety of the house.

If Sister Beatrice refused to take Louise, perhaps she could get a pass to take a bus down to Lyon. When Tante Corinne saw

Louise, she would surely take her in. No one needed to know her mother was born into a Jewish family.

The low hum of an automobile startled her, and she turned around. Dust ballooned on the driveway, tires rumbling across the gravel, and she grasped Louise close to her as she squinted down at the brown cloud that obscured the vehicle.

Had the gendarmes already come?

She didn't want to see anyone today, not while she held Louise in her arms. A black sedan rolled into the courtyard and stopped near her. She glanced wildly around her, searching for a crevice or rock or someplace to hide her empty basket. And stash a child.

But it was too late.

She knew most of the gendarmes in Saint-Lô. How could she explain away picnicking with a child who wasn't hers?

Louise pulled Gisèle's hair as she swiftly calculated her options. There was nothing she could do except stand strong against whoever was in the sedan.

Pushing back her shoulders, she tried to appear taller than her small height. No matter what happened, no matter who emerged from the car, she wouldn't cower.

When the driver's door opened, a young German soldier stepped out, his uniform fitted snug over his slender shoulders. His hair was trimmed short, and he looked like he should be wearing knickers and knee socks.

The soldier didn't acknowledge her, reaching instead for the handle of the door behind him and opening it. A much older man stepped out into the courtyard, his gold-tipped walking stick crushing the gravel beneath it. His uniform was decorated with ribbons and medals, and he had the air of a weathered officer who'd fought many battles. And won.

Tapping his walking stick on the gravel, the officer surveyed the property—the fields laden with flax and wheat, the apple orchard and stone barn. He scanned the château and the *chapelle*, and then his steely gaze focused back on her and her basket. And her baby.

Silently she petitioned Saint Michel for strength.

Towering over her, the officer lifted his black stick and rapped it against his glove. She put her hand over Louise's back, afraid he might poke her with it. "Who is this child?" he asked in German.

She feigned ignorance. They needn't know that Odette taught her the German language a long time ago.

The officer mumbled something about the stupid French, and then he waved another man out of the car. This man's eyes were on the ground, but she recognized the civilian clothing of a Frenchman.

Traitor, she wanted to hiss, but she held her tongue.

The German barked at the shorter man as if he were an animal who could only understand commands. Loud, harsh ones.

The Frenchman faced her, and her heart filled with compassion when she saw the sorrow in his eyes. She had no idea what the Germans had done to him or his family.

The officer continued to shout in the man's ear. When the officer finally stopped, the Frenchman looked back up at her. A hint of amusement replaced the sorrow in his eyes. "The stupid German would like to know about the child in your arms."

"She is my daughter." The lie slid off her lips as easily as the one she'd told Louise about seeing her mother.

The Frenchman translated her words, and then they began to volley the translated words.

"What is the name of your daughter?"

She almost blurted out, "Louise," and the way the major looked at her, it was as if he were waiting for her response in

German as well. But she turned back to the Frenchman again. She had to take extra care in maintaining her ignorance. The French and possibly the Germans would be looking for Louise Batier.

A name rolled off her lips in response. "Adeline," she told him. "Her name is Adeline."

It was a name that reminded her of André and Nadine, a name that would honor both of them. In order to protect the child, she must pretend Adeline was hers, for as long as André and Nadine were gone.

"And where is your husband?" the officer asked.

Both of her parents—and the nuns at her boarding school—had impressed on her the virtues of an honest woman, but in the clarity of this thin moment, she knew she had to pretend with all that was within her that she had a husband. And that he had gone away.

"I don't know."

"*Maman?*" Louise—Adeline said again, but the officer didn't seem to hear the questioning in her voice.

The officer scrutinized the basket in Gisèle's hands and then looked up at the gray mantle in the sky. "Are you picnicking today?"

After the Frenchman translated for her, she replied, "Please tell him I help feed people who have no food."

"Where are these people?" the German asked.

"At the top of the hill," she told the Frenchman. "In Agneaux."

And then she wished she hadn't said that. What if he checked her story?

"Why are you feeding them?" the officer demanded.

"They are invalids," she said. "If I don't feed them, no one will."

The German officer looked over her shoulder as if he were trying to determine where she had come from.

"Would the officer like me to take him there?" Her heart pounded with her words, but she needed to proceed with confidence, as feigned as it may have been. Surely one of the French-women would corroborate her story for her.

The Frenchman spoke to the officer, stretching her story as he relayed it. "She said she would gladly take you there. They are all sickly people, but she said not to worry. Only a few of them are contagious."

The officer took a step back from her, as did his driver. "Perhaps we will go later."

"Certainly." She put down the basket and switched the child to her other hip. Adeline seemed mesmerized by the decorations on their shoulders—or maybe she was afraid as well. As the two German officers conversed, she bent toward the Frenchman. "What is your name?"

"Lucien."

"Why are you here?" she asked.

He shook his head. "I have no choice. My family tried to run from Paris when the bombing began, but the bombs killed my wife and daughter. When the Germans caught me, they almost killed me as well until they discovered I knew German."

"They killed my father during that raid."

Sorrow filled his eyes again. "I'm sorry."

"Stop talking," the German officer snapped at them. "Tell her we have come to visit her house."

The Frenchman hesitated. It seemed as if he was unclear as to whether or not he was supposed to speak again. As she waited, a hundred questions raced through her mind. What did it mean for the German officer to visit? And how long did he plan to stay?

"Tell her," the officer demanded.

The thought of having them in her house for even a moment revolted her. She didn't want to let them inside the front door—their stench, she feared, would linger long after. And how could she entertain the Germans as she cared for Michel?

"You have no choice," Lucien said after he relayed the officer's words.

She stood tall again. Perhaps if she played hostess instead of victim, they would treat her as such. "Tell him if they intend to spend the night, there are empty rooms on the third floor of the servants' quarters and in the west wing of the house."

They would probably take whatever rooms they wanted, but the thought of them sleeping in Papa's room or even Michel's room made her skin crawl. And she didn't want them anywhere near her chamber.

She pointed toward the house. "My servant and I will need an hour to prepare your rooms."

The officer ignored Lucien's words, marching across the courtyard instead.

She kissed Adeline's head as the child played with her sleeve. She didn't have any choice, did she? Not if she wanted to remain alive to care for Michel and the child in her arms. But what would Papa say to her allowing German officers inside?

He would probably tell her to do what she could to survive. Her mother would tell her to demand respect. If they respected her, they wouldn't harm her or Adeline.

She rushed around the officer and put her hand on the doorknob before he touched it.

Then she opened the front door and let the Germans inside.

CHAPTER 28

GUBERNATORIAL CANDIDATE DUMPS FIANCÉE.

I wanted to hurl my iPad across the room, but instead of throwing it, I clenched it in my hands, stared at the lie of a headline on the news site and the picture of Austin and me in front of the Byrd Theatre this past spring. His arm was around me, communicating to the world that we belonged together. Or at least that I belonged to him.

Austin and Olivia and the rest of his staff had probably huddled together in his war room for hours, trying to concoct the best way to announce the end of our engagement. I could almost hear the indifference in their discussion—was it better for Austin to be the victim of a breakup or the instigator? Would he seem cruel to break up with me prior to an election? If he was a victim, it would make him look weak, though some might take pity on him.

Austin wouldn't want pity.

Switching over to Austin's campaign site, I read the statement on his front page, and it was much more nuanced than the news headline.

Due to unforeseeable differences, my fiancée and I have mutually decided to postpone our wedding until after the election. A campaign is a rigorous affair and I am focusing my attentions on preparing to become the best governor for Virginia. This is a private matter between Miss Sauver and me, and we both respectfully ask that you allow us time and space to focus first on the election.

Mutual postponement, my foot.

Austin and Olivia had gambled that I wouldn't retaliate by dragging his reputation through the mud on the talk shows. And even if I decided to tell the truth, it seemed these days that even the career of a married politician survived an affair or two. My story might only benefit Austin in the end and pigeonhole me as a lunatic. A jealous lover's rage over her handsome fiancé's last fling. Some might even cheer him on.

I skimmed the statement again. Ironic that he had used the word *affair.*

Swiveling in the chair, I faced the dark windows. I needed to do something, anything, other than surf for news about the end of my engagement.

Riley had researched me before he came to France, so it was fair game, I supposed, for me to search for more information on him as well. Hundreds of results came up on my screen. My mother was right—Riley had won a bunch of awards for his work, including an Oscar a few years ago. It seemed that he had a fascination for documenting the secrets of World War II, and an even greater fascination for the women he met along the way.

I groaned as the first image filled my screen: Riley cradling a beer bottle in one hand, his arm wrapped around a blonde in a skimpy dress.

I skipped to the next picture. And then the next. Multiple pictures showed him partying with women in various states of undress. A slightly older version, it seemed, of Austin's brother. Or the secret life of my former fiancé.

Riley might have come across as charming, but like Austin,

Riley was hiding his true self from me. And, I suspected, he was hiding the real reason he was doing this documentary.

I turned off my iPad and tossed it onto the bed.

I was tired of people trying to hide things from me. Tired of lies.

Instead of being angry at Austin's deception, perhaps I should be thankful that he showed his true self before we married. I should be grateful that he had gotten careless—or cocky—and I caught a glimpse of the destruction of my future before we proceeded with our marriage.

But right now I wasn't feeling very thankful.

Closing my eyes, I replayed the conversation I'd had with Riley tonight. He had hinted at my engagement, but I supposed I hadn't been honest with him either. I was so frustrated about my suspicions that I'd never stopped to consider that I was hiding information from him as well.

I rolled over on my pillow. It was the second time I'd gone to bed and still I wasn't able to sleep. In contrast to Riley's determination to fight jet lag, I had taken a long nap to fight the change in time, so now, long past midnight, I was wide awake.

It was a good time, perhaps, to explore. Before the interview tomorrow morning.

Pulling on a pair of socks, I padded out into the hallway in my long T-shirt. The light bulb in the hallway had burned out, but in the faint beam of my cell phone's flashlight, I puttered across the second floor, trying to locate my grandmother's bedroom.

I opened two doors, and in each room was a time capsule from the past—some of the décor seemed to be from the past twenty years, while some of the pictures looked as if they hadn't been updated in hundreds of years. Portraits of both men and women hung on the walls, some of them with ruffled collars and powdered wigs. Other pictures were of men and horses alongside their hunting dogs. As I stared into their faces, I wondered which of these people were my ancestors. It was a bit unnerving to see the people who'd gone before me all hanging on the wall, as if they were keeping tabs on their descendants.

As I crept to the third door, I imagined myself to be Mary Lennox in *The Secret Garden*, a stranger to the mysterious Misselthwaite Manor, walking down the dark corridor. Since Mémé couldn't tell me her stories tonight, I pretended she was here, sharing her favorite memories. The wonder of Christmas mornings in the château. The ornery escapades of her brother. The weekend parties her mother used to throw with their friends from Paris. The walls might have wanted to whisper more stories to me, but I couldn't hear them.

"The ghosts refuse to leave this place."

Marguerite had said it so matter-of-factly, as if the talk of ghosts was normal, but in these dark corridors, under the scrutiny of the portraits, my imagination raged. What if the ghosts of the past really were here? What would they say?

I didn't believe in ghosts, but I could almost imagine them watching me here. Perhaps they too were each clamoring to tell their own stories.

The door in front of me creaked open, and my inadequate cell phone light faded out in the vast space of the room. I flipped on the light switch by the door, and the bulb in here worked.

To my right was a canopied bed, and as I stepped left, I saw an antique dresser with rounded edges and a painting of faded flowers on the drawers. On top of the dresser were two tarnished candlesticks and a black-and-white photo of two young women smiling atop their horses. The woman in a light, button-down blouse looked like Mémé.

This must have been my grandmother's room. It seemed untouched, as if Stéphane and his father never stepped inside when they'd occupied the château.

I picked up the wooden frame from the dresser, examining the other woman. Could it be Isabelle's great-grandmother with her? As I studied the photo, their laughter captured on film, I was glad they had no idea about the destruction that awaited France.

But if this was Madame Calvez, playing with my grandmother, why wouldn't she welcome me into her home now?

Opening the armoire, I discovered a dozen colorful hatboxes in two neat stacks. I opened several of them, and spread the hats across the bed—there were felt hats with bows and flowers, a chic black velvet hat, one with netting in the front and daisies on the side. Mémé was always elegant in my eyes, even in these twilight days of her life. I could imagine her sporting any of these hats with a tailored suit or evening gown.

I picked up an ivory hat with a scalloped trim and copper-colored ribbons plaited in the front. Putting it on my head, I posed in the mirror, pretending I was a vicomtesse from long ago, preparing for a visit from a French king and queen. Then I opened another box and found a smart little navy hat. As I lifted it, I realized there was something underneath. A photo album.

The house creaked, and I jumped. I could almost hear the German soldiers shuffling on the floors above and below me.

Was Mémé alone in this house with the soldiers? She had always seemed strong, but with the Nazis under her roof, she must have been terrified.

Shivering, I snagged the photo album and bolted back to the master suite, locking the door. I opened the album and began flipping through the black-and-white pictures, each one secured by faded white corners. There were cursive captions below many of them.

Mother bringing me home from the hospital.

Papa holding me in his arms.

Michel and I collecting Easter eggs on the front lawn.

Nadine and I diving into the lake.

Riding Papillon Bleu.

I held up a picture of Michel beside an old roadster. My great-uncle was a handsome fellow when he was young, his curly hair dipping over his eyes. Mémé said he'd died during the war, but like so many of the other stories, the end of his story was lost, at least to me.

I put down the photo album and opened up my iPad again, to the notes Olivia had compiled for my interview. She'd detailed the German occupation in Normandy and then the destruction of Saint-Lô. Once the Allied troops landed on the Norman beaches, she wrote, Hitler and his men knew defeat was inevitable, yet he refused to surrender. Until he took his life—if he took his life—Hitler had refused to be wrong.

The Nazis wouldn't relinquish Saint-Lô. The Allies initially tried to chase them out of the area from the air, but they ended up fighting a bloody battle in the hedgerows that surrounded the city. Even as the French rejoiced that their enemy had been defeated, thousands of their civilians lost their lives in this final fight.

The darkness of what men could do to one another disturbed me deep in my soul. I had no desire to even try to understand a man like Hitler, but I was intrigued by Riley's idea to document the stories of some of the German soldiers. What if some of them hadn't wanted to fight? What if some of them tried to run?

I turned to the last pages of Mémé's photo album and several colored papers flitted out, falling onto the floor.

I picked up the top one and scanned it. Then I picked up the next one.

❧ *Chapter 29* ❧

The German officer with the golden stick—Major von Kluge—toured the Château d'Epines as if he were the owner surveying his property. He flipped light switches, opened closets, prodded the carpets with his walking stick, all while telling three soldiers about his exploits in the Great War. The soldiers swarmed around him like mosquitoes on a horse's rear, and Gisèle wished she could swat them all away from him and from her house.

After the arrival of the automobile this morning, three canvas-covered trucks had deposited dozens of officers and soldiers onto the château's front lawn. They descended into the crevices of her home like a plague of green locusts. Then the major ordered up dinner. As Émilie scrambled to make a simple meal, Gisèle followed the locusts and their leader through the corridors, lest they forgot they were guests in her home.

At Major von Kluge's command, the men scuttled into the dining hall. The officers took the chairs and the soldiers found their seats on the stone hearth of the fireplace, in cane chairs along the wall. As Gisèle served the men bread alongside sautéed zucchini and squash from the farmers' gardens, she tried to listen to the conversation, but even though she knew German, she couldn't understand the men. They spoke in low tones as they pointed toward the paneled windows that overlooked her valley, her serene oasis of river and trees. The lush hill across the river, the forest above that crowned the beauty—it all felt contaminated by their stares.

When they finished their food, the major pounded the tip of his walking stick on the table as if it were a bell, and when she responded, he sent her to fetch coffee and cognac and cigars, as if no one had informed him of the rationing they'd mandated in Normandy.

At least Adeline was safe from these men. The child played happily in the pen Gisèle and Émilie had found for her in the attic. Each time Gisèle returned to the kitchen, she pecked a kiss on the child's forehead.

The major pointed at his coffee—made from ground acorns since real coffee was scarce. "*Sucre?*"

She shook her head. "No *sucre.*"

It fascinated her that one of the few French words the German man knew was sugar.

"*Oui,*" he demanded.

She turned to Lucien and explained that all their food supplies were low, and just like they had no meat to serve the men, they hadn't had sugar for months. Major von Kluge wasn't pleased when Lucien translated her words. She retrieved a little cream from the supply the farmers brought for them, but she reserved the milk for Adeline.

As she set the cream on the table, she studied the faces of the men around her—some didn't look much older than sixteen, while others, like the major, bore shoulders heavily laden with ribbons and medals. None of the men smiled. Their clean-shaven jaws were set in a grim pattern, their hair shaved at their collar and above their ears.

Could these men in her house, drinking cognac purchased by her father, smoking his favorite cigars, be the same men who had killed him? Hatred welled inside her again—hatred at them and hatred at herself for serving them.

She scanned their sleeves, searching to see if any of them wore an onyx-and-gold cuff link like the one she and Michel found by her father's body, but all of these men wore silver cuff links on their wrists. She didn't know what she would do if she came face-to-face with the man who'd murdered him.

Her glance turned toward Lucien, sitting on a chair by the door, clinging to the cup of tepid coffee she'd brought him. He was stuck, just like her. The Germans had killed his family, just like they killed her father, and then forced both her and Lucien to serve them. If she refused, they might kill her as well. And Émilie and Adeline.

Should she stand for all that was good and refuse them, even if it cost her her life? Or should she continue to compromise her morals to save her life—and the lives of those in her care?

The major commanded his men to follow him out into the main hall and then the dining hall was quiet. She knew not where they went, but after the room emptied, she and Lucien were alone.

Lucien glanced at the open doorway before whispering to her, "There are rumors of people resisting."

She nodded, wishing she could take the man into her confidence and tell him those who resisted were living below their feet. "I have heard them."

"It is making the Germans nervous. They pride themselves on maintaining control, and the more people resist, the harsher they will become. It is not only the Jewish people they will punish . . ."

She glanced toward the doorway. The hall remained quiet. "Do you know where they take the French Jews?"

His eyes heavy with sadness, he gave the slightest nod. "To an internment camp called Drancy."

Her heart began to race. If André and Nadine were waiting at this camp, she could petition the government for their return. Perhaps she could even have someone drive her there to retrieve them. If the French officials knew they were loyal citizens, if they knew they were good parents and André a schoolteacher, if they knew André wasn't even a Jew and Nadine had converted, surely they would let them return to Saint-Lô.

He rubbed his hands together. "No one stays in Drancy for long. They are deported to Germany."

She stood. There was no time to delay then. Father had once had many friends in the government. If any of them remained in the Vichy government down south, she had to contact them right away. If none of them were left, perhaps Philippe could help her. "Where do they go in Germany?"

He shrugged. "They don't talk about it when I'm around." He glanced back toward the door and then spoke again, his voice barely a whisper above the silence. "When we were at the police headquarters, I heard the gendarmes speaking of a baby missing from one of the Jewish families. Her name was Louise."

She shivered.

"They were angry about what happened but too proud to tell the Germans of their loss."

"They can't find out . . . ," she pleaded.

Her worry was mirrored in his eyes. "If you contact the authorities about Drancy, you would bring suspicion on yourself."

She thought of Adeline and how Major von Kluge already seemed to suspect something was amiss. André and Nadine hid their daughter for a reason. She couldn't point the police back to what they'd lost.

Jackboots hammered across the hall, outside the door, and she sprang to her feet, snatching a plate from the table and stacking it on another. Lucien seemed to shrink back into the plaster wall, as if the house might swallow him.

Major von Kluge marched into the room, his eyes sparking like flint when he saw her. Then, in spite of Lucien's attempt to disappear, the officer motioned to him. "Come with me," he demanded. "Both of you."

Lucien went first, and with trepidation, she followed him through the hall and down the narrow steps that led into their cool wine cellar—the *cave*. Two light bulbs illuminated the bricks that lined the arched ceiling, the rounded brick bins on both sides of the narrow hall, and the wine casks stacked in the back.

This underground fortress held Papa's brandy and what remained of the family's vintage Bordeaux. The walkway between bins was only about two meters across and six meters long. The wooden door at one end led up to the house, and the room was filled with thirty of the brick bins on each side. The soldiers were removing dozens of bottles from each one. Another soldier had begun to roll aside the casks, but there was no other place to stack them in the narrow room.

Major von Kluge motioned Lucien forward, around the two soldiers who remained in the *cave*, until Lucien stood under the arch. "Listen!" the major commanded.

The room grew quiet, some of the soldiers cradling the wine bottles in their arms, as they listened to the brick.

"I heard voices," he insisted.

Gisèle placed her hand on the curve of a bin as Lucien translated. Was it possible they could hear the men hidden in the tunnel? After Michel had told her they couldn't keep Nadine's child because of the noise, his own men might betray him.

"Voices?" she asked dubiously, searching the walls alongside Lucien even as she prayed that the men below wouldn't speak again.

Major von Kluge tapped his walking stick on the ceiling and then on the inside of an empty bin. "There were people talking somewhere down here."

"Perhaps it was the wind," she told Lucien.

"No!" Major von Kluge barked after Lucien translated. Then he began to falter, as if he realized how ludicrous his words sounded. "There were voices—muffled voices."

"Ghosts haunt these walls," she said, but the major shook his head, the suggestion of the supernatural seeming to make him even more angry. Sometimes it did seem to her as if the house groaned, as if it couldn't help but tell its story even if those who listened were invaders, but she doubted the noises today were from ghosts.

Lucien pointed at Gisèle. "Perhaps you heard her speaking overhead—with her housekeeper."

A sound from one of the bins startled her, and she held her breath.

What if one of the entrances to the tunnel was in here? What if one of the members of France's resistance stuck his head into a room filled with Germans? Surely none of them would be so stupid . . .

But they had no way of knowing the Nazis were here, on the other side of the wall.

She and the soldiers stepped away from the bin, though Lucien remained, as if nothing could surprise him.

They heard the sound of a bottle rocking back and forth across the ruts in the brick, and one of the men gasped. She held her breath, praying that no one would enter the room. Then she watched as a gray paw stretched out from the depths.

Her cat hopped out, and the soldier next to her leapt backward. With a long meow, Shadow seemed to scold them for waking him from his nap. Gisèle suppressed her grin as he brushed against her leg. She glanced up at the soldier who had jumped, and in the dim light, she saw him trying to bite back a smile.

"She can be a noisy sleeper," Gisèle said, but Lucien didn't translate for her this time.

Major von Kluge's eyes narrowed again into slits, his finger on the revolver at his side. Swallowing hard, Gisèle plucked her cat off the floor and edged toward the entrance. Being insulted by a cat seemed to muddy the major's thinking. If he pulled the trigger, a bullet would surely ricochet off the bricks until it lodged itself into Shadow—or a person.

She rushed up the stairs and the soldiers followed her. They waited in silence in the lobby until minutes later, when the major emerged. His face was flushed red, but his thinking seemed to be clear again. He spoke directly to Lucien. "Tell her we will return in two days."

A hundred questions flooded her mind, but she waded rapidly through them, afraid her intrusion of being too inquisitive would muddle his thinking again. The most pressing question she dared to ask. "How should I prepare?"

He didn't answer her.

She stood in the doorway, watching their trail of dust as they drove away.

If only she knew what God required of her . . .

CHAPTER 30

I lifted the paper from those slipped into the back of the photo album. It was a faded marriage certificate between Gisèle Duchant and Jean-Marc Rausch—my biological grandfather. It was strange to see his name in print, the only link I had to the man who fathered my father.

Out of respect for Grandpa, I suspected, Gisèle never talked about her first husband, even after Henri passed away. But I did wonder sometimes what he must have been like. I had my mother's eyes and Gisèle's wavy hair and my father's love of the water. Did Jean-Marc pass along any of his features or traits to me?

If only there was a wedding picture in this box as well.

I placed the certificate on the desk and picked up another one—a diploma from the University of Caen with Mémé's degree in literature. This I knew about, but why hadn't she taken her diploma when she moved to the States? Perhaps when her first husband died, she no longer needed their marriage certificate, but surely she would have wanted the diploma.

The last certificate was a pink color. A certificate of birth. The names were poorly written, and I leaned closer to the light, trying to read the scrawl. At first, I assumed the certificate was for my dad, but as I read the names, I realized it was for another child of Gisèle and Jean-Marc Rausch.

Adeline Rausch. The baby lost in the trees.

The print swam together in front of me. Mémé had a daughter?

No wonder she was tormented. Adeline would be my aunt. Dad's younger sister.

I thought of my grandmother, begging me to find Adeline. How had she lost her daughter? And after all these years, how could I possibly find her?

I stared down at the name as if Adeline's story might appear on the paper, like the stories on my iPad.

Did my dad know he had a sister? Clinging to the certificate, I picked up my phone and called him.

"It's the middle of the night there," he said with a laugh.

"I'm still on Virginia time," I said, collapsing back against the cushions of the couch. "How is Mémé?"

He paused. "Pamela called this morning. She said my mother keeps asking about Adeline."

"About that . . ." I slid my hand over the certificate. "I found something."

"What did you find?"

"A birth certificate for Adeline."

He hesitated before asking, "Who are her parents?"

In his hesitation, I realized that my dad was afraid of the answer.

"Gisèle and Jean-Marc Rausch." The silence was heartbreaking. "Dad?"

"Gisèle Duchant Rausch?" he asked slowly.

"That's what it says." I skimmed the certificate again. "Adeline was born in February 1941."

"That would have been . . ." He paused again. "I would have been three years old when she was born."

He didn't say it, but I knew what he was thinking. He should have remembered his sister.

I reached for the faded green paper again. "You were born in 1938."

"That's right."

"I found the marriage certificate for Jean-Marc and Gisèle as well. It says they were married in June 1940."

He didn't say anything for a moment, and I feared it was too much. "I didn't know—I was born two years before my parents married."

Was that why Mémé kept her secret? Perhaps she was embarrassed that she had a child before she was married, a child that might not even have been her husband's. I didn't say anything to Dad about the man he thought to be his father. In his silence, I knew he was already considering this shift in his story.

"But you don't remember Adeline?" I asked.

His voice sounded broken. "My memories are like a shattered picture, Chloe. There are all sorts of little pieces, but I don't know how they fit together."

"What did Mémé tell you?"

"That I was born in the château before the war, and my first years were happy. She has pictures of me playing on the lawn and one in a swing."

She had shown me those pictures too. "She must have taken your birth certificate when you moved to the States."

"I have it now," he said. "But I wish I could remember more of my childhood in France."

"What do you remember?"

"I don't know what was a memory and what was a dream, or even bits from a book I read and made my own."

I stared down at the birth certificate again. "Perhaps I could help you piece some of it together."

Instead of answering, he changed the subject. "Your mother wants to know what you think of the filmmaker."

I tapped my iPad and glanced at Riley's cocky smile. And the beautiful woman entangled in his arm. "I think he is competent." I propped my feet on the small table. "Why does Mom want to know?"

"Your mom enjoyed talking with him on the telephone." Knowing Dad, he'd probably shrugged as he said this. He might act casual but something was brewing in his mind. "When she found out he was single . . ."

I shot up. "You set me up!"

"I had nothing to do with it. Your mom thought it would be nice for you to meet Riley before your wedding day."

I groaned. As if I needed my mom's meddling in my relation-ships. She must not have looked at his pictures online. "Please tell her that it's easy for someone to be nice when they want some-thing from you."

"When are you doing the interview with him?"

"Tomorrow."

"Then why don't you come home right after it?"

As I lay down, I mulled over his words. But I knew I wasn't ready to return home yet. Not just because I wanted to stay away from the media and Austin. I wanted to dig a little deeper here, find out what happened to Adeline Rausch. Was it her presence that seemed to haunt the house?

A breeze came through the open window and I jumped as it ruffled the bedcoverings. Standing up, I shuffled toward the window and closed it, clasping it shut. With the lights off, I looked across the hill and saw a light on in the farmhouse.

Was Riley awake as well?

It didn't matter one bit to me.

Leaning back against the pillows, I began to drift to sleep. The breeze skipped across my eyelashes, my cheeks and forehead, as if they were stones in a puddle. In the coolness, I slept, and it wasn't until morning that I remembered I'd closed the window before going to bed.

≈ Chapter 31 ≈

$\mathcal{D}$esperation drove Gisèle to the *chapelle*, Adeline strapped on her back. The major and his men had left last night, but they said they'd return tomorrow. To take over her home.

How was she supposed to entertain their enemy, the very men who had killed her father?

As two of the village women prayed near the altar, she lit candles for both her mother and her father and then knelt with Adeline beside a pew. Her mind racing, she begged God for wisdom, strength, and, most of all, courage in whatever it was that He required of her now.

For so much of her youth, she'd focused on what she wanted—riding her horses when she was a girl and then going to Paris. And one day perhaps marrying and becoming an elegant noblewoman like her mother, returning each year to visit Michel and his family at the Château d'Epines.

The Germans had changed everything. After her father's death, she knew she must care for her brother until the Nazis left France, but how was she supposed to do that with the enemy under her roof?

Above the pew was a stained-glass window, orange and red and cobalt blue. The pieces of colored glass melded together to form a picture of the body of Christ, broken and bloody after being taken down from the cross. The Roman soldiers beat Him terribly and yet He forgave them.

Her eyes wandered to the front of the room and the statue of Mary holding Jesus. Had Christ's mother forgiven the soldiers as well?

Love your enemies and pray for those who persecute you.

The Germans had killed her father and now they were destroying her country. How was she supposed to care for the men who had killed him? And even more, how was she supposed to love them—love evil? She despised everything they were doing.

Jesus had resisted the devil in the desert, but then He showed love to the men who tortured Him, forgave those who killed Him. When was she supposed to love her enemy and when was she supposed to resist? And somehow, in the great mystery of faith, was it possible for her to do both?

She asked God to take her pride and, trembling, she asked Him to take her very life if He had to, like Christ had done, in order to save those in her care from destruction on this earth. But if He didn't take her, she would cling to the hope of her future, that one day God would right all that had decayed in this world.

Her thoughts and prayers wrestled together. The commandment from the Scripture weighed against what she thought God would have her do.

She didn't think it was possible for her to love the Nazis, but perhaps she could pray.

As rain trickled down the stained glass, tears trickled down her cheeks. She wiped away her tears and crossed herself.

In the name of the Father and the Son and the Holy Spirit.

Her eyes closed, Adeline squirming beside her, she recited one more prayer—a petition to Saint Michel.

Saint Michel the Archangel, defend us in battle, be our protection against the wickedness and snares of the devil.

May God rebuke him, we humbly pray; and do thou, O Prince of the Heavenly host, by the power of God, cast into hell Satan and all evil spirits who wander through the world seeking the ruin of souls.

Was it possible to love your enemy even as you hated—as you battled—the wrong that drove them? Perhaps that was what Jesus did on the cross. He forgave those who killed Him and in his death, He also defeated the sin that blinded them.

She could pray for her enemy, but she also had to fight against evil, and she had no doubt that the Nazis embodied the hatred of their führer. Lucien had said she must care for the men or they would claim her property and perhaps send her to one of the work camps as well.

What would Papa think, knowing the Germans were going to stay at their house, and knowing that Michel was planning to resist them? Her heart ached at the loss of the man who had wanted to protect her from all this.

She was glad she didn't go to Lyon so long ago, but sometimes she wondered what would have happened if she had made that choice. Papa would want her to take charge of the property now, and Michel was relying on her for food.

Perhaps in love she could fight.

When she finished, she opened her eyes. One of the women was gone. The other was an old friend of her mother's, Madame Fortier.

Madame Fortier eyed Adeline. "Who is the girl?"

"My dau—" she began to say, and then stopped. The people in Agneaux knew she didn't have a child. "I have told the Germans she is my daughter."

Her eyes widened with horror. "Oh, Gisèle, you must hide her."

Gisèle gazed at the candlelight flickering on the stained glass, the warmth of the blond wood. This was her hiding place, her protection. Those who came here worshipped the same God she did. They were like family. "But no one here would say anything—"

"They might not want to bring harm on you or this child, but if they are questioned . . ." She glanced back toward the door. "They might stumble with their words."

"I will tell them I've hidden her for the past year," she said. "I married a French soldier right before the Germans came, and I feared for her life."

Madame Fortier brushed a lock of brown hair away from Adeline's face. "And now?"

"Now the Germans are coming to occupy the house, and no matter my shame, I must speak the truth."

The woman eyed her again, and Gisèle knew that Madame Fortier was keenly aware of the consequences for repeating this lie.

"I will spread your story, but still, you shouldn't bring her here," she whispered. "People will ask too many questions."

She nodded. "Thank you."

Madame Fortier bent her head toward Adeline and then studied Gisèle's face. "You have the same eyes—I will tell my friends of the similarities."

Adeline rested her head against Gisèle's shoulder. "I pray the Germans will be too busy to concern themselves with her story."

"I wouldn't be too certain." Madame Fortier glanced back at the door. "I fear they may go to great lengths to demonstrate their power, both big and seemingly small."

It was possible that Major von Kluge and his men wouldn't return to the château. Perhaps they would march on to Cherbourg, or perhaps their entire convoy would be destroyed by Allied bombers. She'd heard on the wireless that the Allies were fighting against the Germans. And that the number of people resisting inside France was growing.

But if the Germans did return, she had to be prepared.

After Madame Fortier left the *chapelle*, she almost slipped down into the tunnel, but Michel would be angry if Adeline began crying again. She would go down in the morning and warn Michel before the Nazis returned. The next time Major von Kluge heard voices, he wouldn't believe it was a cat.

She left Adeline in the kitchen, with Émilie, and slipped back down into the *cave*. The light bulb flickered on in the cellar and she wandered down the passage, pressing against the brick and peering inside the bins. The room smelled of damp earth and old wine.

In the casing of cool bricks, she could hear the echoes of voices, muffled shouts of men below or beside them. The ghosts in the tunnel.

Michel had said he was going to leave soon, but when he returned, she feared it would be too difficult to feed him and the other men through the hiding place in the *chapelle*. If she could find another entrance to the tunnel in the house, she wouldn't have to go to the *chapelle* for any other reason than to pray.

Minutes passed as she searched, the faint voices in the tunnel no longer audible. Feet shuffled down the steps, and she turned, thinking Émilie had come with Adeline. But a man stepped through the doorway instead, his wide shoulders ballooning across the doorframe.

The man wore the grayish-green uniform of a German officer, his hair black as ink, his eyes brown. Instead of the Aryan people the Nazis idolized, he looked more like the pictures she'd seen of Hitler.

Her mouth gaped open, but no sounds came out. The Germans weren't supposed to return yet, not until tomorrow night at the earliest.

"What are you doing down here?" the officer demanded in German.

She pressed her lips together and swallowed hard before she replied in French. *"Je ne comprends pas."*

I don't understand.

She hoped he would stomp away in frustration. Or find Lucien to translate.

His torso turned back toward the steps as if he was considering a retreat back up to the dark entrance.

She shifted herself to the center of the passage, ready to hurry upstairs behind him, but he didn't leave. When he looked back at her, she shuddered. In his eyes was something more sinister than desire, like she'd seen in the eyes of the soldier in Saint-Lô. It was a thirst for power. Conquest. And the only thing to conquer in this *cave* was her.

Everything within her cried out for her to run, but it would be impossible to get around this giant of a man. *A man will only respect you if you respect yourself.* Her mother's admonition flooded her mind, and she rolled her shoulders back, trying to maintain the Duchant dignity.

She slid a bottle of wine out of a bin and, clutching it in her hand, took a small step toward him and the exit. "If you would excuse me . . ."

His hulking form loomed over her. She tried to muster confidence, but inside her stomach clenched with terror. If he attacked her, no one above would hear her scream.

Her fingers tightened over the bottle. Her only weapon. What would the major do if she killed one of his men?

Before she could lift the bottle, the man stepped forward and grabbed her arm. The bottle shattered on the floor. Wine splashed across her stockings and shoes.

She shoved him away, commanding him to halt, but he ignored her, pressing his body into hers, pinning her against the jagged edges of the bricks. When he reached for her blouse, she screamed.

He pressed his hand over her mouth. "You scream again, and I will kill you."

She held her breath.

He slid a knife from his sheath and pressed it against her neck. The blade piercing her skin, she began to pray again—to Saint Michel, to the Virgin Mary, to God Himself if He was listening.

"Defend me," she whispered in French. "Protect me against the wickedness."

He pushed the knife deeper into her skin. "Shut up."

Her lips silenced, her eyes closed, she continued mouthing the words. And she pretended that she was far, far away, on the fields behind their house, cantering with Papillon Bleu along a stream. She was far from this madman who wanted to destroy what she'd saved for her wedding night. And probably take her life with it.

His knife slit open her blouse before the blade clattered against the brick floor. She gagged as he groped her skin. The stream—she could see it in her mind's eye. The breeze fluttered over her face and comforted her. She was transported in her mind, hidden in her place of refuge. Secure with her mother and her father and all who had gone before her.

"Halt!"

The command was so powerful, so loud, she thought for a moment that it had escaped her own lips, but she hadn't spoken a word. The man who had assaulted her shoved her to the ground, and she snapped back into the present, her hands sticky with wine, glass cutting her left palm as she hovered over the floor like a dog, her blouse in tatters, her breasts bruised.

In the doorway stood another man. A fellow German officer. Would he join his comrade in humiliating her?

Her mind began to wander again.

The enemy pressed his hand into her hair, her chin digging into her neck. "This doesn't concern you."

"The major said not to harm her."

"He does not care—"

"He wants her to make dinner tonight, and he will care very much if you detain her." The officer's voice was hard.

Her neck screamed in pain as the men argued, her knees and palms ached, but she didn't dare make a sound. Then her attacker picked up his knife and shoved it back into the sheath before his footsteps echoed up the stairs.

She hesitated for a moment, uncertain if he would return, but then she reached for a bin and pulled herself off the floor. Mortified, she wrapped her arms across her bare chest. The officer before her—her rescuer—looked down at his boots.

He could have ignored her scream, could have looked the other way like she'd done in the forest. So many of them had to look away. The other man could have raped her—killed her even—and she doubted the major would care.

Her body trembled as she stood before him. "*Merci.*"

"Are you injured?" he asked.

She shook her head.

"You must stay away from the cellar until we are gone." The officer stepped back toward the exit. "I will have your house-keeper bring you another shirt."

"Will he bring you trouble?" Too late, she realized she had spoken in German.

"I'm not concerned about him," he said. "As long as you are useful to Major von Kluge, you will be safe."

Safe.

It was a strange word to use. She doubted she would ever feel safe again, at least not in her home.

She switched back to French. "What is your name?"

Instead of answering, the man bowed his head to her one more time. And then he disappeared.

CHAPTER 32

Someone pelted pieces of gravel at my window five minutes before eight. I pulled my hair back into a ponytail and crossed the room to reopen the window. Fog settled over the driveway and Riley stood in the midst of it, a backpack slung over his shoulder.

I leaned against the windowsill. "What are you doing?"

He grinned. "Waking you up."

I rubbed my eyes, the images flashing through my mind of him with his arm around multiple women. And his bottles of beer. His smile irritated me even more, as if I would swoon under his charms like the women in the pictures.

I crossed my arms. "Why do you feel compelled to wake me?"

"I thought we could get a jump-start on the interview."

"I'll be ready at nine," I insisted.

He glanced down at his watch. "How about eight thirty?"

"Nine!" I shut the window, refusing to be disarmed.

Slowly I took a bath and washed my hair. The cool temperature of the bathwater revived me, and I dressed in a black skirt and a teal blouse. Then I checked my voicemail messages— eleven of them from friends and fellow teachers who'd read the news. Some offered sympathy while others, it seemed, called mainly out of curiosity. Later I would return the calls to those who cared.

At 9:10, I sauntered down the staircase.

Riley was waiting on the bottom step, wearing jeans and a dark brown T-shirt under his bomber jacket. He seemed like such a different person from what I'd seen in the pictures, but I knew well that appearances could be deceiving.

He held out a white paper bag. "I thought you might be hungry."

I peeked inside to see a chocolate croissant. "Where did you get this?"

He shrugged. "I walked to the village while you were getting ready."

With a quick thank-you, I focused my attention on the pastry he brought. The flavors melted in my mouth—warm chocolate and melted butter and the flaky sweet crust. This was what I loved about France. A keen appreciation for the simplicity and sweetness of life. The French seemed to savor their minutes along with their food.

I leaned back against the railing as I ate. A few moments passed before I realized Riley was studying me. "What?"

"I asked if you wanted me to make some coffee."

"I'm sorry—"

He balled up his bag. "Is everything okay?"

I was so tired of people refusing to tell me the truth. As much as I wanted to tell him nothing was wrong, I would have been doing exactly what was frustrating me. "I couldn't sleep last night."

He leaned back against the steps. "All night?"

"Until about two." I paused. "I decided to hunt around online a bit to uncover your story, since you've already uncovered mine."

His smile faded. "I hate to think of what you found."

"A man who likes to party."

The intensity of his eyes unnerved me. "I'm not that man any-more—"

"You don't have to explain," I said.

He stood up and smiled again, but his smile had lost a bit of its charm. "Grace is a gift I don't take lightly."

He was baiting me, but still I asked. "Why do you need grace, Riley?"

Instead of answering, he picked up his backpack off the ground. "What do you like to do, Chloe?"

"What do you mean?"

He slung the strap of the backpack over his shoulder. "I mean what do you enjoy doing, more than anything in the world?"

I leaned back against the banister. "I like to kayak."

The green in his eyes shone. "If I can drum up two kayaks, will you paddle the river with me?"

I crossed my arms. "You're supposed to be interviewing me."

"I will," he said before stepping toward the front door.

I followed him. "From a chair."

He shrugged. "Chairs usually make for dull interviews."

I wanted to give a decent interview to honor my grandpar-ents. And I wanted to kayak. So I changed my clothes again, this time into my paddling shorts and an REI T-shirt.

A friend of Pierre's loaned us two kayaks, and Riley and Pierre transported them in the station wagon from Agneaux to the river. After Riley stored his camera in a dry bag at his feet and his aluminum tripod in the storage hatch, we began to paddle.

Geese scattered as Riley and I kayaked under a stone bridge, the river meandering through the still morning. Fog swayed in front of us like a sheer veil hiding the pristine valley and the promise of warmth.

I didn't mind the coolness. Sometimes it was easy to settle into comfort, like a lobster swimming in a pot of warm water, minutes before it begins to boil. The bite in the air breathed life into me. I was made for this, the strain on my arms, the pounding of my heart as I cut through the water.

The château was hidden by the fog, but we paddled past the jagged cliffs underneath. As the river cut through farmland on the other side, Riley pulled up his sleeves, and I saw an odd mix of scribblings tattooed under his forearm.

I pointed at the tattoo. "What does that say?"

"It's a word from the Hebrew Scriptures. It means 'revelation' or 'unveiling.'"

"Very mysterious," I replied, but didn't probe.

It was an odd amalgam—a man tattooed with a Hebrew scripture, doing a documentary on German soldiers.

"I have a few questions for you," he said.

I glanced over at the waterproof bag at his feet. "Aren't you supposed to be filming?"

"In a bit."

I shrugged. It was his documentary. "Where do you want me to begin?"

He placed his paddle across his lap and floated beside me. "What do you love about kayaking?"

A bird trilled in the nearby trees and shards of sunshine cut through the mist as I leaned back to savor the morning again, the promise of a slate wiped clean, new beginnings. I stole a glance back over at him. "Being outside on the water and enjoying each minute as I paddle instead of striving to accomplish something new."

"Does your fiancé enjoy these minutes with you?" he asked.

He must not have read the news in the States today—at least not political news. Or were Austin and my breakup considered entertainment?

"Not particularly." I took a deep breath. "And Austin and I aren't getting married after all."

Silence was his response, and I wanted to flee. I'd poured out just a drop of my story, and he was letting it spill all over the ground.

He dipped his paddle back into the water, moving closer to me. "I'm sorry," he finally said. "Ending a relationship with someone you love is gut-wrenching."

We floated past crisscrossed wooden fence posts, and I wanted to run and hide behind them, not from Riley as much as from the torment of the emotions that crashed within me. "It's not so hard when you find the man you planned to marry sleeping with another woman."

His mouth dropped open and then he caught himself. "Chloe, I'm sor—"

I lifted my paddle and waved it slightly to stop him. "You don't have to apologize. I'm really not angry at all men—just Austin."

I shuddered as we floated through another curtain of mist.

"Let's not talk about Austin Vale," he said. "Why don't you tell me about your life pre-Austin?"

I dipped my paddle back into the water and flowed with the current. What was my life like before I met Austin? It had only been a year since the coffee shop fiasco and yet it seemed like a decade ago. I had enjoyed my freedom during those single years, but as my friends began to marry, I'd longed for a husband and children of my own. A part of me had felt like I was in a holding pattern since college, like life wouldn't begin until I met my Prince Charming.

Like Riley, I had once dreamed of the power of story—of using stories in the lives of children to inspire them—but I'd lost my dreams to someone else. To an opportunity that seemed too good to be true, with a man who'd swept me off my feet.

Riley paddled again. "I'm not going to let you off the hook about your story."

I dug my paddle into the slow-moving water and the motion calmed my nerves. I didn't want to tell him my story and yet I was spending these weeks trying to delve into the story of someone I loved who kept her story locked inside her. I didn't want to share my story with a man I didn't trust, but I didn't want to hide either.

"Until last week I was a third-grade teacher and I loved helping children learn new things," I said. "I loved watching when that proverbial light bulb went off and their eyes grew wide as they mastered a hard concept or learned something that ignited their world. In the summers, I used to travel with my best friend and sometimes by myself so I could learn as well, but when I was home, I spent most of my free time kayaking in Virginia."

"I read that your dad owns the top investment company in Virginia."

So many people knew *about* me but few actually knew me. It was easy to read a profile online, but that hardly told you what a person was like. "My parents are both successful because they love to work and they both do what they enjoy. Not because they want to be wealthy."

"There is nothing wrong with being wealthy, Chloe."

And yet there was. Even though my parents never flaunted the money they'd made through their successes, there was a stigma attached to it. They might have been oblivious to it or so wrapped up in their careers that they didn't care, but I felt it when I was in school. It seemed people were either criticizing me or judging me or holding me up to impossible standards. I never wanted the attention, good or bad. When I moved out of our home, I was comfortable in my modest condo by the river and in the steady pace of my work.

A tiny village lay to our right, the stone houses clustered together above the riverbank, and a grove of tall trees stood on the far side of the town, the branches barren except for giant balls of leaves that ornamented them. I pointed toward one of the trees with my paddle. "What do you think that is?"

"Mistletoe," he said. "Should we paddle under them?"

I turned back to him and saw his wide grin. Then I splashed him with my paddle before turning my kayak around. Laughing, he returned the favor.

After today, I would never see Riley Holtz again and I was glad about it.

Together we kayaked back toward the château. The fog had lifted, and we peered up at the castle on the cliff, surrounded by trees. It looked so majestic, like a gateway to the heavens. There were clusters of trees below the house as well.

When I looked back toward Riley, he had his camera out now, filming the château above me. Then he lowered the camera. "You ready to do this?" he asked.

I put my paddle on my lap. "As ready as I'll ever be . . ."

I clipped on the microphone he gave me, and then he lifted the camera again, training it on my face. I pretended I was back in my classroom, ten hands raised to ask questions. This time I would pick Riley.

"What do you know about the history of your family's château?"

I glanced up at the house and then looked back at Riley.

Olivia had put me through hours and hours of exhaustive media training. For my interviews, presentation was more important than content, the trainer had said. I'd memorized the campaign talking points in about an hour, and then the trainer had worked with me on the position of my shoulders and legs, the tilting of my head, the tone of my voice. In front of a mirror, he showed me the differences between a comfortable, warm smile and a strained one.

But there was no studio around me now. No chair.

I flashed what I hoped was a warm smile and began. "The first walls were probably built about a thousand years after Christ, during the reign of William the Conqueror. They named the area Agneaux because legend has it that Saint Martin of Tours prayed for the dead sons of the first Norman family who lived here. After the twins were restored to life, they were known as the Lambs— *les agneaux*—of St. Martin.

"The house probably harbored knights at one time, but three hundred years ago, King Louis XV gave the property to the Duchant family as a reward for fighting alongside him." I pointed toward the river. "Before the French Revolution, our property stretched all the way down to Saint-Lô."

"Did your family live here during World War II?" he asked.

"My grandmother was only twenty-two when the war started. Her mother had already passed away, but her father died during the war and her first husband was killed during a battle."

"Was your father born here?"

"He was, but he moved to the United States when he was six."

The current pushed us away from the château, and he put down his camera. "Should we continue onshore?"

"Sure." I dipped my paddle back into the water, and when I reached the edge, I pulled my kayak onto the grassy bank. We were at the base of the trees and cliff, and Riley set up his tripod and had me stand where he could capture the trees and river behind me. I readjusted my microphone and he began filming again.

"You said your grandmother was a widow at the end of the war," he said, prompting me.

I nodded. "My father was a young boy in 1944 and Mémé was a widow. A friend introduced her to Henri Sauver right after the Allies defeated the Germans in Saint-Lô, and they married about a month later. Henri adopted my father, and their family immigrated to the United States that same year."

"What did your grandfather do during the war?" he asked.

"At first, he fought with the French army as a captain until the Germans defeated them. Then he joined the French resistance. My grandmother said he used to travel all over Normandy and wreak havoc on the Germans."

Riley crossed his arms. "What sort of havoc?"

"He and his men disrupted the German phone service and telegrams and other means of communication."

"With bombs?"

"No, they snipped the lines."

"Did he bomb the railways?"

Mémé once said he did, but I wasn't sure she would want me to broadcast that on national television. Nor was I sure what the resistance had to do with a documentary profiling German soldiers.

I decided to redirect the conversation, a skill I'd acquired both from my media training and in negotiating disputes among third graders. "My grandfather was good at accounting and record keeping. My grandmother said he kept their records in a way no German could decipher, in order to protect all the men in their cell."

"What did your grandfather say about the resistance?" Riley asked.

My own questions resurfaced. I wished Grandpa had told me his stories before he passed away.

But I didn't have to prove anything to Riley or the reporter in Richmond or to anyone else. Mémé was proud of Henri Sauver's military and then resistance record, and so was I. "My grandfather didn't like to talk about the war."

"I wonder why not," he said.

He waited for me to respond. Defend my grandfather perhaps.

I wanted to cross my arms like Riley, but instead I smiled at the camera. My media trainer had shown me dozens of clips from people who'd screwed up their interviews, usually by getting defensive with their body language. Others by stomping off in a huff. "Do you have any other questions for me?" I asked, even though I wanted to stomp off as well.

"How did you say your grandmother met Henri Sauver?"

"On a blind date, at a café in Saint-Lô."

"But after the war . . ." He tilted his head. "There were no cafés left in Saint-Lô."

I'd read about the bombing of the city but had never thought to question Mémé's story. Perhaps I'd heard wrong. "It might have been near the end of the war instead."

He watched me for a moment, and I expected him to ask why a member of the French resistance would be on a blind date, at a public café, while the Germans still occupied the town. Instead, he asked, "Was your grandmother part of the resistance?"

My lips pressed together for a moment before I remembered to smile. "The Germans stayed at the château during the war," I said. "I'm sure she resisted them in her own way."

"Did she ever talk about the German soldiers in her house?"

My smile widened, hoping to engage him along with the camera as I spoke. "Can I ask you a quick question?"

"Of course."

I nodded casually toward the tripod. "Off camera."

His eyes on me, he turned the camera off. My smile collapsed, hardening into a grimace. This time I crossed my arms. "What are you keeping from me?"

"I'm trying to put together a documentary."

"But you know something I don't . . ."

He glanced up at the rocky cliffs towering above us and then looked back at me. "My grandfather flew a B-24 during World War II. He hid in a tunnel under the Château d'Epines with some members of the resistance."

My heart quickened. I didn't know any of the old tunnels had remained through the war. Or that the resistance had hidden in them.

"His plane crashed near a river outside Saint-Lô." Riley glanced back to the fields across the Vire. "He said Gisèle rescued him and brought him into the tunnel."

My gaze roamed over the hillside again, and I wondered at my grandmother rescuing the pilot of a downed plane.

"Was my grandfather there?" I asked.

He shook his head.

"Where is the tunnel entrance?"

"Someplace in the forest." He took his camera off the tripod and began to pack it. "When my grandfather told me his stories, I was at rock bottom and didn't listen to the details, but I heard about redemption through everything he told me. There were second chances for him and others who survived the war."

I eyed him again. Was it possible the man before me was different from the man in the pictures? I hoped he had changed, for his sake, but still I didn't trust him.

He glanced at his diver's watch. "I'm supposed to interview Madame Calvez in an hour."

Madame Calvez had asked me not to return, but perhaps if I was with Riley she would change her mind. Or if she was like my grandmother, she might not even remember that I was Gisèle's granddaughter.

"Can I tag along with you?" I asked.

He raked his fingers through his thick hair. "I suppose, if you let me ask the questions."

I readily agreed.

er rescuer was named Hauptmann Milch. Lucien said the officer had a family in Berlin and was respected among most of his fellow officers, but Lucien knew little else about his background.

Gisèle didn't tell Lucien or even Émilie what had happened in the wine cellar. It was much too humiliating to share with either of them. The only ones who would ever know were Hauptmann Milch and Viktor Braun, the *Fähnrich*—sergeant—who attacked her. Lucien said Braun was a bitter man. He'd asked to join the Luftwaffe to fight Hitler's war from the sky, but he'd been assigned to act as a warden to the people of France.

Even after she bolted her bedroom door—and pushed her dresser across it—Gisèle hadn't slept well. With Adeline in the bed next to her, she replayed her minutes in the cellar over and over. Had her solitude been some sort of invitation to that man? The thought of what might have happened terrified her. If Milch hadn't rescued her, she might have been killed.

How could she live in her home with these men here? She would never feel secure again.

She ripped her soiled blouse into threads. It would be impossible to replace, but even if she could patch it, she would never wear it again. Nor would she ever return to the *cave*.

The morning light brought tepid comfort, enough for her to get up and dress Adeline for the day. As she prepared breakfast, Gisèle determined to avoid both Milch and Braun—one because of her humiliation and the other because she feared what he would do the next time he found her alone.

While Émilie tended to the laundry, Gisèle began making scrambled eggs from the supplies the Germans had carried into her home last night. Not only had they secured eggs, they'd brought a ham smoked in ash, crates filled with vegetables, and bags of flour to make biscuits. She hadn't seen this much food since the war began and didn't dare ask where they had obtained it.

Adeline was sucking her bottle in her playpen when Lisette strolled into the kitchen and hopped up onto the counter, her legs dangling over the linoleum.

Gisèle cracked eggs into a porcelain bowl. "What are you doing here?"

"The Germans requisitioned me to work here instead of in Saint-Lô." Lisette glanced around the kitchen. "Please give me a job."

"Don't they need you to type or translate?"

She shook her head. "One of the new men does most of the typing so I won't see their correspondence with Berlin, and others can translate for them. If I'm no longer useful, I'm afraid they'll send me to work in Germany."

Earlier this year, the government had enacted the Service du Travail Obligatoire—Compulsory Work Service—to force hundreds of thousands of young Frenchmen and women to join their labor force. Lisette would be safer here, under the roof with the German occupiers, than living at a camp in Germany, as long as she avoided places like the cellar.

"I can't go to Germany," Lisette said, her voice trembling.

Adeline began to cry, and Gisèle wiped her hands on her apron so she could pick her up. Their guests didn't need any more reminders that there was a baby in the house.

Lisette reached into the pen. "I can hold her."

Gisèle wiped her hand under the *couvre-chef* that held back her hair. "Thank you."

"It's so sad about her par—"

Gisèle stopped her, pointing to the ceiling. "I told them her name is Adeline."

"Adeline." Lisette offered her a piece of a biscuit. "It's the perfect name."

"They think she's my daughter."

Lisette paused. "I suppose they should think that. I will keep your secret as well."

Émilie breezed into the kitchen. "The major said we should not be late with breakfast."

Gisèle sighed. The Germans were punctual about everything, as if the war would be lost if everything from meals to bedtime were not observed at the precise hour.

Émilie began whisking the eggs, and Lisette sat down at the table with a bottle to care for Adeline. Gisèle was grateful for two women she could trust. None of them wanted to serve the Nazis, but they each had to do what they could to survive.

When the eggs were almost finished, Gisèle retrieved the ham from the oven and sliced it before taking the platter upstairs. Then she came back down for the coffeepot, eggs, and biscuits.

As she served breakfast to fifteen men, she was relieved that Viktor Braun wasn't among them. The *Hauptmann* was there, but she didn't dare steal a glance at him. Part of her feared any acknowledgment from her would put him in jeopardy with his commanding officer. And part of her was ashamed of what he had seen.

She prayed he didn't think she had been flirting with Viktor Braun. From her scream, Hauptmann Milch must have known that she was scared, and yet she hoped he didn't think she had invited the trouble. She shouldn't have cared what he thought—he was a German, her enemy. But even though he was a German, he'd risked his life to rescue her.

The coffeepot in her hand, she filled the cups and stepped back from the table.

An *Oberst*, the major's commanding officer, joined the men for breakfast. Seidel was his surname. The Germans had taken over her father's office, including her *verboten*—forbidden— wireless, but she listened as Oberst Seidel told the soldiers of news from Germany, of the victories they'd had in Italy and the nearby islands. He paid no attention to her as he spoke. Either the major had told him she couldn't speak German or he thought her ignorant.

Fear clenched her stomach again. The men before her really believed they would take over the rest of Europe and then conquer the world. What if the Germans never left? What if this was the rest of her life—serving food to her enemy while she worried about her brother's life?

A few weeks ago, she'd heard a news broadcaster read a speech from Winston Churchill to the people of the United States. "If we are together nothing is impossible," he said. "If we are divided, all will fail."

What was the rest of the world doing right now? She prayed Great Britain and the United States remained strong. Churchill was right. They—the British and the Americans and the Free French—must battle this evil together to be victorious. They could not fail.

Evil would oppose all that was good, she supposed, until the very end of their world, but in the end, she believed with all her heart, good would ultimately win.

She began refilling a cup of coffee for Oberst Seidel.

"We are bringing another convoy from Berlin. The train will arrive in Saint-Lô on Friday." He looked up at her, switching easily to French. "Thank you for your hospitality."

She acknowledged him with a nod, and she felt the stares of all the men on her.

"After breakfast, I must see you in my office," he said.

Questions collided within her as she poured the coffee and she swayed back on her heels, the tiny ripples of coffee splashing against the edge of his cup.

Why did he want to see her?

"*Fräulein*—I believe that is enough," he said. "Fräulein?"

He tapped on her hand, and she jerked back the pot, spilling brown drops on the white tablecloth. Did he want to question her about the incident in the wine cellar? Or did he know something about Michel . . . or Adeline?

If he asked about Michel, she would have to smile politely and feign ignorance. She must convince him that she knew nothing. That she was slow in the mind even. No matter what happened, she mustn't draw attention to herself by acting nervous or scared. It was only by becoming as invisible as possible that she and Adeline—and Michel—would survive.

After she cleared breakfast—and cleaned the coffee stains—Gisèle met Oberst Seidel and two other officers in Papa's crowded office. The wireless was still near the window, but they'd moved his almanacs and maps, replacing them with neat stacks of manila folders and a lone copy of *Mein Kampf*.

From behind the desk, the *Oberst* motioned for her to take a chair as if he were the king of this castle and she his subject. Major von Kluge and another officer stood by the desk, and when the door opened, a third officer joined them—Hauptmann Milch. Even though she didn't acknowledge him, there was comfort in his presence. Still, she prayed he wouldn't tell the others that she knew how to speak German.

Oberst Seidel glanced over her shoulder at the dining hall beyond as he spoke to her in French. "This building is much too large for just you and a housekeeper, no?"

"I don't think of it as a building, Monsieur. It is my home."

He placed his monocle on top of a manila folder. "We have outgrown our headquarters building in Saint-Lô. From now on, we will be using the château."

A protest formed on her lips, but she swallowed her retort. Like Lucien, she was trapped in this web.

If Lisette helped her care for Adeline, hidden away from these men, perhaps the Germans would forget about the child. But how would she continue to care for Michel with German soldiers living and working above the tunnels?

The officer's attention turned to the papers on his desk, and as he skimmed them, she thought of her father sitting in that chair, smoking a cigar as he read one of his newspapers. The images of the Nazis were replacing what she remembered of her father.

How would she be able to erase these memories?

She wanted to cling to the good memories of her home, to the days when she was a child and her father twirled her around the main hall as they listened to jazz music on the gramophone, to the laughter of her mother before her death, the afternoon they tried—and failed—to outrun a rainstorm on their bike ride back from Agneaux. In their drenched clothes, their hair clinging to their faces, she and Mother couldn't stop laughing. She wished the laughter never had to end.

Oberst Seidel opened another folder.

She could almost hear the tinkling of glass as her family and friends celebrated her graduation from the university more than two years ago. They had danced under a tent outside and talked of war, though no one believed that Germany would ever defeat France.

At one time, she'd dreamed of going to the United States after Paris, visiting places like New York City and Los Angeles. When the war was over, she would run away from this château and all the bad memories that were replacing the sweet ones. She would preserve all that was good here in her heart and try to forget all that had been stolen from her.

"Fräulein." Oberst Seidel glanced up and studied her face. "Pardon me, mademoiselle—"

"Madame," she said, correcting him.

"Madame," he repeated as if he were willing to accommodate her in the smallest of ways but didn't seem to put much faith in calling her by the married title of a Frenchwoman. "While I appreciate your service for us, you cannot lie to one of my men. Ever."

She nodded her head.

"And you will not lie to me." He tapped the desk. "People who lie to me are sent away. And they never return."

She looked him directly in the eye. "I understand."

His demeanor was a frigid calm, his gray hair icing the coldness in his voice. Unlike the *Hauptmann*, Oberst Seidel seemed the kind of person who would stand by and watch unaffected while his men murdered Frenchmen tied up in the forest.

Oberst Seidel looked down at the papers on the desk again and then back up at her, continuing to speak to her in French. "I am concerned about some of the facts you have relayed to Major von Kluge."

She tried to recall the details that she'd contrived when she met him in the courtyard. "I will answer any questions you have."

"We have been searching for your brother." He riffled through the papers. "What is his name?"

"Michel."

He looked back up at her. "Ah, yes, Michel. Do you know where we can locate him?"

She balled up her fingers so the men around her wouldn't see them trembling. She wasn't as strong as Michel, but she had to pretend in order to protect all of them. "Why are you searching for my brother?"

"We have pressing business we must discuss with him." He laced his fingers together on the desk, leaning forward. "We fear he is in danger."

The gunshots in the forest seemed to deafen her ears. As if these men would protect him. "Last I knew he was in England with my mother's family."

"Where in England?"

"Kennington." Now she allowed the anxiety to flood her face. "I do not know if he is still there, but when you find him, I would like to speak with him as well."

He sat back a few inches and studied her face again, trying to unnerve her. But she didn't falter. Instead she stared back into the emptiness of his pale green eyes.

"Did you and your brother part on bad terms?" he asked.

She contemplated her answer. "I love my brother, sir, but we did not always agree."

"What was your source of disagreement?" he asked slowly, as if they were chatting by the fireside, sipping afternoon tea.

She tried to mirror his placidity. If he didn't want to rush his words, neither would she. And she needed time to think. The man in front of her seemed to admire strength, and yet if she appeared too strong, he might crush her instead. If she said the disagreement between her and Michel was political, the *Oberst* would think she was pandering to him. "Neither my father nor I wanted him to join the army."

"And he joined anyway?"

She nodded.

"Why didn't you want him to join?"

"I—I was afraid he would be killed."

The *Oberst* pointed at the man standing beside him. "Major von Kluge says that you are married."

"I—"

He didn't let her finish. "Yet my men have found no record of your marriage."

She put her hands behind her back. "There should be a certificate in Saint-Lô."

He reached for a pen. "What is your husband's name?"

Her heart clutched. The name should have been ready on her lips and yet her mind was a blank.

"His name, madame," he repeated.

Then she remembered the boy who had intrigued her in town, the one who she hoped had left Saint-Lô long ago. "Jean-Marc," she blurted. "Jean-Marc Rausch."

The captain's eyes narrowed. "Rausch?"

"Yes, monsieur."

"Good." He tapped the pen on the desk. "I don't have time to spare one of my men to search for your marriage certificate in Saint-Lô, but I assume you have a copy."

"I'm not cer—"

He had no patience for a protest. "Where was your child born?"

"Here," she said. "In the house."

"Then you must have a certificate for her birth as well."

"Of course."

"Excellent!" He put the pen into the top drawer of the desk. "Please retrieve them for me."

She hesitated. "I will have to search for both certificates."

"I'm certain they are not far away," he said. "I will need them by morning."

CHAPTER 34

Isabelle's left eye twitched as she glanced between Riley and me, the door behind her pressed against her back. "I'm afraid Grand-mère can't talk right now."

"You must be the young lady I spoke to on the phone," Riley said.

She smiled at him.

Riley checked his watch. "Perhaps we can visit later today."

"I don't think—"

I stopped her. "I don't need to be here for the interview."

Neither of them protested as I stepped back. Whatever happened in the past must have angered or scarred Madame Calvez for life.

But before I walked away a shaky voice spoke from behind the door. "Let them in, Isabelle."

Riley glanced over at me, and I shrugged. Isabelle slowly opened the door, and Riley followed me inside.

In the living room was a woman crouched over a walker, scooting across a hardwood floor. Her short, white hair was curled neatly and she wore a tailored suit with hose and sturdy shoes.

Riley stepped around Isabelle. "You are Madame Calvez?"

Lifting her head, she flashed a tentative smile. "You must be Riley Holtz."

Riley moved quickly across the floor and kissed both of her cheeks like a seasoned Frenchman.

Then she motioned to me, squinting into the light. "Come closer, child. Age has stolen away my vision."

"I'm Chloe Sauver. The granddaughter of Gisèle Duchant Sauver."

As I walked toward her, she examined my face. "You look like your grandmother."

I kissed both of her cheeks, and then she turned away from me.

Isabelle put her arm around her great-grandmother's shoulders. "Monsieur Holtz wants to interview you about the war."

She nodded.

Riley glanced around the small room, most of the surfaces covered with used cups and dishes. Then he glanced out the window. "Why don't we talk outside?"

He opened the sliding door, and then he lifted Madame Calvez's walker so she could step onto the patio. Riley reached back to grab the backpack he'd left inside.

"It will only take me a few minutes to set up my gear." His eyes met mine. "Will you help me?"

So I stepped out onto the patio, Isabelle behind me. Madame Calvez sat beside a glass table, her walker hidden behind Riley's lawn chair and the bomber jacket he'd slung over the back. A small jungle of potted plants were crowded together on the patio and a sparrow dipped in a bath outside the kitchen window, seemingly undaunted by the visitors in its backyard.

I clipped a microphone on the lapel of Madame Calvez's jacket as he set up his camera on a tripod, chatting with the older woman about her plants. Isabelle brought me a stool, and I sat beside her, close to the sliding glass.

Riley pulled a Moleskine journal from his pack. He opened the journal beside him, and I saw a list of questions that he'd prepared.

Madame Calvez's finger, slightly crooked, pointed at the chair. "Where did you get your coat?"

"It was my grandfather's. He was a pilot during the war."

"From America?"

He nodded.

"The Allied airmen were very brave," Madame Calvez said. "Is he still alive?"

Riley shook his head. "He passed away three years ago, but he told me a few of his stories. Madame Calvez, may I ask—"

She stopped him. "You can ask me anything you want, but I can't guarantee you an answer."

He glanced back down at his notes. "When did you live at the Château d'Epines?"

She fidgeted with her fingers for a moment, and when she spoke again, her voice sounded a bit sad. "I never technically lived there," she said. "Until the end of the war, I kept an apartment in Saint-Lô."

"Did you work at the château?" he asked.

"I was a secretary to the Germans in Saint-Lô, and when they moved their headquarters to the château, I helped at the house."

I leaned forward on the stool, intrigued about what she would say. Perhaps she could give all of us a glimpse into my grandmother's years during the occupation.

"So that would have been in 1942?" Riley asked.

"That's right. Two years before the Allies landed on the beaches. We had no idea, of course, that the end was near. We thought the Germans would be here forever."

"Did you know many of the German officers?"

"Of course." Madame Calvez looked over Riley's shoulder, at the bird playing in the water. "They were my employers."

"Did you have Jewish friends in Saint-Lô?"

"I had acquaintances but no friends. My father had been a farmer on the other side of France, and he didn't like the Jewish people. It wasn't until—" The strength in her voice slipped. "I didn't have any Jewish friends until after the war."

When he glanced over at me, I scooted toward Madame Calvez. "Can I get you something to drink?"

She shook her head, but I still stood up. Isabelle helped me pour two glasses of lemonade and deliver them back outside.

Riley took a long sip before continuing. It seemed as if he was trying to proceed with care, trying to understand her story without pushing too hard. "I read that some Jewish men served in the Wehrmacht," he said.

His words sounded odd to my ears. The Jews were the victims in this war. Why would they be in the German army?

Her gaze wandered to a bird diving his head under the water of the birdbath. "Some were full Jews, but mostly it was *Mischlinge* who served."

He jotted a note in his Moleskine before he continued. "What is a *Mischling*?"

"A partial Jew."

"My grandfather said he would never forget one man he met when he came to Saint-Lô—a Jewish captain named Josef who helped him get his identity card so members of the resistance could smuggle him through France."

Her hands shook as she reached for the lemonade. Isabelle helped her sip it. "So many officers came through here during the occupation," she finally said. "I can't remember all of them."

"Which officers do you remember?" he asked.

Her eyes glazed for a moment and she tugged on the sleeves of her jacket. "None worth talking about."

"I understand if it is too difficult."

Her lip quivered. "I don't believe you do . . ."

I glanced at him to see if she'd insulted him, but he seemed completely engaged. Instead of probing her for his agenda, he was probing her for her story, allowing her to lead him as well.

"You are right," he said, and I was touched by the kindness in his voice. "There is no way that I could understand."

She brushed her wrinkled fingers over the ridges on the glass table. "Some of the soldiers in Saint-Lô were prisoners themselves. They didn't want to be in the army—like most of the Jews."

Riley glanced down at his journal. "What happened to the *Mischlinge* who weren't in the army?"

"They were sent to the concentration camps." Sorrow locked her gaze and for a moment, it seemed she had gone to another time and place. Watching her, I wondered where she had gone. "So many people were hurt during this war. So many of us did things we would never have imagined we'd do—" Her eyes filled with sadness. "You cannot understand."

He agreed. "I cannot."

"It was a terrible, terrible time." She turned toward me. "What did Gisèle tell you?"

"She said very little about the war."

Madame Calvez folded her wrinkled hands together. "Gisèle never forgave me, but she didn't know what happened during the occupation—not the whole story."

Riley didn't move, not an inch, even though I knew he must have been dying to hear the whole story. "Would you like to tell me what happened?"

Isabelle's chair squeaked, and Madame Calvez's eyes flew to meet her great-granddaughter's. When she turned back to Riley, it seemed she was no longer dreaming about the past. "I only remember small bits and pieces now. The rest has faded away."

Riley leaned forward, trying to engage her again. "I want to tell people what you remember of your story, so we don't forget."

"If only Gisèle were here, she would tell you much better stories than I could. And she would probably remember your soldier."

I didn't have the heart to tell her that Gisèle had forgotten most of her stories.

"My grandmother mentioned the name of a child she was searching for," I said, glancing over at Riley before I looked back at Madame Calvez. "Did you know a girl called Adeline?"

Madame Calvez's eyes turned glossy again and it almost seemed as though she looked right through me. "I am sorry—I'm getting tired."

I wanted to ask her again, but Riley's glance silenced me.

"Forgive us," he said as he turned off his camera. "We've kept you too long."

isèle slammed the door shut and collapsed on the floor of her bedroom. Pulling her knees to her chest, she struggled to breathe.

For two years, she and Émilie had maintained the château and fed the men in the tunnels without drawing attention from the Germans. Now their enemy had turned their cruel spotlight on her, and they wouldn't stop searching, she was certain, until they found out the truth about her and Adeline. People didn't lose their marriage and birth certificates unless they were running—or perhaps their house burned down.

She could still say she'd misplaced it, but the *Oberst* wouldn't stop there. He would ask for the name of her doctor.

There was a whole war to be fought, continents to be conquered, and these men were fixated on the birthdate of one child and the marriage of her parents.

She hated living in a world like this—where the officials were more concerned about controlling people than caring for them—but there was no escaping this nightmare. Even if she took Adeline back down into the tunnel, Michel wouldn't let the child stay. It would ruin all he and his men were doing to resist the enemy.

She paced the floor in front of her bed.

How was she supposed to obtain a marriage and birth certificate by morning? The *Oberst* had made it clear what he would do if he caught her in a lie. Perhaps she could stall at finding them. Or perhaps he would be distracted by the convoy, at least until Friday.

But then again, if something happened to that convoy, he might take it out on the rest of them anyway.

She couldn't stay and let these men harm Adeline. If Sister Beatrice would let them spend the night at the orphanage, she could figure out transportation to Lyon tomorrow. The last time they spoke, Philippe had hinted again at marrying her. Perhaps she should tell him the truth—Adeline had lost her parents in the war. If they married, Philippe would protect Adeline.

Her gaze roamed over the grassy hill and trees behind the house. The Germans didn't know the countryside like she did. She was a Frenchwoman with a French daughter. Even if she didn't have papers for Adeline, she could carefully find her way among her people.

Autumn air chilled the room when she opened the window. It would be hard traveling with Adeline in the darkness, with the night patrols guarding the river and valley and the perimeter of the town. Adeline's cries would alert the patrols for ten miles around them.

Perhaps Émilie could give Adeline something to help her sleep.

They would have to leave tonight or it would be too late to run.

— CHAPTER 36 —

"You weren't supposed to ask questions," Riley chided as we walked past a row of brick shops in Saint-Lô. Instead of returning along the river path, we'd followed Isabelle's directions into town to get some coffee and a late lunch.

"I'm sorry, I . . . ." But I had no real excuse except that I wanted to know the truth.

Riley stuck his hands into his pockets as we climbed a hill. "Who is Adeline?"

"I believe she's my aunt, but Madame Calvez seems to be hiding the truth."

"People usually hide what they're ashamed of."

His words resonated with me. We were talking about Madame Calvez, and yet as he spoke about shame, I realized that I was hiding too—at a château in France instead of facing the media questions and Austin back home.

I had thought Austin loved me for who I was, not for what I brought to his campaign. I'd put him up on a pedestal in my heart, and when he fell, he hurt my heart along with my pride. Now I was hiding because I was ashamed of what my fiancé had done. And I was embarrassed that I'd been blind to his wandering.

Riley waved his hand in front of my face. "You with me?"

"Sorry." I blinked. "I was back in Richmond for a second."

"Better company there?"

I shook my head. I had to stop thinking about Austin and focus on the person with me.

"Not at all." I tugged my sunhat down on my forehead. Without the tree covering, the sun scorched my skin. "What were you saying?"

"That people who hide a portion of their story are usually either ashamed or they're protecting someone else. It takes a little time, but if I listen well and try not to judge them for what they've done, people will usually tell me the truth."

"Who do you think Madame Calvez is protecting?"

"I don't know."

Saint-Lô had been rebuilt after the war, but across the street were the remains of a medieval wall that had fortified the hillside in the center of town. We strolled up the steep sidewalk, and the bombed façade of a cathedral and a maze of winding slate streets overlooked the shops.

Riley ordered two *café au laits* at a small café, and as I waited, I imagined my grandparents here, meeting over coffee and cream. But Riley was right. The Allied pilots and soldiers—men like Riley's grandfather—destroyed almost everything as they fought to liberate this town.

Perhaps Mémé got the location wrong. Perhaps they met in another town.

I sipped my creamy *café* as we descended the hill and began our walk toward Agneaux. What would it have been like to live in one of the apartments over the shops during the occupation, German soldiers patrolling the streets below? The people in this town must have been scared to leave their homes, especially those who were Jews.

Did the Jewish people here know there were Jews fighting in the German military? Until Riley and Madame Calvez discussed it today, I hadn't known about it, and I was still trying to sort out the schism in my mind.

"Do you know how many Jews fought in the Wehrmacht?" I asked.

"Some put the number at a hundred thousand."

"But Hitler was trying to kill the Jews—"

He glanced down at the Vire as we crossed the bridge over it. "It's ironic, isn't it? On one hand, he was exterminating the Jewish people, and on the other, he was using them in his army. Sometimes he even 'Aryanized' them."

"How exactly does one Aryanize someone?"

"Hitler declared his Jewish soldiers had German blood, and magically, by the power of Hitler, they had new genes."

"He thought he was God."

Riley nodded. "And the Nazi leaders encouraged his delusion. He was power hungry, but he was also pragmatic. The army needed more soldiers, and if the Jewish men were willing to fight for him, Hitler and his top men were often willing to look the other way. The families of these soldiers were a different story . . ."

We waited at a stoplight before crossing the street with a handful of pedestrians, their arms filled with fresh flowers and bread. "It's heartbreaking."

"Hitler had the power to give life or take it, or, in his eyes, change someone's genes. There is a reason why so many people thought he was a lunatic. Those who confronted him, though, lost their lives."

I took another sip of the *café*. "What I don't understand is after all the terrible things Hitler did to oppress the Jewish people, how a Jewish man could serve under him?"

"An excellent question, and that's exactly what I'm hoping to find out for this documentary."

"I thought you were profiling German soldiers."

"German soldiers with Jewish backgrounds," he said slowly.

So he had been hiding something from me.

"Some of them kept their Jewish roots a secret for the rest of their lives," he continued.

I glanced over at him. "Why didn't you tell me you were going to profile the Jewish soldiers?"

"I didn't want it to taint your answers."

We walked another block before I spoke again. "Are you doing this story because of the man who helped your grandfather?"

"Partially," he said. "My grandfather hated all the Germans until he met Josef and realized that not all of them were evil."

"What was Josef's surname?"

Riley shook his head. "My grandfather never knew."

Chapter 37

Gisèle gathered a small bundle of warm clothes and stuffed them into a satchel. It would be hard to carry Adeline along with the clothing and some food, diapers, and a bottle, but she would do what she must. She'd already poured a little brandy in Adeline's bottle before putting the child to bed and then tucked a flask of it into the satchel. As long as she could keep Adeline quiet, they would be safe for the night.

Shadow meowed at Gisèle as she packed, and then he kneaded the bedcovers with his paws and settled back in again. In her absence, she hoped he would continue to frighten the Nazis. Or perhaps Lisette would take him home.

He would find plenty of food and water near the river, but it made her feel better to think of Lisette caring for him.

Lisette had left hours ago to return to her apartment, and Gisèle and Émilie spent a long evening cleaning up after the officers. Émilie knew something was wrong with her, but she couldn't tell her friend what she planned. When the Germans interrogated them, neither Émilie nor Lisette would have any knowledge of her departure.

When she had gone to the chapel earlier that evening with the food and a letter for Michel, she'd slipped down into the tunnel to find him one last time. The corridors were empty, and in that moment, her scrambled plans became clear. She and Adeline would sneak out to the *chapelle* and take the tunnel back to the beekeeper's cellar. Then they'd escape to the orphanage until she found transportation to Lyon.

But a war still waged inside her, as daunting as the war waging in their country.

How could she leave her brother without someone to help him on the outside? And if she didn't leave, how could she protect Adeline?

"People who lie to me are sent away."

She wanted to rescue Michel and Adeline and all those being hunted by the Nazis, but she wouldn't help anyone if the *Oberst* sent her away. And if Michel knew what was happening, he would insist she run far from here, to save herself and Adeline.

When she emerged from the *chapelle*, the guard watched her kneel in the cemetery, pressing one hand on the patch of weeds on her father's grave and the other on her mother's tombstone as she said good-bye. Her heart ached at the thought of leaving her brother and Émilie as well without telling them good-bye, but she had no choice.

Back in her bedroom, she dressed in black pants and a gray sweater to blend into the night. When her clock ticked past one in the morning, she picked up Adeline and carefully unlocked the door. With Adeline asleep in one of her arms and the satchel secured in her other hand, she snuck down the back staircase to the main floor.

In the dining hall, she stopped, listened for voices, but the night was quiet. She prayed the brandy would keep Adeline silent. If something startled her, her cries would wake the entire house. Then she would have to fabricate yet another lie, that she was going to get warm milk or something else. The Germans would inquire about her attire and the satchel, but after what had happened in the cellar, she would never consider wearing her robe down to the kitchen at night.

She wasn't certain how to explain away her satchel.

The windows on the north side of the hall looked out over the cliff—much too high for her and Adeline to jump—and there were no shrubs to hide behind along the windows that overlooked the courtyard.

She and Adeline would have to sneak out of the window in Papa's office, the one concealed by the hedge. They would wait until the night guard made his next round through the courtyard and then they'd run across to the *chapelle*.

The office door was closed in front of her, and as she neared the door, she heard a voice, low but stern, coming from the other side.

It was the *Oberst* speaking.

"The tracks were destroyed on this side of Caen," he said. "It will take an extra day to fix them."

Then she heard the voice of Major von Kluge. "We must stop these men. They will ruin everything."

She froze beside the door. Was that why the tunnel had been empty tonight? She prayed the Nazis didn't know who was thwarting their plans.

"Our men spotted a half-dozen men running into the woods."

"Did they shoot them?" the major asked.

"Only one," he replied. "But he had no papers to identify him."

She shivered. Michel would never tell her where he was going, but she knew he wouldn't shy away from danger—like blowing up railroad tracks or a bridge so the enemy's train couldn't pass.

"You have his body?" the major asked.

She didn't know if the *Oberst* nodded in response or shook his head. What would they do with the body?

"They cannot stop our convoy on Wednesday," the *Oberst* said. "We need the munitions in Cherbourg."

"That's what I told my men. We don't have enough men to watch every inch of the tracks, but we have ten soldiers guarding each car. The rebels don't have the manpower to fight all of them."

"I wouldn't be so certain," the *Oberst* said. "We don't know how many men they have."

Adeline began to squirm and Gisèle quickly backed away from the door before racing back up the steps.

Her hands trembling, she opened the door and placed Adeline on her bed. Then she slumped against the bedpost. What was she going to do now?

Even if the *Oberst* was distracted by the delay of their convoy, she doubted he'd forget her certificates.

The blackout curtains over her windows extinguished the stars, but she unhooked one of them and looked outside. The crescent shape of the moon seemed to rock in the sky and below it was a narrow strip of rocky land between the back of the house and the cliff that sank into the valley.

Could she throw her satchel out the window and escape? If it was just her, she might have been able to shimmy down a strand of sheets, but even with the brandy, Adeline would never stay quiet. And if the sheets tore . . .

She should run away while she had the opportunity, before the *Oberst* discovered she didn't have the papers. But she couldn't leave Adeline with these men. André and Nadine had to leave their daughter in order to save Adeline's life, but if Gisèle left her now, it would only be to save herself.

Closing her eyes, she leaned back against the windowsill and begged God for help. With so much evil in their midst, it seemed as if God was far away, but she couldn't give up hope that His spirit lingered. He had been in the cellar with her, and she was certain that He was here in her room. She may not have a sword to fight the dragon like Saint Michel, but she could battle with prayer.

Something shuffled outside her door, and her heart pounded again. Had she locked it on her return? She didn't move for fear someone outside was listening for her steps. If the door was unlocked, if an officer opened it, he would find her dressed, a satchel beside her.

But why would one of the men be opening her door at this hour? Perhaps Viktor Braun—the man from the cellar—was coming to finish what he'd started.

She eyed the knob in the moonlight and then carefully reached into her satchel and pulled out her father's knife.

There was a rustling sound outside the door and her gaze dropped to the floor. In the dim light, she saw a brown folder. Slowly she tiptoed across the hardwood and picked it up. Then she hid her satchel in the armoire and turned on the lamp beside her bed, not caring one whit if the Allied planes saw it.

She opened the folder, and her mouth dropped when she saw the green certificate in her hand.

Certified Copy of an Entry of Marriage
Marriage Solemnized at Chapelle d'Agneaux
May 7, 1940
Jean-Marc Rausch, 25
Gisèle Duchant, 22

She shivered. The date of their marriage was weeks before her fictitious husband disappeared.

Below the marriage certificate was a pink one.

Certification for Birth
Château d'Epines, February 25, 1941
Adeline, Girl
Daughter of Jean-Marc Rausch and Gisèle Duchant Rausch

The name of the registrar was a scrawl.

Her hands clutching the certificates, she stared at the crack under the door. The only people who knew about her need of papers were the men in her father's office.

Had Hauptmann Milch rescued her again? If so, where had he gotten the certificates?

It didn't matter, she supposed. As she clutched the papers to her chest, she blessed him or whoever had come to her rescue. She would stay at the château and continue to pray that the Lord would blind the Germans' eyes.

Gently she brushed her hands over the baby's soft hair.

Adeline Duchant Rausch.

The name fit her beautifully. With these papers, perhaps neither of them would have to run away. The Germans would never have to know the truth, and through her deception—*their* deception—they would save Adeline's life and perhaps the lives of many more.

CHAPTER 38

Riley and I found a quiet park in Agneaux and settled under the shade of a tree to eat—two baguette sandwiches and orange sodas from the bakery where he'd found the croissants. On the other side of the fence were three cows, their skin mottled black and pink, grazing in a pasture beside the park.

Riley handed me a sandwich.

"Why don't you tell me your story?" I asked.

"It's messy."

I smiled. "So is mine."

Whatever his story, there seemed to be few similarities between the man beside me and the stereotype of the man I'd seen in the pictures online. I'd asked him to see past the stereotype of a politician's wife. Perhaps I needed to see past the stereotype I had of him as well.

I leaned back against the jagged bark of the tree. "Where does the life of Riley Holtz begin?"

"I grew up outside Detroit," he said as he unwrapped his sandwich. "My dad and grandfather both worked in an auto plant, and by the time I was in middle school, I'd already decided I didn't want to be like them."

He took a bite of his sandwich before continuing. "I had a little success with acting while I was in high school, and I'd convinced myself that I was going to be the next Brad Pitt, so the summer before my senior year, I packed my car and drove to New York."

I eyed him for a moment. He certainly looked like he could be a movie lead and had the confidence that went along with it, but as he lay on the dry grass, relaxed, I couldn't imagine him under the lights of Hollywood.

I bit into my baguette sandwich, bulging with fresh mozzarella, tangy basil, and sweet tomatoes. I could have eaten this sandwich every day and been happy. "What did your family say?"

"They were devastated, but at the time I didn't care. I was thrilled to be leaving town. A long time passed before I looked back, and my regrets were too many to count."

I smoothed my paper wrapping on the grass and set the rest of my sandwich on it. For some reason, I'd expected him to downplay the bad in his life and tell me how incredible he was. It was refreshing to hear the authenticity in his story.

"New York wasn't quite as enamored with my acting abilities as my high school instructor. After a few weeks there, I sold my car to pay for rent and hopped on the treadmill of auditions—I kept running faster and faster but never seemed to get anywhere. When I wasn't auditioning, I was waiting tables to pay for food and a crummy apartment on the Lower East Side.

"It took a full year before I landed a role in a small film. It's not a role I'm proud of now, but I fooled myself into thinking I was a celebrity and began partying like one."

His smile dimmed.

"After that film, I had a few small gigs on the stage. It was enough to keep me pressing on. I was certain the powers-that-be would soon discover I was a star in need of a place to shine.

"The city is filled with lapdogs who lick the crumbs off the floor of the entertainment industry and then wag their tail as they wait for more. I was surviving on the rumors I'd heard about celebrities who'd been discovered off Broadway, but by the time I was twenty-four, I was desperate as well. I didn't realize it then, but I'd begun to hate myself for who I was becoming."

I sipped my orange drink, my legs crisscrossed in front of me. I couldn't imagine this man across from me being desperate enough to eat crumbs from anyone. He was confident like Austin, and yet he was authentic as well about his weaknesses. Austin had always been more focused on my weaknesses than on his.

Riley leaned back on his elbows, his legs outstretched. "At the same time my life seemed to be falling apart, I was hired to work as a host on a documentary. I thought it was my ticket to stardom, but I had no idea what was about to happen."

I leaned forward, curious. "What sort of documentary was it?"

His familiar gaze returned alongside his grin. "A documentary that was supposed to prove once and for all that the resurrection of Jesus Christ was a sham."

I leaned back against the tree again, wringing my hands together. I don't know why I felt so uncomfortable talking about the life of Jesus. I believed Jesus was the Son of God. I believed in the resurrection. I'd attended church every Sunday beside Austin for the past year, but church had become part of the show—like his concern for his constituents, like having a wife.

In essence, Austin Vale worshipped himself, and somehow—like Olivia and the others—I had changed my allegiance to worship alongside him.

I knew the pat answers on religion that Olivia had concocted for Austin and me. Answers that would appeal to those constituents who believed in God but wouldn't scare those who didn't believe.

But Riley, I feared, would see past my script. He was well acquainted with acting, and he could tell pretty quickly that I was a poor actress. If Riley asked me a genuine question, I might fumble.

Instead I would keep the spotlight on him. "Did you go to church when you were a kid?"

He nodded. "But our church preached more about judgment than mercy. My parents followed all the rules set out by our church, and I loathed the anger and perfectionism that masked itself as righteousness."

"So you turned away from your faith?"

"I fled from it," he said. "When I was in New York, I discovered I could pretend to be anyone I wanted, and the last person I wanted to be was the kid who grew up in church or the man who still had questions about his faith. Even after all those years away from home, a quiet voice still beckoned to me. For a long time, I plugged up my ears and refused to listen to its call."

I leaned forward, intrigued now by his story. "What was this voice saying?"

"'Return to me.'" He glanced up at the clear sky. "I was desperately seeking peace, but I had no idea where to find it. I should have gotten on my knees and begged for His help right then, but I wasn't ready."

I took another long sip of my Orangina and glanced back at the cows. They had wandered far away from us, close to the playground at the other end of the park.

I couldn't decide if this guy before me was real, nor did I trust myself to make this decision. The pictures online of him and the multitude of women were proof that he'd had a wild side. I'd seen no pictures that spoke to his reform.

Was he weaving together a tale like Austin had done at our "chance" meeting in the coffee shop? But there was no reason for Riley to impress me.

I could be intrigued by his story, though, without trusting him. It wasn't like with Austin—my heart was too scrambled now to even consider romance.

"What happened next?" I asked.

"While I was filming the documentary, my grandfather came to visit me in New York. I had always admired him and his war stories, and as we talked about faith, he challenged me not to rely on what my parents or friends said about Jesus. He challenged me to find out what I thought about Jesus on my own.

"He also said something I'll never forget—he said we never know what we truly believe until we are standing in a trench, surrounded by the enemy. My trench came two weeks later. After spending the little money I had on alcohol and painkillers, I didn't have enough to make rent and was evicted from a pit they called an apartment during a snowstorm. I had no choice but to spend the night in a homeless shelter, and the next morning, I woke up shaking from a nasty cocktail of freezing temps and withdrawal.

"I'd been offered a job in a movie I knew I'd regret, and in that shelter, I realized I had to choose what I believed in— whether I would sacrifice everything for this obsession of mine or if I would choose to do what seemed right in my heart. I got down on my knees on that cement floor and asked God to reveal Himself. Thankfully, He did."

"And the documentary?"

The familiar smile returned. "The producer never finished it. He was determined to find solid evidence that the stories of Jesus were fiction, but after three years of working on it, he couldn't find the evidence he needed."

Two kids climbed up the monkey bars behind Riley and began swinging. "Did you return to acting?" I asked.

"No. I caught the bug for truth and started work behind the scenes on another documentary. A couple more years passed, and I started producing them on my own."

"So you converted?" I blurted before I realized it sounded like I was accusing him of failure. "I'm sorry—"

"God revealed Himself to me, just as I asked." He tapped on his tattoo. "It was the most painful experience of my life, but the healing started in the midst of the pain."

He tossed his ball of sandwich paper into a nearby trash can.

"My story is dull compared to yours," I said.

"I skipped over the dull parts."

I heard someone laugh, and when I turned, I saw a dozen kids lined up behind the low hedge, ready to invade the park. Riley hopped up and reached for my hand. His demeanor seemed to shift again. "We should probably let them play."

"I don't think they'll kick us out," I quipped. "We're bigger than they are."

He didn't acknowledge my joke, pointing instead to another gate at the back side of the park. "Why don't we go out that way?"

For a moment he reminded me of Sulley, the monster in *Monsters Inc.* who had been terrified of little Boo. "You're not scared of kids, are you?"

His smile was forced. "I'm scared of plenty of things."

I didn't ask, but after all he had been through, I was curious to know what could possibly frighten this man.

I gathered up my sandwich and he reached for my hand, urging me toward the door. I followed him out the gate and it wasn't until he shut it that I let go of his hand.

Chapter 39

The clock ticked mercilessly behind her father's desk as Oberst Seidel donned his monocle. Gisèle held her breath as he examined the certificates, awaiting her fate. If he didn't believe her . . .

There was nothing she could do if he didn't believe her.

He studied both of the papers closely. Then he slid them across the desk to Hauptmann Milch.

Hauptmann Milch lifted both papers and held them up to the light, scrutinizing them even longer than his commander had done. "They are in good order," he finally said.

She bit her lip to keep all her breath from escaping at once.

Oberst Seidel handed the papers back to her. "Do you have a death certificate for your husband?"

"I am not certain he is dead."

He set his eyepiece on the desk. "You have heard of the Compulsory Work Service."

"Yes, sir."

"Instead of sending you away, you and your housekeeper will work for us here along with that woman who was a secretary at our headquarters office."

"Lise—" She stopped herself. "Mademoiselle Calvez."

"Yes, Mademoiselle Calvez. She will join you."

Gisèle clutched the certificates to her chest. She would hide them in her room in case anyone else questioned her about Adeline. Until the Batiers returned, she could prove Adeline was hers.

The *Oberst* dismissed Hauptmann Milch and another officer until it was just her, standing before him alone. He tapped his pen on the desk. "The major also told me that he had one other concern. When he was examining the house, he heard something unusual down in the wine cellar."

"I went down there with him," Gisèle said. "He heard my cat."

"He mentioned the cat to me, but he was certain he heard voices as well."

"I don't know, monsieur. Parts of this house are a thousand years old. You and your men may not believe in ghosts, but some of our past residents have refused to leave. They play pranks sometimes on our guests."

"I have seen many things in my life, Madame Rausch, but you are correct—I don't believe in ghosts."

"And I don't believe that cats can talk, so I'm not sure what to say to Major von Kluge."

"I believe we will have to consider it a misunderstanding." He glanced back at the door again. "Where is your daughter?"

"Mademoiselle Calvez is caring for her."

His gaze wandered over to the window with the broken lock. "I have a wife and three children back in Cologne. My oldest daughter gave birth to our grandson almost two years ago—he would be about your daughter's age."

Conflicting emotions flooded through her. Even though she knew this man would take her life if she was caught in her lies, confusion and something akin to compassion warred in her. It was more like sadness, not for him as much as for all the children and innocent people who were losing in this war. For the little French girl who might never know her parents and for the German grandson of this *Oberst*, the officer who would decide her fate.

Oberst Seidel dismissed her, and as she passed back through the dining hall, she saw Hauptmann Milch sitting at the table alone, pecking with two fingers on the Hermès typewriter. He was quite handsome, with his short dark hair and brown eyes, now intent on his reading. His face was clean-shaven like the rest of the men, and his German uniform would have inspired fear in most people in France, but if one looked close enough, there was kindness etched beneath his Nazi façade.

Even as she stepped up beside him, he didn't look up. She fixed a curtain before leaning down to whisper. "Thank you."

His glance darted back toward the office and then his gaze dropped back to the typewriter. "I have done nothing," he replied, the prickliness in his voice like the thorns that protected the valley trees.

She pressed on through the main hall and down into the kitchen. Émilie was frying ham while Adeline played with blocks in her playpen. Beside her, Lisette was scooping dried acorn grounds into a pot to boil for what they called coffee—the Germans had secured crates of food but they hadn't been able to plunder any coffee beans.

She understood why the *Hauptmann* couldn't acknowledge her, but still it hurt. Perhaps, like a guardian angel, he would have to remain her benefactor in secret.

It might be difficult, but she would pretend as well that he was invisible.

. . .

Instead of taking her picnic basket to the *chapelle*, Gisèle brought a knapsack stuffed with the Germans' food, in case Michel had returned. Most of the officers were out patrolling Saint-Lô and the valley below this evening, but if one happened to stop her, she'd say she was continuing to feed the hungry in Agneaux. They could argue with her charity, as the *Oberst* had questioned her about the ghosts, but she was sticking to her original story.

No one was praying when she opened the door, but four candles continued to burn, the incense a sweet reminder of the way the Spirit moves, wafting into crevices and into the hearts of those willing to listen.

God used ordinary, often unexpected people throughout the Old Testament to rescue others—Esther and Moses and Jael, the woman who drove the tent peg through her enemy's head. Even though God could use anyone, Gisèle had never expected to find an advocate among the Germans.

Kneeling at a pew, she thanked God for using a Nazi soldier to save her life and the life of Adeline.

When she finished her prayers, she locked the entrance to the *chapelle* so no visitors would surprise her. Then she swept the sanctuary, blew out the flickering candles, and gathered the dried flowers into a pile. The aroma from the incense lingered around her as she unlocked the gate to the sacristy.

It seemed so strange to think Michel and his men were below this floor even as the women of Agneaux prayed above them. Michel and the others could hide in the tunnel, but none of them could escape God's presence, above or below the ground. The Nazis couldn't escape either. They might not care now, but one day they would be required, good or bad, to account for all they had done. Just as she would have to account for what she had done.

She slid back into the closet and opened the panel. Before she put the basket inside, she gasped.

Someone was sitting on the ledge.

The man blocked the beam from her flashlight with his hands. "Put that away, Gigi."

She collapsed against the thick coat of robes, scared and yet relieved that he hadn't been the one killed in the convoy. "Don't scare me like that, Michel."

"I needed to speak with you."

Dark whiskers peppered his smooth face. He looked thinner than she had ever seen him, and she wondered how much he'd eaten while he was gone.

"You'd best speak fast," she said as she dumped the contents of her knapsack into the waiting basket. "We have eyes and ears everywhere these days."

"Your last letter said the *boches* had taken over the château."

"Don't call them that," Gisèle whispered.

"I'm not afraid of them."

"You should be." She nudged the basket toward him. "Your men must be quiet when they are near the house."

"Sound echoes all over down there."

"Then you must find another place to hide—"

He shook his head. "This is a meeting place for people from all over La Manche."

She reached for his hand, clutching it in hers. "They will kill you if they find you."

"I am prepared to die, but you cannot." He thumbed her cheek. "You, Gigi, must live a long life and carry the name and legacy of the Duchant family forward."

She shook her head. She didn't want to speak about Michel's dying or the family legacy. She and Michel were both going to survive this war. Michel and Lisette were to marry, and perhaps she would marry one day as well. Their children and even their grandchildren would grow up to be the best of friends.

"Have you seen Lisette?" he asked.

She nodded. "The Nazis recruited her to work with me in the château."

"They haven't—" He stopped. "She is a beautiful woman."

I squeezed his hand. "A beautiful woman who has eyes only for you."

"If something happens to me—" He stumbled on his words. "Tell her that I loved her too."

"Nothing is going to happen to you," she said, trying to reassure him.

"We won't stop fighting, Gisèle, not until the Nazis are gone."

"The officers were talking of another convoy coming through here on Wednesday."

"They are trying to fortify all the Normandy beaches against an invasion."

She prayed the Allies would invade. Soon.

"You can no longer bring us food," he said.

"But you need it—"

"If the Germans find out about this tunnel, it will jeopardize everything."

She sighed. Now she was the one who was dangerous. "How will you get food?"

"The farmers are helping us."

"Michel, I—"

A soft thud pounded on the other side of the closet, and she dropped his hand. It sounded as if someone was hitting the wall with a pillow.

He hopped up. "You must go."

She reached into the small space and hugged her brother before he slipped down into the darkness.

Quickly she replaced the panel and stepped out into the sacristy.

The pounding on the *chapelle* door grew louder, someone insistent about getting inside.

Her hands trembling, she locked the gate and then threw a handful of spent candles and two bouquets of decaying flowers into her knapsack. At the back of the nave, she unlocked the door and shined her flashlight into the faces of two men: Viktor Braun and Major von Kluge.

"What are you doing?" the major demanded.

"I was praying and then cleaning out the nave."

Suspicion flooded his gaze. "In the dark?"

"We have no electricity in here," she said as she held up her light. "Only candles and lanterns and flashlights."

The major stepped into the nave. "What took you so long to answer—"

"I didn't realize it was an urgent matter," she said, desperately trying to keep her voice calm. "The villagers often knock on the door at night, wanting to pray."

She started to step outside, but the major stopped her. "We will take a look around your chapel."

"Of course," she said as he shined his flashlight toward the altar. "You may pray as well if you'd like."

His eyes were filled with indignation, but she ignored it. They reminded her of the rock by the river, immovable and cold. The aroma of the incense lingered. God's Spirit was still here, present in the midst of the evil. She prayed the men would feel the fear that came from Him, the fear of doing wrong instead of that which was right.

She waited by the door as the men tromped up the aisle. Fahnrich Braun stared for a moment at the sculpture of Christ hanging on the wall. The Jew who had been killed by the Jewish people. But even as He hung on the cross, Jesus showed His love for both the Jews and the Gentiles.

The Nazis passed under the picture of Saint Michel and the dragon, seemingly unfazed by the power of the archangel to defeat evil, and then stopped at the sacristy. The major shook the locked gate. "Why is this locked?"

"It's a supply room." She held up her key. "Would you like me to unlock it for you?"

"Right away."

She rushed forward. Any hesitation, she feared, would alert him to the fact that she was hiding something. Inside the sacristy, the major opened the closet, and she held her breath as he combed through the robes. Then he opened the drawers in the middle of the room, rummaging through each one before he turned back to her. "What is in your bag?"

She opened it and dumped the contents onto the small table. The spent candles rolled out across the polished wood, the old flowers piling on top of them. "I always clean up when I leave," she said with a shrug.

Fähnrich Braun searched through the used supplies and when he looked up at the senior officer, she saw disappointment in his eyes.

"Let's go back to the house," the major said.

They waited for her as she relocked the gate and then the main door.

Moonlight crept over the stained-glass windows, and sadness filled her heart as she followed them past the small cemetery into the house. She had fed the Germans, but she'd balanced her work by also feeding the men who resisted them.

But Michel was right—it was too dangerous for her to continue. Until the Nazis were gone, her work feeding Michel and his men was over. Instead she would pray for Michel while she cared for Adeline.

— CHAPTER 40 —

I checked the headlines when I got back to my room and discovered that my breakup with Austin had blitzed the national news. The media seemed preoccupied with the fact that I'd gone missing . . . and that Austin's poll numbers were slipping.

FORMER SHOO-IN FOR GOVERNOR GETS BOOT FROM FIANCÉE.

FIANCÉE OF VIRGINIA'S VALE GOES AWOL.

AUSTIN VALE FREE-FALLING IN VIRGINIA POLLS.

It seemed the monument Austin had built for himself, brick by brick, was crashing down.

My flight back to Virginia had been scheduled for Sunday morning, the day after Riley left, but I wasn't ready to return to Richmond. I called the airline and changed my flight to the following week. Then I emailed the itinerary to my parents.

A few minutes later, my cell phone rang, and I answered my mom's call.

"I just got your new flight schedule," she said.

"That was fast."

"I thought you were coming home this weekend."

"I decided to linger in the peace."

She sighed. "Austin stopped by your dad's office yesterday. He's not going to let you go easily."

"That's why I can't come home yet."

I looked out the windows at the silvery-blue ribbon of water combing through the valley. Today had been a day of questioning for me, but it had also been therapeutic.

"You should stay as long as you want, Chloe."

"I sure wish Dad would come back here with me."

"He can't—" She stopped. "The memories are too confusing for him."

"Did he tell you about Adeline?"

"He did, and I think the truth is scaring him."

I told her about Madame Calvez, about her animosity toward Mémé.

"Something horrible must have happened at the château," Mom said. "Some reason why Gisèle refused to return. It would have been impossible to live through that war unscathed."

I fiddled with the window until it opened. "I wish she would have told us."

"She wanted to remember all that was good about France," Mom said.

But now it seemed Mémé's heart yearned to find out what happened to her daughter, even if the truth wasn't good.

. . .

Riley tossed his duffel bag and suitcase into the back of the Peugeot that he'd rented in Saint-Lô. The sun was barely up, and I clung to the coffee that I'd managed to brew in the kitchen. He said he was headed over to Coutances and then driving farther down into France.

"Who are you interviewing next?" I asked.

"A Jewish officer who fought in the Wehrmacht, and then the

children of four other Jewish soldiers who've passed away," he said. "When are you going home?"

"In a week or so." I hesitated. "You said that Gisèle rescued your grandfather. And that he met a Jewish soldier here at the château."

Riley nodded.

Perhaps his grandfather was a key as well to my past. Through his stories, perhaps I could figure out some of mine. "Did he write down his stories?"

"I don't believe he wrote them down, but he made a video of his stories for my family." He slammed the hatch and rounded the vehicle to stand by me. "Unfortunately, my parents have it."

"Can you get it from them?"

He grimaced. "That would mean I have to call my father."

"Is that a problem?"

Instead of answering, he climbed into the car. "If my father won't send it, I'll make you a copy when I get back to New York."

"When do you go home?" I asked.

"In a week. When I finish my other interviews." He turned the key in the ignition. "They drive on the left side here, right?"

"Only if you want to scare the pants off oncoming drivers." I tilted my head. "You do know how to drive a manual, don't you?"

"Sure I do." He glanced down at the stick shift. "It's just been a few years."

"Can't you take a train?"

He shook his head. "There is no train station where I'm going."

For a moment, I wished I could explore France with him.

"I need to return this car before I take the train back to Paris." He smiled. "If my dad will send the DVD, perhaps we can watch it before we leave."

He shut the door. The gears ground as he shifted it into first. He waved and the poor car shuddered as he steered it up the lane. It died near the top, and Riley started it again.

A few minutes later, my cell phone vibrated.

You want to fly back to New York together?

I stared down at Riley's words.

Fancy that, a man who wanted to get on an airplane with me.

⪼ *Chapter 41* ⪻

"⎍isette!" Gisèle called as she walked through the empty corridor of the west wing.

Cold air slipped under the cracks of the closed doors, and she rubbed her arms. It had been months since she'd been on the third floor. Even though Fähnrich Braun had been reassigned back in November, she was still afraid of meeting another German alone.

When Adeline went down for her afternoon nap, Lisette volunteered to bring up linens to the north wing and clean the two bathrooms. An hour had passed, and Adeline had already awakened, ready for a walk outside before night fell. Gisèle would have taken her, but she was helping Émilie prepare for the evening meal.

Of all of them, Lisette was most comfortable among the Germans after working for almost two years at their headquarters. Since Lisette could translate, the major had sent Lucien on to Cherbourg, and when Gisèle pretended not to understand, Lisette translated for her. After months of serving the soldiers, Gisèle now spoke the basics with them anyway. Unlike Lisette, though, she maintained her distance as much as possible through the barrier of language.

In the past six months, Lisette and Adeline had developed a special bond, and Gisèle was glad that Adeline was well loved, though she still despaired that Adeline's idea of normal was to be living among the German soldiers. Some of the men liked to spoil her, while others instilled fear in her heart.

As the months passed, it seemed as if Adeline had forgotten about her parents. Adeline had begun to call her Maman and Lisette Tante. She was sad that the girl had to forget—and perhaps would never be told of—the parents who loved her. Her lies had become Adeline's reality.

While Gisèle avoided the Germans, Lisette seemed to find a sense of belonging with them and with Adeline. On long winter evenings, after dinner, Lisette told the men some of the chilling stories that Michel had told her, about those who had been murdered in the château during the revolution and about the ghosts who sought revenge. Gisèle cringed when Lisette told them about a tunnel underneath the castle that harbored dangerous trolls and how they came out at night to haunt the floors above them. The Germans laughed at her stories, and yet they kept coming back around the fireplace to listen to more.

Sometimes Gisèle wondered if the men were coming to hear Lisette's stories or if they were there to admire her beauty. Lisette had always been beautiful and she'd matured into a lovely woman, with her blond curls and shapely figure that was so unlike those of many of the hungry Frenchwomen who'd become shadows of themselves. The way Lisette flirted back with some of the soldiers made Gisèle's stomach roll, and she prayed Michel never found out how the woman he loved had toyed with them. They all had to lose a bit of themselves to satiate the enemy, she supposed, but she prayed that in their hearts, they all would remain true to God and to France.

She knocked on the bathroom door. "Lisette?"

There was no response.

Most of the men were patrolling in the valley and town, and she wondered for a moment if Hauptmann Milch was among them, though she had learned through Lisette that when he wasn't needed to type correspondence, Hauptmann Milch worked in the registration office in Saint-Lô, issuing identity cards and certificates. He avoided her, speaking only when it was of utmost necessity, but even with his brusqueness, he intrigued her. Sometimes she wondered if he was trapped like the French people who had no choice but to entertain the men they despised.

Then she heard laughter from across the hall. And a woman's voice.

A door opened, and someone stepped into the hall. Gisèle slipped back into the alcove to avoid the German. But an officer didn't walk out of the bedroom door. It was Lisette.

Usually they would leave fresh linens outside the doors, but perhaps Lisette had felt the need to make the beds. Yet that couldn't be right. She should never have gone into a room alone with one of the men.

A wave of nausea swept over her.

In the village, Gisèle had heard rumors of Frenchwomen consorting with the German soldiers in exchange for petty favors—lipstick and sugar and silk stockings—but she prayed not here in her house, with her friend.

Gisèle stepped into the corridor and Lisette whirled around. The winter light illuminated the smeared mascara under Lisette's eyes, and Gisèle wondered for the first time where her friend purchased mascara when there was none to be had in Saint-Lô. And where she found her seemingly endless supply of cigarettes.

"What are you doing?" Gisèle asked.

Lisette brushed her hands over her skirt. "I was cleaning the rooms."

"The men can care for their own rooms."

"Some of them need assistance." Lisette's hands flew to her throat, straightening the pink scarf crumpled around it. Gisèle should have felt sorrow for her friend, for the years lost and their dreams ravaged by war, but more than compassion, anger raged within her. Anger for Michel, who had remained faithful. Anger that Lisette hadn't remained strong.

If the Germans had forced themselves on her, like Braun tried with her in the cellar, her heart would have broken for Lisette, but her friend's laughter echoed in her ears. How could she give herself freely to these bastards? And then laugh with them?

"Michel is the one who loves you, not these men."

"This has nothing to do with love," Lisette replied, the passion stripped from her voice.

"Why didn't you tell me? I could have helped . . ."

"This is my secret, Gisèle. Just like you have secrets."

Gisèle hugged her arms close to her chest. "You give yourself away for nothing . . ."

Lisette's eyes narrowed and she pressed together her lips as if she teetered between anger and tears. "Don't act like a saint, Gisèle. It's not like you've taken a stand against them."

"I had no choice but to let them live here." She clenched her fists. "I don't sleep with them."

"If you think I want to do this—"

The door behind them opened, and the *Oberst* walked into the hall. He looked at Lisette with a mixture of appreciation and ridicule. The man had said he had a wife at home . . . and grandchildren. He looked much less distinguished with his untucked shirt and missing monocle. And when he tweaked Lisette's thigh.

"Stop it, Rolf," she hissed.

He ignored Gisèle, his gaze hovering on Lisette. "You'll be back tomorrow?"

"Of course."

Gisèle turned away from them both, disgusted at what was happening under her family's roof . . . and to the woman her brother loved.

CHAPTER 42

With Mémé's photo album in my arm, I trekked back up the drive to Madame Calvez's house. Riley had been gone for two days now, and in his absence, I scoured the recesses of the house, the closets and nooks, as I searched for information about Adeline. And I'd tromped through the forest, searching for any hint of the tunnel that Riley's grandfather remembered.

My search proved futile, but the woman I guessed could answer my questions was still alive, less than a mile from the château. She may not have wanted my company, but perhaps she would answer a few of my questions, if only so I'd stop bothering her.

After I knocked, Isabelle swung the door open, grinning at me.

"You lost a tooth," I said.

She grinned even wider.

I glanced behind her. "Where is your great-grandmother?"

She pointed down the short hall. "In her bedroom."

In the dimly lit hall was a photograph of three women. The oldest woman was Madame Calvez; her blond hair was bobbed and she wore a pale green pantsuit. The middle woman had long sandy brown hair and a smile that warmed the picture. Her arm was around a young girl who looked a lot like Isabelle. The girl wore a yellow ribbon in her hair and a matching bow on the wide collar of her neck.

I pointed at the girl. "Is this your mother?"

Isabelle nodded.

I tapped on the glass. "And this must be your grandmother."

"It was my grandmother—she and my grandfather died in a car accident before I was born."

"I'm sorry to hear that."

Isabelle grinned with pride. "My mother says I'm just like her."

"Where did your grandmother live?"

"Paris. My whole family lived in Paris until the government gave Grand-mère this house."

"Why would the French government give her a house?"

She shrugged as she opened the door to a small bedroom.

We found Madame Calvez in a recliner, a game show blaring music from the small television set at the foot of her bed. Isabelle turned down the volume and climbed up on the bed. Then she folded her hands in her lap like a young lady. It seemed like Isabelle was watching her great-grandmother more than Madame Calvez was watching her.

In spite of the warm air, a blanket rested over Madame Calvez's lap, and her short hair stood up around her ears. She attempted a smile when I sat on the edge of the bed. "I'm afraid I can't offer you any tea."

Leaning forward, I kissed both of her cheeks as Riley had done. "I'm not thirsty."

Madame Calvez closed her eyes for a moment and then reopened them. "The girl next door usually plays with Isabelle in the afternoons, but she took the flu."

"Are you ill?" I asked.

"No," she said. "Just old."

I held out the photo album. "I found some pictures in Gisèle's room."

Isabelle opened the cover and pointed to two women mounted on horseback. "Who's that?"

"This is my grandmother," I said. "And I believe that's your great-grandmother."

Madame Calvez leaned forward and squinted at the photo.

"It says, 'Nadine and I riding along the Vire.' I thought your first name might be Nadine."

"My name is Lisette," she replied, her voice sad. "That was Nadine Batier."

"I've never heard of Nadine."

Madame Calvez leaned back in her chair. "That's because your grandmother forgot about us all."

Shaking my head, I leapt to defend her. "I'm sure she didn't—"

Madame Calvez stopped me. "How is Gisèle?"

I took a deep breath, trying to calm myself. "Not well," I finally said. "Her mind is slipping away."

She started to say something else but stopped herself. Instead she asked, "Can you describe the pictures for me?"

With Isabelle helping me flip the pages, I told Madame Calvez about each of the photographs. Of Nadine and Gisèle sitting in the garden. Of my handsome great-uncle by his fancy roadster, and my grandmother and Michel posing by the front door after his first Communion. Of Michel looking every bit the aristocrat with his fancy riding clothes and horsewhip and hunting dogs.

"Michel was full of life," she said wistfully, and in that moment, I wondered if Madame Calvez had been in love with my great-uncle.

In her interview with Riley, she hadn't spoken of her husband or even of her daughter. If she had loved Michel, it must have broken her heart when he died.

"What do you remember most about Michel?" I asked.

Her gaze wandered to the blinds over her window. "It has been a long time."

I nodded. "My grandmother said he was fearless."

"But sometimes fear is a good thing. It keeps us alive." She paused. "There's more I would like to say, but to you, not the camera."

"I don't have a camera."

She blinked, nodding slowly. "At the beginning of the war, I thought your great-uncle Michel and I would marry, but I was never a patient woman. Four years is an eternity when you're young and you think the world is about to end."

"What happened?"

She stretched out her hand and took Isabelle's. "Could you find some cookies for our guest?"

Isabelle hopped off the bed. "The pink ones?"

"The pink ones would be just fine." Madame Calvez waited until Isabelle scrambled out of the room before she turned back to me. "When you feel powerless . . ."

I sat with her in the silence until she was ready to speak again.

"You must understand, the Nazis ruled and reigned over us. They had absolute power over everything except . . ." She swallowed, and I knew of what she spoke. "I sold my soul to the Nazis in exchange for power and a promise of protection. I thought I could save myself from them, but I discovered the hard way that the Nazis weren't very good at keeping their promises."

I closed the photo album. "After the war, were you still afraid of what they could do?"

"I wasn't afraid of what they would do to me, but I was afraid of what they would do to someone I loved."

"Who were you afraid of?" I asked quietly.

She glanced back toward the door, but Isabelle was still gone.

"I was afraid of your cousin—Philippe Borde."

I'd seen that same fear in my grandmother's eyes when she spoke his name.

"What did Philippe do?"

When she shook her head, I ventured one last question. "Did you know Gisèle's daughter?"

She leaned back against the chair, her energy seemingly spent. "Gisèle didn't have a daughter."

"But what about Adeline?"

"Adeline was . . ." She closed her eyes, and a few seconds later, her chin began to bob against her neck. I had already stayed too long.

Isabelle crept back in the room, carrying three pink meringue cookies on a chipped plate. When she offered me one, I took it and nibbled on the edge. Madame Calvez's eyes were closed, and I glanced over at Isabelle who watched her as well. "Did I tell you I'm a schoolteacher?"

Isabelle shook her head, and I saw just a hint of admiration.

"And my favorite place in the whole world is, of course, the playground."

Isabelle clapped. "Mine too."

I reached out and gently squeezed Madame Calvez's hand, rousing her. "Would you mind if I took Isabelle to the park?"

She mumbled her consent before she fell back to sleep.

Isabelle skipped toward the door.

~ *Chapter 43* ~

Gisèle stared at the man in the front doorframe of the château, the February snow falling down behind him and his black trench coat. His fancy black *coupé* had trailed muddied tire tracks through the white carpet of snow.

Émilie usually answered the door, but after three months of working for the Germans, she obtained a pass to bicycle to her sister's home in Cahagnes and never returned. Gisèle mourned her leaving, but Émilie had taught her well. Now it was just her and Lisette, serving the Germans in silence.

"*Bonjour*," Philippe greeted her as if no other words needed to be spoken.

He had matured since she had seen him last, his face stockier and forehead balding. He looked a decade older than his thirty-two years.

He motioned toward the entryway. "May I come in?"

The familiar fear twisted in her gut again. She couldn't explain away Adeline as a friend's child now, not with the Germans occupying her house. Perhaps Philippe's visit would be short. And Adeline would remain hidden.

"Of course," she said, but she wished she could run away, like she'd done the night of the blitzkrieg. Except now, there was no place left to run.

She hadn't talked to Philippe in more than a month, but Tante Corinne wrote that Philippe had taken an important position in the Vichy government. Doing what, she never said.

Adeline toddled up to her when they stepped into the drawing room, jingling a silver bell one of the officers had given her. Her arms outstretched, Gisèle had no choice but to pick her up.

Philippe stared down at the child. "Who is this?"

"Adeline . . ." She swallowed hard. "She is my daughter."

"Your daughter?" Fire flashed in his eyes. "How old is she?"

"Two."

He glanced at the window, and she guessed he was calculating the months in his mind. It had been two and a half years since she'd seen him last. She should have said something about Adeline, during one of their brief conversations on the telephone, so he wouldn't be shocked. But with transportation so difficult now, gasoline almost impossible for a French citizen to obtain even with the coupons, she had never guessed he would show up at her door.

"Where is Lisette?" she asked, praying she wouldn't say upstairs.

"In the kitchen."

"Why don't you go play with her for a bit?"

Adeline nodded her head before she toddled toward the kitchen.

Everything had changed that afternoon Gisèle found Lisette with the *Oberst*. Lisette continued to work at the house, helping with Adeline, and she visited the servants' quarters almost every day while Adeline napped. But Gisèle and Lisette rarely spoke.

When Philippe turned back to her, the fire in his eyes was gone, replaced with a coldness as bitter as the winter air. "Is this the reason you never came to Lyon?"

"One of them."

"You should have told me you were pregnant."

"I knew you'd be angry."

His fist pressed into the back of a chaise longue. "Who is the father?"

"A man from the village. You don't know—"

His eyes blazed again. "What is his name?"

"It doesn't matter anymore."

He unbuttoned his trench coat and took it off. "I will find out."

Gisèle didn't know where Jean-Marc Rausch was, but she hoped he was far, far away. She stared at the coat on the chair. Was there another reason Philippe was here?

"I've heard you've been entertaining soldiers," he said.

"I have housed them, Philippe. Not entertained."

"Does your *amour* know?"

Irritation flamed within her. "He is my husband."

"Your husband?" His laugh crackled with sarcasm. "Of course, you must have been married to have a child."

She stepped back toward the main hall. "It's time for you to leave."

He didn't move. "You may tell people you were married, but I know the truth." He straightened the porcelain urn on the sideboard. "Where is this husband now?"

"I don't know. He was a soldier . . ."

He turned back toward her. "I don't believe you."

"You don't have to." She crossed her arms. "Why are you here?"

"I came to discuss our marriage, but I see it's no longer possible for us to marry."

Even if she wasn't pretending to be married, the thought of marrying Philippe repulsed her. Whether or not she had a child, the idea would be revolting to him too when he realized she had been slaving in the kitchen to serve the German officers. In his mind, serving the soldiers was probably as bad as sleeping with them.

The Germans may have occupied her country, her village, but until she decided otherwise, neither Philippe nor anyone else would occupy her heart.

Major von Kluge stepped into the room, and when he saw Philippe, he lifted his palm. "*Heil* Hitler."

When her cousin returned the greeting, she cringed. Then he introduced himself. "I am Philippe Borde. Gisèle's cousin from Lyon."

Something passed between the two men, an odd look of understanding. Did the Germans already know she had a cousin living in southern France?

The major directed him toward the office. "May I have a word with you in private, Monsieur Borde?"

"Of course."

As they walked away, she heard the major say, "Your château has been most accommodating for us."

His château? The château wasn't his—

But then a terrible thought came over her. If Michel didn't return—and she disappeared as well—the château and all the Duchant property would become Philippe's. She shivered. Philippe wasn't here to check on her—at least not in a caring sort of way. He was here, she feared, to see what could be done about securing this property for himself. He knew she hadn't been married when they fled from the château that June. What if he found out that her marriage certificate read May 1940? He could have her deported for her deception.

Would her own cousin send her to a work camp? She didn't know to what extent he would go to get rid of her, and it seemed they were sending away the French people without any sort of justice. The yellow stars in Saint-Lô had been extinguished and others had disappeared as well—those who refused to hail the god Hitler. She often wondered about the children at the orphanage and the little boy who'd refused to give his name, wondered if they had been taken too. And she wondered about André and Nadine, and Nadine's parents, and her old friend Odette.

When Lisette brought Adeline back to her, Lisette nodded toward the office. "Who is here?"

"Philippe Borde."

Lisette backed away from her. "I must go."

Gisèle picked Adeline up, and the girl patted Gisèle's hair. "Sad, Maman?"

She kissed her cheek. "There is no reason to be sad when I'm with you."

Adeline looked back at the office door, and when she stuck out her tongue, Gisèle rushed her away from the hall. "It's time for your nap."

As Adeline rested in her small bed, Gisèle sang softly like her mother had done for her years ago. When Adeline fell asleep, she stepped back into the hallway and peered down into the courtyard as Philippe drove away.

Was he here on government business as well as to inquire about the property?

Gisèle was no longer the girl who had run with Philippe during the bombing. The château was her father's home. Her brother's refuge. Her family's legacy.

One day good would defeat the evil in their midst. She didn't know when, but she clung to that hope. Philippe might expose her, but she had no regrets for what she had done.

It was too late for her to go back on her story about the marriage and there was no place for her to run. She didn't know how much longer she could hold together the pieces before everything unraveled, but like her brother, she would continue to fight. Resist.

Even when she was afraid.

CHAPTER 44

The quaint chapel had been beckoning me for days. The place where my parents and I had prayed with Mémé so long ago.

Out my bedroom window, I watched as strangers strolled down the long path from Agneaux every morning and slipped through the door. Marguerite said she unlocked the door so villagers could pray and tourists could explore the medieval treasure.

This afternoon I dressed in jeans and a T-shirt, the color of fire, before strolling across the courtyard like the locals. I wasn't alone. Madame Calvez didn't want to see me again, but Isabelle's friend was still sick, so for the fifth day in a row, Isabelle and I spent the afternoon playing at the same park where Riley had lain back in the grass and told me how God rocked his world. The quiet time, the laughter, had soothed my heart.

Isabelle made me smile, and she made me forget for a few hours all that had transpired back in Virginia. It had only been two weeks since my mom called and asked me to come to France, but it felt like a million years ago. I never could have imagined that I would be exploring the corridors of our family's château, visiting the parks with a ten-year-old, and beginning to dream about a future without Austin.

Oddly enough, I was content.

It wouldn't be long before I had to face my reality and get back on an airplane, but what I would do in Virginia now, I had no idea. There was enough money in my savings account to cushion the blow of unemployment, and my parents would let me tap into my trust fund if I drained my bank account, but I wanted to support myself. It was the Duchant in me, I supposed.

The breeze rustled the trees as Isabelle and I walked along the drive. Dozens of messages had flown back and forth between Riley and me this week. The château seemed empty without him here. Even though my own faith had been shaken, I took shelter in his and Mémé's and my parents' faith.

Tombstones were clustered together in a small yard outside the chapel. We found the graves for Vicomte and Vicomtesse Duchant—my great-grandparents—and placed wildflowers Isabelle and I had picked on top of each of them. Michel rested beside them, and I had the faintest memory of Mémé and me putting flowers on these graves before I'd left her alone to her tears.

She'd said something odd to me as we stood in front of the chapel so long ago. Something about secrets. A secret that shielded their family.

Dad thought childhood memories shouldn't be trusted, but something about this memory pricked my mind, like the thorn that had stung my finger.

I read the epitaphs on the twenty or so stones, wondering if the girl Mémé remembered might have been buried with the rest of the Duchant family, but there was no Adeline.

I pushed open the wooden door to the chapel, and Isabelle scooted around me to get inside. We were the only ones there, but the smells from time past permeated the old wood—wilted flowers and incense and dirt from the fields. The stone floor was worn

smooth from years of shoes scouring it, and near the altar was a picture that captured my attention. It was a pencil drawing of a man
with wings—there was a sword in one hand and the head of a
dragon in the other. I suspected he was an angel, but he looked like
a warrior. A sculpture of Christ's body hung on the wall, his head
missing. An old gate stood open at the side.

She tugged on my hand, toward the pew. "Let's pray."

Isabelle knelt like an old pro.

Until my grandmother became bedridden, she'd attended
Mass every Sunday and often during the week as well. I remembered going with her to a chapel in the months after Grandpa died.
The chapel overlooked the Potomac River and I would stare down
at the water. Tears had streamed down her powdered cheeks as she
prayed in French, and I determined then—as a thirteen-year-
old—to master the language my grandmother loved.

Isabelle folded her hands in front of her, and I did the same,
though I wasn't certain what to say. Ever since I'd begun attend-
ing church with Austin, my faith had become sterile. Riley had
been so passionate about his faith, but I felt like I had lost my passion for just about everything.

I wanted it back. My passion to love kids and see the world.
My desire to talk to God and not run the other way. To love again
and not hide. To revel in the honesty of being able to share my
story.

Isabelle prayed quietly beside me in French, and I prayed as
well, that God would reveal Himself to me as He did with Riley.
That He would show me what to do next.

When she finished praying, Isabelle crossed herself, and I followed suit. I didn't want to leave though. The château was full of
mystery, but the chapel was different. Instead of questions, there
was peace here. Answers, perhaps.

We lingered at the foot of the cross, and I knew . . .

I was at a crossroads like Riley had been. No matter what happened when I returned to the States, no matter if I never married or had children, I would have to trust God. Only He could fill those empty places left in my soul.

My peace was disturbed by the sound of gravel crunching outside. I didn't want to move, but Isabelle took my hand and urged me toward the open door.

I expected to see Pierre or Marguerite in their station wagon, or a delivery truck, but instead a black Mercedes crawled like a spider across the courtyard, searching for prey.

The door opened, and when the car's driver stepped onto the gravel, I cringed.

Austin Vale had stepped back into my world.

PART THREE

*To love another person is
to see the face of God.*

—VICTOR HUGO

LES MISÉRABLES

Chapter 45

May 1944

Below the château a torrent of flames fractured dusk's fading light. Gisèle swallowed her gasp and almost dropped the bowl of mashed potatoes onto the lap of the officer in front of her. The row of paned windows in the dining hall framed the blaze, but the men were all focused on their discussion and their plates instead of on the fire raging on the hillside across from them.

The Allies were pushing hard into France, their planes becoming more daring the past few weeks as they flew farther inland with their bombs.

Had a German plane crashed near the river? Or was it a Royal Air Force plane?

The Allies, Oberst Seidel said, knew Château d'Epines was a Nazi headquarters, and he feared they would target the house. She'd heard the planes overhead at night, but the rattling of the engines didn't bring her fear. Instead they inspired her with hope. Michel had said they must do anything they could to help the Allies win this war. "Hitler has mandated that we increase the deportation of Jews," the major told his men.

"I thought the French police already sent all the Jews in Saint-Lô to work camps," Hauptmann Milch said.

"He is convinced there are more hiding here."

Gisèle would have been alarmed at their discussion had her attention not been solely focused on the fire.

As the men talked about Hitler's new mandate, she switched on the electric lights and then stepped carefully toward the windows, taking care not to gawk at the glow. The Germans in her home may not have seen the crash yet, but someone in Saint-Lô must have.

Still, if it was an Allied plane, she might be able to help the crew buy a little time.

Instead of waiting until after dinner to pull the blackout curtain across the rod, she closed them. None of the Germans even glanced up from their meal.

She stole away from the table, down into the kitchen. Adeline was asleep in the playpen, and Lisette was washing pans.

"I must run an errand," Gisèle said. "But I'll be back within the hour."

Lisette dried her hands on a towel. "It's past curfew."

"If they ask, tell them I went to lock up the *chapelle*."

"You never lock up before the nineteen hundred hour." Lisette tossed the towel onto the counter. "They will ask questions."

She couldn't wait for another hour to go out. "Then tell them I'm unwell and have to rest in my room."

"But—" Lisette began to protest, but Gisèle was already out the door. If the crew had survived, there was no time to spare.

While the men were still eating, she retrieved a flashlight and locked her bedroom door before rushing outside and down the smoky path. The flames had subsided, and on the other side of the river, her flashlight beam rested on the blackened shell of the downed plane. At the edge of the river was a broken wing, but instead of a hooked cross painted on it, there was a star.

Her heart pounding, she clicked off her light. There was no time to waste. If the Germans hadn't seen the blaze, someone from town would surely report it to them soon.

"Is anyone there?" she shouted in English. Her mother's language.

When no one answered, she tiptoed forward until she reached the footbridge. There was no use crossing the bridge to search inside the plane—no one could have survived the impact of those flames. If they didn't parachute out, the crew would have perished.

In the moonlight she scanned the valley and hillside for any movement. If there were survivors, they would need a place to hide right away or the Germans would find them. Would they send the airmen to work camps like they did the Jews or would they execute them like they had her father and the men in the forest?

She stepped into the ribbon of trees by the river, calling out one last time. "I can take you to a safe place, but if you don't come with me now, it will be too late."

Seconds crept by, and still no one answered. Disappointed, she turned back toward the path. She'd been hoping she could help the Allies and selfishly, she had been hoping for some news of their fight. If the men weren't here, she prayed the crew had bailed out in a safe place where people would care well for them.

She had to hurry back to the house now. The Germans might not search for her in her room, but if they found her down here, they would know with certainty that she was collaborating with their enemy.

"Psstt . . ."

The whisper came from behind a hawthorn, and her heart plunged to her toes. She turned on her light, scanning the branches. "Who's there?"

A tall man limped onto the path, his forehead bloodied. Balled up in his arms was a parachute. "How do you know English?" he asked.

She swallowed. "I only know a little. My mother was from England."

He stuck out one of his hands. "My name's Eddie. From the US of A."

She studied his face in the light, the thin mustache over his lips and the bloody gash over his right eye, before extending her hand. He gave it a hearty shake.

She pulled her hand back to her side. "You have a nasty gash on your forehead."

"I'm in much better shape than *Deborah D.*"

She examined the grassy path behind him. "Where is Deborah?"

"Over there." He pointed toward the river, at the smoke still pouring from the plane. "We've flown eighteen missions together."

She wasn't sure how one was supposed to mourn the loss of an aeroplane.

A dog barked in the distance, and she shivered. "We must hurry."

"Are the Krauts near?"

She turned off the flashlight. "There are almost twenty of them. Staying on top of this hill."

He whistled.

"Stop!" she said, and her command silenced him. "Only Americans whistle like that."

He stepped back toward the trees. "My navigator injured his arm when he landed."

"Where are the rest of your men?"

He shook his head. "I don't know."

The dog barked again, closer now. Whether or not the animal was searching for them, in minutes a host of Germans— and perhaps some of her fellow French citizens—would clamor near the river to hunt for survivors. With their lanterns and flashlights, rifles and dogs, the Americans wouldn't have a chance.

Somehow she had to find a way to get them up the cliff, and then while the Germans were searching by the river, perhaps she could sneak them into the *chapelle*. She'd heard the rumors about loud Americans, but as she followed Eddie into the hawthorns and apple trees, she prayed these men knew how to be quiet as well.

A second American, a young man named Daniel, sat on a log close to the river, cradling his arm.

"Did you break it?" she asked.

He forced a smile. "Technically, a tree broke it."

Just what she needed, a smart aleck. If these men didn't take the Germans seriously now, they would soon. "We must hide your parachutes first and then I'll take you to a safe place for the night."

Not far was a wide crevice cutting through the cliff. She and Eddie stuffed the chutes into the gap and then camouflaged it with leaves and branches.

"The Germans will search all night for you," she told both men.

"Where will we hide?" Daniel asked.

She motioned him forward. "You must come with me."

The navigator hesitated.

"If you don't, they will kill you."

Daniel stood and collected his backpack, ready to follow her, and the responsibility weighed heavily on her. These Americans had decided to trust her with their lives.

If they could cross over the path before the Germans arrived, she could take the airmen west along the river, crossing under the shadow of the château before they snuck back up the forest on the other side of the house and into the *chapelle*.

But when they stepped forward, she saw a flare of lights through the smoky air, descending down the hill toward them like a swarm of bees. And then she heard Major von Kluge shouting orders.

There would be no going through the *chapelle* tonight. They had to run as fast as they could in the opposite direction.

"Hurry," she commanded.

When they heard boots hammering down the hill, Eddie and Daniel collected their backpacks and this time, they followed her quickly through the forest. She didn't know if Major von Kluge knew about this narrow path, set back from the river, but she guessed it wouldn't take his men long to find it.

Eddie lagged behind them for a few minutes, as if he needed to pay a final tribute to his plane. Then he caught up again as they hurried through the trees.

Before they moved right at the river's bend, toward the Batiers' house, she crept to the edge of the forest and scanned the bottom of the valley to her left. A pool of lights collected on the valley floor. It wouldn't be long before the Germans spread out to comb every inch of the forest and cliffs.

Would any of them wonder why she hadn't returned from the *chapelle*? Hopefully they would be too distracted by the aeroplane . . .

Still, she needed to hurry home.

It was too late to take the airmen to the locked door at the *chapelle*. For a moment, she considered trying to hide them in the Batiers' home, but the gendarmes knew about the house in the forest and if they didn't already, the Germans would find it soon. They would search all the vacant homes and the occupied ones as well until they found the crew.

There was one other place nearby that she could hide the Americans.

She prayed the cross around her neck would open the door.

CHAPTER 46

Isabelle didn't stick around for the showdown. Right after Austin stepped out of the Mercedes—and informed her that he was my fiancé—she asked if she could return home. I'd kissed her on both cheeks and sent her on her way.

If the Plaza had never happened, I'd have been flattered by his resolve to fly across the ocean to see me, like I'd felt the night he literally swept me off my feet and proposed. This time his determination wasn't romantic. It was maddening.

Now he paced in front of the château. His button-down shirt was slightly wrinkled, but he held the composure of an attorney who usually got his way. I couldn't physically remove him from the château's property—and I had a suspicion that as long as Austin wasn't threatening to hurt me, the local police wouldn't want to get involved with two Americans disputing over whether or not they remained engaged.

He leaned back and glanced up at my family's château again. "It looks like a castle."

"It is a castle!"

His gaze remained locked on the building. "How much do you think it's worth?"

I put my hands on my hips. "You flew all the way to France to ask how much the château is worth?"

"No—I came to apologize," he said, turning back to focus on me. "I still want to marry you."

"You *still* want to . . ." I said, appalled at his audacity, as if he was willing to humble himself. "I told Olivia the wedding is off."

He shook his head. "It's only been postponed."

"Austin—" I crossed my arms and asked the question I should have asked a long time ago. "Why do you want to marry me?"

He paused, his handsome eyes squinting as he seemed to search for an answer. "I need you."

"That's a lousy reason, Austin."

He seemed shocked at my retort.

"Let me help," I said. "You want me to marry you because you think I can somehow help you win this election."

"It's not just about me, Chloe. It's about us. We make a good team, a team that will last far past this election."

He was asking me to play on his team? He might have thought he was being winsome, but the blinders had been ripped from my eyes. He didn't love me. He loved the idea of having a team-mate—and a cheerleader who knew when to look the other way.

I cleared my throat. "Have you broken off things with Starla?"

He leaned back against the wall. "I will be a good husband to you, Chloe."

"Not if you're sleeping with other women."

"I will end it with her."

I thought of Isabelle, jumping from stone to stone in the park, giggling as she raced down the metal slide. What if I hadn't found out about Austin's affair? We could have been having this conversation six or seven years from now, after we had a child of our own. His infidelity would have shattered our family.

"But for how long will you end it?" I asked.

His eyes hardened for a moment and then he met my gaze again, his smile creeping back. "I won't be like my father, Chloe. Once we're married, I will be faithful to you."

I wanted to believe him, I really did, but it was impossible. Even if I forgave Austin and became his wife, his betrayal would cast a shadow over our entire marriage.

When I married, I wanted to love my husband with all my heart, knowing he would be faithful. It shouldn't have mattered—didn't matter—if my husband was the governor of Virginia. President of the United States, for that matter. I wanted to treasure the man I married, along with our children.

"I can't marry you, Austin." Why was it so hard for me to say it? "I thought I loved you, but I've discovered I don't—not as a wife should love her husband."

He didn't seem fazed by my words. "It doesn't matter, Chloe. Love is such an ambiguous word."

"But it matters to me. I want to love well in my life. I want my husband to love me." I paused. "Why didn't you ask Starla to marry you?"

"She's not from Virginia, nor is she—" He stopped. "I wanted to marry you."

"That time in the coffee shop, when you spilled my latte." I swallowed. "It wasn't really an accident, was it?"

At least he had the decency to look down at his shoes.

He should have been ashamed.

"You'd already researched me."

"Chloe—"

"You needed a wife to run for governor, and on paper you thought I would make a decent addition to your little team," I said slowly. "So you staged our meeting."

"Olivia thought you would be good for the campaign, but once I met you—"

"It was all smoke and mirrors."

My phone vibrated in my pocket and I pulled it out. There was a text from Riley.

Headed back to Saint-Lô.

When I smiled, Austin glanced at my phone. "Who is it?"

I looked up at him, the strength surfacing again. "It's time for you to leave."

Instead of getting into the car, he stepped toward the château. "I'm not leaving France without you."

. . .

Riley strutted into the formal salon an hour later, his grandfather's bomber jacket slung over his shoulder and his Moleskine journal clutched in his hand. I probably should have warned him about Austin's arrival, but I was afraid if he knew Austin had dropped in, he might bypass Saint-Lô for the airport.

The smile on Riley's face faded when he saw the man in the formal high-back chair sitting across from me.

Austin leapt up as if he was about to tackle Riley. "Who are you?"

Recognition flickered in Riley's eyes. "I'm Riley Holtz."

"Ah, the filmmaker." And with that, Austin dismissed him.

Riley tossed his jacket over the back of the couch. "And what is your name?"

He sat back in the chair. "I'm Austin Vale," he said as if he was Prince William and Riley was the pizza delivery guy waiting for a tip. Then he pointed at me. "Chloe's fiancé."

I shook my head. "We are no longer engaged, Austin."

Riley glanced at me again, and I could see the concern in his eyes. "I was expecting a package from my parents. I thought it might have arrived—"

Austin stepped up to Riley. "If you would excuse us, we were in the midst of a discussion."

Discussion wasn't quite accurate. It was more like a congressman filibustering a vote. The familiar pounding had returned to my head, and I pressed my fingers against it. Oddly enough, my head hadn't hurt after I ended the relationship with Austin, only when he showed up in France and refused to leave without me.

Clearly Austin Vale had no regard for people telling him no.

"Chloe . . ." Riley motioned toward the hallway, his eyes vacillating between worry and angst. "Could I speak with you for a moment?"

Even though he no longer had any say as to where I went or with whom, Austin still swore under his breath when I agreed. Without a glimpse back, I slipped down into the kitchen.

Riley sat on the counter. "I thought you broke up with him."

"I did." I paced the floor in front of the fireplace. "He showed up here and somehow thought he could convince me that we should still marry."

He searched my face. "Do you still want to marry him?"

"Of course not," I said, but the concern in Riley's eyes had turned into doubt. He didn't believe me. "I'm still processing . . ."

Riley rubbed his hands together. "Will Austin love you for who you are or is his love dependent on what you will do for him?"

"It's dependent on what I do for him."

"So really Austin loves himself." Riley hopped back down

from the counter. "You have to decide with certainty what you want for your future."

"I've already decided."

"Then why is Austin still here?" His dark green eyes seemed to sink into mine, and my skin flushed. In that moment, I wasn't thinking at all about the man waiting for me upstairs.

Questions knotted together in the pit of my stomach, and strength began to fill me again. Wonder at the man in front of me. I reached for Riley's hands, like he'd done with me at the park. But this time he jumped away from me. As if I'd burned him.

I pulled back my hands, crossing them under my arms. Tears began to pool in my eyes, and I squeezed them shut, willing my emotions to flatline.

I wanted—I didn't know what I wanted except . . .

Right now, I wanted to be alone.

Riley leaned back against the counter. Quiet.

"I'm sorry . . . ," I finally said.

He shook his head. "You didn't do anything wrong."

I stepped toward the door. "I'm going to tell him to leave."

The tears were gone as I stood in front of Austin and told him once and for all that our relationship was over. There would be no wedding—not even a postponed one. And this time Austin believed me. Before I finished talking, he rushed out of the château and climbed into his car.

I stood in the dust, and for the first time since I'd left New York, I was grateful. Grateful that he'd cheated on me. Grateful that I'd been able to tell him how I felt. Grateful that he was gone from the château.

But I wasn't sure what to do about the man still left inside.

Chapter 47

The starlight made the tree limbs look like spindly gray webs painted on a black canvas. The village of beehives was silent for the night, but twigs and dried leaves crackled under the feet of the airmen. Each time the forest broadcast their presence, the Americans stopped and listened.

The hawthorns became denser along the path, and Gisèle urged them along quickly, her own heart beating at a rapid pace as she whispered prayers to her mother, begging her to petition God for guidance. She hadn't been back to the cellar since she'd found Adeline.

Eddie stopped in front of a beehive. "Where are we?"

"Near a friend's house," she whispered back.

"But—"

"You must trust me, but I must trust you as well. You can tell no one of this place."

A dog barked in the direction of town, and both men readily agreed.

Glowworms sprinkled green light in the grass, and she heard one of the men whisper, "They look like fireflies."

She hushed him and listened again for the sound of German voices, the pulse of foreign footsteps nearby. All she heard was the rustle of leaves in the wind and the steady flow of the Vire.

The root cellar had to be close, somewhere among these hives. If only she could shine her flashlight into the trees, but with the houses in town shrouded in blackout curtains, it would be a beacon to the enemy and to the Allies alike.

So she stumbled forward in the darkness, feigning confidence in what she could not see, trusting her heavenly Father to guide her. She didn't dare tell the Americans her fears. If she couldn't find it, they would all be taken away.

There were no markings to guide her, but the moonlight glazed a silver sheen along the path. The next time she pushed back a spray of branches, she saw a rock pile in front of them.

Relief escaped her lips in a long sigh and she reached for the rope handle of the stone room, tugging the door open. It was brilliant of her ancestors to put this entrance in a cellar, hidden among the beehives. The people of Saint-Lô had probably avoided this place for centuries, and foreigners would certainly avoid the hives.

The room reeked of moldy potatoes and animal droppings, but she was more concerned by the rustling of tiny feet, shuffling into the corners.

Moving aside a stack of empty baskets, she found exactly what she'd hoped for—a small door set into the floor. She tugged on it, in case Michel had left it unlocked, but it didn't budge. As she removed the rosary from her neck, she prayed that the same key that opened the *chapelle* and the iron gate and the closet in the sacristy would open this lock as well.

She turned it slowly, unlocking the hatch, and when she lifted the door, Eddie whistled.

"Hush," she commanded again.

This time he responded with a low rumble of a laugh. "I'll apologize later."

She flipped on her flashlight and urged them quickly down the ladder, into the cavern. Along the tunnel, they stepped over pans and newspapers and passed by small rooms cluttered with bedrolls and clothing, the crevices where her ancestors and some of the townspeople hid during the French Revolution.

The next time Eddie whistled, she didn't scold him. "Who lives down here?" he asked.

"Members of the French Resistance."

"We've heard rumors about them . . ."

She stepped over another stack of papers. "I don't know that word. *Rumors.*"

"It means 'stories.'"

"Ah," she replied. "*Rumeurs.*"

He shrugged.

"The *rumeurs* are probably true."

The stench of rotting food and urine drifted through the tunnel, and her anger flared. How could her brother and the other men live like this? It was atrocious that the gentlemen of France were forced to huddle down here in this stench like rodents. Trolls. Even as they fought for France, they were refugees in their own country. The Germans were making animals out of them all.

"How is your arm?" she asked of the man trailing behind them.

"Tolerable."

"My brother will know how to help you."

Daniel tripped, and Eddie caught him. "Is your brother down here?"

"He travels much, but he is in charge of the men who stay here."

There was pride in her voice, and she realized it was the first time she'd been able to tell someone about Michel's work. He could have hidden away in England with their grandparents, ignored the plight of his country to protect himself. For almost four years the Nazis had tried to stop him, yet he chose to continue the fight for France and for the people being persecuted in their country. So many had given up, resigned themselves to their occupants' presence, but he never quit. These Americans were fighting hard in the skies for her country, and she was immensely proud of the work her brother was doing on the ground as well.

"Perhaps your brother can help us get home," Eddie said.

"Perhaps . . ." She slowed her walk. "How long will the Allies fight?"

"Until Hitler is gone," Eddie said.

His words brought her peace. "Sometimes it feels as if the Germans will never leave."

"There are thousands upon thousands of soldiers across the Channel, waiting to fight," Eddie said. "It won't be long before the rest of our men will join your brother in fighting on French soil."

Every day she woke up afraid the Germans would find out she'd never married, that Philippe would return again and take Adeline from her, that they would uncover her brother's hiding place.

She was tired of living in fear.

The stench of human waste grew stronger, along with a cloud of cigarette smoke that hovered in the narrow tunnel, but they pressed on until the dull light in front of her merged with the edge of her beam.

"Wait here," she commanded before tiptoeing forward.

She peeked into the large room where she'd found the cigarette butts and bedding before. This time, the room was packed with men, about thirty of them, leaning against the walls or huddling around the lanterns on the floor, reading newspapers or quietly playing cards. Most of them were terribly thin, with clothes more like strands of thread dangling from their skin.

Where had they all come from? Her pittance of food wouldn't have done much to feed this many men, but it had been something to support them, to show she was resisting instead of just strengthening their enemy.

When she stepped into the room, the men quieted and they all turned to stare at her.

Michel elbowed his way through them. "Gigi, I—"

She stopped him before he began to lecture her again about coming into the tunnel. "The Nazis shot down an American plane in the valley."

His mouth dropped open before he spoke. "Were there any survivors?"

She nodded slowly. "At least two of them."

He stepped forward, his eyes wide. "Where are they?"

She cleared her throat. "In the tunnel, behind me."

In the dim light, she watched his gaze falter between frustration and curiosity and perhaps even hope. "You weren't supposed to tell anyone about this place," he said, but there was no threat in his tone, as if he was speaking out for the sake of the men waiting behind him.

"I had to hide them, Michel." She glanced at the faces of the men. "And it seems like half of Saint-Lô already knows about your tunnel."

He swept his arm out beside him. "I trust my life to any of these men."

"And you told me to trust the Americans as well."

Michel buttoned the top button on his shirt. "We were just preparing to leave for the night."

She shivered. What were they planning?

"Perhaps they can rest here until you return." She hesitated. "One man has injured his arm."

When Michel stepped into the corridor, most of the men continued whispering or playing their card games. Except one man. His gaze rested on her face, and even though his face was smudged with dirt like the others, his jawline shaded with whiskers, this man smiled at her.

When he stepped forward, her stomach somersaulted. "Do you remember me?" he asked.

She was almost afraid to speak with him but forced herself to answer. "I believe I do."

"I'm Jean-Marc," he said. "We went to primary school together."

"Rausch." She wrapped her arms across her chest. "Your name is Jean-Marc Rausch."

He smiled again, as if he were pleased that she remembered him. She was pleased as well—that he was safe, hidden in the tunnel, and that the Germans, or Philippe, couldn't interrogate him down here.

She rubbed her arms. "A lot has happened since primary school."

"What has happened to you?" he asked.

She almost told him what she had done, how she had taken his name as her own, but Michel stepped into the room, the two airmen behind him. "Daniel's arm is broken, but our doctor can set it," he said to her before he turned back to the airmen. "If we can find someone to make you *papiers d'identité*, I have a friend who can escort you down to Spain and arrange your transport back to Great Britain."

"We will need photographs to make identity papers," Gisèle said.

"We have pictures." Eddie opened his backpack. "In our emergency kits."

Gisèle took the photographs from him and Daniel. "Then I'll try and obtain papers for both of you."

Eddie hugged her and Daniel carefully shook her hand. She might never see them again, yet they were all fighting together.

Michel escorted her toward the ledge. "Where will you get the papers?" he asked.

"I have a friend . . ."

"Be careful, Gigi."

She nodded. "Are you afraid?"

In the dim light, she saw compassion in his eyes. "Of course."

"Yet you continue to fight . . ."

"Courage doesn't mean you stop being afraid." He kissed her cheeks. "It means you continue to fight, even when you're terrified."

All these years, she'd thought her brother wasn't afraid of anything.

As she climbed the steps to the *chapelle*, she tucked the men's photographs into her brassiere and brushed the leaves out of her hair, the dust off her skirt. No matter how worn she was, no matter how afraid, she would continue to fight.

"Madame Rausch!" the patrolman called out as she moved through the cemetery. "It is not safe for you to be out tonight."

Taking a deep breath, she turned to face him. "It is not safe to pray?"

He shook his head.

As he escorted her back to the château, he didn't seem to notice the smell of damp moss or perspiration on her clothes. Nor did he notice the trembling in her hands or the prayers that slipped from her lips.

It might not have been safe to pray, even in the darkness, but on nights like this, she needed to pray even more. For courage for herself, in spite of her fears. For Eddie and his navigator. For Jean-Marc and Michel. For André and Nadine. And for all those aboveground with her trying to keep the earth from cracking wide open and swallowing the people they loved.

CHAPTER 48

Riley and I trekked down the hill beside the château, to the path along the Vire, so he could record footage of the river and the valley beyond it. My headache was already gone, replaced instead with an odd giddiness, as intoxicating as the nectar-laced honeybees that danced around the hawthorn blossoms.

Riley didn't say anything else about Austin or mention our awkward exchange in the kitchen, but after he filmed the valley, he began to ramble on about a man he'd interviewed named Benjamin Tendler, a part-Jewish officer who had served in the Wehrmacht.

"Mr. Tendler knew the last name of the man who helped my grandfather with his papers. He said it was another German Jew in the Wehrmacht, a man named Josef Milch. Apparently, Milch falsified what was called an *Abnenpass* for Mr. Tendler to prove his Aryan lineage. With this document, he could stay in the military."

"I still don't understand why a Jewish man would stay in the German military,"

Riley returned his camera to his backpack. "The rest of Mr. Tendler's family was killed at Auschwitz."

"So he hid behind a German uniform?"

"How can you judge him, Chloe?" A look akin to torment flashed through Riley's eyes. "How can any of us judge?"

I instantly backed down, and we began walking again toward the town. How could I judge a man's decision to choose life over certain death, even if it meant he had to compromise what he valued? I'd hidden many times, even when the reasons for hiding weren't life-and-death.

"You're right," I said. "I can't judge him or Mr. Milch."

"Mr. Tendler said he had a picture of him and Josef someplace. He's going to try to email it to me."

"If your grandfather met Josef Milch here, perhaps my grandmother knew him as well."

Riley stopped and looked at me. "Mr. Tendler was in Saint-Lô the weeks after D-Day. He said he saw Josef here, sneaking through the night with a group of children."

"Where were the children from?" I asked.

"There was a Catholic orphanage outside of the city that had taken in Jewish children after their parents were sent to concentration camps. The Nazis raided it in the days before the Americans liberated Saint-Lô, but the children were gone."

"I wonder what happened to them."

"Mr. Tendler didn't know, but I want to get some footage of the place," he said. "I'm hoping Madame Calvez can tell us where the orphanage is."

"I'd like to go with you."

He nodded.

"Can I ask you a personal question?" he asked as we neared Madame Calvez's home.

I laughed. He'd never bothered in the past to obtain permission before asking after my personal life. "Why not?" I said. My pride had already been wrecked.

"It seems to me——" He sounded a bit nervous. "Well, what did you see in a guy like Austin?"

Instead of hiding behind my polished shield, I decided to be gut-wrenchingly real with him. "Everyone wanted Austin." I took a deep breath. "But Austin——I thought he wanted to be with me."

And with those words, I realized that Austin was not the only selfish one in the relationship. Austin wanted to marry me for what he thought I could offer him, but I too wanted to marry Austin for what he could give me. Somehow I'd mixed up my worth with Austin's love.

He turned to me. "You are valuable, Chloe. Without him."

I kept walking, no longer wanting to talk about me. "Did you leave behind a girlfriend in New York?"

He was silent for a moment. "It's been a long time since I had a serious relationship."

"Not enough women in New York for you?" I quipped, the online pictures of him looping through my mind again. He was certainly handsome enough, and confident enough, to get mobbed by a horde of single women.

"I have no desire to be in a relationship for the sake of being in one," he said. "I've made mistakes in the past, terrible ones. The next time I date a woman, I hope it's for keeps."

For some reason I blushed. Perhaps it was the intensity in his words. Or because I was still trying to figure out my upside-down emotions in the kitchen.

"One day, a man is going to try to earn your trust again, Chloe," he said. "But the only one who won't fail you is God."

A verse flooded back to me, one that Mémé used to quote for me.

Trust in the Lord with all your heart, and do not rely on your own insight. In all your ways acknowledge Him, and He will make straight your paths.

Maybe I did need to learn to trust Him completely before I trusted another man.

When Riley stopped again to film along the path, I heard laughter in the trees. Hiking a bit farther down the path, I saw Madame Calvez's house. And then I saw Isabelle on the swing, her long hair flapping in the wind as the swing pitched her toward the sky.

"Mademoiselle!" Isabelle shouted, and then switched to her English at the peak of her swing. "Miss Chloe."

I waved.

Her arms were flapping as she leaned forward and swung back toward me. "I'm flying."

She flew past me, pumping up toward the sky.

"Is that man gone?"

I shouted up to her. "Which one?"

"The mean one," she hollered as she swung past me again.

"He is."

Her swing slowed. "I didn't like him one bit."

I smiled. "I'm not particularly fond of him either."

"He said you were supposed to marry him."

"I've changed my mind."

"Good," she said. "I think you should marry Monsieur Holtz instead."

"I—"

Riley cleared his throat, and I wished I could fly with Isabelle. Far, far away.

When Isabelle saw him, she hopped off her swing and raced toward him. Kissed him on both of his cheeks. He looked as if he wanted to fly away as well.

"I will go find Grand-mère," she said, skipping toward the back door.

Riley and I stood there in an uncomfortable silence. It was strange how one minute of time—one awkward comment—put us both back on edge. I couldn't erase that moment, so I decided to make light of it. "For some odd reason, Isabelle likes you."

His smile hung crooked with his shrug. "I suppose I am irresistible."

I rolled my eyes. "Really, I think you're just plain irritating."

He laughed, and it felt so good to laugh with him.

We sat down on the patio again. "I'll wait here," I said. "Madame Calvez won't tell you anything if I go inside."

The back door slid open, and Isabelle hurried outside. Her brown eyes creased with worry, her smile erased.

I jumped up from my seat. "What is it?"

Her voice shook. "Something is wrong with Grand-mère."

Riley and I rushed inside.

Chapter 49

*A*deline squealed when she dipped her toes into the cool lake water, and then she began twirling, both hands overhead. Gisèle spread her khaki blanket across the grassy shore and then lay down, closing her eyes as she listened to Adeline splashing in front of her and the gentle rustle of leaves overhead.

This had been her favorite spot to play in as a child, but she hadn't returned since—

She opened her eyes and looked up at the spring buds bursting from the branches, at the afternoon light that gently filtered through them and danced among the pods of green. In the past four years, she'd tried to forget that terrible night when she and Michel had found her father's body, wanting instead to remember her father when he was alive. But on days like this, her heart still ached.

Adeline splashed water toward her, and Gisèle smiled. When she was younger, she and Michel and Nadine used to jump from the dock and hold their breath under the water for as long as they could, competing to see which of them was the most tenacious. Their parents were haunted by their memories of the Great War, but the three of them weren't weighed down by the burdens of warfare. Nor were they worried one iota about their future. They had each other, a beautiful lake, and the summer sun. At the time, nothing else mattered.

The good memories of her childhood were beginning to fade. One day she would leave this château, and when she did, she wanted to remember all the laughter before their loss, before Michel joined the resistance and Nadine disappeared. Before the woman her brother loved began spending her afternoons in the servants' quarters.

Two German fighters darkened the sunlight, and she looked over to see if Adeline was frightened, but the girl only glanced up at the sky in annoyance. Then she continued playing in the shallow water. In the shattered world of her childhood, Adeline's life among the German soldiers and the aeroplanes flying were as normal as the summers that Gisèle had spent swimming in the lake.

The major had been raging for two days about the aeroplane that crashed into the valley, searching for its missing crew. But more Allied aircraft flew overhead now, both day and night, and the Germans seemed to be growing nervous.

She hadn't been able to obtain the identity papers yet, but she prayed the men in the tunnels were all safe. If she'd learned nothing else during the past four years, she had learned that life was as fleeting as dandelion seeds in a storm. In her heart, she'd begun saying good-bye to those she loved, even before they were gone.

A shout from the ridge above shattered the silence, and before Gisèle could react, a rock plummeted through the branches, hurling toward them. She lurched forward and grabbed Adeline as the boulder crashed into the lake, several meters from where Adeline had been playing. Before she could pull Adeline to shore, another rock catapulted over their heads, spraying water on both of them.

Adeline clung to Gisèle's neck, sobbing, as Gisèle scanned the ridge above them. She couldn't see anyone in the trees. Either someone was threatening them or they didn't know she and Adeline were here.

"Stop," she yelled up in French and then in German. "There's a child down here."

The woods grew still, and she sat back down on the shore and held Adeline on a towel, drying her tears along with her soaked feet. She was so tired of running and hiding and trying to protect those she loved. But when she heard the stomp of boots on the branches, she stood with Adeline clutched beside her. No matter how exhausted she was, she couldn't stop fighting, for Adeline's sake.

A solitary soldier descended the hill, and when she saw it was Hauptmann Milch, she released her tight hold on Adeline.

"Forgive me," Milch said when he stepped beside her. His German accent was strong but his voice sounded broken. "I did not know you and your daughter were here."

She looked up into his swollen eyes, and her breath caught when she realized that tears streaked his clean-shaven face. Even though she thought she had nothing left to feel, the pain in his eyes resonated in the hollows of her heart.

Adeline clapped her hands together. "*Guten Tag*, Josef."

Gisèle glanced at Adeline and then looked back up at the man in front of her. "Josef?"

He shrugged. "She asked my name . . ."

She didn't know which disturbed her more—that Adeline was learning German or that she'd begun calling the officers—their enemy—by their first names. At least this friend was the man who'd saved her life. "Why are you throwing rocks?" Gisèle asked.

He crumpled a piece of white paper in his hands. "Something happened, and I—I didn't know what else to do."

She kissed Adeline's hair and scooted her back toward the water. "You can play again."

The pull of the water and perhaps the sight of Josef seemed to soothe Adeline's fears. When she began splashing again, Gisèle pointed the officer to her blanket. His long legs stretched across it.

"What happened?" she asked.

He tossed the paper onto the blanket. "Have you heard of the Gestapo?"

She nodded slowly.

"I just found out—" His voice cracked. "They deported my mother from Berlin."

The air seemed to deflate out of her. "But why—"

"She's not like—" He paused. "We're not like the other Germans."

She studied him again, the sadness that consumed his warm brown eyes, the boyish features that would have intrigued her if she'd met him at the university. She'd already known that Hauptmann Milch was different from the other Germans occupying her house, obsessed with fear and destruction. His secret kindnesses for her and Adeline had given her peace in the midst of the turmoil. He may not have had Nadine's dark hair and distinguished nose, but slowly she realized why the German secret police had deported his mother.

"You're Jewish," she whispered.

He nodded. "My mother was born into a Jewish family."

"What about your father?"

His gaze wandered back to the water. "When they married, my father was an officer in the German army, and my mother owned an art gallery in Berlin. Twenty years later the government began harassing the Jewish people, but instead of standing up for his wife, my father took my younger sister and brother and moved to Frankfurt."

"You were left to care for your mother."

"It wasn't a burden," he said sharply. "I wanted to care for her."

In the soft light, she didn't see a Jewish officer in a German uniform. She saw a young man who had refused to abandon his mother. A man like André, who stood by his family even when it could mean death.

"My mother is stubborn," he said. "She didn't want my help, but after the Nazis closed down her gallery, she had to rely on me until there was no place for me to work either. I tried to obtain visas from the U.S. embassy, but we were denied. They said we weren't sufficiently threatened. When the Germans began deporting the Jews who lived in the ghettos, we knew it wouldn't be long . . ."

He wiped his face with the back of his hand, and she looked toward the lake, not wanting to embarrass him.

"I was conscripted into the Wehrmacht, and I went willingly," he said, his voice weighted. "It was the only way to protect both of us."

"Does the army know your mother is Jewish?"

"The major knows, but he doesn't want to tell the others under his command. They might revolt."

"Why didn't you falsify your papers?"

"Because I thought if those in command knew who I was . . ." He picked up another rock and threw it into the water, far from where Adeline was playing. "I thought that out of respect, they wouldn't deport the mother of a *Hauptmann*."

She wrung her hands together. "They don't respect anyone."

"For the past four years, I've had to serve under a madman—" His voice broke again. "I've seen horrific things, and no matter how much I wanted to stop it, I could not."

"Because they would kill you?"

He raked his fingers through his short hair. "Because they would kill my mother."

How could she tell him that he never should have joined the German army, that he should have sacrificed his life along with his mother's? She didn't know how to respond, but no matter how much she hated the Germans, no matter how she wished the Allies would crush every Nazi in the Wehrmacht, she couldn't hate this man.

"If the war ends soon," she finally said, "there is hope that your mother will remain alive."

He nodded slowly. "That is why I must stay in the army."

And with his words, she knew he was also imploring her to understand. No one else except the major knew he was even Jewish. Defecting from the German army would mean certain death—for him and his mother. He'd trusted her with his secrets. He wanted her to understand.

"We must do what is right before God," she said. "Not before any man."

He sighed. "I no longer know what is right."

"It is right to sacrifice yourself to save another's life."

"But in order to do that, I must fight for a country—a man—who puts no value on life."

It was as if a net had dropped over all of them, trapping them together, suffocating them as they fought. Every day they had to make choices. In order to survive, she and Josef and others like them had to choose the least of the evils to do the most good.

She leaned forward, her eyes focused on the lake. "I must cook and clean and house my enemy to sustain them, even as they kill those I love and destroy my beautiful country."

"Gisèle—" When he reached for her hand, her heart leapt against her will. "I am sorry for what we have done to you."

"You haven't done anything wrong," she whispered.

"But I have—I am Jewish but I am also German."

"Josef—" She stumbled. "I'm sorry, I meant—"

He stopped her. "No one except your Adeline has called me Josef in a long time."

"I won't say it again."

"Not in the house," he said. "But out here, it is nice to hear."

She leaned forward, meeting his warm gaze so he understood. "I forgive you, Josef."

The pain eased away from his eyes. "Thank you."

Adeline's laughter brought them both back to reality, but he didn't release her hand. "What happened to her parents?" he asked.

She wanted to lie to him as she had all the others, tell him that Adeline was really her daughter. Yet as he held her hand, as he trusted her with the secrets of his past and his heart, she couldn't do it.

"The French police took them away during the roundup." She took a long breath. "I had no place to hide her but here."

Adeline picked up a rock like Josef had done and tossed it into the water. "Are both her parents Jewish?"

"Only her mother."

His hand grew tighter around hers. "I wish we could rescue them all."

She pulled her hand away and wrapped her arms around her knees. Her life was already tangled in the web; she couldn't allow her heart to be as well. "Me too." She paused. "But there is something we can do to help end this war."

"What is it?"

Turning, she reached inside her blouse and pulled out the photographs of Eddie and Daniel. His eyes grew wide when he saw them. "They need identity cards," she said.

He waved his hand. "Don't tell me anything more."

"Can you help them?"

He nodded slowly as three planes flew overhead. The shelling from antiaircraft cannons pulsed in the distance, trying to bring their enemy down.

"More aeroplanes are coming now," she said, watching the sky.

He hid the photographs in his letter. "The Allies are preparing to invade at the Pas-de-Calais."

She rubbed her bare arms. "Will they succeed?"

"I don't know," he said as he stood. "The Nazis are doing everything in their power to defend it."

"So they are worried—"

"They are always worried." He brushed off his trousers. "Major von Kluge told me to return in an hour."

Only an hour to sort through his questions. His sorrow. It was more time, perhaps, than Lucien and others had to grieve their losses, but it wasn't nearly enough.

She stood up beside him. "Thank you for helping me—for now and for the papers you made me before and for helping me in the cellar."

"In the cellar—" He looked away, and she realized that like her, he was ashamed of what happened that day. "I am sorry about that as well."

"That was not your fault." She reached for both of his hands, imploring him to look back at her. "Neither of us did anything wrong, but instead of running away—you rescued me."

He took a step away. "It is too dangerous for us to speak to each other in the house."

Dangerous—that was exactly why she wanted so badly to leave.

"When I pray at the *chapelle*," she said, "I will pray for your mother."

He kissed the top of one of her hands. "She would have liked you, Gisèle."

It wasn't until he was gone that she realized he spoke of his mother in the past tense. Perhaps in his heart, he had already said good-bye.

CHAPTER 50

Riley and I found Madame Calvez balled up on the carpet in her living room. Her arms clasped around her chest, she rocked back and forth, muttering to herself. I couldn't understand what she was saying.

Isabelle clung to my arm as I glanced up at Riley. A lot of men would have fled back out the door, but Riley didn't run. Instead he slipped onto the floor beside her. "Madame Calvez—"

She edged closer to the wall. Terrified. "Leave me alone."

"No one here is going to hurt you."

"Yes, they will," she said, her voice clear. "You lied . . ."

Riley looked at me, but I had no answers for him.

I grabbed my cell phone from my pocket. "I'll call an ambulance."

Isabelle tugged on my arm. "My mother already called an ambulance."

"Where is your mother?" I asked.

"Driving here from Paris," Isabelle whispered.

Madame Calvez's eyes surveyed the room. "You can't take me away," she cried. "Someone must care for Adeline."

My stomach clenched. Was she grieving for Adeline as well?

Riley slipped his arm over Madame Calvez's shoulder. But instead of finding comfort in his protection, she gasped and began to pummel him with her knobby fists, crying as she fought. Riley retracted his arm to protect his face against her blows, but he didn't move away.

Then, as quickly as she'd begun to hit him, Madame Calvez stopped. Her eyes flickered for a moment, and I watched as both her hands fell back to her sides, her gaze locked on the black engraving on Riley's skin. Mesmerized. He lowered his arms, and her eyes followed his tattoo.

Slowly she reached out one of her hands. For a moment, I thought she might strike him again, but her fingers gently touched his forearm. The fear in her gaze melted into compassion. "You were there."

This time Riley didn't look back at me. Instead he gently placed his hand over her fingers. "Where was I?"

She curled the sleeve on her left arm and slowly pushed it up above her elbow.

Dear God.

Etched on Madame Calvez's forearm was a series of faded numbers. The mark of the beast.

The elderly woman leaned close to Riley, whispering, one friend empathizing with another. "Birkenau," I heard her say.

He cradled her in his arms.

❧ *Chapter 51* ❧

Instead of raiding Pas-de-Calais, the Allied troops stormed the northern beaches in Normandy. On the morning of June 6, German troops awakened to a swarm of aeroplanes that blackened the sky and thousands of soldiers emerging from the treacherous waters, attacking their fortresses on foot.

Major von Kluge had been raging for weeks, ever since they'd found the remains of *Deborah D*. Now, with the Allied troops fighting on French soil, he was inconsolable. Every night he berated his men over dinner as if they'd personally invited and then escorted their enemy across the English Channel.

But tonight was different. Tonight Gisèle waited outside the dining hall, a roasted chicken on her platter, as Major von Kluge ranted about the ineptness of the German military.

Shivering, she glanced up at the clock. It was already fifteen minutes past the eighteenth hour. The Germans were never late—not for their morning routine, not for patrol, certainly not for dinner. Tonight she took a bit of comfort in their lateness. The deficiency in the German army must have rattled Major von Kluge to his core.

When it appeared his tirade wouldn't end, Gisèle stepped back toward the kitchen. Lisette was sitting by the hearth in the kitchen, a cigarette in her hands. Adeline was playing on the floor with Shadow.

Lisette motioned toward the chicken. "They didn't like it?"

"Kluge was yelling at his men. Apparently the Allies are almost to Saint-Lô."

Lisette swore under her breath.

"I thought you might be pleased at the news," she said as she set down the platter.

But Lisette's face remained grave. "It's going to get ugly, Gisèle."

Gisèle glanced down at Adeline. "Why don't you and Shadow go play in the pantry?"

Adeline groaned in response, but she reached for the cat's front legs and dragged him into the pantry. Gisèle closed the door partway.

Lisette took another drag on the cigarette and then lowered her voice. "Hitler won't let his men retreat."

"How do you know?" she asked. Then wished she hadn't.

Lisette fidgeted with her scarf before meeting Gisèle's eyes again. "One of the men I know—" She paused. "He said that no matter what happens, they won't leave. As if I would be pleased with that news. They're preparing to fight, right here among the hedgerows."

"What about all the civilians?" Gisèle said, glancing over at the cracked door to the pantry. Adeline was lecturing the cat inside.

Lisette flicked ashes into the fireplace. "The civilians will be collateral."

Gisèle shuddered. "It is sick," she whispered. "They kill innocent people for no reason—"

"The Nazis are depraved and desperate." Lisette eyed the door, her hand trembling along with her cigarette. "And they hate the innocent."

"Perhaps they will have to leave the château."

Lisette's laugh sounded sour. "Only after the Allies have bombed it."

Gisèle sat down on the hearth. It had been four years since the Germans' bombs crashed down around them. They'd lived in fear of their enemies for so long; she'd never considered that the Allies might have to take their town by force as well. If the Germans refused to leave, her house would become their target.

Gisèle pointed toward the pantry. "We must protect her."

Lisette nodded.

"But where can we take her?"

"That's simple." Lisette puffed on her cigarette and the smoke drifted over her. "We can take her to your hiding place."

She stiffened, too stunned to respond at first. "What hiding place?"

"I'm not stupid, Gisèle. I know you've been hiding Michel." Lisette closed her eyes, leaning back against the bricks. "I loved him with all my heart, but you hid him from me."

Gisèle sighed. "Michel hid himself."

"Because he didn't trust me."

Gisèle shook her head. "Because he was trying to protect you."

"It's too late now for Michel and me, but I love—we both love—Adeline. Perhaps we can hide her wherever you hid him."

Gisèle thought about Adeline's cries when she was hidden in the cellar, of her fear of dark places. She may have been three years old now, but sometimes she still cried in the dark. "They will hear her there."

The cigarette trembled in Lisette's hand again. "We can't let them hurt her."

She may have lost her friendship with Lisette, but she had no doubt of this woman's love for Adeline. "What if you take her to your apartment tonight?" Gisèle asked.

Lisette pointed her cigarette toward the ceiling. "But if I don't return—what will you say?"

"Nothing at all," she said, "unless they ask."

Lisette considered her words. "Eventually they will ask."

"Then I'll tell them the truth. We want to protect Adeline from the Allied bombs."

She heard the boots on the steps and she shut the pantry door with a solid kick. Major von Kluge stood before her, his eyes ablaze. "You are late," he barked.

Gisèle reached for the cold chicken. "I didn't want to interrupt your meeting."

"Who told you to wait?"

"I—" She stumbled on her words.

"Who?" he demanded.

She shook her head. "No one."

He slammed his palm on the kitchen table. "Why can't you people do as you're told?"

When he turned, Lisette rolled her eyes and then stepped toward the pantry. As she followed the major up the steps, Gisèle hoped the Allies would hurry to and then quickly through Saint-Lô.

— CHAPTER 52 —

Riley insisted that he was fine, but after Madame Calvez was stabilized, the paramedic refused to leave until she'd cleaned up the scratches on Riley's face and his bloodied nose. The man I'd seen in the pictures online was gone. Transformed. I'd never forget how he had comforted Madame Calvez in the depths of her pain, her horrific memories of the concentration camp.

After the ambulance left for the hospital, Isabelle clung to my hand until her mother arrived. Then she raced into her mother's arms.

"My name is Monique," Isabelle's mother said in English before directing Isabelle to her car. "Isabelle calls you the lady of the château."

I wasn't sure if Monique meant her words to be a slight, so I chose to ignore them. "Your daughter is a delight."

Monique peeked out the window at her car. "Isabelle adores her great-grandmother, but I don't know how much longer I can send her here. These episodes are becoming more frequent."

"I can't imagine how hard it must be—"

"France wants to forget what happened to many of her people, but my grandmother will never forget. It almost seems—" She paused. "The older she gets, her memories seem more clear."

My frustration at Mémé's fading memory seemed trivial in

that light. Perhaps, instead of the memories plaguing her in her last years, there was mercy in the dullness of her mind.

Monique thanked both Riley and me for our help, and as we stepped outside, I asked her, "How long was your grandmother in a concentration camp?"

"The Germans didn't send her there until after D-Day, but as the Allied forces moved closer to the camps, they kept sending their prisoners west. It was nine months before they set her free."

"Why did they send her away?" I asked.

Monique took her car keys out of her pocket. "Someone was afraid she would talk."

.   .   .

The silver thread of river glistened in the setting sunlight as Riley and I walked back toward the château, the silence of contemplation our third companion.

The man beside me was nothing like the man I'd been engaged to marry. Instead, his sincerity and steady confidence, and even his kindness, reminded me of my father. I wasn't trying to earn Riley's approval. I was simply enjoying his company.

He had asked me to fly home with him, but I couldn't leave yet, not until I found out what had happened to my grandmother and Madame Calvez and Adeline. Somehow they were all connected, by the thread of their stories. Like the villages on the Vire.

But how were they connected?

Madame Calvez said she was afraid of Philippe Borde. Had he sent her to a concentration camp? And after the war, why did the French government give her the home of a Jewish family?

I wished I understood where Mémé was when Madame Calvez was taken to the camp. Had she fought for her friend?

Riley said we couldn't judge, and he was right. But after seventy years, it seemed the wounds were still fresh. And somehow, Adeline seemed to be the source of both women's pain.

Mémé may not remember much now, but at one time, she had. Was it shame that made her keep her secrets, perhaps like some of the Jewish men who'd kept their family's secrets as they served under Hitler?

"What do you think happened to Adeline?" I asked.

"I'm afraid the Nazis might have killed her," Riley said.

I nodded. It made sense. My grandmother's agony. Why she never told me about this child. She was grieving for her daughter at the end of her life.

I glanced over at him. "Are you going to the orphanage tomorrow?"

He pulled out his phone and clicked on the calendar. He stopped walking, staring down at the date.

Riley Holtz was a complicated man. Cute and charismatic when he wanted to be. Unassuming when not. And seemingly undaunted when he sat by a woman sixty years his senior, sharing her pain. Something haunted him, and while I didn't know if I'd earned the right to know what it was, I wanted to give him the gift he'd given to Madame Calvez.

"Is something wrong?" I asked.

"Tomorrow is June 24."

"Do you have another interview?"

"No. It's a . . ." He dug his hands into the pockets of his grandfather's jacket. "It's an anniversary."

But there was no celebration in his words. "The anniversary of what?" I asked quietly.

He glanced over at me, sadness etched in his eyes. "Of my daughter's . . ." His voice trailed off, but I assumed he meant his daughter's birth.

≈ Chapter 53 ≈

ootsteps drummed up and down the hallway outside Gisèle's bedroom until long past midnight. The footsteps didn't stop at her door, but their persistent pounding reminded her of the wind rattling against her windows, trying to force its way inside.

No matter how long she closed her eyes, trying to sleep, rest evaded her. Shadow rested beside her in the darkness, but it seemed so strange not having Adeline asleep in the bed below her. She was grateful Adeline was safe tonight with Lisette, but she'd grown used to having the girl in her room at night, acting as a mother.

When the war ended, Adeline would no longer be hers. Every night she prayed for the end of the war. For André and Nadine and their return home. But even though she thought her heart was numbed, it ached tonight at the thought of losing the girl who'd become her daughter.

She couldn't stay in the room for another moment, thinking about Adeline and the Germans and the bombs that could be dropped on her roof tonight. She had to go to the *chapelle* and pray.

Dressing quickly in pants and a blouse, she slid her rosary beads over her head and marched down the steps and out the front door, silently daring any of the soldiers to stop her. The stars flickering in the sky above the château reminded her of vigil candles, their steady blaze reminiscent of God's unfailing, unwavering love in spite of the storms.

There were no blackout curtains over the stained glass in the *chapelle* and the Germans forbade the glow of candlelight after dark now, so she knelt at a bench in the starlight and petitioned Mary to pray for Adeline and her parents. Then she asked Saint Michel to fight for her and Josef and her brother.

The door to the nave opened behind her, but instead of heavy boots pounding over the stone, there was only the soft pad of footsteps.

In the dim light, she recognized Josef. "What are you doing—"

"May I pray with you?"

"Of course," she said. "Where are your boots?"

"I left them beside the door."

He knelt beside her in reverence, clutching his hands to his face. Stunned, she couldn't focus again on her own prayers. She'd yet to see any of the men in her home pray.

Josef wasn't like the other men though. Since their encounter at the lake, he had done nothing to acknowledge her, and she'd tried to pretend as well that he wasn't there, but she always felt his presence. Sometimes it calmed her. Other times it confused her. But his presence never frightened her.

He reached for her hand and with his whispered prayers, he begged God for guidance. It wasn't until he released her hand that she realized she was trembling.

"Are you cold?" he asked, and the concern in his voice terrified her. He could not care about her. Nor she him.

"Why are you here?" she whispered.

He sat up on the bench. "The Allied soldiers are drawing near."

"I heard Major von Kluge—"

"Hitler is desperate for control and so are his commanders."

Her heart quickened. "Don't they control enough already?"

"Their appetite is insatiable." He paused. "Hitler has demanded we find more Jews to send to the German camps."

She rubbed her hands over her arms. The roundups in the past two years had stolen away all the Jewish people in their community. "There are none left."

"There are rumors of a Catholic orphanage outside Saint-Lô—"

She gasped.

"I'd hoped you might know of it," he said.

"What business do they have at an orphanage?"

"The major believes the nuns are hiding Jewish children among the other orphans."

She stood up in the darkness. "They cannot harm those children."

His focus remained on the sculpture of Jesus in front of them. "He is sending me and my unit out to find it tomorrow."

"But he knows about you . . ."

Josef shuffled in his seat. "The major has begun to doubt my loyalties."

She shuddered. "It is a test."

He nodded.

"But the children are not Jewish," she insisted. "At least, not all of them . . ."

"It doesn't matter what you say, Gisèle. He must send someone to the camps."

She crossed her arms. "I can't allow him to do this."

He rubbed his hands together, his gaze still on the crucifix. "Neither can I."

And then she remembered the reason he was in the German army. The woman he'd sacrificed everything for. "What will they do to your mother?"

"If my mother still lives—" His voice broke. "She would tell me to save these children."

She sat down on the bench beside him. "You are a good man, Josef Milch."

"*Nur Gott ist gut*," he said. *Only God is good.*

They sat in silence together at the foot of the cross.

Evil might have coursed through the veins of the Nazi leader and his minions, but God was good. She might not be able to rescue everyone, but He would want her—her and Josef—to try to rescue these children from the evil.

She fingered the key in the middle of her rosary beads. Adeline was safe at Lisette's house for the night. The Germans didn't know she helped the Allied airmen. Perhaps they wouldn't find out if they hid the children in the tunnels.

But how would they travel with so many children?

For with God nothing will be impossible.

Her mother often quoted the words from the Book of Luke when she prayed. Jesus loved the Jewish children, welcomed them to Him in the Scriptures. If nothing was impossible, she prayed He would help them protect these children.

Josef interrupted her prayers. "Major von Kluge sent me out here to find you. He wants to . . ." He paused. "He wants to interview you."

She nodded, understanding. "I won't go back to the house."

"How far away is the orphanage?"

She hesitated, knowing she must trust him and yet still afraid that Josef would deceive her. That he would tell the major her secrets in order to protect his mother.

But the Germans would find the orphanage without her. And she couldn't rescue these children without his help.

"About three kilometers on the main roads."

Eddie would have whistled, but Josef kept his eyes on the cross. "How about the back way?"

"If we take the footbridge across the river and go over the hill, it's about one kilometer."

He silently contemplated her words. "Even if we could make it there, we have no place to hide them."

She wrapped her fingers over the key again.

This was not just Michel's tunnel. It was their family's tunnel. Her tunnel. They each had a part to play in fighting this war. Michel and his men were intent on resisting the enemy, but she wanted to rescue people—the Allies and the children.

If they were caught tonight, the Nazis would send her and Josef to one of their camps—or kill them. But she'd never forgive herself if she didn't try to save the orphans.

"I have a place," she whispered. "But if you go with me, I fear there is no turning back."

He lingered for another moment, his hands clutched together as he whispered his prayers. She couldn't imagine the conflict in his soul, the unknown awaiting the mother he loved and the mandate to send defenseless children to their death.

Finally he stood up beside her, his voice strong. "I won't turn back, Gisèle."

He retrieved his boots by the door and then she locked the door to the nave.

"Come with me," she said, and she guided him through the sacristy and down into the secret spaces under her house.

"The major did hear voices," he said as they crept through the tunnel.

"Indeed."

Josef's laughter escaped his lips, and it warmed her heart. It was the first time she'd heard him laugh.

They passed quickly by the large room and then the smaller alcoves. Michel and the other men were gone, and the stench had tapered back into a more tolerable earthy smell.

"The children will be safe here, from the Germans and the bombing," he said.

She nodded. Others fought with bombs and guns to kill their enemy, but she could fight with her heart.

CHAPTER 54

I'd never heard anyone call the date of someone's birth an anniversary. But Riley didn't say anything else about his daughter, and I didn't press him.

His sorrow ballooned between us as we hiked back toward the château. The questions in my mind unanswered. Had he somehow lost his daughter, like my grandmother lost hers? And did this mean he once had a wife or was he still married?

It shouldn't have mattered to me, but as I'd watched him tonight alongside Madame Calvez, something had shifted inside me. If I ever fell in love again, I wanted it to be with a man like this who genuinely cared about people, not just about their vote.

Riley lingered beside the door to the château, but before we said good-night, my cell phone rang and I saw my dad's number on the screen. With a quick wave, Riley headed back toward the farmhouse.

"Chloe?" my dad asked as if someone else might answer.

I confirmed that it was indeed me.

He didn't bother with pleasantries. "I just got served papers, from an attorney in Paris."

My mouth dropped open. "What?"

"Stéphane is suing for the property."

I sighed. Even though Mémé, for whatever reason, had allowed Stéphane's father to live here, Dad wanted nothing to do with the Borde family. The château had been in my family's custody for three hundred years and French inheritance laws were strict. Property like this would pass down to a nobleman's son or grandson before a distant cousin retained it. I couldn't imagine any judge siding with Stéphane, but then again, Stéphane lived in France and we were strangers in Normandy.

I heard the crisp unfolding of papers in the background. "It says that I cannot inhabit the property nor can I inherit it because I'm not a biological heir."

"Of course we're biological heirs—"

"Stéphane has new information, but I don't know what it is." The line crackled again. "He should have waited to serve these papers until after my mother is gone."

"Dad," I said slowly. "Do you remember an orphanage near the château?"

He paused. "Perhaps."

"Riley is hoping to film there tomorrow."

"What does the orphanage have to do with his documentary?"

"He's doing a story about the Jewish men who served in the German military. Riley said one of the soldiers helped rescue the children in the orphanage before the end of the war."

When my dad spoke again, I heard the brokenness in his voice. "One of my recurring dreams is about a large group of children, sneaking through the woods."

A tremor of fear mixed with sorrow sparked inside me. Perhaps one of the children was his sister.

"What happens in your dream?" I asked.

"I'm hungry and cold and terrified, frankly, until your grandmother takes my hand. And then—" He stopped.

"What is it?"

"There is a German soldier in my dream, but he doesn't scare me. He reminds me of your grandfather . . ."

"Maybe it was at the end of the war," I said, "when you were leaving."

"Perhaps, but I'll never know. My memories are like a prism, Chloe. All fragmented in the light."

Why did everything have to be so complicated?

"I'm afraid we might lose the château," my dad said. "But I'm even more afraid of what else Stéphane will dig up about the Duchants."

"We are a family," I said, "and we will love each other, no matter what happened in the past."

Chapter 55

The ramparts of the old Norman forest shielded thirty orphaned children and their five chaperones as they snuck toward the river valley. When the aeroplanes rattled overhead, they would duck under the mantle of leaves, waiting until they passed.

Glowworms clung to the leaves above them and to blades of grass at their feet, lighting their path, but Gisèle still wasn't certain how the children had managed to walk so far that night. Perhaps some of the children thought it was all a dream. It was as if they were all sleepwalking, dazed from Sister Beatrice awakening them long before dawn.

The nuns had prepared them well for a nighttime evacuation. The older children dressed quickly and rolled up their bedding. Gisèle and Josef assisted the younger ones who lagged behind, and the nuns quickly prepared sacks of food to carry.

Now Sister Beatrice and two other nuns prodded their wards gently along while the older children helped those who were younger, picking them up when they stumbled. Gisèle held the hand of the boy she'd found in Saint-Lô and the hand of a girl who wasn't much older than Adeline. Josef carried the youngest child, a two-year-old boy, who'd fallen asleep on his shoulder.

Gisèle glanced over at the man beside her, towering over all of them in his uniform. The child now cuddled against his chest. At first, the children had been terrified of the German officer and initially Sister Beatrice had been furious at Gisèle for leading him to the orphanage. It hadn't taken Gisèle and Josef long to convince her of the gravity of what might happen if they didn't leave right away.

Soon Sister Beatrice was more angry that after all these years of hiding, when the Allied forces were so close to rescuing them, the Germans were coming after her children.

A light shone at the edge of the trees, and at first Gisèle thought it was the starlight, welcoming them, but she quickly realized that it was much too bright.

"Get down," Sister Beatrice commanded, and the children sank to the ground.

Gisèle held her breath as four vehicles passed by them, waiting to hear the slamming of car doors, but only silence remained.

Josef motioned for all of them to wait as he stepped out onto the road. "Gisèle," he whispered.

Seconds later, she joined his side. The taillights of the vehicles had disappeared, and no lights glowed in the valley below, not even in Saint-Lô.

"Why are they using their headlights?" she asked. An Allied plane could see them for miles.

Josef scanned the valley in front of them. "They are in a hurry."

She shivered. When Josef didn't return to the house, had the Nazis rushed out to find the orphanage without him?

He glanced down at his watch. "They'll patrol the footpath below in a half hour."

"Should we wait?" she asked. It would take the children at least twenty minutes to get down the hill.

He put his hand on the back of the sleeping boy in his arms. "When they find the orphanage vacant, they will comb the forest and valley until they find us."

She remembered the lights when they were searching for the airmen. The barking of the dogs. The Germans had searched for weeks for Eddie and Daniel. If they didn't get these children to the tunnel right away, they had no chance against the dragon.

"We must go," she said.

Josef whispered to Sister Beatrice, and she arranged the children and adults into small clusters. Then, with the child in his arms, Josef led the clusters quickly down the hillside. Gisèle crossed the footbridge first and ushered the children across the footpath and back into the covering of the hawthorns while Josef waited on the far side of the river until everyone was safe in the trees.

But then she heard the hammer of the boots she'd heard outside her bedroom door hours ago.

"Halt!" A man shouted, and her heart plummeted.

The German patrol had arrived.

"Who is it?" a man barked in German.

Gisèle glanced at Sister Beatrice, who was tucked back in the limbs of an apple tree. The nun didn't say a word, turning instead toward the children, outstretching her arms as if she could protect every child in her care. Gisèle clung to the rosary beads and the key around her neck as she murmured her prayers.

"It is Hauptmann Josef Milch."

They were so close to the cellar. So very close . . .

Should she join Josef? No, that would only give away the location of the rest of the children. Perhaps Josef could convince the patrol that he'd been sent on official business.

But that would be impossible. Josef still held a child in his arms.

When the man spoke again, his voice was much lower, and she strained to hear his words. "The major is looking for you."

"Benjamin?" She heard the relief in Josef's voice.

"*Ja.*"

"Von Kluge ordered me to raid the orphanage."

"I see you have followed his command." And Gisèle could imagine him looking at the child in Josef's arms. She prayed the man was a father. And that a seed of compassion remained in him.

"*Ja,*" Josef said, "but I will not send this child to the camps."

She couldn't hear Benjamin's response.

"Where are the others?" Josef asked.

"The major sent everyone else out tonight."

She shivered. Would others be awakened by German soldiers commanded to send them away?

One of the other children coughed from the trees, and the men stopped talking for a moment.

"I could not do as I was commanded," Josef whispered.

"They will search everywhere for you."

"They will not find me."

After a long pause, Benjamin spoke again. "Godspeed." She released her hold on the rosary beads, and Sister Beatrice's arms relaxed beside her.

Seconds later, Josef marched through the branches. The child had awakened, but his arms were clutched around Josef's neck.

"Why did he let us go?" Gisèle asked.

Josef held back a branch so it wouldn't cut the child. "He is a friend."

Another fleet of aeroplanes charged down from the north, and with the ground trembling under their feet, she directed the children swiftly through the thorny trees.

— CHAPTER 56 —

Riley and I found the abandoned manor house hidden back in the forest north of Saint-Lô, hemmed in by an iron fence and canopy of trees. The sisters who worked there, Marguerite told us, had hidden Jewish children among their wards.

The front gates were open, and Riley parked his rental car inside before he dug out his camera. I took a picture of the front of the house with my phone, but I would wait to text it across the Atlantic. If it did jog my father's memories, I wanted Mom to be near him.

The front door was locked, but there was no knob or latch on the back door, so I pushed it open. The ceiling sagged precariously over ten wooden tables and benches, convincing me not to step inside, but I stood at the doorway and took another picture.

Had the children here survived the war or had the Nazis taken them away?

I knew it took a lot of courage for my father to share his troubled dreams with me. It was humbling to forget one's childhood, especially when it was replaced with a confusing set of memories and dreams that prompted only questions. Snatches of children grouped together. Escaping in the night. The airplane ride to the States.

Another thought thundered through my mind.

Stéphane had said that my father wasn't the biological son of Gisèle Sauver. The Duchant heir.

Was it possible that my father hadn't come with his mother to help the orphans? It was plausible that he may have been one of the children needing help. Perhaps he was supposed to replace the child that Mémé lost.

If that was the case, no wonder his childhood was like a prism. Mémé, in her love for him, had invented a beautiful story about his father—the French soldier who died in the war—and a childhood growing up at the château. A story she deemed safe. She had wanted him to forget the truth and he had. Until he began to dream.

Turning, I wandered over to an old playground. With his camera on his lap, Riley was spinning slowly around on the rusty merry-go-round. He looked up at me, and I saw tears in his eyes. All the pride I'd seen in his pictures online, the cockiness that I'd once accused him of, all of it had been stripped away.

Riley wiped his tattooed arm across his face before he slowed the merry-go-round. I sat down beside him. The seconds passed in silence, the two of us watching the branches sweep across the roof of the old manor house. Somehow, in the mystery of this house, I suspected there was healing as well.

"What happened to your daughter?" I asked.

He took a deep breath. "I told you that I moved away from home before I finished high school."

I nodded.

"I wanted to act, but there was another reason I left. My girlfriend was pregnant, and I talked her into having an—" He choked on the word. "I wanted her to end her pregnancy. We were too young to have a child . . ."

I crossed my arms over my chest, not knowing what to say.

"Twelve years ago, I drove Helena to the clinic." He stood up, his eyes on the swing set. "And then I didn't even wait a week. I packed up my beater of a car and didn't just walk away from my girlfriend. I ran, all the way to New York."

I stood beside him, and he pushed a rusty bar on the merry-go-round, watching it swirl around. "My parents were furious, and I tried—I tried desperately to forget them and Helena and most of all, my lost baby. I threw myself into my own search for success, and when I failed miserably, I tried drinking and drugs and more women, as if that could somehow patch up my bleeding soul. It wasn't until my grandfather came to find me that I knew I had to stop running.

"My grandfather rescued people, but I—" His voice broke again as he pushed the rail. "I thought I'd killed my child."

My skin bristled.

"I didn't think I could forgive myself, but then—" His voice cracked. "Helena was killed in a house fire two years ago, outside Chicago. She died making sure her nine-year-old daughter wasn't trapped in her bedroom."

I shivered. "She didn't abort?"

He shook his head.

My arms slowly fell back to my sides, the wonder in his voice drawing me into his story.

"She lied to me in the clinic and then after I left, she and her family moved away. Last year, my father got a call from Helena's father. His wife had grown ill, and they couldn't care for their granddaughter anymore. My parents didn't tell me what happened, but they invited her to live with them."

I leaned back against a tree, trying to bear his burden like he had with Madame Calvez.

"Last week, when I called home to ask about my grandfather's video, my daughter answered the phone."

"What is her name?"

"Abigail." He pushed the merry-go-round again. "Her name means 'the father's joy.'"

"Oh, Riley," I pleaded. "You have to go home."

"I can't go back now. I wanted to abort her."

I tugged at his sleeve until he looked back at me. "You are no longer that man. God has given you a second chance."

He sat back down on the merry-go-round.

"Abigail needs her dad," I said. "But even more, I think you need Abigail."

Chapter 57

Gisèle tried to rub the pain out of her head. They'd been in the tunnel for more than four hours, and most of the children were asleep now on the floor. Adeline was at Lisette's apartment, but what if the Germans took Adeline from her, thinking the child was Gisèle's? Would they punish both Lisette and Adeline because Gisèle had disappeared?

She had to sneak out to Lisette's apartment and bring them both back here.

Josef studied her as he picked up two of the canteens left on the floor. "I will get water for the children and another flashlight."

Gisèle motioned him farther down the path so they could speak without any of the children hearing. The flashlight they'd found in the tunnel was still glowing, but Josef was right. The batteries wouldn't last much longer. Still, she didn't want him to leave. "They'll find you," she whispered, terrified at what the Germans would do to him.

"The children are safe," he said, his eyes upon her, tenderness in his voice. "You are safe."

"Adeline isn't safe."

"I will search for her."

How she wished she and Josef were both students at the university, five years ago. They could laugh and flirt and toast to tomorrow where neither of them had a care. The cares of today felt impossible. Overwhelming. They must find Adeline, but she did not want to lose Josef. It felt as if her heart would tear into two tattered pieces.

"Michel will return soon," she insisted. "He will help us find her."

He raked his hand through his hair, his voice sad again. "I fear your brother won't be returning."

Her pulse quickened. "Why not?"

"Major von Kluge was expecting another convoy today from Germany, but the resistance fighters blew up the tracks."

"What about Michel?"

"The train was carrying hundreds of soldiers from the front and they jumped out when the train derailed."

When he hesitated, her stomach clenched. "Josef?"

"Someone sent a wire to the major. It said that both Michel Duchant and Jean-Marc Rausch had been killed."

She clung to the side of the tunnel, the shell that had protected her brother for the past four years, gasping for breath. "Why didn't you tell me before?"

"The major wanted me to find these children, but even more, he wanted me to find you."

The realization sickened her. "He was going to hurt me."

"Your brother was found to be a leader of the resistance party and your husband was a member as well. You are guilty by association."

"Not by association, Josef. You know I am guilty, at least in their eyes."

"But innocent in the eyes of God."

She wanted to scream so loud that it would echo through the tunnel, all the way up through the wine cellar and shake the halls of the château. She wanted the men upstairs to feel her pain.

She'd known it was coming, that Michel would join their parents soon. In her heart, she'd said good-bye long ago, but with the war so close to the end, she'd hoped, desperately, that perhaps he would survive.

Josef clutched both of her hands and held them to his chest. "I will come back for you, Gisèle. For you and all of these children."

"Please find Adeline," she begged before giving him directions to Lisette's apartment. Then she slipped her rosary beads off her neck and placed the crucifix in his hand. "This is the key."

He held it to his own heart. "Indeed."

And as he left, her heart warred with itself. She knew she probably should say good-bye to him as well, but she couldn't.

. . .

Gisèle sat at the base of the cellar in the darkness, clutching the neckline of her blouse as if it was her rosary beads. Josef had been gone for hours now, much too long for checking on Adeline and filling up the canteens. Had Major von Kluge or his men found him?

She couldn't think about what might happen if they did. Her brother was gone now, and if she lost Adeline and Josef too—

She wouldn't be able to survive.

The roof of the cavern rumbled, the ground shuddering. Were the Germans bombing Saint-Lô, or was it the Allied forces who were trying to take it back from the Nazis? It didn't matter, she supposed. A bomb from the good guys or the bad guys was still a bomb. The Allies wouldn't want to kill the children like the Nazis did, but neither could they control precisely where their bombs fell. And they didn't know there were children under-ground near the château.

The bombing had shaken the tunnel for hours, and she feared the roof might cave in, but still they couldn't leave. As she waited, she prayed—for Josef and Adeline and for all the children in her care.

A candle flickered in the tunnel, and she looked up to see the little boy whom she'd taken to the orphanage two years ago, the one who had clung to her hand all the way down the hill last night and snuggled beside her until he fell asleep.

"What are you doing up?" she whispered.

"I don't like the bombs."

"Me neither."

He climbed into her lap.

"What is your name?" she asked as she had in that alleyway so long ago.

He leaned back against her, and this time he answered. "Michel."

"It is a good name," she said softly, wondering if that was his real name or if he'd acquired it when Lisette said he looked like Michel. "Were your parents French?"

"I don't know."

He was so young. Like Adeline, he probably wouldn't re-member his parents when he grew up, but perhaps it was good that he couldn't remember. Perhaps she should pray he did forget—the bombing and the hatred, the abandonment and the fear, the hunger and the grief.

She pushed his hair back away from his eyes. "Do you know the story of Saint Michel?"

"A little."

"I used to tell it to my brother when he was younger."

"He is an angel," the boy said.

"Not just any angel. Michel is a fierce archangel, and the leader of God's army." She swallowed. "He defeated evil once already and the Scriptures say that one day Michel and his army will fight this great dragon again and defeat it for good."

"I will fight too," he told her. "Like Josef."

She prayed he would stand up against the evil in their world. "Do you want to pray with me for Josef?"

He closed his eyes. "Please help us fight," the boy prayed. "Help us not to be scared."

Then he looked back up at her.

"My brother once told me that courage doesn't mean our fears are gone. It means we continue to fight, even when we are afraid."

She might be scared as well, but she could no longer hide in this tunnel while Adeline was out there. If Josef couldn't find her, then she would have to.

The hatch rattled above them, and as they leapt to their feet, her heart rejoiced, thinking Josef had returned. But then she realized someone with an ax or another weapon was hacking away at the lock on the door. There was so little fight left in her, and yet she had to protect Michel and the other children.

She shoved him away from her. "Run!"

She would tell the Germans she was the only one down here, that she was hiding alone. She would tell them—

Michel edged back to her side. "I will fight them."

"Not now," she said, chiding herself for telling him about the archangel. "When you are older, you can fight."

But still he didn't move.

A flashlight shone down on her face, and she covered her eyes. How was she supposed to protect the children now? The

Germans had killed her father. Her brother. Major von Kluge and his commander would take her life in a heartbeat if they thought she'd helped the resistance and the Jews. But like Michel—her brother and the little boy beside her—she wouldn't cower.

"Gisèle," the man above her called. She blinked in the light.

"Who is it?" she asked.

"Don't tell me that you forgot me already." The man dropped down beside her, and she could see his face, the sliver of a mustache over his upper lip. It was the pilot from the American plane. Eddie McAllister.

And he was smiling.

She dropped her arms to her sides, relief washing through her. It had been such a long time since she had seen anyone smile. "I told you not to tell anyone about this place," she said.

His grin grew a little wider. "I thought you might need a friend."

She pointed down the tunnel. "There are thirty children hiding back there. They all need a friend."

He shouted up to whoever was above him, and a group of soldiers flooded past her.

"We'll get them out."

They ran past her, and when she looked up, she saw the faint light of morning above.

She hurried up the ladder.

— CHAPTER 58 —

The day the delivery truck arrived, Lisette Calvez was waiting by the window in the drawing room of the château, sipping a glass of red wine. "Chloe!" she called from the bed one of her grandsons had brought down when he visited from London.

I rushed down the steps from my room.

Riley had hoped the package would arrive yesterday, but it was held up at customs. Lisette and I had been watching for it all morning.

After Lisette was discharged from the hospital, I asked her to stay at the château with me. At first she had balked at the idea of living here, but Monique told her grandmother she could not continue living on her own, so she finally agreed to join me, as long as she could sleep in one of the rooms on the first floor. She'd been living with me for more than a week now. When I returned to the States, she would go back to Paris with Monique and Isabelle.

There was a story she wanted to tell me before she left, but the nurse who visited twice a day told her to stay away from stress. And the best way to avoid stress right now was to avoid talking about the past.

But Riley said Lisette and I should watch his grandfather's interview together. When I asked about stress, he thought it would bring healing instead. I figured he should know a little about healing. In the past five days, he'd texted me at least ten pictures of the most beautiful young lady smiling back at him. She had his green eyes and long honey-colored hair that she tucked back in colorful headbands.

Outside I signed for the package and clutched it close to my chest. We'd discussed having him put the interview online, password protected, but he planned to use some of the footage for his documentary. The rest of it, he said, I probably wouldn't want online either, even with a password.

I made a pot of vanilla almond tea for Lisette and me, and we sat on two upholstered chairs in the drawing room, the cups of tea between us. My heart began to race as I inserted the DVD into the laptop I'd borrowed from Pierre.

On the screen emerged a picture of the man I assumed to be Eddie McAllister, wearing a decorated hat and coat from World War II. His face was wrinkled with age, but I could see Riley in the sharpness of his eyes and, as he began to speak, the confidence in his voice. The girls must have swarmed around him in France after the war as they did Riley in New York.

At first, Eddie spoke about his early years growing up outside Detroit and about training to become a pilot for the U.S. Air Force. Then he talked about the night his plane crashed into a valley near Saint-Lô.

I leaned forward.

"My navigator and I were rescued by a lovely gal named Gisèle," he said with a smile. "She hid us—well, I promised her I wouldn't say exactly where, but she took Daniel and me to her brother and then she helped us get identity cards. Her brother

Michel got us on what they called *the line*, and we were escorted by another lady all the way down to Spain, where our boys flew in to pick us up."

A voice off camera asked him what happened to the rest of his crew. "Two were shot by the Germans, but four others were hidden by farmers and eventually sent back to England too." He straightened his hat. "After D-Day, I came back to Saint-Lô. The Germans refused to leave that city, and the fighting was atrocious, but I owed it to Gisèle to help her. I had no idea what I would find there . . .

"I asked Gisèle to marry me." He laughed. "But she turned me down. It seemed she was in love with another chap, a German officer."

I stared at the screen, my head struggling to sort out his words. My grandmother, in love with a Nazi?

That wasn't right. She loved Henri Sauver.

Was this German her first husband? No, that didn't seem right either. Marguerite had said that the Germans were friendly in the beginning of the war, but my grandmother had never been in love with one . . .

She'd married Henri Sauver in 1944 after the war, but my grandfather was French. He'd resisted the Germans.

Eddie continued. "The officer was part Jewish, and he'd been the one to make us the identity papers. And I remember this little boy with us the day we went back. An orphan. He wouldn't let go of Gisèle's hand.

"The world was crashing down around her, but Gisèle refused to leave France without him. She also wanted us to find a woman named Lisette and another child, a little girl." He paused. "I can't remember the girl's name, but it was too late. They'd already been deported. It was one of my biggest regrets of the war, not being able to find them."

The voice off camera asked what happened to Gisèle. "I don't know," he said, sadness heavy in his voice. "The airplane took her to England, and I never saw her again. But I owe my life to her and Josef."

"Stop," Lisette whispered.

I turned off the DVD.

❦ Chapter 59 ❦

Saint-Lô was on fire.

Buildings burned around Gisèle, the hedgerows flattened and charred by the bombs. Townspeople were screaming. Fleeing. The nightmare of the blitzkrieg returned, except this time the Allied forces were fighting back.

Planes blazed overhead. Gunfire echoed through the streets. The shadows of Nazi soldiers shifted among the flames.

Gisèle took no care for herself. She had to find Lisette and Adeline and Josef. There was still time to flee in the confusion.

She wouldn't tell Lisette about Michel's death, not until they were safe in the tunnel.

The door to the apartment building had been torn from its hinges, and she rushed toward it.

"*Bonjour*, Gisèle."

She whirled around, and Philippe stepped out of the shadows.

"There are a lot of people searching for you," he said.

"I don't know why—"

"Are you looking for your daughter?" His voice was cruel. Malice wrapped around every word.

Her heart froze. "Where is she?"

"Far away." He clicked his tongue. "You shouldn't keep secrets from me."

She glanced wildly around them. Where had Adeline gone? Perhaps she could catch whoever had taken her.

But she couldn't move, couldn't run. The Nazis had taken everything from her. Everyone she loved. She'd done all she could to protect them and yet it wasn't enough. The dragon was still crushing them.

"The château is mine, Gisèle."

She felt sick. After all this, he wanted the house. "You can have it."

"Thank you." She saw the muzzle of his gun, pointed at her, and then the glint of a diamond on the end of his cuff, surrounded by black onyx and gold. She flashed back to the night she'd found her father in the tunnel. Her brother showing her what he'd found in the cave. The cuff link she'd thought a German officer left behind.

"Philippe—" She clutched the sides of her skirt. "When did you replace that?"

He lowered the gun a few centimeters. "Replace what?"

"Your cuff link."

He shook his head. "It doesn't matter."

Her resolve hardened. "You went back to the château, didn't you? The night we got stopped in Saint-Lô."

"Perhaps—"

"Did you kill my father?"

In his silence, she knew. The Germans hadn't killed her father that night. It was her cousin who'd beaten him up by the lake. And then pulled the trigger. Michel was right—Philippe would do anything to get the Duchant property.

A child cried for her mother, and Gisèle's heart clenched. She had fought as hard as she could and she had lost. She had pushed through her fears, but still she'd failed.

She heard the shuffle of feet and a little boy stepped in front of her. Michel. He must have followed her from the tunnel. "Don't touch her," he said.

Philippe's gaze flickered down to the boy. "You seem to be collecting children, Gisèle."

She put her arm around the boy's shoulders, pulling him close to her. "He hasn't done anything wrong."

"Bravery I admire, but not stupidity."

The boy lurched forward, his fists clenched in front of him, but she held him back. She was so proud of him, standing resolute in front of her, ready to die for someone he loved.

A German soldier stepped into the smoky light. "I will take over."

Philippe's pistol shook. "She is mine," he replied in German.

Josef wrapped his fingers around her arm. "No, she is Oberst Seidel's."

She'd never heard Josef speak with such authority, as if there was no doubt that Philippe had to obey.

But Philippe refused to concede. "I will take her to the *Oberst*."

A bomb hit the prison behind her cousin, and in seconds, the centuries of stone collapsed into rubble. If Philippe didn't shoot them, it wouldn't be long before one of the soldiers or a bomb took all of them. The bombs didn't differentiate between enemies and allies.

"I said I will handle this." Josef yanked on her arm, and she lurched toward him. "You are Philippe Borde, are you not?"

Philippe's eyes narrowed. "How do you know my name?"

"Major von Kluge is searching for you." He glanced both ways before he spoke again. "He fears he might have been mistaken about the death of Michel Duchant."

Philippe dropped the gun to his side. Then he raced the other way.

Josef clasped both arms behind her back and did the same with the boy, prodding them both down the sidewalk. His two prisoners until they reached the end of town.

Then the three of them ran.

It wasn't until much later, when they reached the *chapelle*, that she saw fresh blood pooling on Josef's sleeve.

CHAPTER 60

"After the war . . ." Lisette whispered. "Gisèle never returned or tried to contact us. I didn't think she cared about what happened to Adeline. Or to me."

I reached over for Lisette's hand and we sat in silence for a moment, processing Eddie's story, which collided with both of ours.

"Hauptmann Milch was a hero," Lisette said.

"Why did you tell Riley that you didn't know him?"

"There were a lot of German men named Josef."

I sipped my tea. "But you knew who he was talking about in the interview."

"I figured Josef wanted to keep his story secret, like I didn't want anyone to know mine."

I let her words settle for a moment as I stared at Eddie's face, paused on the computer screen. "The orphan boy was my father, wasn't it?"

"The Germans put me on a train," Lisette said. "I don't know what happened after I left."

But I knew Stéphane was right. My father wasn't the biological child of Jean-Marc and Gisèle Rausch, nor had he helped Gisèle rescue the Jewish orphans. He was one of the orphans.

An insect landed on the table, and Lisette watched it for a moment. "In the last days of the war, the Nazis went crazy, deporting everyone they thought to be Jewish or those who they thought were harboring the Jews or members of the French Resistance. They raided the orphanage, but all the children were gone."

"Where did they go?" I asked.

She shrugged. "Perhaps your father knows."

I understood that my grandparents might have been afraid to tell people their son was a Jew after they immigrated, in case there was another war, but why had they harbored the secret for so many years after the fighting ended? They should have been proud of his heritage.

"What happened to Adeline?" I asked.

Lisette's hands trembled as she sipped her tea, the cup clattering against the saucer when she placed it down. Then she nodded slowly, as if she'd decided to trust me with the rest of her secrets. "Adeline was just a baby when Gisèle and I found her. Her mother was Jewish and her parents were deported during the war. Gisèle cared for her at the château during the war." She scooted back on her chair. "Did you know Philippe tried to marry Gisèle?"

I shook my head.

"She refused, but Philippe was deeply in debt and he needed the Duchant property to maintain his lifestyle. After he took the life of Vicomte Duchant, he determined to kill both Gisèle and her brother so the château would be his." She paused. "Have you heard of the Milice?"

Again I shook my head, feeling foolish for knowing so little about what Mémé had faced. And for being frustrated at her for not telling me what happened.

"The Milice were the French version of the Gestapo and they were a nasty bunch. Philippe joined them during the war and began to research Gisèle's story. He found out that Jean-Marc Rausch, the man she'd said she married, had been fighting in northern France on their wedding day. He tried to deport Gisèle before the Allied troops freed Saint-Lô, but she ran away. And she left Adeline in my care."

"Mémé thought you'd been deported—"

"At the time, all I knew was that she was gone and Philippe was at my apartment. I had known him from before, back when he visited the château . . ." When she paused, I told her I understood. She didn't need to tell me more. "No one in Saint-Lô knew he was with the Milice except me. Philippe knew that the Germans would be gone soon and he feared the French would send him to prison when they found out about his role. He had me arrested, but he kept something—someone—for when I returned."

I shivered. "Adeline."

"She was collateral for my silence." She looked down at her hands. "Philippe's mother died soon after the war. He moved into the château, and I went to Paris with Adeline. For almost seventy years, I guarded his secret and he guarded mine."

I glanced out the window. "Monique's mother was Adeline."

"I changed her name back to Louise," she said. "She knew her biological parents were killed during the war, but she didn't know that her mother was Jewish. The Germans had already attacked our country twice. I wanted to protect her, in case they returned again."

"What happened to Louise?" I asked.

Lisette smiled. "She grew up in Paris and trained to be a nurse for the Red Cross. In 1966, she married a fine man. A doctor. They had five children who decided they wanted to change the world in their own way."

"You never married?"

"The only man I ever wanted to marry was killed in the war," she said. "But my friends in Paris thought I was a widow."

I reached for my cup and took a long sip of the tepid tea. "Isabelle said the government gave you the cottage."

She nodded. "The children of deported Jews began receiving compensation from the government ten years ago. By that time, Louise had passed away and I didn't want money, so I asked them for the cottage where her parents had lived before the war. No one had lived in it since 1942, and I think the local officials were pleased to have someone renovate it. I was pleased that my grandchildren and great-grandchildren could learn a bit of Louise's story."

My phone beeped and I saw a text from Riley. It was a photo, he said, that Benjamin Tendler had emailed to him. A picture of Benjamin and his friend Josef Milch.

I stared at the two men in uniform, standing in front of the hedgerows. All my life I'd been told that Henri Sauver was a French soldier, a resister of the Germans, but as I stared at the photo of the German officer next to Benjamin, there was no denying the truth. My grandfather had served Hitler in the war.

What would have happened if my grandparents' American neighbors found out that Henri had been an officer in the Wehrmacht? And that his son, my father, was a Jewish orphan?

They had to guard their secret.

I texted Riley back, asking him to wait to finish the documentary. I wasn't afraid to let the world know my father's family was Jewish, but I was horrified to tell anyone that the grandpa I loved had been a Nazi.

✍ *Chapter 61* ✍

Josef collapsed on a pew in the *chapelle*. He'd been shot in the shoulder, the blood seeping through the American bandages. As one of Eddie's friends worked on him, Gisèle wondered silently if the Americans had been the ones to shoot him as well.

"We have to take him to a hospital in London," the man said.

She knelt beside Josef, taking his hand. She couldn't lose him too.

He kissed her hand. "I'm not going to leave you."

At one time she couldn't imagine loving a German officer, but she loved Josef Milch with all of her heart. She loved him for the way he cared about the Jewish children, for the way he served under an evil man in order to protect his mother, for the way he fanned an ember of warm light for those trapped in the darkness, for risking his life to save her.

"Well, I was going to ask you to marry me," Eddie said from behind her. "But a man knows when he's been defeated."

She looked back at the American pilot through her tears. "You'll make someone a fine husband, Eddie."

He shrugged. "Maybe after this war is over."

She squeezed Josef's hand. "The Allied soldiers are taking the children to London."

Flak echoed outside the *chapelle* and she heard a bomb explode nearby. She leaned closer to Josef. "I must find Lisette and Adeline before Philippe does."

He shook his head. "They are already gone."

"But where—"

"Benjamin said they'd been taken to the trains."

Dear God. She felt as if she would be sick. "They're deporting Adeline?"

"I'm so sorry, Gisèle."

She looked toward the door. "We must get to the trains."

"It's too late."

She found Eddie's eyes again, hoping he could find Adeline and Lisette as he had Josef, but all she saw was remorse in his gaze. "The Germans still control the train station."

She shivered. "We can't leave her and Lisette."

"I have a plane ready to fly you out of here," Eddie said. "To London."

"We must find them first."

"The trains already left," Josef said.

Her heart felt as if it had shattered.

Another bomb hit nearby and she heard the terrible crash of a building caving in upon itself. Loneliness pierced the fragments of her heart.

"It's only a matter of days before we defeat the Nazis," Eddie said. "Then you can search for your friends."

"I'll search with you," Michel said beside her.

She looked back and forth between Josef and this boy who risked everything to save her. And she realized that she was no longer alone.

If Josef was right, if the trains had left, they would never be able to find either Lisette or Adeline. At least not now.

Josef rested his head back against the wooden arm of the pew. "We will find them after the war."

Gunfire ricocheted outside her beautiful *chapelle*, and she didn't want to move. All this killing, this horror, would it never stop?

Eddie held her chin in his rough hands, looking her in the eye. "You and Josef must hurry."

She pulled Michel close to her. "This boy belongs with us."

Another bomb rocked the ground, and Eddie urged all three of them out of the *chapelle*. "Go quickly."

She would pray all the way to London for Lisette and for Adeline. And the moment the fighting was over, she would find both of them.

CHAPTER 62

Dad and I spent hours searching through the boxes in his parents' attic. It seemed my grandparents had kept every piece of memorabilia they'd collected since they reached the United States, along with all of Mémé's classroom papers, bills, and sixty years' worth of the *Farmers' Almanac*. Rain streaked down the dormer windows of the attic, and my dad and I laughed and cried together as we remembered.

I thought Dad would ask Riley to stop the documentary when he found out his father was an officer in the Wehrmacht. Instead he called Riley after I flew home from France and thanked him for telling the story of Josef Milch. In Dad's eyes, Henri Sauver—his father—was a hero.

Riley's documentary about the Jewish soldiers was scheduled to air the first of the year, and now he was trying to track down other orphaned children who had been rescued during the war.

But before he started filming his new documentary, there was another project he wanted to complete first.

My father opened a file and then he whistled. "Bingo."

I scooted over to him and saw a birth certificate for Henri Sauver. Born in Paris. August 8, 1918.

"Josef must have forged that," I said.

Instead of using Milch, he'd changed his German last name to a French one that meant "salvation."

There was a marriage license for Gisèle and Henri in the folder, and the birth certificate for Michael Sauver. It slowly occurred to me that Josef had forged my father's birth information as he had Adeline's.

I leaned back against a post. "They never adopted you."

"Perhaps not legally," he said. "But they were my parents."

"They should have made it legal . . ."

My father shook his head. "It doesn't matter now."

But it did matter, at least for their case against Stéphane. My grandfather had forged the papers for Dad's birth, perhaps to bring him to the United States with them, but châteaus in France were passed down through the bloodline of the old families. Even if Josef had the best of intentions, the French courts wouldn't side with a German officer who had taken one of their children and run away.

Josef Milch had rescued an entire orphanage of French children and raised one of the orphaned Jews as his own child. But he still should have legally adopted my dad.

"Look at this," Dad said.

I leaned over and saw the other papers in his hands. They were carbon copies of letters, inquiring after Lisette Calvez, André Batier, Nadine Batier, Charlotte Milch, Odette Laval, and Adeline Rausch. I slowly read through the responses to Henri's letters.

Lisette Calvez had returned to Paris in May 1945, one letter reported, but Odette Laval had been killed in Paris during the blitzkrieg. Nadine Batier died on a train before she reached Buchenwald, three months before André died. Charlotte Milch was killed in the gas chamber at Dachau. And according to the last letter from the French government, they had found no record of a child named Adeline Rausch.

My grandparents hadn't forgotten those they loved, the people they had left behind. They'd found out what happened to everyone except Adeline. No wonder that, in these years when memories blurred, my grandmother thought Adeline was still lost in the trees.

"Chloe!" Marissa shouted from the base of the stairs, and I hurried down to my best friend. Her hair was tied back in a knot, and the apron she wore over her jeans and T-shirt was coated with flour. She held out my cell phone and I saw two missed calls from Riley.

"Do you know what happened?" I asked.

"Of course not," she said with a laugh. "Your mom is trying to show me how to make a lemon soufflé."

As Dad and I worked, Marissa and my mother had been inspired to concoct all sorts of French desserts in Mémé's kitchen.

I called Riley back.

"Turn on your TV," he said.

"Are you certain?"

He sighed. "No."

I'd been avoiding the television all day, but with Riley on the phone, I finally braved the network news. Red and blue balloons trickled down the screen, and I saw Austin Vale on a stage with both of his parents and his sister, all their arms raised in victory. In the close-up shot, his smile almost stretched across the television screen.

Austin hadn't just charmed me. He'd charmed the entire Commonwealth of Virginia.

In that moment, I thanked God for filling the empty places inside me with contentment and peace. I was incredibly grateful to be in my grandparent's home tonight with people I loved instead of on that stage, forcing a smile alongside the new governor-elect and his dysfunctional family.

The camera panned across the front of the crowd, and I searched the screen for Vos and Wyatt. I didn't see Austin's brother or brother-in-law, but there, two rows back from the front, sat Starla Dedrick, pampered and pressed. She wasn't smiling.

"Are you okay?" Riley asked.

"I'm relieved," I said, muting the volume on the TV. "Immensely."

"No regrets," he asked, part question and part statement.

Marissa and my mother laughed in the kitchen. "Not a single one."

"I was thinking . . . ," he said.

"Thinking about what?"

"Thinking that I would like to come back to Virginia soon."

My stomach fluttered. "I'm sure Mémé would love to see you again."

"Yes, well . . ." He paused. "I want to visit her, of course, but then, I wondered if I could come down to Richmond to spend time with you, or better yet . . ."

"Yes?"

"I was thinking you might want to come up here and meet Abigail."

I sat on the bottom step. Riley's relationship with his parents was slowly mending, and it seemed he'd begun to forgive himself for his selfishness in the past. He hadn't known his daughter was alive, but the guilt for encouraging his girlfriend to abort their daughter had turned into guilt for abandoning her.

Even though Abigail was too young to hear the entire story, Riley had begged her forgiveness for missing the first eleven years of her life. Their reunion had been bumpy, he said, but Abigail was slowly beginning to forgive him.

"Or we could all meet in France," he said, and I could hear his smile.

"Why are you going to France?"

"Lisette wants me to do an interview with her about Philippe Borde and the undercover work of the Milice."

"Stéphane will be furious when he finds out."

"It's Lisette's story to share," he said. "Besides, it's a good excuse for me to return to Normandy. I hear there's decent food over there."

I laughed. "Pretty good wine too."

"And a whole lot of cows."

"You should definitely go back to see the cows."

"Come to France with me," he said, his voice low.

I glanced at the television screen again, at Austin's victory smile. Instead of the lights of the television cameras, the glamour of the celebration parties to follow, my heart longed for Normandy, for the beauty and the history and the time to savor all of God's gifts, for the stories that I knew about and the stories that remained untold.

"Perhaps I will . . . ," I said.

But this time I wouldn't be running away.

This time I would be running alongside Riley and his daughter, I hoped, to the place where my heart had begun to mend.

— EPILOGUE —

Three Months Later

All five of Louise's children attended the memorial service for Gisèle Duchant in the Chapelle d'Agneaux, each of them telling my father how much they appreciated all she had done. Lisette read a beautiful tribute to her and so did my dad. I'd tried to read the tribute I wrote, but Riley had to step up and read it for me.

Mémé's body now rested in the small plot by the *chapelle*, beside her parents and her brother. And my father had arranged for the remains of Grandpa to be returned to France as well, so he could be put to rest beside his wife. His epitaph read:

Henri Sauver, also known as Hauptmann Josef Milch
A man of God
And a protector of God's children

As the priest recited the Rite of Committal in front of Mémé's grave, my father clutched my hand. After my return from France last summer, I'd waited for months to tell Mémé about Adeline. With peace in her heart, I feared she would finally let go of this life for the paradise beyond.

I don't know if Mémé understood when I shared Adeline's story, but three days later, Pamela opened the window in Mémé's room and when she turned around, my grandmother was gone. It was as if she'd hitched a ride on the breeze and sailed away to those who'd been waiting for her for so long.

I imagined Josef and Adeline and Michel and my great-grandparents crowding around her, kissing her on both cheeks, showering her with their hugs. I imagined her remembering again all that happened in her life, but with joy instead of pain, for in the end she'd conquered even death.

I imagined Christ welcoming her with open arms, saying the simple but profound words.

Well done.

Along with Mémé's will, Dad had received a letter from his mother explaining much of her story in case Philippe—or his son—tried to fabricate it. No one else except Philippe had known Henri Sauver was a former Nazi officer. Just as Philippe kept Madame Calvez's secret, he kept the secret of Josef's and Michel's histories, as long as Gisèle didn't expose that he'd murdered Vicomte Duchant. And allowed him live in the château.

Philippe hadn't told Stéphane all the details of the past before he died, but he'd told his son that Michel wasn't a Duchant by birth so Stéphane could fight to retain the château.

Gisèle had clung to the good memories of her home and the *chapelle* she loved, but with the exception of honoring her brother almost twenty years ago, she never wanted to return. Still, she wanted to keep the château for her son, hoping he and his family would love France as she had once loved it.

Enclosed with her letter and will was another paper, stamped by the Commonwealth of Virginia. In 1948 Henri and Gisèle had legally adopted Michel, and—much to the dismay of Stéphane

Borde—adopted children in France now received the same inheritance as biological kids. Both the United States and the French government would treat Michel Sauver as Gisèle's legal heir.

Two days ago, after Stéphane had dropped his lawsuit, Dad offered to let Lisette stay in the house year-round, but she declined; her memories inside the château were too overwhelming. This evening Monique was taking her back to Paris.

But Dad was dreaming again—this time about using the château to house other orphans, older kids in need of a home. Mémé's spirit may have been embracing those she'd lost during the war, but her legacy was alive here in Saint-Lô.

When the service was over, Abigail and Isabelle raced off to play in the park. They'd become inseparable since they had met at the airport. Both of them needed a good friend.

As Dad and I walked away from the cemetery, he slipped something into my hand. "She wanted you to have this."

I smoothed my fingers over the amber beads of Mémé's crucifix "Are you certain?"

He nodded. "Look at the cross."

I held it up and realized it was also a key.

He nudged me toward the *chapelle* door. "She said to find Cair Paravel."

The ruined castle in Narnia, before it was rebuilt.

Riley's hand enclosed mine as the two of us stepped into the *chapelle* and then through the iron gates at the side. Dust clung to the old sink and table in the sacristy and it streaked across the large closet at the side of the room.

I thought of the times my grandmother had read the Narnia books to me and how fascinated I'd been with the magical world behind the wardrobe. Oftentimes we'd create our own worlds where good always triumphed over the bad, where death had no victory.

Cair Paravel could only be found in one place within the *chapelle*.

I opened the door to the large wardrobe and the smell of mothballs flooded out. I pushed aside the robes and other vestments, and at the very back, I knelt down and searched the wall until I found a tiny keyhole on a panel. Riley shone the light from his video camera into the closet, and I used the cross to open the door.

We'd found Mémé's tunnel.

Riley's light illuminated the walls for us as we descended under the ground. They were packed with dirt, the air musty and cold. We crept forward until the passage opened into a room with old newspapers, shoes, blankets, and cigarette butts scattered like muddy snowflakes on the ground.

"It's like a time capsule," I whispered in awe.

Riley swept the room with the lens of his camera and then he zoomed in on me. "How long do you think it's been since someone was down here?"

"Probably when my grandparents hid my father and the other orphans. Seventy years ago."

I leaned down and picked up what looked like a wallet. Inside was an identity card for Michel Duchant and I stared at the look of abandonment in my uncle's eyes, the windblown hair that he hadn't bothered to comb. Behind the card was a slip of paper, folded in half, addressed to Lisette Calvez. I smiled. Perhaps my uncle had loved Lisette as much as she had loved him.

I stuck the note in my pocket to take up to Lisette.

In front of Riley and me, the tunnel had caved in, from the impact of a bomb I assumed. Where it led I might never know, but here I felt my grandmother's presence, her passion and purpose, to rescue when the enemy was determined to destroy.

I followed Riley up the steps, and when we got back into the nave, I found a broom and began to sweep the floor. When I looked up, he was watching me. "What?" I asked.

"You may not be a Duchant by blood, but you have the heart of your grandmother." He stepped closer to me, and my stomach fluttered again as it seemed to do these days whenever he drew near. He glanced over at Saint Michel and then at the stained glass glowing against the gray walls. "This would be the perfect place for a wedding, don't you think?"

I tilted my head. "Are you planning to get married?"

"Only if you'll marry me."

Riley pulled me close to him and kissed me with the tenderest of desire, as if he feared he might hurt me. And I kissed him back.

In the past months, God hadn't given me what I thought I wanted. Instead he'd given me exactly what I needed—a man who loved me and a daughter I adored, hope for the future and a peace that settled deep in my soul. And He'd blessed me with the gift of my family's story.

As Riley held me in his arms, I glanced back up one more time at Saint Michel and his defeated dragon.

Mémé's story was finished at the Château d'Epines—the château of thorns—but the Duchant family legacy, I prayed, would live on in the children of France.

AUTHOR'S NOTE

On a rainy evening in March, I wandered alone through the halls of an old mausoleum in Normandy. While visitors swarmed the white crosses above Omaha Beach, honoring the lives of courageous Americans, the German cemetery was a lonely, grim memorial to twelve thousand Nazi soldiers who'd died on French soil.

It was curious to me that the French people chose to honor their enemy with this beautiful plot, set on a hill overlooking the island of Mont Saint-Michel and the English Channel, but during my visit to France I learned something new, something the French know well. While many of the German soldiers chose to battle for the Third Reich, others were forced to fight for a madman, like those French citizens forced to make weapons for Germany and the Russian prisoners forced to build roads.

As I stood in that eerie place, reading the epitaphs of soldiers as young as sixteen, I wondered who among them had been trapped in the German army. And who were the Jewish soldiers who fought and died for Hitler, believing that by joining the Wehrmacht they could protect themselves or someone they loved?

Until I began researching this novel, I had no idea that so many men of Jewish descent were in the Wehrmacht. No one knows the exact number—many of these men probably took this secret to their grave—but Bryan Mark Rigg in *Hitler's Jewish Soldiers* estimates that 150,000 Mischlinge fought during World War II. He interviewed a number of these men in recent years. Some of their stories were courageous, others cowardly, but all of their stories fascinated me.

The past slowly may be forgiven in France, but it will not be forgotten. What Hitler and his fellow Nazis did to the people of France was evil. Seventy-six thousand Jews were deported from France during World War II, eight thousand of those children. Only 3 percent of those "sent east" returned home. Horrific . . .

While visiting France, I heard stories about the Germans who occupied France for four years and I heard the stories of the resilient French people who chose to resist them. Thousands of men and women, conflicted in their hearts, stood against evil and sacrificed their lives so others could live. Some were shot. Others sent to concentration camps. Many of them refused to talk about their service even after the war.

This novel is loosely based on the life of one such heroine—a noblewoman named Genevieve Marie Josephe de Saint Pern Menke. Genevieve was raised in a medieval château outside Saint-Lô called Château d'Agneaux. The tunnels under the de Saint Pern home are no longer accessible, but the stories of her heroism are being passed down through generations of Menkes.

As a young woman, Genevieve rescued Allied airmen and volunteered for the French Red Cross as a driver and medic. She was awarded two Croix de Guerre medals for bravery in war—the first one for courageously telling a German officer that "an honorable man would not kill innocent people" and then successfully negotiating the release of the villagers in Germolles from execution by firing squad.

Genevieve married an American officer and moved to the United States after the war though she returned often to France.

She passed away in 2010, but her legacy of courage and kindness continues on through her children and grandchildren. I hope this glimpse into her story and the stories of so many other heroic men and women during World War II inspires you as much as it has inspired me.

ACKNOWLEDGMENTS

Thank you to the entire Menke family for gifting me with Genevieve's remarkable story. To Kellee Menke Hernandez, who first told me about her beloved grandmother, and her parents, Doug and Ann Menke, who graciously answered my many questions, shared their favorite memories of Genevieve, and critiqued my rough manuscripts—I am so grateful for all of you. To both Darwin and Emmanuelle Menke for their hospitality—I loved spending time with your family, overlooking the lights of Paris. To Liz Menke for helping me navigate the French language, and to Anthony (Tony) "Yany" Menke, the oldest of the five Menke boys, for sharing the memories of his mother as well as educating me on the landed aristocracy in France. And a huge thank you to Herman Menke, an American lieutenant who fell in love with a French noblewoman seventy years ago and moved from Washington State to France with her in their twilight years. Herman asked me to portray the marvelous things his wife did in this novel, and I hope I have given her the honor she greatly deserves.

Thank you to my agent, Natasha Kern, for her enthusiasm for this story, and to my wonderful editor, Beth Adams, for all her wisdom in helping me build it. To my dear friend and sister Ann Menke, who invited me to spend an unforgettable week at her family's *manoir* and shared her love of Normandy with me. To my other "sistas"—Orlena Ballard and Mary Kay Taylor—who ventured to France with us and ended up stranded in a spring blizzard. Thank you for your flexibility and laughter, and for rescuing me when I got trapped behind the barbed wire on the Norman coast . . . Apparently *"sortie de secours"* does not mean "exit to the beach."

To my new French friends who shared their heroic stories with humility: Serge and Marie Charlotte Letourneur, the daughter and son-in-law of leaders in the French Resistance, thank you for welcoming us into your home and sharing both your stories and the pieces of an Allied parachute found after D-Day—I will treasure our day together. Jean ("Bobby") Veuillye for sharing your love for America with us and your childhood memories of the war. And Monique Lopez, who welcomed Darwin, Ann, and me with a warm heart and a kiss on each cheek. She remembered well the German occupation, but those memories were too painful for her to share.

To Martha DeLong for sending me her father's stories about fighting in France. George Edick passed away while I wrote this novel, but his legacy lives on . . .

To six amazing ladies who journey with me through every manuscript—Michele Heath, Nicole Miller, Leslie Gould, Dawn Shipman, Kimberly Felton, and Kelly Chang. I can't tell you how much I appreciate each one of you! To Julie White, my longtime friend and elementary schoolteacher extraordinaire—thank you so much for sharing with me the many reasons you love teaching. To Lyn Beroth and Paul and Sheila Herbert for their gracious help with the authenticity of European birth and marriage certificates. To Sean and Adam at the Hillside House for the peaceful retreat and for spoiling me as I worked on this book.

Thank you to my family and friends for their consistent prayers and support, and my dad, Jim Beroth, who flew out to Portland to help care for my girls while I was in France. And thank you to my husband, Jon, for his love and encouragement, and our sweet daughters—Karlyn and Kinzel—for cheering me on. I am so blessed by each one of you.

He will wipe every tear from their eyes, and there will be
no more death or sorrow or crying or pain.
All these things are gone forever.

—REVELATION 21:4

Thank you most of all to our Savior, Jesus Christ, for His promise that one day all things evil will be destroyed.

CHÂTEAU OF SECRETS

Melanie Dobson

INTRODUCTION

Gisèle is a young noblewoman whose world changes abruptly when German invaders bomb her hometown of Saint-Lô. Her beautiful home, the Château d'Epines, becomes the local head-quarters for German officers. What no one else knows but her is that underneath the château are winding tunnels where her brother and fellow French Resistance fighters hide. Secrets abound within her heart, the walls of the château, and the snaking tunnels underneath.

Gisèle's granddaughter, Chloe, lives a life far removed from the times of war that her grandmother endured. After calling off her engagement to a prominent political candidate, Chloe agrees to participate in a documentary featuring her family history and the château in Normandy. She is surprised to learn that the documentary filmmaker, Riley, is interested in uncovering the story of Jews who served in Hitler's army. How would that relate to her family? And she is even more shocked to learn that there are tunnels under the Château d'Epines that saved lives.

As Chloe follows Riley on the documentary journey, she discovers secrets held by both her grandmother and the château that encompass profound depths of love, loyalty, and sacrifice entwining their generations.

TOPICS AND QUESTIONS FOR DISCUSSION

1. The idea of secrets is introduced early in the novel. Gisèle considers the following question: "When did a secret cross over the gray wasteland between protecting one you loved and destroying him" (page 4)? In what ways did Gisèle's secrets protect the ones she loved? In what ways did Gisèle's secrets harm or cost the ones she loved, such as Lisette or even herself? How have you seen a secret destroy?

2. Initially, Chloe is engaged to marry Austin. Chloe acknowledges that she has lost herself in this relationship though, "Somewhere along the line, I'd forgotten exactly who I was, silhouetted by those with greater dreams than my own" (page 71). How do Chloe's romantic choices and consequences compare and contrast to Gisèle's, both in her refusal of Philippe and in her love for Josef? How does each woman's choice affect her identity?

3. The events surrounding Gisèle's young adult life differ drastically from those that surround Chloe's. Different generations experience diverging degrees of luxuries, experiences, hardships, and upbringings that define their thresholds of "norm" and pain. How do you think someone from Gisèle's generation views those of today's generation? How have you judged someone in an older generation? What have they faced that you have not?

4. In an eloquent comment on World War II, Gisèle says, "Hatred, it seemed, was a powerful unifier of even the greatest enemies. Hatred for the Nazis had also unified those resisting them" (page 106). Love is also a powerful unifier, seen in Josef's desire to protect his mother and those who sacrificed their lives to protect Adeline. Describe how you have experienced the unifying power of both hatred and love.

5. After witnessing members of the resistance being shot to death, Gisèle thinks twice about being able to fight the Germans. "She might not be able to fight the dragon, but perhaps she could rescue this boy" (page 121). How do you see Gisèle continue to "fight the dragon" against the Germans even after she thinks this to herself? Describe an experience in your life that despite its trauma, you continued fighting the dragons.

6. When the Germans come to live at the Château d'Epines, Gisèle asks herself, "Should she stand for all that was good and refuse them, even if it cost her her life? Or should she compromise her morals to save her life—and the lives of those in her care" (page 180)? What decision would you have made if you were in her shoes? Why? Describe an experience in your life when you felt judged by others for making a decision that seemed the lesser of two evils.

7. In Chapter 30, Chloe tells her dad about finding Gisèle's marriage certificate and Adeline's birth certificate. How do you think this made him feel? Describe a time when you learned a secret that impacted or involved others. How did it make you feel?

8. Gisèle wrestles with the biblical command to "Love your enemies and pray for those who persecute you" (page 191). When was she supposed to love her enemy and when was she supposed

to resist? And somehow, in the great mystery of faith, was it possible for her to do both? Do you think Gisèle did both? Explain. Do you think it is possible to do both in the Christian faith? Have you ever received love from a perceived enemy or prayed for an enemy? Describe the situation.

9. Riley tells Chloe, "It tells a lot about a person when you find out what or who they're willing to die for" (page 164). In light of this statement, how would you describe and characterize Josef? Do you think Josef or Gisèle went too far to protect those they loved? How do you personally draw the line between protecting, serving, or loving others against sacrificing too much of yourself?

10. Riley's grandfather tells him that "we never know what we truly believe until we are standing in a trench, surrounded by the enemy" (page 243). Identify the "trenches" in Chloe's story that facilitate her discovery of who she truly is and what she believes. Were these events challenging, painful, or untroubled events? How have the "trenches" in your own life shaped you?

11. Philippe's debt drove him to make horrific decisions in order to obtain the château. How does his self-centered behavior contrast to the selfless actions of Gisèle's brother Michel? Secondly, consider and discuss the effects of their choices on the generations that follow. Describe an area in your life where you are influenced by a family member's prior decision(s).

12. Josef is a rescuer in numerous ways. At what cost to himself did he become the unlikely hero and of whom? Describe how you would feel to know that a soldier of one nation begins fighting *with* and *for* the perceived enemy. How do you see this occurring today?

13. Imagine Gisèle and Lisette being able to see each other later in their lives prior to Gisèle's memory loss. What do you think the women would share with each other? What do you think each woman would feel toward the other?

14. Consider the novel being told from the *Oberst's* perspective, a man defending and sacrificing for his country, beliefs, and family. How do you judge and compare his level of sacrifice?

ENHANCE YOUR BOOK CLUB

1. Two of Gisèle's favorite quotes were the following: "You've never lived until you've almost died" by Guy de Maupassant and "I have learnt that all men live not by care for themselves but by love" by Leo Tolstoy (page 138). Discuss which of these quotes speaks the most to you. Why? Decide as a group a way everyone can lovingly serve someone this week, be it with time, money, or skills.

2. Outline your family tree to the extent that you can. Which two people in your family lineage inspire you the most? Why? What mysteries remain in your family tree, if any? If there are gaps in knowledge, seek out the information.

3. The main characters in *Château of Secrets* make weighty decisions, often at great expense. "They all had to lose a bit of themselves to satiate the enemy . . . but that she prayed that in their hearts, they all would remain true to God and to France" (page 258). Discuss how you relate to this in the spheres of your vocation, relationships, finances, or time. What "enemy" do you feel like you must satiate for a greater purpose? Make one change if you believe you have sacrificed too much in a particular area and ask the group for accountability.

4. Write a letter of thanks to a U.S. soldier or veteran. If you do not know one, visit the websites "Letters to Home," "A Million Thanks," or "Operation Gratitude" to participate in sending words or small gift packages to a soldier, veteran, or wounded warrior.

5. Document your own personal story, either in its entirety or segments. Your story is a piece of history and significant to loved ones. Share a portion of it with the group.

A CONVERSATION WITH MELANIE DOBSON

1. How did you first come to know of the story of Genevieve Marie Josephe de Saint Pern Menke on whom this story is loosely based? How do her children and grandchildren describe her?

After Genevieve passed away in 2010, her granddaughter shared Genevieve's stories of courage and faith with me. I was captivated by Genevieve's bravery in standing up against the Nazis when they could easily have killed her, and by the stories of her hiding the French Resistance underneath the family's château while the Germans occupied it. The Menke family partnered with me as I wrote this novel, and Ann Menke, Genevieve's daughter-in-law, graciously invited me to their family's *manoir* and former château in Normandy. Genevieve left a beautiful legacy as an elegant, courageous, feisty Norman woman who was strong in character and devout in her faith. Her husband, children, and grandchildren adored her, and I hope readers are inspired by her story as well.

2. Do you always visit the places where your books are set? Why is it helpful? What did you love most about your trip for this book?

I always visit the main setting of my books to discover what makes the place unique. The Internet is fantastic for accumulating general details about a location, but good sensory description—the local sights, smells, sounds—breathe life into a novel. And once I can see the setting in my mind's eye, I no longer get stuck on the details. My brain is freed to focus on the story.

I enjoyed everything about my trip to France—eating the crusty bread and local cheese, biking through the villages, staying in a medieval château with three dear friends. Also, I loved spending time with Genevieve's family and visiting with new friends in Normandy who welcomed us into their homes.

3. This novel is steeped in the historical detail of World War II and the Battle of Saint-Lô. What was your research process like?

Before I started writing *Château of Secrets*, I read through a stack of resources about the war as well as a number of interviews with Jewish men who fought in the German army. To help me visualize the details, I obtained photographs of the Battle of Saint-Lô along with film footage of Frenchmen resisting the Germans. My time in Normandy was the most important step in the research process. I learned a tremendous amount by exploring the Utah Beach D-Day Museum, strolling through Saint-Lô, and visiting with men and women who shared their memories of the occupation and the war.

4. Many of the main characters in this novel make great sacrifices for freedom, be it tangible or emotional. What does freedom mean to you?

Years ago a friend asked what I valued most in life, and my quick response was *freedom*. In hindsight, what I really meant was independence—the selfish freedom to do what I wanted, whenever I wanted. Much has happened since I answered that question, and the freedom I value now is more internal—freedom from anxiety and bitterness and fear. Instead of striving for things that deplete me or allowing my thoughts to whirl with anger and frustration, I try to focus on what God has called me to do and rely on Him for provision, direction, and peace. I don't always succeed at letting go, but this renewed faith in Christ has given me great freedom on the inside.

5. *What would you describe as the main theme(s) in* Château *of Secrets?*

The heart of this novel is about sacrifice—what happens to those willing to risk their life to rescue others and what happens to those who betray innocent people in an attempt to save themselves. Some of the characters lost their life in this story while others found healing in their later years. In the Book of John, Jesus said these beautiful words, "Love each other in the same way I have loved you. There is no greater love than to lay down one's life for one's friends."

6. *What do you want readers to experience or take away from this novel?*

Château of Secrets is about seemingly ordinary people who stood against evil, often working in secret as they fought against the Nazis and protected innocent people marked for death. As I wrote this story, I was reminded that we have many opportunities today to stand against evil and protect those who are suffering. We may not be risking our life, but it is always extraordinary to sacrifice finances, time, and even our pride to help someone in need.

7. *With which character do you relate the most? Why?*

I'd like to say that I relate to Gisèle's heroic choices to rescue Adeline and other orphaned children, but since I've never been in her situation, I can't honestly say what I would do. I do identify deeply with the mixed emotions of many of the characters—Gisèle's faith and fear, Chloe's anger and relief, Michel's optimism in spite of the circumstances, the conflict in Josef's heart over his terrible dilemma, and both Lisette and Riley in their regrets and ultimately redemption.

8. Michel tells Gisèle "Courage doesn't mean you stop being afraid . . . It means you continue to fight, even when you're terrified" (page 298). How do you personally strive to live this out?

Fear is the personal dragon that I fight daily. Sometimes it's fear of failure or the unknown. Sometimes it's fear for my children or my husband. Sometimes it's seemingly ridiculous things that keep me up at night.

Last year my family spent Christmas serving orphans in Uganda. I was afraid of countless things before and during that trip, but I knew we were supposed to go in spite of my fears and the experience changed our lives. God, in his faithfulness, continues to help me fight against this dragon, and I'm incredibly grateful that He never leaves nor forsakes us.

9. How does your degree and background in journalism influence your writing of fiction?

I pursued a career in journalism because I love to learn. Writing was and still is a fun outlet for me to dig deep as I research both historical events and contemporary people and places. I approach the writing of each new book as a journalist, delving into the time period and details of the events and location first. After a few weeks of research, my characters and plot begin to emerge from the factual accounts of the past.

10. A line from your website highlights your gift as a writer: "My issue is not about finding time to write. It's about finding time to live around my writing." With a passion for writing, what are the things that can stifle your creativity? What or who inspires and energizes you again?

Faux busyness stifles my creativity. Often when I'm on deadline, I'll lose myself to all sorts of seemingly urgent tasks like vacuuming the house or cleaning out the garage. In order to eliminate distraction, I like to escape to a coffee shop with a steady buzz of noise or a quiet hotel where I can immerse myself in my imaginary world. As a family, we also try to keep the Sabbath each week. After a day of rest, I'm rejuvenated and ready to write first thing Monday morning.

11. *What will you be working on next?*

I've just started a novel about a forty-five-year-old woman named Heather who returns to England to prepare her childhood home for sale. As she and her daughter work together, Heather discovers that her parents hid a terrible secret from her and their village when she was a girl. In spite of the risks to her heart and her future, Heather decides to pursue the truth about what happened in the beautiful gardens behind her family's cottage and in the gardens of the castle next door.

12. *When you are not writing, what do you do for fun?*

I love exploring new places, hiking in the mountains, playing Settlers of Catan with friends, line dancing, working in my garden, taking yoga classes, reading novels with surprise endings, and most of all, laughing with my family while we dance, hike, or explore together.